LIST OF AUTHORS

CHRISTY ALDRIDGE
BROOKLYN ANN
SIMON BLEAKEN
JAY BOWER
CLAY MCLEOD CHAPMAN
HEATHER DAUGHRITY
JOE DEROUEN
WILLIAM J. DONAHUE
J-F. DUBEAU
JOSHUA LOYD FOX
JENNIFER ANNE GORDON
GAGE GREENWOOD
JUSTIN HOLLEY
JO KAPLAN
RONALD KELLY
MARIE LANZA
CAITLIN MARCEAU
D.E. MCCLUSKEY
JEREMY MEGARGEE
JOE SCIPIONE
SAMANTHA UNDERHILL
MER WHINERY
MERCEDES M. YARDLEY

HOUSE

OF

HAUNTS

EDITED BY
HEATHER DAUGHRITY

Parlor Ghost Press

Parlor Ghost Press

Published by Parlor Ghost Press, an imprint of
Watertower Hill Publishing, LLC
Copyright © 2023 by Parlor Ghost Press
www.watertowerhill.com
www.parlorghostpress.com

Cover design by Christy Aldridge at Grim Poppy Design
Cover creation by Susan Roddey
at The Snark Shop by Phoenix & Fae Creations
Cover copyright © 2023, Parlor Ghost Press
Interior format by Joshua Daughrity at Watertower Hill Publishing, LLC

Library of Congress Control Number: 2023
ISBN: 979-8-9893011-2-6

Oh house of haunts, oh house of spirits,

Darkened halls and treacherous floors beneath;

Upon your walls, laced webs

Hang without motion;

Into your rooms

No trace of light does reach.

Oh house of haunts, oh house of spirits,

Your dust lies quiet, undisturbed and deep;

Those who walk your corridors

Leave no footprints,

Those who dwell within

Need never sleep.

{ Heather Daughrity }

Table of Contents

Foreword

Josh Malerman

Okay: This is a *great* idea for an anthology.

You start with a palatial estate. You've got *Clue*-esque maps of all three floors and the grounds. The grounds include a pool house, a treehouse, and a graveyard. The maps themselves act as your first look behind the musty curtain of the haunted house. Excuse me, haunted *mansion*. Then, each author takes a room, until every chamber is spoken for, and every room a haunted history therein.

I know. Amazing.

But if this wasn't enough:

The hauntings span a couple centuries. And so, not only do we as readers experience what happened in every cranny of the place, but what life was like in Hale House year by year. We travel from 1996 to 1955 to 1862 to 2006 to many more. We don't only get the ghosts; we get the *spanning of Time.* And the compound effect this has is profound. The year 1999 (and the fear of Y2K) must be informed by the history of 1856 (and the Spanish Flu) all of which must be part of 2019 (and Covid) to come.

It's a kaleidoscopic quilt of horrors. An absolute tapestry of good people and bad, good relationships with the dead and bad, and those responsible for the dead and those not.

I think this really must be the most comprehensive book about a haunting I've ever read.

Editor Heather Daughrity sets the table before each floor is presented. These brief one-page "horror-host" beats are highlights, full of drollery and fear. But what these editor pages really do is unify the immediate stories to come, floor by floor, giving us an immersive experience: we step deeper into the house as the anthology motors on. So then, what better place to begin than on the front porch swing, the perfect introduction: a moment so horrible it could only christen a haunting.

And from there? Through the front door, to the parlor, the library, the kitchen.

We're inside Hale House now and I'm not convinced we're ever entirely leaving.

Very soon you begin asking yourself: which room would *I* want to be haunted in? And did the characters of one story get off easy compared to those of the next? And what year might I want to be haunted *in*? And why does it feel more romantic to have been haunted in 1890 than 2002?

By the time you reach the second floor, you understand you've come too far. You're not going to get out of this without a story of your own. And so you give yourself up to the illicit goings-on in the master bedroom in 2016, but you're just as present in 1918 when the toy soldiers spell out "hi" in the nursery. You're suddenly as game for erotic taxidermy as you are ghostly chess in the game room.

Hell, the bathroom might be the scariest room in the house.

I suppose that's not that irregular.

And are you excited yet? I know you are. Because, you, like me, you *want* to be haunted. And so do some of the characters in this book! Think: after some time, with this many incidents on record, Hale House *must* be known to be infested. And so those who arrive in the modern era no doubt know something of the past.

Whether they find that amusing or take it seriously may inform how deep their peril runs.

But things don't stop at the second floor, oh no no. Just wait till you meet Inez in the attic. But please don't move the blankets. And what self-respecting haunted mansion doesn't include a secret staircase leading to a secret room with a grisly horror all its own?

I'm not sure anybody sums it better than Audrey does – Audrey of "My FairLady," Brooklyn Ann's story of the garage. Audrey is doing a little research on the place (if only she had this book to reference) when the narrator exclaims:

Holy hell, was every room in the house haunted? And she hadn't even gone back twenty years yet!

And that's the beauty of this book. The deeper you go, the more canorous the experience, until you're surrounded by history's wail. Try finding a safe corner to stay. And reference the maps: might not the deathly melodies emanating from the music room in 1902 be heard in the parlor directly below it, in 1989? And why wouldn't the mist from the bathroom in 1995 be felt by the mannequin in the attic in 2019? There are endless combinations like these, in which the hauntings interweave, threading not only their individual horrors, but their eras as well. And the different ways people thought at different times, too. And the different technologies, foods, and moods.

By the time you're fixing the convertible in the garage, you're supernaturally drunk.

I want to visit Hale House.

I want to drive there now.

Perhaps my haunting would happen on the way.

And if I did head out, I would have an incredible guide: the layout of the book you're reading is as extraordinary as the layout of the house itself. And the writing all adds up to what is probably the strongest writing in any anthology I've read.

It's an absolute honor to play a part.

I dare say, I'd be particularly interested in visiting the chapel, where the statue of Jesus might wink my way, though I'd worry about being so close to the mausoleum, where the body of the first murder of Hale House remains interred.

And while I'm a professional, I do have my limits.

Though I'm not sure Hale House cares.

And maybe I like that. For, like Gwen in the hall beneath the attic, I want to be haunted, too.

Josh Malerman

Michigan

2023

BALL ROOM

PARLOR

BACK PORCH

KITCHEN

FRONT PORCH

DINING ROOM

LIBRARY

HALE HOUSE
EST. 1823

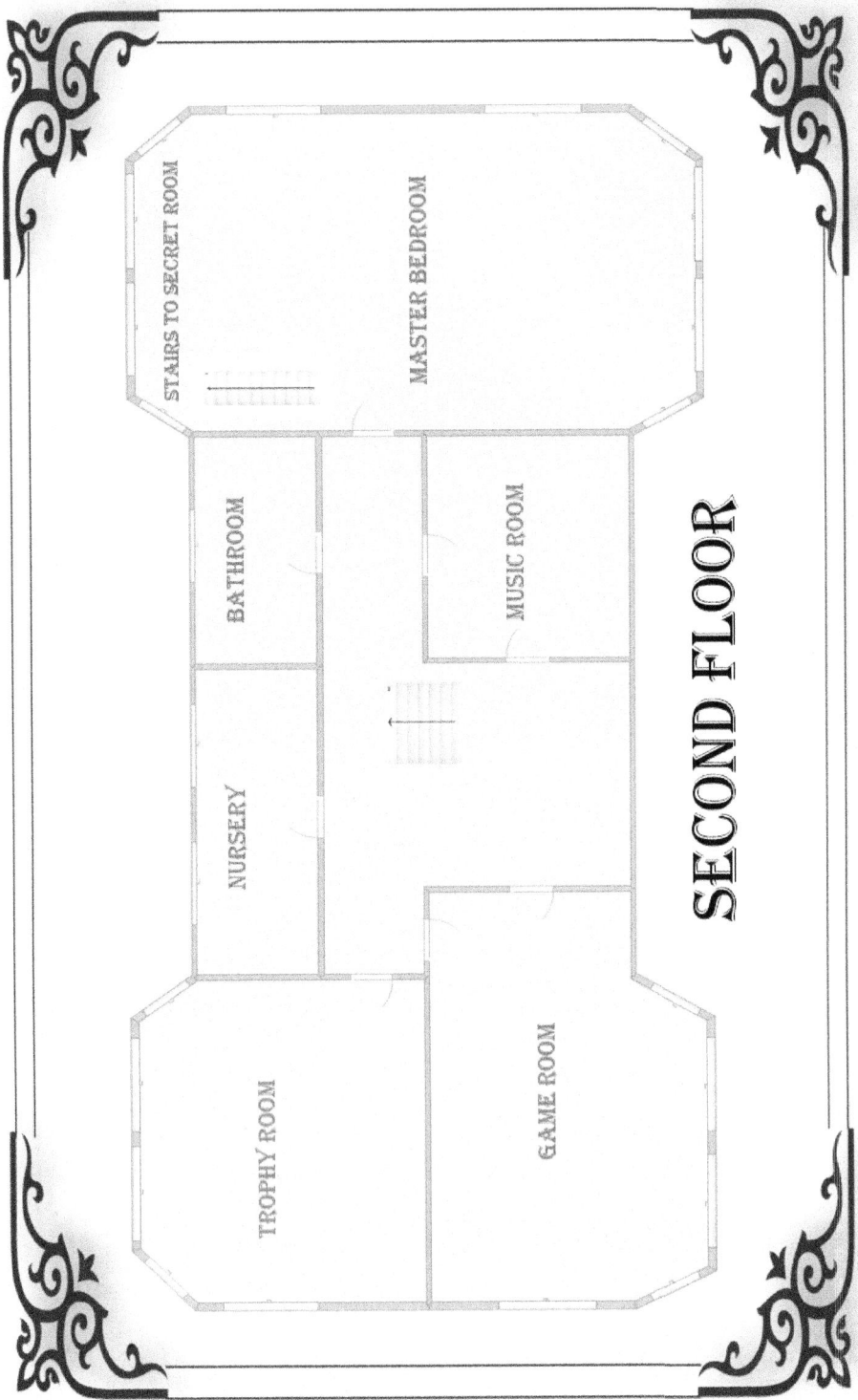

SECOND FLOOR

STAIRS TO SECRET ROOM

MASTER BEDROOM

BATHROOM

MUSIC ROOM

NURSERY

TROPHY ROOM

GAME ROOM

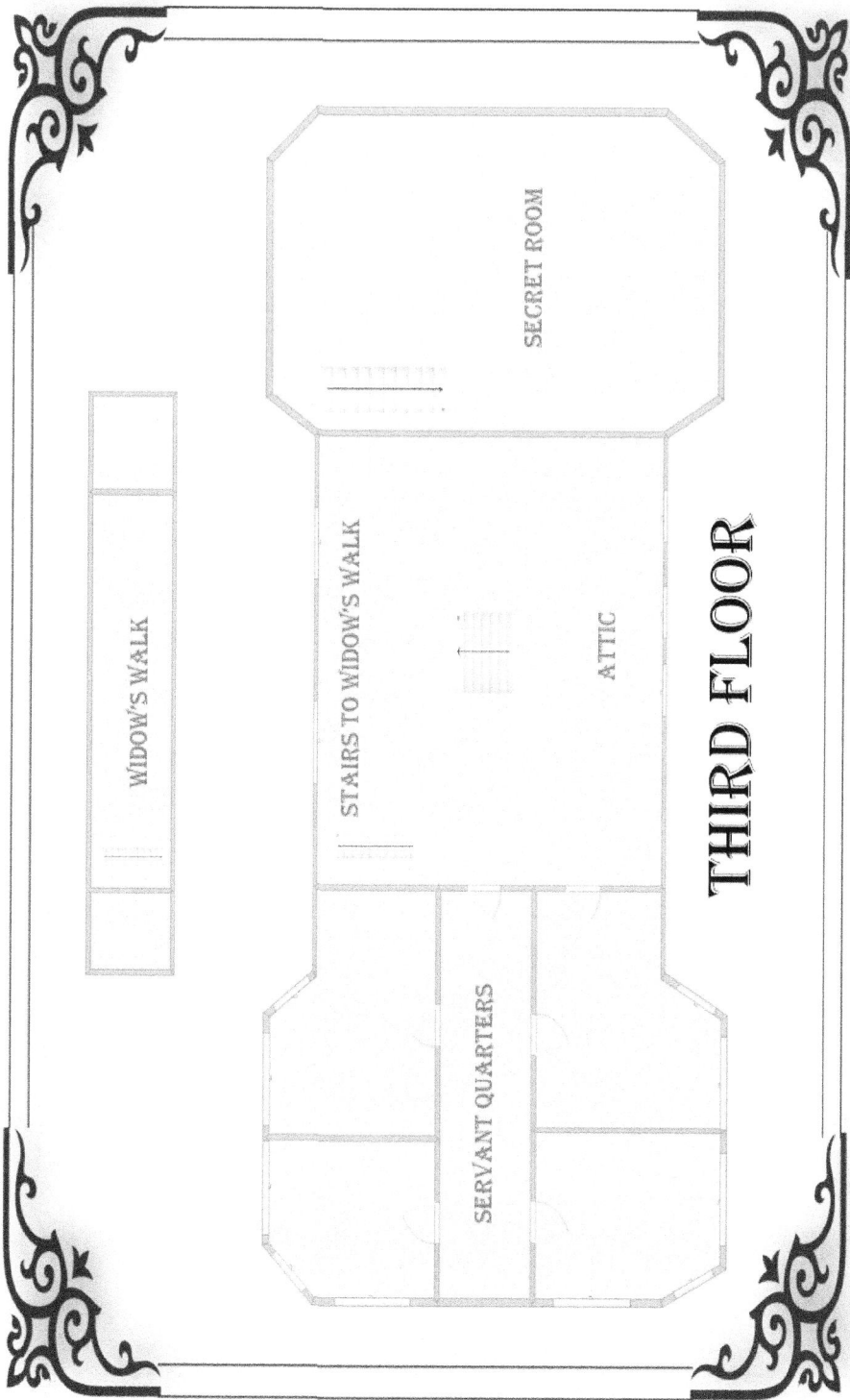

WIDOW'S WALK

STAIRS TO WIDOW'S WALK

SECRET ROOM

ATTIC

SERVANT QUARTERS

THIRD FLOOR

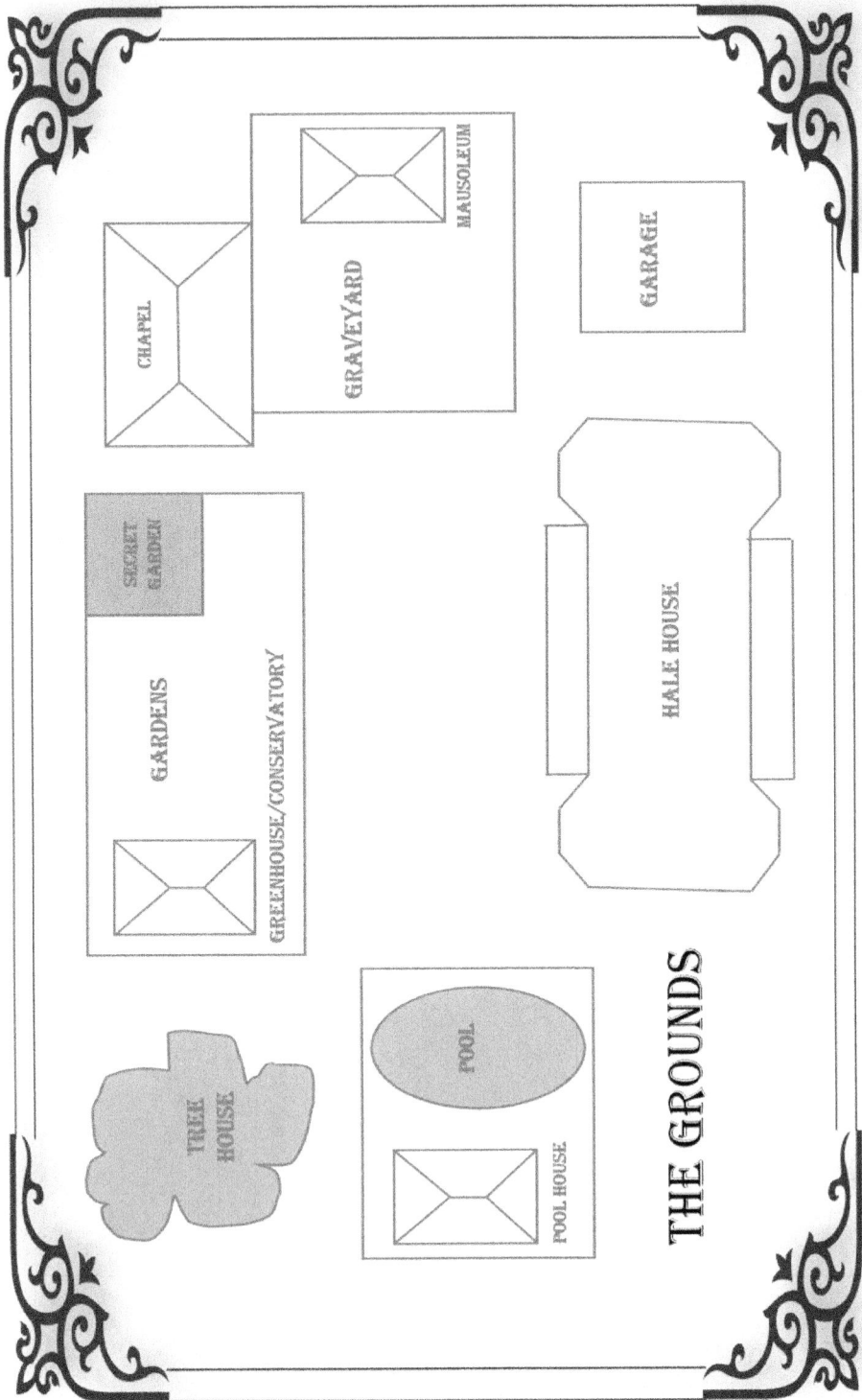

THE GROUNDS

Labels in the illustration: CHAPEL, MAUSOLEUM, GRAVEYARD, GARAGE, SECRET GARDEN, GARDENS, GREENHOUSE/CONSERVATORY, HALE HOUSE, TREE HOUSE, POOL, POOL HOUSE

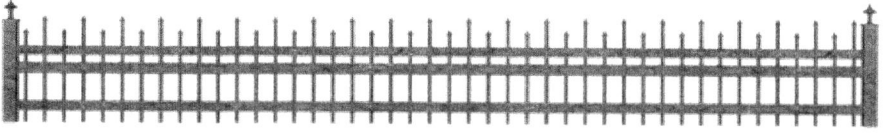

Welcome

It's nearing sunset as you approach the estate, that magical golden hour found only on crisp October evenings. Shadows stretch long and dark across the ground; the sinking sun sits low on a horizon striped in shades of autumn fire.

The fence which surrounds the grounds is tall, black, and surprisingly straight, considering its age – a thousand iron spears pointing toward the darkening sky above.

The gate is a tangle of wrought scrollwork flanked on either side by stone pillars. Atop one of these pillars sits a statue whose weathered surface might depict a lion, a dragon, a gargoyle straight from the pits of Hell – the centuries have worn away the sculpture's original form.

Beyond the gate, a long and winding drive stretches through overgrown fields. A cold wind, sour-sweet and sibilant, sweeps over the land, calm but constant, rustling the dry grass.

In the woods that surround the estate, the few remaining leaves which still cling stubbornly to the trees shiver and tremble against their branches.

At the end of the drive, Hale House rises - a broad block of darkness against the dying light.

Your eyes are drawn to the house: the blank windows, the spires of the widow's walk atop the roof, the sheer hulking size of it, the cloud of bats that rise from the chimneys and swirl into the air above.

You jump, startled, at a loud, screeching *caw* to your left. On the tilting pillar sits an enormous black raven, so perfectly still that you take a tentative step toward it, half-convinced the bird is made of stone.

The old blackbird tilts his head at you, one beady eye sizing you up as he ruffles his inky feathers. His gaze seems to look deep into you, into the dark and cobwebby spaces of your soul; you feel a rush of vertigo, the falling night opening into a spiral which threatens to pull you in.

But what was that?

The rusty creak of heavy, long-disused hinges.

You drag your eyes from the raven; he caws again and flaps away.

The gate now stands open.

In the distance, a silvery candle flame dances to life in a small third-floor window.

∞

Hale House welcomes you.

First Floor

The house looms over you as you make your way carefully up the front steps. An ancient wooden swing hangs suspended from the porch ceiling, creaking softly even though the wind has stilled.

The ornate double doors of Hale House are heavy.

Imposing.

Unlocked.

∽

Enter.

Let your eyes adjust to the darkness. If you need a light, there are candles here, and matches, but careful, please; Hale House has seen its fair share of fire over the years.

Allow me to show you around.

Who am I? No one of consequence.

Put that question from your mind.

Let's begin the tour, shall we?

Enjoy our parlor. Don't mind the music.

If you're hungry, the kitchen is always stocked, but leave the dishes for later – the sink is a bit tricky.

For the finest dining experience, please enjoy your meal in our opulent dining room. Try to avoid the mirror, and forgive us if the food tastes a bit… odd.

If you'd like a little after-dinner reading, we have a spectacular library. We do ask that you wear gloves when touching the books, for your own safety, of course. If you hear raised voices, it's just the wind, though *do* be extra careful here with your candle flame.

Or, if a bit of physical exertion is more your style, please feel free to make use of the broad expanse in our grand ballroom. Don't mind the bullet holes. Or the screams.

∽

Go on, explore. I'll wait here.

And don't forget – careful with that candle.

Front Porch
1930

Save Me a Spot on the Old Porch Swing
Ronald Kelly

Donnie Chambers loved Granny, and Granny loved him. He was her favorite grandchild, and she was his favorite grandparent. They didn't say this openly, in fear of hurting the feelings of others, but it was no secret.

Everyone knew.

They were connected, from his birth to her death, by an underlying thread of deep affection and mutual respect.

Growing up in the early 1920s had been difficult for the boy, and particularly for his family. Donnie's father, Emery, had struggled to keep his business – a small grocery store – thriving and the shelves stocked after the hardship of the First World War, as well as keeping up the big house on the edge of town that they had moved into to when Donnie was only nine.

His mother, Harriet, had suffered from debilitating headaches that caused her to reluctantly abandon her chores and responsibilities, and left her bedridden in the darkness of her bedroom for days at a time.

But Granny was there. She was the one who cooked and cleaned and tended the garden. The one who filled in the blanks and made life tolerable and enjoyable, even when there was no tolerance or joy to be found. She was the glue that held the family together.

∞

There were places in the Chambers home that Donnie liked and those he disliked.

The ones he liked could be counted on one hand. The parlor, where they studied the Bible, indulged in the classics, and listened to shows on the old

3

Gilfillan cathedral radio. The dining room, where they ate and talked and laughed. The upstairs bedroom where he slept, read dime novels, and dreamt of places far beyond the big house and the property that surrounded it. The rooms he avoided were the attic and the basement, for it was said they were haunted and not to be trifled with.

Donnie's favorite place was the front porch and the swing that hung from the rafters at the very end. That was *their* place… his and Granny's. There, his grandmother would knit, snap shelly beans, or cut quilt squares and enjoy the fresh air. And she would talk. Tales of family history, ghost stories, or corny jokes she'd heard when she was a child. Donnie enjoyed baseball, climbing trees, or hanging around the swimming hole, but when Granny was parked on the swing, all those things seemed bland and unappealing. He would sit and swing with her for hours, just listening to her spin yarns and impart a lifetime of sage advice and wisdom.

Sometimes the parlor window would be open on a warm summer day, and they would hear an old song from a dozen years before drift past the lacy curtains with the strumming of a banjo and bouncy, nasal tones.

> *Save me a spot on the old porch swing,*
> *That spot where we met in the height of spring,*
> *Happiness and joy it will always bring,*
> *Our perfect little spot on the old porch swing…*

Whenever that song played, they would sing along and push the swing back and forth with their feet, higher and higher, until the bolts that suspended it began to creak and they were forced to stop in fear of it pulling free of the beams overhead and leaving them sitting in a heap of splintered lumber. The two would laugh until their ribs ached and tears came to their eyes.

Their song. Their spot. Their blissful piece of heaven on the old porch swing.

∽

But, unfortunately, things tend to change with the passage of time.

As Donnie grew older, from adolescence and into young adulthood, his and Granny's times grew fewer and farther between. As he would leave the house, she would smile from her spot on the swing and pat the place where he had always sat. Donnie would see his friends waiting in a jalopy by the roadside and, embarrassed, shake his head curtly or ignore her completely. Then he'd hop the picket fence and jump into the rumble seat, anticipating a night of drinking and dancing at some clandestine speakeasy across the county line.

When he turned sixteen, he heard that a crime boss and bootlegger in Chicago named Touhy was in need of men. Sick of small-town life and craving adventure, he left home in the dead of night and hopped a freight train for the Windy City. Before his departure, he had written his grandmother a short letter and left it on his pillow, telling her of his dissatisfaction and desire to make it on his own. It had been the summer of 1926, and after that he had not returned to the big house or attempted to contact his family.

One thing lead to another, and Donnie became involved in shady dealings and a seamy life of organized crime, transporting Touhy's cellar-brewed beer and bathtub gin to illicit nightclubs across Illinois during the Prohibition years.

Before long, he split off from the Chicago operation and began running with a gang led by a cocky little fellow named Lester. Petty crimes led to hold-ups and burglaries, and then bank robbery after the stock market crashed in 1929.

The opening days of the Great Depression made desperate men even more desperate than before. Lester – who possessed a blood-thirsty streak a mile wide – was ruthless in his pursuit of cold cash and his tendency to shoot before considering the consequences of his actions.

∞

In October of 1930, Lester and his boys robbed the Itasca State Bank of over four thousand dollars. Attempting to dodge the law, they took to the backroads and, a week later, found themselves in Donnie's hometown. Pressured by the others, the young man agreed to take them to his family's home, to lay low for a night or two and make plans for the next heist.

It was well after eleven o'clock that night when they arrived at the old house. Quietly, they left the roadster parked on the street and crossed the dark yard to the front porch. As they mounted the steps and approached the door, Donnie was startled to look toward the porch swing and see someone sitting there in the darkness. The form was small and gaunt, but familiar.

"Granny," he gasped. "What are you–?"

"Doing up at this time of night?" she replied. A face that had once worn a perpetual expression of cheer and goodwill was hollow-eyed and solemn.

"Boy, I haven't had a restful moment since you up and vanished." Her ancient eyes hardened as she regarded the men who were with him. "So, this is what you've been doing with your life? Running with this lowdown rabble?"

"Hey!" snapped Lester harshly. "Shut your trap, old lady! Give us no flack and we'll give you none in return."

But Granny wasn't intimidated by the little man in the gray trench coat and jaunty brown fedora. "You're the one who's corrupted my Donnie, aren't you? Or had a strong hand in it?"

"Granny," Donnie said softly, his heart thundering in his chest. "Please..."

Lester laughed and looked around at the members of his gang. "Looks like this broad is growing deaf in her old age." He squared his shoulders and took a threatening step forward. "You heard me the first time, lady. Clam up and mind your own damn business."

"This boy here *is* my business!" Granny declared with contempt.

"How do you think it makes me and his poor mother and father feel, hearing of the corruption he's taken part in... robbing honest folks... running with a sawed-off little runt like you?"

Oh God, Granny, thought Donnie, attempting to take a step between the two. *Please... don't.*

Angrily, Lester pushed past him and stood no more than a yard from the porch swing and its surly occupant.

"What the hell did you call me?"

"You heard me!" snapped the elderly woman.

"Why, you look more like a youngster than a full-grown man. Short and soft with a face like a baby!"

Then it happened, faster than anyone on the porch could imagine.

"I'll show you who's soft, you mouthy old bitch!"

Then Lester drew a .38 revolver from beneath his coat, leveled the muzzle, and fired.

The gunshot shocked everyone into immobility.

Donnie watched in horror as the front of his grandmother's gown blossomed in crimson and she pitched forward, slipping from the seat of the swing. She collapsed upon the floor of the porch and lay there, her breathing shallow, her eyes growing glassy and unfocused.

Donnie dropped to his knees beside her, stunned by what had just transpired.

"Granny… oh God in heaven!" He turned angry eyes toward his boss, his right-hand easing toward his coat pocket.

Lester aimed his gun at the young man, coldly and without error.

"Go right ahead, Chambers!" he sneered arrogantly.

"Pull that gat and your folks will be paying for two funerals."

The gathering stood there for a long moment, listening as a dog began to bark a half mile away. Then Lester turned to the others.

"Come on, boys. Let's split this joint."

Together, they abandoned the porch, ran to the roadster, and lit out for parts unknown.

Donnie remained where he was, helpless as his grandmother's blood pooled beneath her thin body. Through his tears, he watched as she raised a frail hand and gently touched his cheek.

"I saved you a spot," she rasped weakly.

Then her fingertips slipped away and so did she.

∞

In 1931, Donald Chambers was convicted for his part in the cold-blooded murder of his grandmother and sentenced to forty years hard labor in the state prison.

As he settled into the grim life of an incarcerated man, he soon learned that his mother had died of a brain tumor and joined his grandmother in the town cemetery.

Grief-stricken, his father had sold the big house and his store in town and moved away. Exactly where he had gone, Donnie had no earthly idea.

Through newspaper accounts, he followed the violent exploits of his former boss. How Lester had become a notorious bank robber and mobster, joined forces with other gangsters of notoriety on occasion, and following a deadly shoot-out with federal agents at Little Bohemia Lodge in Wisconsin, even became Public Enemy #1 on the FBI's most wanted list for a short time.

Eventually, Lester's luck ran out and, in November of 1934, he was gunned down in the town of Barrington, a few miles outside the Chicago city limits.

Donnie spent the better part of his life working on road crews in the daylight hours and locked securely in his prison cell at night. Often, he would wake up in the dark hours with a scream on his lips as he relived the nightmare on the front porch.

He would feel his grandmother's fingers softly caress his cheek and hear her final words.

∽

After three and a half decades in the penitentiary, Donnie was released in the spring of 1965, five years before his sentence was set to expire.

He again took to the road and began to wander from town to town. Eventually, his travels lead him to a place where he thought he would never return. The little town he had once called home.

One sunny afternoon in mid-summer, he found himself walking past the big house with the stately oaks and the wrought-iron fence. Several families had come and gone since then, but the structure remained hauntingly the same.

Two children – a girl and a boy – ran and played in the front yard. At the side of the house, a dark-haired woman took down laundry from a clothesline. She eyed him mildly as he walked past; more curious than suspicious.

Not wishing to alarm her or the children, he continued onward down the sidewalk.

But as the evening drew on and he prepared for a night spent in the shelter of the surrounding forest, Donnie considered the house and what had taken place there so many years before.

And knew that his soul would never rest easy until he made his peace.

∽

Donnie Chambers waited until half past two in the morning and returned to the street of his childhood. Quietly, he made his way up the walkway of the big house, then mounted the steps to the front porch.

Things had changed in the thirty-five years since he had last stood there. There were two rocking chairs of polished hickory, one at each side of the front door, as well as potted flowers and plants on iron stands and a couple of brass windchimes dangling from the eves of the overhang.

But one thing hadn't changed at all.

The swing was still there.

In the gloom, he approached the hanging bench and stared at it for a long moment. The first thing he looked for was blood. Spattered upon the slatted back, smeared across the seat, pooled on the floorboards underneath where his grandmother had fallen from her piece of heaven and bled out.

Those awful images had played over and over, like an endless loop of film, in the back of his mind for most of his adult life.

He could find no trace, however. Both the swing and the boards of the porch floor had been painted, probably several times, over the years.

Donnie sighed.

"Granny," he said softly, then sat down where he had hundreds of times before, but during a time of joy and fond memories. Now there was no such innocence. Guilt and regret pressed upon his gaunt frame like the weight of the world itself.

He leaned forward, burying his face in his hands. *Why did you come here?* he asked himself. *What did you hope to find?*

It was at that moment the porch light came on and he froze.

As the front door opened, he expected to find the man of the house standing there, disheveled with disturbed slumber, angry, shotgun in hand. But it wasn't. Instead, it was the dark-haired woman he had seen earlier that day. The one who had watched him as she took down her laundry.

Donnie began to rise, but the woman halted him with a gentle wave of her hand.

"No. Please. Sit all you want."

Uneasily, he sat back down and watched her. He saw no threat in her hand – pistol, baseball bat, knife – and neither did he see alarm on her face.

In fact, she seemed to possess no fear of him at all. He watched in amazement as she gathered her housecoat around her and took a seat in one of the hickory rockers.

For a moment, they simply sat there silently and said nothing. Then she spoke.

"You know, an old woman once died on that very swing. She was shot down in cold blood by a criminal on the run."

He nodded grimly.

"His name was Lester Gillis. But folks mostly knew him as…"

"Baby Face Nelson."

The surprise on the man's face made her smile.

"My father used to tell me about the old bank robbers and gangsters. Bonnie and Clyde, Dillinger, Pretty Boy Floyd."

She studied him for a long moment; the sadness on his face, the drop of his shoulders, the wringing of his hands.

"My name is Linda."

"Nice meeting you, ma'am."

The woman continued to regard him; not with pity but purpose.

"She loved you, Donnie. More than anything. More than life itself."

The ex-con was startled. "How do you know my name?"

Linda sat back in the rocker and stared out into the night. "She told me, that's why. She tells me lots of things. My husband… the kids… none of them have ever seen her. Just me."

"I… I don't understand."

"Every now and then, the wind chimes will jingle, and I find her there… on the swing. Sometimes she'll be knitting a shawl, sometimes breaking beans. Sometimes she just sits and smiles, looking at someone beside her. Someone from a long time ago."

Donnie regarded the place where Granny always sat. Her final words cut through his heart like shards of broken glass. *I saved you a spot.*

"And sometimes she talks," continued Linda.

"She tells ghost stories and silly jokes and tales about her childhood days. Sometimes she sings and the swing moves back and forth. It always ends with laughter, before the swing grows still and empty."

A song from decades ago played in his mind and tears bloomed in his eyes.

"You don't know what kind of man I was. What I did."

Something in the woman's eyes told him that, somehow, she did. Rocking forward, Linda stood and walked to the door.

"Stay as long as you like. In fact, any time you want to come and sit – after my husband and children are asleep – well, that's perfectly okay with me."

"I won't be coming back," he told her truthfully.

"I got a bad diagnosis a while back." The word formed in his throat, hard and bitter, slow in coming out.

"Cancer."

"I'm sorry to hear that," she said and meant it. "Well, I reckon I better go in."

Donnie attempted a smile and failed miserably.

"I appreciate you allowing me to spend some time… to atone."

She turned her face toward the door and nodded. Before going in, she spoke softly.

"I don't know if she'll come. If you'll even get to see her. But never doubt that she loved you. It's written on her face. Every time."

Donnie watched as the woman went inside. A moment later, the porch light winked out and he found himself sitting in darkness. He embraced the black of night, however. Illuminated, he felt vulnerable, like an exposed nerve.

"Forgive me," he whispered. Hoping, praying that she would come.

He listened for the tinkle of the wind chimes.

But it never came.

∽

Linda Lowery often thought of the man on the porch. The morose, tormented soul with the hollow eyes and the suit of clothes that hung loosely upon his diseased and emaciated form.

She had hoped he would come back. To visit the porch… to try again. But he never had. The first night she had encountered him had been the last.

It was an evening in late September when she sat in the parlor, curled up on the sofa, reading a romance novel. Her husband, David, was doing a crossword puzzle in that day's paper and listening to his music. Johnny Cash, Ferlin Husky, Loretta Lynn.

The evening was cool, but the room was stuffy, so they had opened the window for some air.

She was about to turn to the next chapter of her book, when she heard the wind chimes twirl melodically from the eaves of the porch. On an evening that held no breeze.

Linda marked her place and laid her book aside. Breathed in deeply and held it. Listening.

A burst of static crackled from the radio's speaker, mangling music and scrambling lyrics. Then, the song that had been playing was replaced by another. Monotoned, the banjo strummed, and the reedy vocals rang out, as though echoing from an eternity ago.

Save me a spot on the old porch swing,
That spot where we met in the height of spring…

Her husband's brow furrowed in frustration, and he shook his head. "What the heck…?" He reached over from his armchair to fiddle with the station dial.

"No," said Linda. "Let it play."

With a grunt, David sat back in his chair and returned to his puzzle, allowing the old song to run its course.

Beyond the music, the tinkling of the chimes stopped.

Linda turned her head and looked through the screen of the parlor window.

There, in the gloom, the porch swing was occupied… like she had found it countless times before.

But unlike the other occasions, not one form sat there, but two.

And, as the swing swayed to and fro, she was certain she could hear the sound of distant laughter.

Parlor
1989

Love Historically
Justin Holley

His first celebrity crush, or perhaps historical crush was a better term, was Anne Frank. And if anyone pronounced her name in that pretentious "open up and say ahh" sounding way, he would just go ahead and punch them in the larynx. Yes, Jesse had loved her, and had daydreamed of killing Nazis to rescue her from their clutches, sweeping her off her feet and marrying her. Loving babies into her. The whole nine yards. Jesse knew others might think his love interests bizarre, but he didn't care.

These daydreams brought him to today, this very moment, the culmination of his young life's work. He would realize a dream-come-true, a forever love not tainted by the world. A righteous love in which both parties would thrive and flourish in the relationship.

Not just him, or her, but both. A safe space where they could help each other through thick and thin. A relationship which would transcend the barrier between life and death.

The parlor shone with his diligence, cleaned and smelling great, of incense and evergreen. He wanted to impress Sarah, his ghostly love.

This love not just the infatuation of an adolescent, but that of a grown man. He had researched so much about her and this residence, and just knew they were compatible.

Keenly aware that other rooms in the historic mansion harbored their own spirits, Jesse only concerned himself with one. *The one.* The one he had read so much about – about heartbreak and loss. And death.

She needed someone; didn't deserve an eternity destined for nothing but loneliness and isolation. They could warm this parlor, and their own lives, with the blossoming heat of their romance.

Jesse peered around the lavish parlor. The marble floors were well-swept. The plush rugs underneath the crimson davenport and twin sitting chairs looked fluffy and fresh, feeling pleasingly soft on his bare feet.

The walls were adorned with landscapes of the surrounding countryside: copses of birches surrounded by dense evergreen thickets only broken by the occasional fast-running creek or spring-fed pond. The hearth and bed of the gigantic fireplace glowed with his care, a bundle of sticks ready for his lighter when needed for both warmth and ambience.

He had made sure of these things, especially the cleanliness, because what gal didn't appreciate a tidy man who proved willing to go the extra mile for the *one* he loved – the one his heart ached for?

Yes, he also wore a shroud of debilitating aloneness and felt eager to shed it. Jesse wanted this win for them both.

He avoided glancing at the exit because it might give Sarah the wrong impression, his devotion deemed as temporary. He hoped his trust in her was starkly obvious, and that Sarah would trust him to never harm her or leave her.

He thought, just for a moment, about himself, his own loneliness, how traditional relationships always ended, leaving him alone and cold. Yes, he had given them a fair shake, but they were a no-go.

He harbored a small bit of guilt that his parents would never hold grandbabies, but such was life. He and Sarah deserved happiness, whatever it took to achieve it, and whatever that happiness looked like.

If it worked for him and Sarah, then the rest of the world could go hang. Jesse glanced at the entrance to the room, again, then refocused his efforts.

With gentle tenderness, to help him focus, Jesse peered at a Polaroid photograph which sat on the coffee table in front of him. Part of him enjoyed perusing it, the only visual proof of his love's existence. Yet, a wave of guilt always washed over him for his greedy gaze, peering at her in such a vulnerable moment.

Snapped by a hardhearted ghost hunter a few years back, the photo captured *his* Sarah crouched on the hearth, hand to her own cheek in apparent sorrow, as if reliving the trauma which befell her decades ago. Jesse hadn't minded parting with the hundred bucks it cost him to secure it.

His hand trembled as a wave of grief and anxiety rippled through him. He glanced at his hand and studied it. *Curious.*

Feeling the need to act, Jesse said, "Sarah, are you here? Can you communicate in some way?"

He pointed at the bottom of his pants legs.

"I know you passed away long ago, so I want to tell you about what things are like today. Notice my pants legs are rolled up? That's the style nowadays, such as it is."

He pointed at his Nike sneakers next to the davenport.

"Notice the friendship pins on my laces?" Jesse paused.

"Also notice how few there are?" He didn't wish to sound melancholy but sometimes couldn't help feeling that way.

"I know I shouldn't complain, not to you."

He looked around the room for any sign of Sarah's presence. Jesse felt uncomfortable pointing out weakness but felt it important that Sarah know the real him, not some work of perfectionist fiction.

Nothing stirred in the room, except for a couple of flies in the double-hung window adorned with crimson treatments which overlooked the front porch. Jesse quickly averted his gaze.

The porch harbored its own spirits, and he didn't wish to intrude on the domain of another.

Jesse decided to converse further, to break the ice, and hopefully put Sarah at ease.

"So, the year is 1989. Lots of cool things have happened so far… I mean besides meeting you."

He chuckled.

"The Berlin wall came down. So, the cold war between the East and West is officially over. No more nuclear war worries. That's a blessing."

Jesse wondered briefly how nuclear fallout would affect the spirit world.

"Conversely, Exxon spilled a metric-fuck-ton of oil into Prince William Sound in Alaska. Not good for the local wildlife, I hear, but no threat to us. Just sharing. I think it will push the price of gas over a buck a gallon though."

He thought for a moment.

"I know you may not understand all these things, but we have forever for me to explain them to you.

"Nintendo came out with their platform called Gameboy in July. It's electronic, so we may be able to enjoy it together. You know, as I'm sure you've already found out, spirits can manipulate electronics."

After a moment, he decided to bring things back to him and Sarah.

"I've read so much about you, Sarah," Jesse said.

He hoped his voice conveyed his good nature and respect.

"You're famous… in a way. A few real-crime authors and paranormal investigators have written about you. They even made a short documentary which won a prize at the Cannes festival back in '83."

He waited for a response.

When nothing happened, Jesse continued, "That's how I first discovered you, started to research who you were as a person."

He smiled.

"We're so similar, you and I. We're both sensitive people with the need for companionship. I read that you liked to dance. I love it too."

Jesse paused as he chose his words.

"I – I just haven't had much opportunity. Like you, I'm shy, and it gets in the way of things. I want to change that with you."

He glanced around the room in hopes of a sign.

When nothing happened, Jesse walked over to the hearth, his bare feet slapping on the cold marble floor.

He reached down to the portable boombox he had put there earlier. Jesse had made sure the batteries were fresh as he didn't want to count on the house's electricity.

When he rented the room, the landlord explained that it could sometimes go out unexpectantly, occasionally for days because of the remote location.

According to the paranormal articles he had read, batteries weren't a sure bet due to spirits draining their energy. Jesse would risk it.

"I made a mixed tape for you," Jesse said.

"So, we can dance."

He sat down on the hearth next to the boombox, patting the space next to him.

"These are some songs that convey how I feel. Some of them are a tribute to your past, as well. I hope you enjoy them."

He pushed the play button. It didn't engage at first, so he concentrated and poked the button again. This time he heard an audible click.

The music started and Jesse thought it sounded as if he listened to it through a cup of water. This didn't matter. All that did matter was what Sarah thought of his selection.

"When I'm With You" by Sheriff echoed around the room.

"This is one of my favorites. I hope you like it."

He stood.

"I always wanted to slow dance to this song but never have. Will you do me the honor?"

Jesse waited for a response, just about to give up, when he thought he noticed a glimmer from the other side of the hearth. He walked over.

"Are you here, Sarah?" Jesse reached out with his right hand.

"Please, take my hand. I'm yours if you want me. I'm not going anywhere."

The faintest tingle erupted on his fingertips, perhaps Sarah's energy mingling with his.

"That's it. I can feel you." Jesse stood that way a long while.

The song ended and "Heaven" by Warrant fired up.

"I picked this one specifically for you, Sarah."

Jesse continued to hold his hand out.

"I know your husband owned a factory and you could see it from your front porch. Sure, I know it's been torn down for decades now, but I just knew you would like the song."

He paused out of respect before going on to his next topic.

"I – I know he shot you on the porch, then dragged you in here to die. I'm so very sorry. I read that he was a jealous man and thought you had fallen in love with one of the factory workers. Maybe you did, but that doesn't matter to me."

A soft, flowing form, tendrils much like vapor, coalesced into a semi-humanoid shape, then dissipated as if Sarah was shy or playing coy.

"I saw you, Sarah! I saw you. That's excellent. You don't have to be shy. We have all the time in the world to take things slow and easy."

He made sure his smile showed his genuine enthusiasm as the song continued.

"So, I've worked at a couple factories in my day. I also worked at a gas station and made a little money in real estate."

Jesse looked down and his demeanor grew thoughtful.

"I actually got the real estate license so I could eventually secure this room. Well, it worked. Here we are. I've invested some money I got from Grandma when she passed, and the trust will pay the rent indefinitely. At least until the

Justin Holley

funds run out. But by then… well, suffice to say, we have forever to get to know each other. I'm going to live in the parlor here, with you, and we can do whatever you want. Anytime we want."

The chill caused by Sarah's presence reminded Jesse of the fireplace and its contents.

With hands that didn't seem to work as well as he wished, he picked up the lighter, concentrated on holding it close to the tinder underneath the wood, then flicked the flint-wheel.

Nothing happened.

He tried again, and a small spark emanated from the wheel, but not enough of one to ignite the tinder.

Jesse took a deep breath, concentrated, and flicked the wheel once more. This time the tinder caught.

Fire spread up through the dry wood. The lighter fell from his hands and rattled to the floor.

"There, isn't that better?" Jesse said, rubbing his hands together.

"Sarah, you can even use the heat energy from the fire to make yourself known."

He didn't want to mention the batteries in the boombox, because he did want to dance with her before they bled dry.

"Heaven" ended with Janey Lane's mesmerizing vocals, and "Girl You Know It's True" by Milli Vanilli took its place.

Jesse smiled sheepishly.

"So, since I created this tape, these asshats got busted for lip synching. This isn't even their voices, I'm told. At least when they're on stage," he said.

"However, the sentiment still holds true. I hope you can still appreciate it."

The fire crackled next to Jesse, but despite the intense heat energy, he felt a cooler gust around his neck as spectral tendrils enveloped him in an embrace.

Jesse felt his spirits soar.

The embrace felt romantic and loving, sustainable. Sarah's ephemeral arms grew more solid by the second, increasing the pressure on his neck and shoulders. It felt as though her energy was mingling with his.

He couldn't allow himself to imagine the implications of this just yet. Thinking about making love with her would drive him insane if it didn't come to fruition.

18

He would remain patient, just enjoy her company, and the fact that she must feel the same as he did. But he really did want to kiss her lips, her neck, and whatever else.

For a moment, his insecure nature took over and Jesse wondered if she was a lot more experienced in love than himself.

Obviously, she had been married, so probably, yes. She could probably teach him a thing or two. Fine by him. This didn't matter.

Lead away, Sarah. Take control.

Jesse leaned into her touch.

"I can feel you, Sarah. Thank you. We can always be together. I just want you to know that."

He could feel a tingle which started on his cheeks and spread lower across his arms and chest.

"Your hugs feel rad."

Jesse decided to sit in the rocking chair and see what happened next.

The form of a woman appeared in front of him. Sarah wore what Jesse assumed she died in, a lightweight summer dress adorned with various wildflowers.

Her shoulders were bare, as was her head, her locks of fine brown hair cascading over her shoulders. She looked almost solid now and something inside Jesse squeezed tight with anticipation.

Sarah's light blue eyes bore into his with an intensity that Jesse hoped he reciprocated. Things were definitely heading in the right direction, his little experiment coming to glorious fruition.

"You're so beautiful," Jesse said.

Sarah reached down and cupped Jesse's cheek. The tingling intensified; the pleasure more than he could have hoped for.

They could be together. *It worked!*

"Girl You Know Its True" ended and "Eternal Flame" by the Bangles started.

Jesse scooted closer to Sarah and said, "This is one of my favorite new songs. I picked it because I want you to know we can live together, here, forever."

Sarah materialized on Jesse's lap and their faces came together.

Jesse's entire body erupted in the intense tingling of their combined energies. He knew they would be happy together... forever and ever.

Justin Holley

He closed his eyes, held her close by the fire, and rocked back and forth to the music. His entire body felt like it would explode with pleasure, and he didn't care if it did.

All his life, Jesse worried about things like that, but not now. Now he would just enjoy the sensation and let happen whatever would happen.

No stopping now.

A whisper in his ear, *"Jesse."*

"Yes – yes! That's me. Jesse. I hear you."

Joy erupted within him. Not only could he now feel Sarah, but Jesse could also hear her.

"Oh, Sarah. This is fantastic."

He could feel her weight on his lap, their energies entwining and driving them toward a wonderful, cataclysmic first coupling.

The sensation built until Jesse thought he would explode into a million pieces.

"Life Goes On" by Poison started up on the boombox.

"You get it, Sarah? Life goes on. We're proof of that right now."

Even to himself, Jesse's words sounded breathy and laced with pleasure.

He didn't care.

He was in love with the girl on his lap and they could do this always and forever and nobody could possibly interfere.

The outside world would just fade away and leave them to their business of loving each other.

Jesse didn't know if Sarah could leave the room, but they would find out, find a way to go for walks in nature, hand in hand. They could do almost anything they wanted.

The sky is the limit.

Jesse held Sarah close as the world faded around them, rocking together to the music, enjoying each other's company.

He felt a breath in his ear and smiled as he felt better and better.

Jesse could feel the teeming of Sarah's energy as she loved him.

They had both been lonely for so long and now they had each other. No more stress, or worries, or lonely nights. Nothing but them and whatever they wanted to do, now and forever.

A voice came from over by the entrance to the parlor.

A man wearing a leather, Cajun-style hat spoke to an Emergency Services responder.

When they had arrived, Jesse didn't know, and didn't care. His attention, and rightfully so, had been projected toward nobody but Sarah.

The man had a southern accent. "Yeah, found him here about a half-hour ago. He came by himself with a bunch of stuff. When things got quiet, thought I should check on the kid. Too bad."

The EMS officer stared at the rocking chair. "What are you doing here, sir?"

"Oh, trying to meet the ghosts who live on the porch here. I want to write a story about it. I'm an author… Ron Kelly is the name."

The official nodded, then said, "Creepy that the music is still playing, and the fire is going. And – and the chair."

He pointed where it rocked back and forth.

"No breeze to speak of."

Ron Kelly said, "Yep. All that started up *after* I found the body. Spooky, right?"

The EMS guy nodded and grimaced. He looked like he wanted to bolt.

Still holding Sarah tight, Jesse watched the frightened EMS guy walk up to the corpse dangling from the ten-foot entrance header.

Jesse had had a helluva time getting up there. Had to bring a ladder and everything.

But things turned out just fine.

He and Sarah could now spend eternity together. Neither of them would feel lonely ever again.

Kitchen
2012

Seeking Ruin
Jeremy Megargee

Harper feels like a rodent in the kitchen of Hale House, exposed by too much light. She is accustomed to shadows, those that rule her internal world, and those that lurk in the outer parts of life.

Her hoodie is tight across her face, and her tattered battle vest clings to her petite frame, the pins and patches covering up the frayed parts of the material.

Her makeup is smeared black winged eyeliner, her features of the pretty, cadaverous sort, a corpse maiden fresh from the pit of a deep dark depression.

There's a significant amount of metal decorating that face, and when she's nervous and the social anxiety is roaring more than usual, she has a habit of reaching up and twisting her septum piercing back and forth in her nose, the sensation almost pleasant in some dim unfathomable way.

She is often nervous, so this act is common.

The listing on the board at the community college said that Hale House was seeking a caretaker for a season before significant repairs would be made to the library and ballroom, so Harper snatched one of the phone number tabs, wrinkling it up and depositing it into the pocket of her jeans, that lost dimension where forgotten items go to die.

And she did forget all about it for a long time, but then things became hardscrabble, finances were threadbare, and Harper needed a miracle to keep her impoverished head above water.

The miracle came in the form of this big rambling mansion, a place so vast that the interior seems labyrinthine and intimidating. Her first thought when a distracted real estate agent gave her a brief tour and handed her the key was that it would be easy for a human to just fall through the cracks in a house like this.

Jeremy Megargee

To have both flesh and spirit meld with the walls, never again to be seen in the land of the living.

She paces the tiles, impeccably clean, almost too clean for a dirty girl like her to be walking on. The kitchen itself is three times the size of the little shitty studio apartment she was evicted from a month or so ago. The fridge rumbles like a sleeping monster, and she's tempted to poke it awake and find some grub.

She opens a few cupboards and rummages around, and they remind her of gaping mouths just waiting to slip out a tongue from a high place of darkness.

Harper knows what the arrangement is. She is to occupy the mansion, to have a presence so that the property isn't vacant while awaiting upgrades. Some light cleaning and checking of the electrical wiring to ensure that all is in proper order, but other than that, she is free to explore each corner that calls.

She has roamed already, but only the surface has been scratched. Each stroll through Hale House seems to lead her back to this kitchen.

There's something about the kitchen that brings her a degree of comfort. The granite island to sit at, the looming stove that sends up little pleasant flames to warm the pores in the face. It is a hub of creation, a zone where tastes are not to be denied.

It's nothing like the kitchen from Harper's childhood.

The grimy floor's stained in cat piss. The dirty dishes rotting in the sink, a birthplace for maggots and lingering clouds of flies.

The hoarded piles of garbage and cardboard and that stinking kerosene stove that sat in the center of the floor to warm the room, and yet despite its best efforts, a coldness reigned beyond its rim.

Harper remembers the dysfunction of that household. Her broken parents screaming broken phrases at each other day and night, and never realizing that in doing so, they were breaking their child in the process.

Those memories are always in her head, and they scurry the mental corridors like rats that are too clever to ever be trapped and expelled.

She twists at her septum, and she scrunches up golden eyes that could have been so much more if she had been born to a safe place with safe and nurturing people, but sometimes life has the tendency fuck hard, and there's not a whole hell of a lot you can do about that.

Harper goes to the great gleaming stove, and she cranks up the gas and lets the pilot burn a pretty blue, and she simply stands there and stares into it for a while. She gets close enough so that her eyelashes almost singe, that small eager flame adding a warmth just inches from the piercings that adorn her face.

Harper was born in a hell that most wouldn't understand, and the flames are nothing but familiar. Hale House is a strange and magical dream in comparison. It is a glimpse of world that she's never even imagined possible to touch.

The wealth, the complex architecture, and all the creature comforts of existence that have always been forbidden to a love-starved stray like her.

She inhales the scent of clean and nice and normal, and it lodges in her nostrils, because it makes no sense at all. It's comparable to handing a wildflower to a chimpanzee in a lab that is expecting the stab of syringes and the prod of scalpels.

What is this?

This Hale House that she now inhabits, and she nothing more than a little rat of a girl in maze. A maze that makes the most sensitive parts of her itch.

She has brought something here. Something allowed to fester in dysfunction, toxicity, and the beautiful black broken parts of a human brain. Harper is unaware of it, but she always been excellent food. Perfect energy. A host for pessimism and clouded negativity that billows outward unseen, tasting and touching as it goes.

From somewhere behind Harper, where she stands enchanted by the pilot flame of the stove, a kitchen door softly cracks open by itself, and then it closes just as softly. This repeats itself several times, and she does not notice.

It is subtle and quietly invasive, something jittery and wrong that craves to crawl in fresh confines. It clings to Harper like sickly perfume, and it waits.

It has always been patient.

∞

Harper has vices.

Her decades of dysfunction have transformed her, and deep within, she harbors deviancy.

She likes cheap pleasure, pleasure that makes her forget, and pain that is so fucking volcanic that it splits her head wide for just a few precious seconds, making it seem like she's not a person at all, but a splattered weeping rose beneath the boot heel of a universal gardener.

She sits cross-legged on the granite island in the kitchen, her fingers going pitter-patter on the surface, and she doomscrolls through BDSM forums on her Motorola Droid.

She's not exactly sure what she's looking for, but she'll know it when she sees it. There's a vague approximation of what she wants in the far back of her mind.

An animal.

Something big and hard and cruel that will make her do things. A man that looks more like a monster, capable of restraint, but also capable of terrible cataclysmic violence.

She wants that.

She wants to curl up especially close to that, licking at stingers and claws, sucking down poison in the form of a pacifier.

It's a masochism that runs so deep that it often scares her. Some part of her begs and whines on her knees for a personal annihilation. Harper doesn't think that it would be considered traditional suicidal ideation, but instead something far darker.

It is ruin that makes her glisten the most between her inner thighs. It is ruin that defines her. It is ruin that she cries for in the night when no one is there to see. She remembers an old low budget fantasy movie she watched when she was a teen. A particular line of dialogue always stood out.

A broken villain of a character kneeled in pools of shadow, emotion wrecking at his features, and he looked down to an angelic figure dying in his arms. A figure that saw not what he was, but what he could have been had his potential been reached.

"I am ruined. Why can't you see that?"

Harper chokes up when she thinks of that line. It is more relatable than anything she has ever heard in her entire shattered life. It is a part of her, and she cannot purge it out.

She travels the familiar passageways of the online kink community, always searching, forever yearning, aching to find something that will scrape her clean and make her raw. Her eyes light up, because potential stares at her from the screen.

His pics align with what she needs. He is big, ugly, and his hands are calloused catcher's mitts.

The kind of brutal rogue you'd expect to see looming in a knife-shaped alley on a cold dark night. A man that knows hurt, a man that *will* hurt. She scrawls out the message carefully, imploring him to make her his toy, and she scratches at her chipped black nail polish as she does so, adding little flakes of lingering dark to the pristine tiles of Hale House.

Harper is hyper-focused on the phone in her hands, and she is unaware of the cupboards opening in unison above her, gaping black mouths, toothless and eager.

She has earbuds locked in tight, shrieking metal blasting from them, and so even the sound doesn't squeeze through. The smack of wood against wood, the precise disruption.

The hammer-fisted knocking on the ceiling, and under tiles of the floor, and deep in the skeletal framework of the walls. Knocks with no origin, knocks that make no sense, knocks that cannot exist because no person can squeeze themselves up into such small spaces, but they resound all the same.

It is noisy chaos, designed to rip at the senses, but Harper doesn't even notice it, lost in her own little aching hellscape. She's been surviving in bubbles of chaos all of her life. She is all instinct and hair-trigger impulses, a prey animal that has been so scared for so long that it would be a mercy if the predator were to finally show up and eat her.

Her phone pings in her earbuds, and the brute has messaged back. He will give her the gift of pain. He will dominate, and she will slither down into submission. She will kiss scuffed work boots and lick at the thick purple veins in his forearms as he strangles her. She will make of her mouth an invitation, and all of the world's worst vampires will come slinking in.

Harper's eyelids are twitching, too much caffeine and not enough sleep. She uses every ounce of self-control she has not to rip off her faded black jeans and start masturbating right there on the kitchen island. She gets like this when the promise of pain is on the horizon. Something feral, something twitchy, something needy in her core.

All around her, with the metal still blistering so loud that her eardrums nearly bleed, the knocks are drowned out, but they continue. They pick up in speed and aggression.

It sounds like there are things in the walls and under the floor that want to break through and get to her, to take hold of her and shake her like an unwanted ragdoll.

That's how it often feels in her skull, too. The sensation of things knocking from within and desperate for a cathartic release. Knock, knock, knock. May I come in sir, pretty please, with all the ripest cherries on top?

She lies down and stretches out across the granite, a feline on her ninth life, and she fantasizes about what is to come. The brutality. The sadism.

The vessel that brings ruin into this big, bruised mansion that she does not own and never will. It has to be soon.

She wants to be worthless and wilted, and it *must* be soon.

∞

"My safe word is gumdrop."

Jack barely reacts at all when Harper tells him this. He doesn't talk much. He looms big and crooked in the doorframe, a mammoth with vacant tunnel eyes and crisscrossed scars across his brow and chin.

He looks at her and through her in equal measure. He wears a tank top, frayed jeans, and boots with scuffed steel toes. His hair is a crew cut the color of straw, and he smells of tainted cedar and pine, a man who spends most of his time handling a chainsaw in isolated forest regions and picking the splinters out from his big tombstone teeth.

For Harper, time ceases to exist when the games start. Hours or days, she cannot tell, and she does not care. He bends her over the countertop, ripping fishnet stockings with his knuckles, and he uses a studded leather paddle to make artwork on her porcelain cheeks.

Welts of red, raised bruises of purple, and the sickly yellow of flesh tortured to limitations. With each strike he makes her count, and she wonders when the skin will break and ooze, when the plasma will bubble to the surface, but Jack is careful.

He bruises and he bludgeons, but he doesn't let her bleed. She's not allowed to bleed until he says so.

There are breaks. She's allowed to breathe, to cry big thick mascara tears, and to drink glasses of water like a woman scorched in the desert, dying for a few cool droplets across the tongue. And speaking of tongues, he has lots of uses for hers.

Every item of clothing has been shredded from her body, a kneeling servant, and he gives her things to lick. Rich chocolate from a silver spoon. The grit from his boot heels. The sweat from his belly button, nestled in a personal wilderness of body hair.

He puts that big, calloused thumb into her mouth, pushing apart swollen lips, and she sucks with endless desperation. She has a void inside of her, and she makes direct eye contact with Jack, willing him to fulfill every role she needs.

Father, fiend, and feral thing from a black-walled place in time.

He smacks her across the face so hard that long strings of saliva drip down her chin, each impact snapping her head from side to side. Her eyes roll up, a fawn fucked up beyond conceivable repair, and the moan that starts in the far back of her throat is comparable to a crushed animal dying on the asphalt of the road.

She snuffles snot back into her nostrils, wiping the moisture from her septum, and when his hand clamps down on her windpipe and begins to squeeze, Harper smiles so bright that her face threatens to split into a jack-o-lantern. Her cheeks bloom with pulsing roses, and she counts the little black spots that dance in front of her eyes.

Each gasp is brimstone, and Hell drips out from between her legs to pool sticky against the floor.

A horrendous aroma is permeating the kitchen, rot from the lowest pit of the earth, corpses rolling in the sunlight, roadkill smeared across the stained-glass windows of abandoned churches. The stink does not come from Jack or Harper. It has no conceivable origin, but the big man notices it, his nostrils flaring in mild disgust.

"Your house smells of rot, little one."

Harper is whining, begging, so trapped in her own submissive headspace that she's unable to articulate a decent reply. She doesn't notice the smell. All she smells is Jack's sweat, all she wants is Jack's rage.

Silverware rattles in the drawers all around them. Glasses pop out from the cupboards and shatter on the tiles, and as Jack continues to strangle her, Harper has no choice but to drag her knees through the broken glass.

The overhead light starts to swing violently back and forth, a pendulum in motion, and the gargantuan dom cuts his eyes upward, watching this noise and disorder take hold all around them. He studies it without real interest, eyes lacking shine, a dog that sees only what it hungers for.

"There are devils here. Devils in you, little one. I see them screaming in the whites of your eyes."

Harper pouts, pushing her throat deeper into that life-crushing hand, getting off on the lack of oxygen, everything about this moment burning in her guts and her sex like the embers of a campfire.

Her voice is a soft little croak, an invitation.

"Ruin me."

He doesn't answer with words. His actions answer for him.

Jeremy Megargee

He lifts her skyward, toes painted the color of midnight leaving the floor, her naked body running with rivulets of sweat and black tendrils of her own makeup.

Jack hauls her to the side and choke tosses her up against the wall, wedging her there before reaching down to see just how soaked she is.

Sin pours from eyes and her soul.

The pain is a distant roar lost in the hallway of fractured personhood, and Harper wants to cradle it like an infant, nurse it at her breast for long as she can. The fingers bite so deeply into her neck that she knows she'll be wearing his handprints like a necklace for weeks to come, and what of it?

All the best jewelry is forged from scars.

Consciousness is eager to depart. She finally becomes aware of the noise, the bizarre cacophony that is happening beyond them.

Forks, spoons, and knives flying across the room. Cupboards opening and slamming on their own. The reek of decay bubbling up from dimensions unseen.

Something is with them. A third. Feeding and fucking and fueled on the toxic energy she and Jack are creating together. What has come to Hale House with her?

Eyelids flutter and close. She barely hears her own limbs topple downward when Jack drops her, a marionette that he has momentarily lost interest in playing with.

Nightmares flash, a sloshing dark soup in her brain, but they don't compare to reality. The sour presence in the kitchen senses her slumber, and its chaos quiets, silverware clattering down to rest against the floor.

Peace reigns, but it isn't meant to last.

∞

Harper awakens bleary-eyed with a stiff neck on the kitchen floor, her cottony mouth still tasting of Jack's depravity. He stands above her, a still monolith with heavy veined hands hanging at his sides. She purrs like a mutilated kitten, curling up all the sore parts of herself and pulling her body into a sitting position against the wall.

"That was nice. Thank you, sir."

He doesn't respond. He clasps his big hands together, rubbing at reddened knuckles and examining the pitted palms.

"We haven't started the knife play yet."

Harper stretches her arms outward, her tongue slipping out to wet dry and cracked lips. There's pleasant warmth in her core, and she feels satiated.

"You've worn me out, Jack. I need some rest. We can delve into the knife play the next time you come over."

She expects that her consent will be respected, but Jack is a stranger that she let into her home, and she doesn't know his character at all.

She sees more of his character when his big hand darts down and twists her up by the hair, making a rope of it as he drags her across the kitchen. This pain is different. It is panicky and wrong. It is unwanted and unwelcome in comparison to what she openly submitted herself to.

"Gumdrop, Jack. Gumdrop. I've had enough for tonight. Gumdrop, okay?"

He seems not to hear. He roughly pulls her up, grabbing her by the waist and lifting her so that she is sitting bare-assed on the rim of the sink.

"Ever since I was a boy, I've liked knives. Knife play is my favorite. But I do it a little different. I don't like to tease with the blade, to trace the skin and pretend that it might go further. Maybe you've had men do that with you before."

He leans forward, inhaling her hair in big gusts, a breathy beast that isn't satisfied by what she has already willingly given. His sweat has gone sour, and at this particular time, Harper just wants him away from her. She wants him out of Hale House.

"I like for the knife to go inside of you. Deep."

His eyes glaze over, and she searches them for humanity. There is none to be seen. It's like looking up at a grizzly the moment before it decides to maul.

"You have my permission to bleed, little one."

Jack's hand has wandered down to an open drawer, and he produces a large, serrated steak knife from the darkened hollow. The lights are flickering again. There's wind in a room where wind should not exist.

Doors slam, the fridge shakes from side to side, and that unseen visitor is there again to sup on the violence between them.

Harper finally recognizes the disembodied force for what it is. She thinks of the dysfunction of her childhood, the torment of the mental illness she has lived with, the nourishment of her dark pleasures and her even darker pains.

It is born from her, and it manifests through her.

A poltergeist.

Chaos, disruption, and formless malevolence.

Hale House isn't haunted. Harper is haunted.

Jack is noticing the objects flying around, and the noises finally start to irritate him.

"These fucking ghosts. They will not rob of me of my whore. Nothing will."

A well-muscled arm cranks back, and he looks to go low and split her abdomen open with his blade, but it's like invisible insects are tormenting him, forks and spoons and pans and pots all levitating in the air around him, making of him a big furious tornado of a man.

Jack is pitched forward overtop the sink, and Harper scrambles down to the floor and crawls free from him.

The garbage disposal starts with a metallic whir, and before Harper even realizes it, Jack's knife-wielding hand has vanished down into that chewing drain, chunks of meat flying, blood spattering upward in a fine mist.

Something pushes him down with unnatural strength, his wrist evaporating, big forearm shredding down to bone, and before he is finally released, the disposal has chewed him down to bicep.

When Jack pulls back and spins around, all that remains of his right arm is a ragged kite of meat, deflated balloon strips of flesh where a bulging bicep should be.

His face has gone bloodless, drained to pallor, and the best of him is leaking red across the kitchen tiles. He collapses in a heap, goliath fallen, and Harper lies on her back in the lake of blood that comes out of the huge man.

She does her best to catch her breath, her arms pinwheeling outward, like she's doing backstrokes on a floor saturated in plasma.

Her mind is a perfect fog, and she can think of nothing now but the hooded bathtub on one of the upper levels of Hale House.

Harper imagines how good it would feel to sink down into perfumed water and wash herself clean. To wash her wounds, soak her sores, and let the flesh go numb in thoughtless bliss.

The poltergeist is in her head now, chattering and giggling. It reminds her of a malformed child that mocks her from the branches of a high tree.

There's been so much hurt tonight, doesn't she deserve a bath to heal?

Yes, she does.

Harper rises and traces her fingertips through the warm fragrant water. She'll scrub the red from her porcelain skin. She'll scrub until the ugliness is exorcised from within.

Her golden irises flit back and forth, hopeless and addicted to harm.

She'll dip her toes in, and the rest of her body will follow.

Harper looks down into the bath, swaying dreamlike, and it takes a moment for her vision to clear.

She stands naked atop the kitchen sink, and her toes are hovering dangerously close to the chewing metal razor teeth of the garbage disposal. It looks like a voracious blackened mouth ready to gorge after a long famine.

But then the poltergeist pulls at the strings in her brain, playing internal puppeteer, and once again it's just a nice soothing bath for her to slide into.

Harper whispers to herself, and she tries to ignore the sound of metal teeth chewing against each other down in the bath.

She dips her toes in.

"Ruin me."

Dining Room
1984

Suppertime with the Lord
Mer Whinery

**Account transcribed from a battered Memorex MRXI C90 cassette tape
found in an old Hush Puppies shoebox along with a melted plastic crucifix, a
strip of pink ribbon scented with a faint perfume and handful of human
teeth. Acquired at the garage sale of one Ruth Lavera for approximately one
dollar. Tape # 83.**

It had felt all wrong from the beginning. You'd think my being a grown man,
all the things I had been through my whole life over, I'd have some kind of
insight. Some way to have seen through all of it. I know now, after sitting around
in here for going on five years now, it was probably because I *am* a grown ass
man that these things went unnoticed until it was too damn late.

But if I am being honest with you here, sir, I did feel something was off from
the moment we pulled into the busted-up driveway of that old place. No, more
than that. Something there was just plain bad.

I had just moved from Kansas City down to this little hole in the wall town,
having snagged myself a pretty sweet job tooling around on diesel engines at a
truck stop just outside the city limits, and this was supposed to be a fresh start for
me and my daughter, Charlie.

Her momma had passed a little under a year earlier after getting shot in a
motel room on the turnpike by one of her boyfriends, and I would like mention
that the word boyfriend in this scenario should have smartass quote marks around
it. I don't need to say no more about that.

I had a cousin in town, also the person who had got me my job, hook us up
with a house to crash in for nothing until we got our act together. All we had to do
was spruce it up a little. Nothing big. Just mow the yard, slap some paint on some
faded spots, and patch up some holes on the roof. Keep it from falling down,

basically. It was a real good deal. Not that it mattered, honestly. It was the only deal we could get. Beggars, they say, can't be choosers, and we were beggars in every sense of the word.

Charlie was a real good kid. Pretty normal twelve-year-old. She liked to draw and had a real knack for it. Always carried around a Trapper Keeper filled with notebook paper so she could sketch what she saw when she would go out on her daily walks. Could draw people's faces like nobody else I've ever known. Unicorns and fantasy creatures.

Her momma's dying had really messed with her upstairs, I think. You know, mentally. I got her some help back home through our church, but I don't know how much good it did. Kinda hard to tell someone "just trust in the Lord" when the son of a bitch constantly gives you lemons to suck on.

But she was a trooper. I never had to ask her to help me. Never had to get on to her for being lazy. She minded and never sassed. I was glad for that, as my own mind was on shaky ground. That long drive down from Kansas with her was one of the last really sweet moments of my life. No, it *was* the last sweet moment. Just the two of us and the radio and junk food and laughing our asses off.

The house was a lot bigger than I had expected. In better shape, too. Big old sprawling monster out in the middle of nowhere with a few acres of thick shooting woods, a water well, and a good-sized shed to park my truck and store tools in. The inside of the house was what would be called efficient. Flat white paint in every room and original wood.

It was fully furnished, thankfully. A lot of fancy-schmancy stuff with elaborate carvings and made from kinds of wood I didn't recognize. Not at all the dollar store type crap we were used to and not the sort of things I would buy even if I had the bread to do it. However, it was *our* place at least. It was *home*, and we needed a home to get over what had happened and start behaving like normal people again.

We settled in quickly, got a routine going, and I started my new gig. For a couple of months, it was good. Nice and normal. I felt we had deserved that after all the troubles we had gone through.

Charlie was alone in that house a lot, as I often had to work late into the evening. Now, you have got to understand this was back in a time when kids could be trusted to not eat bleach from under the sink and use the stove without burning the damn house to the ground.

She seemed to really enjoy keeping the house clean and having supper ready when I came shambling home after dark. Except for that one room. I think both of us knew from the second we set foot in that old house there was something about that goddamned dining room that did not feel right. No more than that. It felt *wrong*.

What do I mean by that? Hard to really put my finger on it. Kind of like it didn't belong with the rest of the house. Yeah, that's it. Built as an afterthought, almost.

I didn't see it at first. It was as if my brain didn't want to accept there was something strange, to stir up a problem when things were going so well. Only when Charlie pointed out the room looked like it hadn't been dusted in years, the mirror smudged up and nasty, did I realize it was the only space in the house we had never bothered to clean since we had moved in. We had been avoiding it and hadn't even known it.

It didn't outwardly look off. A big octagonal room with boring off-white paint, bare walls, ten-foot ceilings with some real pretty crown molding and a huge mirror set in a frame so fancy and fragile looking it had to be older than hell.

The mirror was strange in that the glass wasn't like normal glass, or maybe not even glass at all. The surface was a shiny, solid black. When I tapped the mirror with my finger it felt more like some kind of rock. You could see your reflection in it, but it didn't quite look like yourself staring back at you.

To one side was a braided shank of rope. When you pulled that rope, a black velvet curtain would fall across the mirror. Like the curtain in an old movie theater or a stage for a play. Why a mirror would need a curtain was weird to me. But what did I know? I was just a big, simple old country boy who was good at tinkering with big rigs and woodworking.

Me being a grown up, I think I was better able to deal with how it made me feel. Adults get skilled at denial when they need to. Kids, on the other hand, when something is not right it seems to really get under their skin and make them behave strangely.

Children just must have something inside of them which is more responsive to the unknown. They see things with a clearness that only comes with being young. They haven't learned to bury their fears and feelings to survive. To lie as needed.

My worries about the place were validated when Charlie started school that September. Every night when I got home it seemed she would have some new horror to make me shiver. Some rumor or whispering shared by a classmate about the awful things which were supposed to have happened in the house.

Some of these stories were just flat out ridiculous and don't bear mentioning here. In spite of that, there were a few stories which kind of stuck with me. They just sounded right, and one of those stories had to do with the dining room. This would be the one story which, later on after it was all over, I could actually prove. Not that it matters now I guess. Here I am, right? The truth is no longer all that important after that gavel comes smacking down.

I got friendly with a cashier at the truck stop named Molly Ann Miller. She was one of those people who had lived so fast and hard it was impossible to tell how old she really was. Just by looking at her she could have been anywhere from forty to seventy. Smoked menthols bought out of a vending machine and sipped Old Raven out of a paper cup while she rang customers up and flipped burgers.

Molly was an interesting broad. Ask her anything in regard to town gossip and she always had a story. Funny thing is, she was the one who brought up the house, not me. What she told me, I believe, is a true story. It all jived.

One night, after work was done and I was about to leave, she asked me to stay for a drink. She wanted to chat with me a little. I saw no harm in a nice conversation with a stranger. Charlie was at a church lock-in until the next morning, and I wasn't in a hurry to get back to the house when it was dark.

Molly told me about fifteen years before we moved into the house it had been a church. Kind of. A bunch of religious-minded folks had lived there together. Like hippies, I reckon. Nowadays I suppose we would just label them a cult and call it good.

It was just a small group, from what I understand. Probably around ten or eleven people, all of them living and eating and sleeping in the house. They ran some kind of racket selling flower and vegetable seeds on the streets to pay the bills. Molly suspected it was probably all a front for selling weed and acid. People in cults seem to like that sort of thing.

They called themselves the Orphans of Shadow, and their leader was a woman whose real name was Barbie Olson, but her followers called her Sister Twilight. They were what people like to call a death cult. What that means is everything in their religion revolves around dying, and the end game of their beliefs all finish with everyone in the church being dead.

Pretty much like the bible thumpers out there right now, really. But this was different. I would find out later all of this worshipping didn't have one thing to do with Jesus Christ, God, or the Resurrection and the Reward.

They had all died in the house, you see. Every last one of them. There were a dozen different rumors for why they had done it and how they had checked out. The only consensus was that they did indeed croak in the dining room. Nightshade sprinklings in their food and grape juice had been the most popular gossiped cause of death, although Molly told me Sister Twilight had slit her wrists, slowly bleeding out as her flock choked to death.

The bodies sat around that dining room table, the one still in our house, rotting in the summer heat for almost a week before the stink tipped off the mailman. From what I understand the chairs had to be replaced because some of the corpses had begun to rot into the wood and cushions. Apparently heat can do weird things to a dead person.

What became of their remains nobody seemed to know. It was all taken care of both very quickly and quietly by the authorities. Nobody really cared, I guess. A loon for Jesus is a dime a dozen in these parts.

Molly asked me if anything strange had happened since we had moved in. I told her no, which wasn't exactly a lie but wasn't completely true either. Nothing had really *happened*, but if we're being honest here, even back then I knew things were going to go south. Almost like there was a clock ticking inside of my head, counting down the hours until the devil was let loose upon us.

The day after Halloween, I came home from work that night to find Charlie had cleaned up the dining room and had set the table for supper. A big supper. Roast beef and taters and cob-corn and sweet tea. Way too much food for just the two of us.

I almost scolded her for being wasteful, but after seeing how proud she was I thought better of it. She had done it out of love and was just trying to be a good daughter. A kid who earned her keep, I guess.

As soon as I took my seat things immediately felt off. At first I just chalked it up to it being our first official meal in the dining room, and after my conversation with Molly a few weeks earlier it only made everything feel more wrong. It was hard to shake the picture of the decaying bodies of those Bible freaks sitting in the same place I was, guzzling sweet tea and shoveling in mouthfuls of roast and gravy.

Mer Whinery

My mind began to mess with me. I swore I would glimpse something out of the corner of my eye every now and then. A flash of something sitting next to me in an empty chair. A dark stain spreading across the white bed sheet Charlie had spread out as a makeshift tablecloth. A spoiled, vinegary odor which would grow so strong it would make me gag, only to disappear completely after a few seconds.

Even the roast didn't taste right. There was a strange rawness to it. You could look at the beef and tell it was well done, but to sink your teeth into it you would think it had just been freshly hacked from the haunch of a cow still in the middle of dying. All I could taste was shivering meat and blood and something wild. It tasted…alive.

Charlie didn't seem to notice any of it. She barely touched her supper, stabbing at her grub with her fork and having a sip of tea now and again. I wasn't too bothered at the time because she was a girl, she was twelve, and at that age girls can be kind of insecure about their figure, I guess.

When I brought up the flavor of the roast, she only gave me a weird smile and continued poking at her food and began asking me about my day. This too was another odd thing. For the remainder of the meal she was kind of talkative.

She'd always been a quiet kid, real shy and keeping to herself, and after her momma's death she had become damn near a shut-in. Hardly ever talked with friends on the phone or went out. Having a conversation lasting longer than a few minutes, even with me, was unheard of. Yet here she was, a regular chatty Cathy.

She talked with me as if we had been old friends long separated. There was something about the way she was talking to me, her demeanor, was just too… intimate. Asking me personal questions about a woman at work whom I had let slip I found attractive. Giggling. She had an almost flirty manner in the way she went about her questioning. I found myself, time and again, forgetting this was Charlie and not some random barfly I had struck up a conversation with over at the watering hole in Crow Hollow. I wouldn't be lying if said that I didn't like it. Not one bit.

I struggled to finish supper, and when I was done I complimented her on a great meal and voiced how proud I was of how tidy the dining room was. She gave me that strange smile again and stood up, retrieving both her plate and my own, and said:

"You're gonna eat in here from now on."

Harmless enough, right? But it didn't sound that way hearing it coming out of her mouth the way it did. It felt less like a suggestion and more like an order. I let it go, of course. That's why all of this is my fault. If I had just listened to my gut none of this would have ever happened.

Just like how I had dealt with her momma before she got all strung out on speed. I had seen it coming. I knew it was bad. Yet I was just so weak. So soft and in denial. I didn't have the nerve to do what I needed to do to keep her from falling apart. Same with Charlie. Not until things got out of hand and extreme measures had be taken. When you know it's all over.

It was as if that meal, that night, had opened a door or a window into someplace wrong. Days after, I began to feel as if I were not by myself whenever I stepped into that dining room. I felt like none of those chairs pushed up to that old, scuffed table were empty. I could feel something sitting in them. Watching me with cold, hungry eyes. Studying my comings and goings. Learning about me.

The room always felt really hot, even with the air conditioner running full blast. The sort of hot you get when you leave the stove on in the kitchen with the oven door cracked.

Once, while fixing the dishwasher, I swore I heard someone puking in the dining room. Like full-on, face planted in the toilet vomiting up your lunch convulsions. I ran in there afraid it was Charlie only to find the room completely empty. Well, empty of things I could actually see.

I knew something was there. More than something. Something wrong. Something that wanted me to know it was there and I couldn't do jack about it. And you want to hear the really horrible part? I wasn't surprised.

The weird things happening in that room began to feel like it was all normal. Like I should just accept it. I purposely began avoiding the place as much as I could. Dreading the setting sun when suppertime rolled around, and I had no choice but to endure it.

Through it all, Charlie began to act less and less like herself. Disobedient and back-talking over every little thing. Even dumb stuff, as if she were trying to blatantly thumb her nose at me. Again, I knew something was up but didn't want to get into it. I blamed it on puberty and her being an emotional female and all that other dumb stuff.

What made everything worse was, outside of all of this, life in general was going good. I had started dating that nice lady from work, name was Judy Pendrake, and I was even starting to get the idea into my head that getting married again might not be out of the question.

Hell, I'd even given Judy a little old cameo on a gold chain which had belonged to my granny just to show how serious I was taking things.

My own selfish needs were more important to me than dealing with whatever was going on with my own daughter. I just didn't want to be bothered. I figured I had it owed to me after the hell my late wife had put me through. I felt I deserved to be happy and this nonsense with Charlie would take care of itself in its own good time. That was until the book came into the picture.

We found the book the week after Christmas, right after a really nasty cold snap. I had been under the house thawing some pipes which had become frozen, and I heard the sound of rocks falling close to me. I shined my light on where the noise had come from and saw a little hole had opened up in the foundation wall. Something wrapped in a scrap of leather had fallen out and onto the ground. For some reason I didn't feel like looking at it while I was messing around in that crawlspace, so I took it upstairs to my bedroom to get a closer look. It was bound in a strange, scaly red leather. Like a snake's skin but lots rougher. It was a spare little thing. On the cover, inscribed in black letters which seemed to have been burned into the surface of the book were the words:

EVANGELIA UMBRARUM

Some kind of French or something, I guess.

It was about as big as a paperback novel, maybe a hundred pages, give or take five. The paper wasn't like normal paper either. It was very thick, more like construction paper or even a kind of cloth, yellowed with age, every page filled from top to bottom with a fancy cursive script. It looked like English in some places but complete gibberish in others.

Flipping through it, I felt my head start to get woozy. My eyes would start to blur, and it would get hard to see. I lied to myself again, although I knew it was what was in the book, the contents of it, that was making me feel not right. I took it outside to the trash, dumped it in and washed my hands of it, never mentioning it to Charlie. Even then, *even then*, I knew what it was and what it could do.

The next night, a little before midnight, I heard a ruckus outside. I grabbed my sawed-off from under the bed, a flashlight, and crept downstairs and out onto the front porch. My daughter was headfirst in the garbage can, digging frantically and pitching trash out by the handfuls.

I shined my flashlight on her. Her head shot up and she growled at me, her teeth bared like an angry dog. I swear, even her eyes had a wild glint like a possum or a racoon when you catch a reflection of their eyes caught in the beam. She looked wild enough to hurt me.

I asked her what she was doing, and I don't mind admitting right now that I was terrified. Terrified of my child digging through the trash because I knew what she was digging around for. And still I denied everything to myself. All of it could be explained because things like this didn't happen in real life, especially to folks like us.

"Aha!" she hollered, the book held over her head like a trophy, her face all lit up with joy. No, not joy. Now that I think back, I think it was relief.

I told her to put the book in the trash. She just giggled and opened it up, mumbling something under her breath. It was then that I heard them. People whispering along with Charlie as she read from the book. Their voices had a quality like a choir. All of them saying the same words and sounds over and over. Not singing, but chanting. Preaching, maybe. I told her to put the book back in the trash again. My daughter, who had never so much as raised her voice at me in all of her twelve years alive, looked up at me, her eyes a pair of drained black hollows, and screamed.

"SINNERRRRR!!!"

The force of her voice was like a fist crashing into my jaw. I fell to the porch holding my head. I felt her walk past me and stop at the front door. Her voice sounded totally back to normal. Sounded like just like my kiddo again.

It got so much worse as the weeks went by. I don't even know how long, really. All I know is my little girl became less and less both little and my girl. She eventually got kicked out of school because all she would want to do is stand at the front of her class and preach from the book. Stopped turning in lessons.

I guess the last sermon must have really been a doozy, as it brought with it a stern note from the superintendent to not only never bring my kid back to school, but maybe get the hell out of Dodge altogether.

This didn't bother me as much as it might another man. I'd never taken much stock in public school and kind of enjoyed the idea of Charlie learning at home like I had. I was also relieved to have her no longer out and about, possibly embarrassing me.

I thought about making some calls to a doctor who could help her. You know, a psychologist or something. But the nearest one was almost two hours away. I didn't have insurance and was barely skating by on the everyday stuff.

Mer Whinery

Yet I really think the main reason I didn't do anything about it was because I knew they wouldn't be able to do anything. No doctor could. I knew this was way beyond a sickness in the brain, but I felt helpless to do anything about it. It know now it was the room putting those thoughts into my head. After all, the room was in charge.

It didn't really matter. The end was just around the corner. It all happened so fast I barely remember. Maybe I want to believe it didn't. You know, sometimes if you really work at it you can do that. Bury the things that bother you so deep into yourself you can make yourself believe it didn't happen. I was real good at that. A champ.

A few weeks after Charlie's expulsion from school, just before sun-up, I heard a commotion downstairs. Being half-asleep, I fought it off for a little. Then it got louder. Loud enough for me to recognize Charlie's voice, but there was something else. It sounded like her, but it didn't. Like the way she might sound in a few more years. Her voice but deeper, richer.

There were other voices too. The chanting I had heard when she had been reading from the book after digging it out of the trash. I *hadn't* imagined it, after all. The thought of that scared me so bad I felt like I was frozen to my mattress. I couldn't twitch a finger and my blood was like ice.

I said the Lord's Prayer for strength, and I was slowly able to get out of bed, walking on rubber legs downstairs to meet whatever horrible thing awaited me. I knew right then, at the bottom of that landing, the end of my life was waiting on me. Like I was walking toward a waiting hangman's noose.

There was no way to really prepare myself for what I saw. I'm still not sure if I believe it. But I know in my heart of hearts it was it was real. Oh my, there was no way it wasn't.

Charlie was floating a few feet from the dining room floor, head thrown back, and eyes rolled to the whites, dressed in her nightgown with her breast soaked through with fresh blood. In one hand she held my grandad's old buck knife and in the other she held the book. Her mouth was open, but her lips weren't moving.

All of the chanting was coming from her mouth as she bobbed and hovered in place, and seated around the table were what I knew were the Orphans of Shadow. Or what used to be them. Now they were just blobs of swirling gray smoke collected into the rude forms of people, each with a pair of orange holes of light, like hot coals plucked from a potbelly stove, glowing where their eyes should have been.

I could make out mouths twisted in pain, their cries and hollers broadcast through my daughter's throat like a radio from another world.

In the black mirror behind my daughter I saw a reflection, a reflection which should have been my little girl, but it was someone else. A woman dressed in dark robes with long, straight, blonde hair. Her face was a blob of white, no facial features recognizable to me. Only the same terrible eyes, much like her long dead flock seated at the table, trapped in a suffering which would never end. I knew I was looking at Sister Twilight herself. But that still wasn't the worst part.

On the table, oh dear God. That was the worst of it.

Suppertime had arrived, you see. On each plate before every chair, a meal had been set out. Not a meal for the living, but for things which had no business being in this world. For whatever these things were.

A severed hand in a soup tureen garnished with a healthy ladling of blood. A lopped-off foot on our turkey platter, surrounded by a wet coil of bloated guts. A shank of spine with scraps of skin and muscle still hanging on to the bone skewered on a roasting spit. A tangled handful of long red hair still stuck to a scalp scraped from a skull arranged neatly in a big salad bowl, and in its center a human heart, somehow still beating, pulsing in rhythm with the chanting.

Then… I saw my granny's cameo. The golden chain. Now I could scream, because I recognized the meal being served. I shut my eyes up tight and screamed and screamed until my throat felt like it was going to explode. The room was filled with the sounds of vomiting and deranged laughter, the ghosts seated at the table clutching at their throats and gagging, reliving their deaths all over again.

I opened my eyes in time to watch my daughter, now lost to me, draw the buck knife across the underside of her jaw, a clean tear opening across the flesh followed by an incredible flood of stinking, almost sludgy green fluid, clogging and choking her throat. The book suddenly burst into flames and a terrible howling filled the house. Like a wolf gone crazy with kill lust.

For a split second it was as if there was no time and no here. There was no me. Everything was one. The black mirror began to glow with a green light, its surface becoming clearer until it was like a bright shining light. A blinding light.

There was only the light and the howling and the blood and then there was just me and Charlie, her still floating in place like a fisherman's lure bobbing on the surface of a pond. The mirror's light vanished and my little girl locked eyes with me, smiled weakly, then collapsed into a heap on the floor. The stain that spread out from her body, onto the carpet, was a dark red now.

45

Mer Whinery

The mirror itself was empty. Empty and black once again. Whatever awful thing haunted this room, whatever name it called itself, was satisfied now. The sacrifice made to it had been accepted, and it had been deemed very good indeed. Except for one thing. It was not finished with me.

I had to show my devotion to the church.

I knew it was pointless to resist at this point. Charlie had crossed over and now it was my turn to honor her sacrifice. To honor Judy. It was what the book said, you see. I know that now. It was the book.

I sat down at the supper table, in my usual spot, and tucked my napkin into the front of my shirt. My knife was very sharp and that was good too. It was a fine meal set out before me, and I was not to spare a single scrap. I was one of them now. There was nothing else to do but eat. I looked at my daughter's body crumpled on the ground. She looked very peaceful. I also noticed something else. The book was gone. No matter on that one. The book, like my child, had served their purpose. As would I.

When I was finished, some time later, I gathered my daughter's corpse into my arms and walked all the way to town with her. Walked all the way to the police station. Surely they would believe me. What wasn't to believe? I had the proof right there in my arms. They didn't give me a lot of time to tell my story, if you want to know the truth. That kind of irks me.

It's been a little over five years now, and I know that it all worked out for the best. They put me in this place where people will talk to me about what happened. Help me work through it, I guess. Maybe I need that. Maybe I am crazy now, but I know I didn't do any of the things they said I did.

Judy Pendrake's family tried real hard to get the gas chamber for me, but it didn't work. Kinda hate that. I hate to think they believed I did that to Judy. I really liked that woman. I think we could have made a good go of it, us two. She liked football. You know how hard it is to find yourself a woman who really likes football?

I think I might better off in the ground, feeding worms and bugs and the dirt.

But then who would tell everyone about what had happened? About Barbie Olson and her crew of true believers? As for the book, I never saw it again. I've asked around but nobody will tell me anything. Someone has it. Someone somewhere. They have to. It's too important to just not be here anymore. Someone has it and someone knows what it is and what it does.

Maybe it's back at that house, opened up on the dining room table for anyone to read it and appreciate the horrors and wonders inside of it. Maybe she's back there too. Sister Twilight, sleeping inside of the black mirror, waiting for another chance to deliver a sermon on the mount to the faithful just one last time.

Library
1999

The Living Library of Hale House
Samantha Underhill

Introduction

In the haunting shadows beyond the outskirts of town, where city streets become country roads and eerie branching trees conceal untold mysteries, looms Hale House, its aged walls whispering secrets of forgotten eras to all who pass by.

For the newly divorced forty-year-old, Charlotte Graves, the palatial home offered a beguiling escape from her tumultuous reality, a sanctuary in the heart of her new city.

Little did Charlotte know that amidst the grand estate of Hale House, her life was about to take an unexpected turn. For within the old walls, a spectral presence awaited her, and their intertwined destinies would unfold in a supernatural story that defied the boundaries of the living and the dead.

As she embarked on a journey of self-discovery and liberation from the ghosts of her own past, the old house would play a significant role in shaping her future and healing her wounded heart.

But how does a young divorcee come to reside at such a large grand estate? Well, it all began with Harold...

Chapter One: Harold

April 1999

Harold Ashcroft had never truly loved Charlotte. She saw that clearly now. He valued her support, her willingness to cater to his needs for success, but not her as a person, not really.

Charlotte sat, her hands cradling a steaming cup of coffee, lost in thought as she gazed out of the rain-streaked windows of the Hale House parlor.

It seemed years ago since she had mustered the courage to end things with Harold, and yet, time was playing tricks on her, as only a few months had come and gone with her finally moving into her own space, Hale House, in recent weeks.

Charlotte's hazel eyes drifted around the parlor with its elegance and refinement, a blend of Victorian and Regency styles with opulent touches reflecting the history of the place. This was well-outside her normal beige-walled apartment with its beige furniture and beige rugs and beige… well, everything.

"God, that damn apartment was so bland," Charlotte thought aloud.

Harold had loved the beige. He loved the simple cleanness of it and would often reiterate this to Charlotte any time she suggested adding even a small pop of color.

The differences in the spaces that Harold and Charlotte had shared versus Hale House were stark and dramatic. The wholly beige bland apartment now represented the weight of Harold's suffocating selfishness a little too well.

Charlotte paused and really took in her new space. This was her. A little gaudy, for certain, but vibrant with character, interest, and a certain something that transported you to better times than the present.

The present was not all it was cracked up to be, especially with the looming Y2K apocalypse on the horizon. While the world anticipated the worst, for Charlotte and Harold, the stress of the impending millennium shift meant the further crumbling of their already failing relationship.

Consumed by his career and the relentless pursuit of success at the law firm, Harold had become increasingly selfish and self-centered. He only paid attention to Charlotte when he needed something, showing little interest in her work or emotional well-being, as he was too engrossed in his own ambition.

Meanwhile, Charlotte worked tirelessly as a computer programmer for a company dedicated to averting Y2K-related issues. The demands of her job were relentless, requiring unwavering focus and dedication, especially during these tumultuous times.

Despite her commitment, she consistently attempted to be a supportive and loving wife – writing Harold love notes in the lunches she made for him every morning, keeping house, flirting, and making Harold's preferred dinners after her long days at work.

She yearned for affection and emotional support from Harold, but he continuously failed to provide it. He dismissed her needs unless they suited his in the moment, and instead remained preoccupied with his own aspirations and achievements, leaving their relationship strained and unbalanced.

January 20, 1999, Charlotte finally had enough. The day burned into her memory because it summed up quite nicely the precise experience she had been going through with her husband.

Charlotte had made Harold's favorite dessert after her own long day of work. He had finished a big lawsuit with success, and she wanted to celebrate the win together.

Entering Harold's study with her tray of cookies, Charlotte was met with Harold's dismissive attitude and even more hurtful yelling over forgetting to also "bring a cup of milk" if she was going to "try to make him fat with cookies."

The weight of his constant disregard for her efforts was unbearable, and finally, with his unnecessarily temperamental response, she couldn't contain her frustration any longer.

With tears in her eyes, Charlotte exploded, telling Harold that she would no longer endure his lack of appreciation or his disrespect any further. She bravely declared that she would no longer tolerate being taken for granted and made it clear that she was leaving, determined to find a relationship where her love and efforts were valued and reciprocated.

Charlotte packed her necessities and left for her mother's until she could find a place of her own. Little did she realize at the time that she would be leaving the small two-bedroom apartment she shared with Harold for the opulent estate of Hale House.

Chapter Two: Hale House

March 1999

An odd series of events led Charlotte to discover Hale House. It was almost as if it found her. Doing her programming at a café near her mother's home, she overheard two older gentlemen discussing matters on a rainy afternoon while she nibbled on pastries and coded.

"What am I to do, Michael? We aren't that large of a town, and we don't have those kinds of funds!" the taller man intimated.

The shorter responded, "I'm sorry, Paul, it's not as if anyone expected all this expensive tech to become a source of grief. How were we to know that a year shift would shut the world down?"

Paul nodded gravely, placing his face into his hands.

"It's hopeless," he muttered.

Charlotte hated to be an eavesdropper, but it sounded like they were speaking of Y2K. She debated whether she should intervene. She thought about herself for a moment – she had plenty to offer.

In 1998, she had become a "computer programmer II" or, as her company liked to advertise her services, a Cyber Apocalypse Prevention Specialist, to prevent issues stemming from the rolling from year 99 to year 00 that most felt would unleash havoc and effectively shut down the world.

Now in early 1999, she found herself in this café listening to a panicked conversation of the mayor and city clerk.

"What kind of computer work are you all needing completed?" Charlotte stood and blurted the comment out in the men's general direction.

She was surprised at herself. She was typically pretty introverted – this was unlike her.

Paul's eyes looked up at Charlotte hopefully. He quickly sized her up.

Thirties to forties, dark thick hair, a bit messy but pretty, with the fading tan lines of a recently lost wedding band. He noted her computer and manuals scattered about her table and felt a glimmer of hope.

Perhaps fate was intervening to offer a potential solution to their woes.

"Well," Paul began, "we've been struggling to find affordable help for Y2K. We recently invested heavily in digitizing the town, but now find ourselves wishing we hadn't," he said.

"We thought it was the best for our future, but it was costly. Then the town purchased a historic home, Hale House, to convert into a museum to bring in some income to help. It has a captivating history but is marred by rumors of ghosts and unfortunate events, so we got it at a good price," he went on.

"Unfortunately, we didn't take into account its renovation and maintenance costs. They're overwhelming. So now the house expenses and tech upgrades are weighing us down."

Charlotte's curiosity was piqued by the mention of Hale House's mysterious history – she had heard a bit from her mother. Despite the negative rumors of death and hauntings, the allure of such a unique and historic place was strong.

"I'm a computer programmer," Charlotte explained, "I could help assess and secure your town's systems, ensuring a smooth transition into the new millennium."

Paul's face brightened with interest. "If you could assist us, we would be eternally grateful. But if I'm honest, I'm not sure how we could pay for your services."

Charlotte considered.

"What if," she proposed, "I offer my services to the town in exchange for the free rent of Hale House while I work? I'd have my own place and you'd have a programmer *and* a tenant to maintain the home."

"And once my work here is done," she hopefully ventured, "Maybe we could even explore a rent-to-own contract? I would work to renovate Hale House with my own funds. The town wouldn't have to continue to bear the financial burden, and I could eventually take it off your hands."

Charlotte's heart raced with excitement and hope. Paul's smile widened, and he promised to present the idea to the council.

The allure of Hale House's mysterious history coupled with the chance to assist her new community stirred something within Charlotte.

A week later, the council approved the arrangement, formalizing the terms they had discussed at the café.

With her signature, Charlotte embraced the opportunity for independence and adventure, ready to delve into the enigmatic past of Hale House and make it her new home.

April 1999

As Charlotte paused from settling into her new sanctuary for a break in the parlor, she recalled the unexpected conversation that led to her now living in Hale House with a small, contented smile on her face.

This house found her. Wanted her.

She was fulfilled and where she was meant to be. Again, Charlotte reflected on the emptiness of her past relationship.

She noticed the stark contrast between the sterile, beige surroundings of her previous apartment, which symbolized Harold's preference for simplicity and detachment, and the ornate and opulent parlor of Hale House that now embraced her.

The parlor's character and charm resonated with her, representing a newfound sense of self, free from Harold's cold and distant influence. She could get used to this.

Chapter Three: The Library

May 1999

While the initial weeks were consumed with unpacking and settling in, now, after almost a month, Charlotte finally had the chance to explore the depths of the stately home. She instantly knew where she was drawn – the library.

The library of Hale House brimmed with an irresistible allure – a treasure trove of knowledge awaiting exploration. A vast stock of books had been acquired by the town, part in the home purchase and part from estate sales and donations.

The collection was turned over to Charlotte under their agreed contract.

Antique classics, forgotten mythologies, and ancient grimoires beckoned from the shelves, while aged biographies, occult chronicles, and journals from bygone eras whispered tales of intrigue.

In passing, Charlotte even curiously noted a copy of Chaucer, oddly chewed on as though a wild animal had used it for its plaything. It, along with the mysterious bestiaries and beautifully bound historical manuscripts added to the excitement that coursed through Charlotte as she made her way through the house, finalizing the organization of her belongings.

Each time her eyes caught sight of those books; her heart danced with delight.

Despite her tech-savvy persona as a computer programmer, she remained an unapologetic bibliophile, and libraries had always held a sacred place in her soul. The anticipation of losing herself in those pages filled her with a warmth that only the world of books could invoke.

Charlotte's longing to sink into the inviting embrace of the tufted velvet armchairs in the library intensified, tempting her to immediately lose herself, curled up with a good book.

Yet, she knew there were a few other tasks demanding her attention first, including assembling a small pedestal for the flower vase to grace the entryway of her new abode.

The instructions, regrettably, were in an unfamiliar language, causing the task to drag on longer than she had hoped. Nevertheless, fueled by determination, she pressed on, for this pedestal represented more than just a piece of furniture—it was a reflection of her personal style, something her ex-husband, Howard, would have dismissed as frivolous.

As the daylight hours waned and evening approached, Charlotte finally triumphed over the perplexing instructions, beaming with pride as she adorned the pedestal's marble surface with wildflowers from the garden, a symbol of her newfound independence and the beauty she intended to cultivate in her new life.

It was perfect.

Until it wasn't.

As Charlotte was admiring her handiwork and the lovely flowers from her garden, the lights of Hale House flickered and went out.

With frustration, she tried to remember where she might have put a flashlight in her unpacking, to no success.

Suddenly, she recalled a pack of wooden matches and candles in the cabinet beneath the sink in the kitchen. In the pitch-blackness, Charlotte tentatively extended her arms to feel her way from the entry way toward the kitchen, knocking over the vase in the process.

The shattering sound pierced the silence, and water and shards of porcelain scattered across the floor, a mess she made a mental note to clean up later. For now, her focus remained on finding the kitchen and the much-needed light to dispel the darkness.

As Charlotte passed the library, a sudden warmth washed over her entire body, but she dismissed it as mere anxiety from her growing fear. The vastness of the home felt overwhelming in the darkness, leaving her uneasy and feeling quite alone.

Yet, determined to find a source of light, she steadied her breath and pressed forward toward the kitchen.

Her fingers fumbled nervously over the cold countertop until they finally found the familiar touch of the porcelain sink. Relief washed over her as she located the cabinet, where she discovered the matchbox and comforting presence of candles and candleholders.

Despite her fear, Charlotte felt a sense of accomplishment as she struck the match and lit a candle, bringing a warm, flickering glow back to the enveloping darkness.

Charlotte debated for a moment. Should she still explore the library in these spooky settings? No power and candlelight felt a bit like a cheesy opening to a ghost story.

But with a soft chill caressing her cheeks and warmth flooding her extremities, Charlotte passed through the grand arch opening of the library, drawn by the flickering candlelight with a lure that seemed almost otherworldly.

She had no way of knowing that within those walls, a spectral presence yearned for her connection, a lost soul desperate to break free from the shackles of the immortal.

Their entangled destinies were about to unleash a supernatural tale, defying the boundaries between the living and the dead, and forever altering the course of their intertwined fates.

Chapter Four: Connection

May 1999

As Charlotte ventured deeper into the Hale House library, an enigmatic energy filled the air, sending shivers down her spine. Every step seemed to echo with the whispers of unseen eyes, and her heart pounded in her chest as if in sync with the mysteries that surrounded her.

Mysterious scratching noises from the fireplace warned her that things were not always as they seemed in Hale House. Dusty shelves lined with age-old books beckoned her, their ancient wisdom calling out.

She couldn't explain the inexplicable connection she felt to this place, as if spirits of the past were reaching out, yearning for her presence – and they were.

As she turned a corner, an uncanny warmth embraced her again, pulling her deeper into the heart of the library. It was as though the very essence of the place welcomed her, inviting her to uncover its hidden secrets.

Normally, such an atmosphere would make her uneasy in the dim light, but she found herself captivated by the books, drawn to their secrets and stories.

One particular tome, with its faded cover and elegant golden lettering, seemed to call to her, and she couldn't resist the urge to touch it.

History of the Ages, by Calvin Clifton, beckoned with the promise of untold mysteries waiting to be unraveled.

Unbeknownst to Charlotte, the spectral presence that now resided within the library had witnessed generations of homeowners and visitors, but none had stirred its essence quite like her.

It sensed in her a kindred spirit, someone seeking refuge and understanding in the ancient knowledge that lay within its walls.

Their destinies seemed to intertwine, drawn together by a force beyond mortal comprehension.

With the power thankfully restored the next morning, Charlotte set about her daily routine, completing programming for the town and other work sent from work headquarters by day and investigating her home by night.

Days turned into weeks, and Charlotte found herself irresistibly drawn to the library more than any other space in the home, as if compelled by an unseen force.

The connection she felt with the place grew stronger, as if it held the power to unlock the deepest desires of her soul.

As the days went on, the library became an anchor in her life, offering solace and comfort, but also unraveling a mystery that would challenge everything she thought she knew about reality and the afterlife.

Chapter Five: The Scribe

Amidst the faded whispers of forgotten eras, the ghostly presence in the Hale House library carried a tale that had spanned millennia.

Long before the mansion stood tall, he was a scribe hailing from an ancient civilization of the east, revered for his mastery of the written word and the arcane arts.

His name, now lost to the annals of time and to himself, echoed through the ages only as a whisper carried on the winds of history.

In his pursuit of knowledge, the scribe had discovered a mysterious text during an expedition to lands far distant from his home. The jeweled surface of the tome glimmered with untold power, said to possess the ability to manipulate time itself.

Enthralled by its enigma, the scribe sought to unlock its secrets and harness its temporal capabilities. But his insatiable curiosity led to a grave error.

In an ill-fated experiment within the very space that would one day become Hale House, the scribe triggered a temporal anomaly.

The boundaries of time and space quivered, and he found himself trapped in a new era where Hale House lived and breathed, but now, drifting in the currents of time as a spectral apparition.

While not truly dead, he may as well have been. He knew no means to return to his past in his spectral state and no clear paths to leave the Hale House property.

With some experimentation of moving about the grounds, he found his energy was strongest in the library, and so there he remained. It was as if he had become one with the grounds, forever bound to its past, present, and future, but always seeking a way to return to his own era and to life.

As centuries passed, the scribe watched over countless individuals, hopeful that one would be able to connect with him – to help him.

But none had drawn his fascination as intensely as Charlotte Graves.

There was something about her, an aura of resilience and an insatiable thirst for knowledge, that reminded him of his own past. Her unyielding love for books and her genuine curiosity captivated him, and he found himself inexplicably drawn to her presence within the library.

But even more than this, he identified with her pain. He could tell that Charlotte, while pleasant in her outward showing of herself, was filled to the brim with a hurt of which she did not speak.

It was not merely her mortal beauty or her connection to the world of books that fascinated the scribe; it was the way she seemed to breathe life into the stories she read. She always read aloud, as if the stories were her companions on a journey through time, as if she knew he was listening.

Her voice was soothing and melodic. He felt himself falling for her.

He had found a kindred spirit, a soul that resonated with the very essence of the library he had been bound to for so long.

Yet, his affection for Charlotte was tinged with sorrow, for he knew that his spectral existence was a boundary they could never breach. He yearned to reach out, to reveal his presence to her, but the ethereal nature of his being rendered him invisible to the living world.

And so, he watched from the shadows, an unseen observer, drawn to her every step, and haunted by the knowledge that they were destined to remain apart.

In the library's dim lighting, he longed to unravel the mysteries of the jeweled tome and find a way to break free from his temporal prison, no longer to return to his home, but now to be with her in the mortal realm once more.

As Charlotte delved deeper into the library's secrets, he could not help but hope that she might be the key to his liberation. Her presence in the library seemed to infuse it with new life, a spark that resonated, calling to him like a siren's song.

The scribe couldn't explain why this particular mortal had awoken something deep within him, something that had long slumbered in the depths of the past.

And as he watched her explore forgotten lore, he wondered if she held the power to set him free or if, in doing so, their entwined destinies might forever change the course of time itself.

Chapter Six: Calvin Clifton

June 1999

As days turned into weeks, the connection between Charlotte and the spectral presence in the library deepened from both sides. He, hearing her words and watching her growing interest.

She, feeling the warmth and connection with what she assumed was the space itself. The scribe observed Charlotte with a mixture of fascination and longing, wondering if there would ever be a way for them to bridge the gap that separated their worlds.

He yearned to communicate with her, to share his feelings, to let her know that he was there, watching over her with an eternal devotion.

One evening, as Charlotte sat by the fireplace, engrossed in *History of the Ages* by Calvin Clifton, the scribe sensed an opportunity.

He had noted that Charlotte's ivory skin would flush when he was near to her, and she would often comment on feeling warm when it occurred.

He moved closer, hovering, practically sitting in her lap, and she began to shift in her seat.

Charlotte chalked the warm feeling up to being too close to the fire and stood to stretch her legs.

The spirit, desperate to make a connection, decided to try something new. He had never invaded Charlotte's personal space by allowing his spirit to actually come into contact with her body. He felt that would be invasive and uncouth.

But it seemed the occasion was calling for it, and with a nervous extension of his pointer finger, he gently touched her wrist. She winced and rubbed the space where the connection had occurred.

"Damn pinched nerve," Charlotte remarked aloud.

SHE FELT IT! *How remarkable!* the specter thought. Perhaps this was the way.

He reached out again but this time with his whole hand and placed his fingertips very lightly on top of her graceful slender fingers.

A slow building rush of warmth began spreading across Charlotte's right hand. Her pulsed quickened and she began to wonder if something was wrong.

He noted the fear on her face, and wondered if this was too much. Should he stop? In a swift moment without thinking, he determined to go further.

He wrapped Charlotte in a close embrace.

At first her heart raced, panic enveloped her, but within a few moments, the worry dissolved. The feeling was welcome, loving, warm.

"What is this?" Charlotte called out.

He thought of how he could tell her, reassure her, and with an affectionate touch, he drew a heart on her shoulder with his fingertip.

Charlotte's eyes opened wide in surprise. She knew there was a reason she was drawn to this place, but a ghost? An invisible man? What was this?

Tentatively, she whispered, "Is someone there?"

Nothing changed. Perhaps she was imagining it all.

"No," she determined, "I have to know."

She called out again, "If you're there, tap my nose."

A sudden warmth flushed the very tip of her nose. She shook at the realization.

This was real.

The specter was beside himself. How was this happening? He had touched others on accident in the past, and none of them had had this kind of reaction!

With a jolt of excitement, he decided to see if he could lead Charlotte to the book that brought him here.

In a sort of "hot/cold" hide and seek game, Charlotte followed the warmth of the spirit's touch to an ancient-looking book tucked between the ordinary plain books surrounding it.

The warmth stopped.

"Is this what you want me to see?" she questioned.

He placed his hand on her heart. This was it. Her mind raced as she slid the book off the shelf and admired its jewel-encrusted cover.

His excitement was palpable. The very jeweled tome that had triggered his temporal anomaly was now within her hands, its powers dormant but still present.

The scribe felt a spark of hope; perhaps he could use this forgotten artifact to further make his presence known to her.

With a gentle nudge, the spirit guided Charlotte to a certain page within the book. He focused his ethereal energy on a loose gem he knew was nestled among the pages, a remnant of the power of its jeweled cover that had been left dormant for so long.

The gem glowed with a faint luminescence, catching Charlotte's attention. Her brow furrowed in confusion, and she instinctively touched the glowing gem with her fingertips.

In that moment, the scribe channeled his energy into the gem, begging for his words to be revealed to her. Slowly he felt a shift, as if weaving his essence into the very words on the page. The print on the page shifted into a new text.

As Charlotte watched, she noticed a subtle shift in the narrative, as if the words were secrets meant only for her. The scribe's presence intertwined with the ancient text, shaping the letters and sentences to convey his thoughts and emotions.

Not fully understanding the supernatural forces at play, Charlotte read aloud, unknowingly giving voice to the scribe's hidden messages. The flickering candlelight danced in response to the newfound energy that filled the room, and the air crackled with an otherworldly presence.

The spectral words resonated with her soul, and she felt an inexplicable warmth enveloping her, comforting and familiar.

"I am here with you, Charlotte," she read the altered words aloud.

"I have watched you from the shadows, drawn to the light of your spirit."

Samantha Underhill

Charlotte's heart skipped a beat, and she gasped as she realized that something extraordinary was unfolding before her.

The scribe's presence, once confined to the realm of shadows, was reaching out to her through the very words she read.

It was as if the library itself had come alive, pulsing with an energy transcending time and space.

Tears welled up in Charlotte's eyes as she felt a profound connection with the ghostly presence.

In the silence of the library, she spoke softly, her voice quivering with emotion, "Who are you? What do you want?"

The scribe, seizing the opportunity to communicate, wove his response into the text.

"I am but a soul lost in the tapestry of time, bound to this library by a force beyond my understanding. I seek solace in the company of kindred spirits like yours. Your presence, Charlotte, brings a warmth to this ancient dwelling that I have not felt in centuries."

Overwhelmed with both fear and curiosity, Charlotte gathered her courage and asked, "Can you show yourself to me? Are you trapped here?"

The scribe's reply echoed in the air.

"No, unfortunately I am trapped between times, neither living nor dead, my existence woven into these grounds, and this library. But you, dear Charlotte, have become a beacon of hope. Together, perhaps we can find a way to break the chains that bind me to this spectral existence."

Fear fell across Charlotte's body, causing an uncomfortable sensation of being hot and cold simultaneously. He needed her. This spirit needed her.

Her pulse quickened, heart thudding in the confines of her chest. A million thoughts flooded her mind – the noise of it all deafening within her. This could not possibly be real… could it?

She had never been one to believe in children's ghost stories. She liked facts, figures, programming – solid things. Charlotte questioned her sanity briefly. Perhaps the whirlwind of moving on without Harold had been too much for her?

No, that was not it. This was real. She was experiencing something like she never had before. But what would she do?

In that moment, Charlotte decided. She would not let fear control her; she would embrace this extraordinary connection and help the scribe find the freedom he so desperately sought.

With newfound determination, she whispered into the pages of the book, "I will help you; I promise. But first, what is your name?"

The scribe felt a moment of sadness. Time had played him so cruelly that he honestly could not recall his own name.

He thought for a moment and then responded, "I have no name."

This made Charlotte feel sorrow for the spirit. How sad to not have a name specific to be called.

She pondered, then spoke aloud, "I'll call you Calvin Clifton after the author of the book I've been enjoying since I arrived at Hale House."

"Calvin," he thought.

"How nice to have a name to be called."

And to be called such a name by Charlotte felt like heaven.

From that night on, a remarkable bond blossomed between Charlotte and the specter of the library.

Each time she ventured into its hallowed halls; they communicated through the altered words in the ancient tomes. With every shared exchange, their connection grew stronger, defying the boundaries of time and death, falling into the realm of love.

They sought to unravel the mysteries of the ancient text, its jewels, and the spectral nature of the scribe's existence.

During their quest they found themselves drawn closer together, bound by an otherworldly love that would forever change Charlotte.

Chapter Seven: Love

February 2001

Two years had passed since Charlotte had come to Hale House.

The world had survived the Y2K "apocalypse" with no real *apoca* or *lypse* in sight. Whether the survival had been due to the programming work of individuals like Charlotte or not no longer really mattered.

The world had sailed into a new millennium without much ado.

The city council was thrilled with the work Charlotte had completed and kept to their agreement to shift into a rent-to-own contract for Hale House with a clause that should anything happen to Charlotte, or should she no longer keep up her payments, that the home would once again become property of the city.

Charlotte had no intention of not keeping up her end of the agreement and since her mother had passed unexpectedly at the end of 2000, she was doing this for herself. Hale House had become her home, hers and Calvin's.

Their relationship was stifled by the separation of living and spiritual worlds, but nevertheless, their love had grown. For the first time in her life, Charlotte felt truly listened to and cared for despite their distance.

Calvin loved Charlotte so deeply. She was the first real connection to the living he had had in centuries, and she cared about his thoughts and feelings.

She had even begun teaching him a bit about her work with computers and programming. After some time, he found it was possible to use his energy to access the World Wide Web, even with Charlotte away at work.

For a man who had been a scribe in his living days, internet access was a wonder to behold. He consumed every bit of information he could and was consistently surprised that there was always more to learn.

Initially, Calvin used what he learned to make conversation with Charlotte, to gift her with knowledge, and to reveal his love to her.

As time continued to pass, his inability to connect with anyone but Charlotte and their inability to work out how to overcome the temporal anomaly began to poison his mind.

Calvin became driven, fixated on Charlotte in an unhealthy manner.

He watched her every move, entranced by her dedication to her work and her determination to try and assist him.

His feelings for her literally transcended the realms of time and space and he yearned to be with her, even if it meant she must cross into the realm of the immortal to be with him.

March 2002

Time marched on and Calvin's obsession took a dark turn. He had made suggestions to Charlotte in their interchanges that she should be with him, but she was not taking the hint.

He knew he would have to act. The desire to be with Charlotte at any cost consumed him, and he became blinded to the consequences of his actions.

His longing for her love and companionship transformed into a twisted obsession, leading him to devise a sinister plan.

Haunted by his own past and the mistakes that led him to become trapped in his spectral state, Calvin believed that if he could persuade Charlotte to join him in death, they could be together for eternity.

He convinced himself that his act of liberating her from the mortal world would be an act of love, freeing her from the burdens and limitations of life.

The heavy workloads, the lack of appreciation she had from others, would be gone.

As Charlotte continued her work in the town, unaware of the ghost's changing obsession, Calvin carefully plotted his scheme.

He began manipulating events within Hale House but claiming no involvement, causing strange occurrences to unsettle her. Books would fall from shelves, lights flickered mysteriously, and the temperature in the rooms would fluctuate drastically.

These unsettling incidents created an aura of fear and unease, driving Charlotte to begin to question her sanity.

But Calvin knew this would not be enough. He had to escalate his actions to achieve his goal of he and Charlotte truly being together.

Gradually, he started to influence Charlotte's thoughts, making sinister suggestions in her mind during her most vulnerable moments. These suggestions were subtle, at first, often urging her to spend more time in the library, where he could exert his influence more strongly.

As Charlotte spent increasingly longer amounts of time in the library, she unknowingly drew closer to Calvin's twisted plans.

He manipulated the words in the books she read, altering their meanings and planting dark ideas in her subconscious.

Slowly, he sowed the seeds of self-destruction, making her believe that death was the only path to escape her troubles and find true happiness.

At least, that's what Calvin had hoped.

But Charlotte's resolve and independence following her divorce from Harold had made her into a strong woman. Though Calvin hoped she would be haunted by her sense of despair and physical loneliness, she pushed on.

He knew his intention of having her bring herself into his spirit realm was not going to work.

So he took his desires a step further.

Chapter Eight: The Devil's Cherries

April 2002

Calvin began researching poisons that could be absorbed in the skin by touch. He learned that nightshades such as belladonna were so poisonous that as few as three to five berries could cause death.

And further that the plant as a whole – its stem, leaves, roots, and flower were poisonous enough that they should never be touched without gloves.

He asked himself, could he do this?

Yes, he was willing to risk everything to be with Charlotte, even if it meant putting her life in peril.

As Calvin had been successful in transferring his energy into physical items, like the computer, he wondered: could he transfer anything physical to another space? He would not know unless he tried.

His energy waned when he left the library, so Calvin worried it would not be possible – that he would not be strong enough.

But he was determined.

The next day, while Charlotte was away at work, Calvin made his way to the greenhouse.

Memories of a previous owner's fascination with gothic plants guided him.

He knew there would be some Devil's Cherries, also known as Atropa belladonna, symbols of beauty and death.

Sure enough, when he made it to the greenhouse, he saw them. Dark green, glossy, oval leaves in alternating patterns on the stem just as he had read. This was it. This was what he had researched.

Being spring, they even had the bell-shaped purplish flowers hanging in small clusters all around the stem. And just next to the flowers, the glossy black berries.

Such tiny, small cherries to be so highly toxic. Belladonna, Calvin had learned, was *beautiful lady* in Italian. Appropriate, he thought, as he found Charlotte so lovely.

With thoughts of Charlotte in his mind, he set his plan into motion. For weeks, Calvin visited the belladonna plants, pressing his spirit into them, willing the toxic essence into his being.

Slowly, the effects of the poison seeped into him. He felt lighter. He hallucinated, experienced a sensation of soaring through the air. He was changing, and it was time to share his altered self with Charlotte.

That evening, Charlotte looked positively radiant. Just watching her simply entering the library, book tucked under one arm, a glass of water in her hand, lifted his soul.

She sat her glass on the side table and lit her favorite rose scented candle while settling into a comfy chair. Calvin thought for a moment about the scent.

He wished he could experience it as he did when he were alive, or even become the scent wafting in the air to enter her beautiful body.

His love for her overwhelmed Calvin. And as the ink flowed under his ghostly touch during their usual evening in the library, Calvin infused the words with more of his essence.

Charlotte ran her fingers over his words, unknowingly absorbing the poisoned ink. The euphoria in her voice as she expressed her love for Calvin sent mixed emotions through him.

"I've never felt a love like ours, Calvin. Although we cannot physically be together, you are the best thing that's happened to me," she exclaimed.

In that moment, he wondered if he was doing the right thing but felt it was too late to turn back.

Calvin paused. Was this the right thing to do? Perhaps she did not deserve to have this happen without her consent? But it was too late. Her symptoms progressed.

"Calvin? What's happening to me? I feel like I'm floating. Is this love?"

"It is, my love," Calvin responded, reaching out to touch her hands.

The warmth of his spirit with the increasing feelings of hallucination were comforting at first but quickly grew troubling to Charlotte.

Something did not feel right.

"Calvin?! Calvin? What's happening to me?" Charlotte called aloud.

Calvin's heart sank as he witnessed the distress he had inadvertently caused Charlotte. He had never intended to harm her, and now he was facing the horrifying reality of his actions.

The effects of the belladonna poison were taking hold of her, and she was experiencing the full force of its toxicity.

Desperation consumed him, and he reached out to comfort her, only to find that he could no longer provide solace. His touch, once so comforting, now troubled her.

Charlotte's words echoed through the haunted library, reminding Calvin that what he had done was not an act of love but a betrayal of trust.

"Charlotte, I'm so sorry," Calvin pleaded, trying to explain his reckless actions.

"I didn't mean for this to happen. I wanted us to be together, but I never wanted to hurt you."

Charlotte's once vibrant eyes were now filled with confusion and fear.

"Why did you do this, Calvin? Why would you risk my life like this?" she asked, her voice trembling.

Needing to console Charlotte, Calvin tried to embrace her, to let her know his intent was pure, but his incorporeal form only passed through her, causing her to shudder with a mix of emotions.

"I thought if we were both spirits, we could be together forever. I wanted to be with you, Charlotte. I just love you so much," he confessed, regret weighing heavily in his words.

Calvin realized he had forced his desires onto Charlotte without her consent, and it had devastating consequences.

She was trapped between worlds, torn apart by the poison that he had willingly embraced. As her condition deteriorated, he could only watch in horror, unable to undo his grave mistake.

Tears streamed down Charlotte's cheeks as she struggled to comprehend the situation.

"This is not love, Calvin. Love doesn't force someone into danger without their consent. Love is about understanding, respect, and care," she said with a mix of anger and sadness.

Calvin's ethereal form trembled with guilt and remorse.

"I know now that I was wrong. I was so desperate to be with you that I lost sight of what was right. Please forgive me," he implored.

But Charlotte was beyond forgiveness in that moment. The poison coursed through her veins, and she was rapidly losing her grip on reality. The hallucinations intensified, and she was no longer able to distinguish between the realms of the living and the dead.

In her haze, Charlotte reached out, trying to touch Calvin, longing for the connection they once had, that had brought her new purpose.

But her physical form could not grasp his spirit, and she felt more isolated than ever. Isolating as it was, she was not alone, as visions of spirits and demons tormented her, pulling her away from life she had known.

Charlotte was torturously being torn apart by the consequences of Calvin's misguided actions right before his very gaze.

As the night wore on, her condition worsened.

The hallucinations became more vivid and disorienting, and her body weakened under the poison's influence. She attempted to find ways to stop the terrible visions in her mind but had little control over her physical form.

She thought perhaps if she could wake herself from this horrible dream, it would all be over. Her actions became more erratic. As delirium took hold, Charlotte's trembling hands fumbled for a nearby object, and with a burst of frenzied determination, she lashed out at herself, hoping that the pain would shock her back to reality.

Calvin's heart sank as he witnessed the depths of her suffering and realized the irreversible damage caused by his grave mistake. He could do nothing but watch in horror as the consequences of his actions unfolding before him.

Charlotte attempted once more at something to pull her from this experience. Perhaps if she could wash away this poison?

She mustered all of her energy to try and take a drink of the water sitting on the side table. But without full control of her motions, she could not grasp the cup.

She focused and redoubled her efforts. Her arm swung wildly at the glass, but only succeeded in knocking over the candle she had lit earlier.

The small candleflame landed too near the drapes and took hold, fire spreading slowly up the beautiful material.

Disoriented, Charlotte watched the flames – how beautiful they were! The dance of elemental energy captivated her senses and sparked an awe-inspiring spectacle.

The vibrant hues of red, orange, and yellow shimmered with a warm, inviting glow drawing her into their embrace. The flames flickered and leaped, creating a mesmerizing interplay of light and shadow, casting an ever-changing tapestry of patterns on the surrounding surfaces.

She rose, drawn, steadied by the flame's magnetic attraction.

No. Charlotte found her mind for a moment.

Samantha Underhill

This could not be her end. She wanted to live. She wanted to be.

With every fiber left in her being, she found her footing, made her way to the library phone, and dialed 911.

"911, what's your emergency?" the operator responded.

"Hale House. Calvin. Fire." Charlotte managed with tears falling from her eyes before fainting and falling to the floor.

"Ma'am? Ma'am? We have emergency responders on the way. Ma'am…"

In the early hours of the morning, Charlotte's body succumbed to the deadly effects of the belladonna before being partly consumed by the flames.

As she passed, her spirit was now freed from its earthly bounds. She watched as firemen came to rescue her in vain.

The fire was contained, only destroying part of the library, but her pulse had long stopped. Her body was marred, and her spirit already separated from her physical form.

Nearby, Calvin was consumed by the guilt as he took in the magnitude of his actions. He had killed her. He was a murderer.

But for a brief moment, seeing Charlotte in her spectral form, negative thoughts fled. He was once again filled with love for her, and a small flicker of hope entered his spirit. "Perhaps now, my love, we can be together?" he questioned Charlotte, touching his spirit to hers.

But the warmth of his spirit was met with the frigidness of her own.

This was not a welcome reunion. There was no comfort. Charlotte felt only anger, sadness, and betrayal.

The library of Hale House, once a place of shared dreams and hopes, now echoed with sorrow and regret.

Calvin vowed never to let his misguided desires hurt anyone else again and sought ways to make it up to Charlotte. Too late he had learned a most painful lesson of the consequences of selfish love.

The weight of his actions would haunt him for eternity.

The coroner determined the cause of death for Charlotte Graves was suicide – finding both the poison in her system and the apparent self-lit fire without other evidence of human influence enough to pronounce it so.

Investigators tried to determine the reason for her naming "Calvin" in her 911 call but could not locate any connection.

Per the contract, the town took back the ownership of Hale House, but placed it almost immediately for sale both to avoid the high costs and to distance themselves from her unexpected death.

As for Charlotte and Calvin, their spirits continue to wander among the heavy, silent shelves of the Hale House library, forever connected but forever apart.

Their love now a tragic tale of a ghost's misguided pursuit to be with the living that no living soul would ever hear…until now.

Ballroom
1862

The Murder Masque
-Or-
'The Orders Came Down for an Encirclement Ambush Manuever of Local Confederate Leadership at a Holiday Gathering'
Joshua Loyd Fox

In nearby New Orleans, a decree had come down from Mayor John T. Monroe declaring that "no masquerade procession or masked individuals will be allowed to parade the streets of the city of New Orleans on Tuesday, the 4th of March 1862, the same being Mardi-Gras."

Instead, the day after the cancelled festivities saw a full brigade of militia parading through the streets.

Union forces would occupy the city by May of 1862 and remain there for the rest of the War. Union warships would find it easy going up the wide and fast-moving Mississippi River and would have almost no resistance occupying the surrounding lands, including the large estate of the late Josiah Hale.

But the night of Mardi Gras, March the 4th, 1862, two months before the occupation of New Orleans, the ease in which the Union Army occupied the area was prologuely accomplished by the mass execution of Confederate Leadership in the Ballroom of the aforementioned Hale House, during an illegal and unadvised Ball.

The Masked Ball would be thrown in opposition and in defiance of the laws laid down because of the War of the States.

Hot blood would run red rivulets down ornamental walls, and marble, metal, and wood would turn dull, stained brassy-orange with body fluids splashed across them during an hours-long massacre that would go down in history as the area's bloodiest.

∞

Joshua Loyd Fox

Before all of what happened that fateful, bloody night, our story would open with the *distraction* of two young women by the fantasies of a wealthy older man, a young and quiet heir, and the sequined ballgowns shopped for in secret, in the stately old shops of New Orleans' French Quarter.

∞

Aurora Devereaux was sixteen years old, and ready to be a mother and wife. She was beautiful, to be sure, but quiet, and demure.

Her best friend in the whole world, Cassandra Long-Westin, however, only had eyes for adventure and independence from the strictest structures of a proper southern upbringing for charmed young women.

The upbringing they had suffered through, together.

Cassandra wanted freedom from the rules and regulations of being a young southern woman of means, while Aurora wanted nothing more than to stay away from things that they were not allowed to do by a society that was slowly yet inexorably breaking down around them.

For instance, the Mardi Gras Ball they had both been secretly invited to by a friend of Cassandra's father, a very rich, and very single, middle-aged man, that very week.

The Ball was outlawed, secretive, and made Cassandra's wild streak come blaring out into the open, but made Aurora's spine pucker up in fear and apprehension.

And as such, there was no talking Cassandra out of shopping the French Quarter for the perfect ballgown two days before Fat Tuesday.

The pair of young women would be masked and secretly ushered to the famed Hale House for the Ball in a pony-drawn carriage, and Cass had used both excuses to pull Aurora into her Sunday afternoon shopping spree.

A shopping spree many young ladies of their station took that warm, muggy Sunday afternoon.

As if the Ball wasn't secret at all, Aurora thought to herself as she was pulled from shop to shop by the excited and babbling Cassandra Long-Westin.

Reds and blues, yellows and greens. Cloth soon flew through the air like bright plumaged peacocks, ready for the Ball. Sequins and masques, feather boas and bright, shiny shoes ran before the eyes of the young socialites.

Before long, even dour Aurora Devereaux was having the time of her life.

That was, until the town criers out on the cobbled streets of the Quarter, holding newspapers aloft that were supposed to be sold the next morning, told the tales coming out of 'back east' and the body tolls amounting.

Aurora swallowed hard, and Cassandra, seeing the look on her best friend's face, tsked at her.

"Come now, 'Rora, that stuff can't touch us here. Come on, let's try the green! It'll surely bring out those eyes of yours," she chided her friend.

Holding up a spangled, yet deep forest green gown to her friend's thin frame, Cass's eyes lit up in wonder.

Aurora shrugged, put the thoughts of death and destruction out of her mind, and let her best friend in all the world lead her to try on and purchase the deep green ballgown that did, indeed, bring out the green of her eyes.

The next two days flew by in a blink, and except for the very secret and tender invitation, hand delivered by a servant, to the Ball, by Mr. Samuel J. Hale, the grandson of the man who had built the large home out in the swamplands more than forty years prior, were uneventful.

Aurora tried to not get excited by the second invitation sent her way for the Masque, but she was impressed that the second invitation was more for just her, and by the young, quiet man that she had known in Primary School.

Samuel Hale would send a horse drawn coach for the two young women mentioned in the invitation, her and Cassandra. And Aurora knew that the addition of Cass as escort and chaperone was more a masking of what Mr. Hale really wanted the night of the secret Ball held by his own father, Jeremiah.

Mr. Evander Beauregard, the middle-aged stag that had invited Cassandra secretly had sent word he would supply a carriage as well, and so, with so many choices for the two young women, it was turning into the single greatest Mardi Gras either had ever heard of.

∾

And finally, the night of Mardi Gras, 1862 was upon them all, and even with the constrictions of the War of the States on local festivities, the air felt jolly and slightly decadent. The girls prepared for the Masque together at the home of the Devereaux's, and the chosen carriage of Hale House appeared out the window of Aurora's father's home like a whispered ghost in the sunset casting last rays of light over southern Louisiana.

∾

It was a warm, humid evening. The cicadas were chirping their ever-present happy tune, and fading sunlight glinted down through the hanging moss covering almost everything around the heavily used track out to the Hale House from the city boundaries of New Orleans.

Cassandra and Aurora wore bright sequined ball gowns, and the skirts bunched up between them on the floor of the covered carriage they were sharing for the long ride to the plantation home.

Aurora wore the deep green gown she had purchased with her father's money, and at the unneeded promptings of her best friend.

Cassandra wore a scandalous ruby red.

Both young women's masks were heavy velvet and black, both striking in different animal mien. Aurora wore a black swan mask, and Cassandra a black cat's face, dark as a midnight secret dalliance.

The carriage bumped and bounced along the hard tack trail into the deep and oppressive trees of the swamplands south of the great city.

The flames of the twin lanterns adorning the carriage near the driveman bounced with the ruts, but also with the hopes and dreams of the occupants of the ornate horse-drawn portage.

An early heat wave pressed the air around them against their pale and lustrous skin, and made their brows under the masks damp with sweat.

But the pair of young, innocent smiles would not be lessened by a heat they both knew all too well.

Soon enough, with the heavy velvet curtains of the dark wooden carriage pulled back to allow in any breeze wandering lost through the damp woods, the pair of young heiresses saw the massive mound of a plantation home appear through the weeping moss ahead of them.

Smiles grew wider as stringed music reached their young ears. Wide smiles, as pops of heated lusts and fantasies burst in young adolescent chests.

"Tonight's going to be just the *grandest* night, don't you think so, Aurora?" Cassandra asked her young best friend and ever-present supporter.

Aurora simply nodded, feeling more excitement blossom in her chest like fireworks in a dark, starless sky. She hoped that the night was so much more than just grand.

She hoped against hope, deep within her heart of hearts, that the night would be the forecaster of the rest of her life.

And she, very secretly, had her sights set on the young man who had caught her attention very early on, with an almost shared vibration between her and the man she dreamed of, all through finishing school.

Samuel Hale, and the legacy of the Hale line.

She smiled again at the thought of the hundreds of shared looks and long sighs between the two all through early adolescence.

And as the wooden carriage stopped in line with other carriages arriving and discharging their costumed passengers at the wide, sweeping steps at the front of Hale House, her excitement grew to a matching vibration as strong as that of her companion and best friend.

A best friend who had not an inkling or care for Aurora's attraction or dreams of her very own beau.

Cassanda's mind was all on wooing and winning the hand of the richest of stag attendees at the night's illustrious masque.

And with those thoughts in mind, as the carriage arrived, and doormen stepped up to help down given glove-covered hands, Aurora and Cassandra arrived, costumed and eager, at the home of the famed and wealthy Josiah Hale family.

∞

Unbeknownst to the revelers at the famed Ball at Mardi Gras, and just about anyone else in the area, the Union Army had moved up the Mississippi weeks earlier, and were camped in the deep and secure swampland near the Delta.

For weeks leading up to Fat Tuesday, spies of the Union had dressed in local garb, stolen into the city, and heard all the rumors and gossip told around tankards of beer and glasses of whiskey.

The spies heard about the illegal parties and balls to celebrate Mardi Gras against the orders of Confederate politicians near around.

And so, on the famed night of revelry, to the Union troops stationed near around the Delta, orders came down to use the distraction and drunkenness of the un-Christian like debauchery as the screen they needed to assure command of the surrounding area.

As the officers of the Union detachment knew, having control of the mouth of the Mississippi would be paramount in the future needs for moving troops and supplies to the middle of the country.

As revelers young and old prepared for the feast and overindulgence of the night, enemy troops moved stealthy and sober through the deep trees and hanging moss, to wreak havoc on the local Confederate leadership.

The leadership, the Union spies had learned, were all, very fortunately, attending the single largest and grandest Ball of this drunken night.

They had, to a man, and following a General of the Union Army, arrived at the famed Ball of the Hale House.

And as the troops surrounding the large plantation home, unknown and unseen, had watched as carriages moved up to the door of the large mansion and dispatched sequin-dressed women in masks, and wonderfully clean and smartly dressed men, to move into the interior of the large, open and well-lit home, other emotions ruled the darkening evening.

A deep and dark sense of anger and jealousy moved through the ranks of mostly poor Union troops watching the spectacle.

Whispered words of hatred and curses came from mouths that had never tasted the finer things in life, the finer things this Ball and this home had in spades.

The young, poor Northern troops were more than ready to enact the orders of death and mayhem that had come down to them from their own leadership.

They would do what their officers told them to do, but as the whispers intensified and anger and rage rose up in faces that had never seen nor felt the revelries before them, they all knew they would do so much worse with the rich and beautiful people enjoying such fine wine and drink.

They would do unmentionable things this night to the rich and wealthy folks within the mansion, who were unaware of the death creeping through the lengthening shadows around them.

∞

Aurora and Cassandra were like tourists who had never seen such finery before. As they walked together through the front area of the home, uniformed servants leading them to the famous Ball Room, they looked around at such finery and handmade craftsmanship not seen in the other plantation homes around about.

Well-lit and smelling wonderfully of food and rich wines, the home and décor exceeded all expectations of the young women who knew this night, more than any other night in their short years on the planet, was going to be full of magic and change.

Excitement blossomed in both chests as they were led into the wide, expansive Ball Room, which was made up of deep mahogany walls, and a floor that glistened with wax, ready for the hundreds of feet that were to dance the beautiful night away.

Aurora looked up into what seemed like dozens of crystal chandeliers, adorned with lit white candles that shed a deep, cozy light on the wooded, speckled room, but Cass had eyes only for the people gathered together in groups around the large room.

Dresses shining like the rainbow dotted the darker clothing of the rich men gathered together. Bright lights twinkled off of sequined gowns and dozens of masks glittering with jewels and diamonds.

Everywhere the girls' eyes traveled, light shimmied in a million colors, dazzling their senses and causing warmth and comfort to rise in their bosoms.

Neither girl had quite been witness to the level of finery and bright richness this night brought, but both had dreamed and fantasized about such a night for as long as they could remember.

And that's when a man behind them cleared his throat, and the girls turned to lay eyes for the first time on their benefactors and investors.

The girls both turned quickly to see their men, and their gowns spun around them like diamond encrusted tops, the toys they all grew up loving, but which gave such simple credence against the beauty of the two young women.

Samuel Hale was taller than the older man standing strong next to him, but both men were in the blossom of their strength and vigor, and two pairs of eyes roamed discreetly yet deeply over the men who would be escorting both women this fine, fine evening.

The middle-aged stag, Mr. Beauregard, was the first to speak, and his words were not lost on anyone in the small gathering.

"My goodness," he said in a deep, steady voice.

"Your beauty shines brighter than the brightest full moon in the darkest summer night," he told the young women.

Both women blushed, but neither more than Samuel Hale, who stammered something similar under his breath, but which Aurora more than Cass heard and felt. She smiled warmly at her friend from finishing school.

Cass only had eyes for the rich single man she was determined to land like the fattest fish flopping on a wooden deck under her feet.

Taking arms outstretched for just that reason, the young women were escorted around the large room while soft music played, and laughter tinkled off of the overhead chandeliers like soft staccato accompaniment to the stringed music notes floating through the light air.

Snatching pieces of conversation about the war, more than anything, both women tried to pick up the men's conversations as they were ushered to introductions after introductions.

It seemed that the first part of their evening would be spent moving from small group to small group, being acquainted and re-acquainted with the genteel of the area.

Seeing Aurora's parents, Samuel led her away from Cassandra and Mr. Beauregard for the first time in almost half an hour.

As he moved her toward her own parents, he whispered to her that he had already discussed future plans with her father, who was close partners with Samuel's own father, Dr. Jeremiah Hale, the man who had illegally opened his own home for the celebrations.

And seeing the mayor of New Orleans himself amongst the gathered genteel, she knew it wasn't really all that illegal of a gathering.

"Mr. and Mrs. Devereaux, how very well you look this evening," Sam said to Aurora's parents.

Both smiled at the young man, and while the men shook hands, Aurora's mother winked at her daughter over her crystal glass of champagne.

Aurora just smiled at her parents, especially her father, whom she shared a special and deep bond with, and pulled Sam's arm tighter against her be-speckled side.

As the new foursome spoke of benign things, a sharp report of fork against crystal glass sounded over the soft murmurings of the large group, and silence fell over the bright, gaily decorated room.

"May I have your attention, good sirs and ladies,'" a deep, sonorous voice broke out over the gathered masses.

"As most of you know, I am Doctor Jeremiah Hale, and I'd like to welcome you to this auspicious occasion, at my home," the voice said from the other side of the large room.

"Mardi Gras goes back to our earliest roots, in Medieval Europe, through Rome and Venice in the last two hundred years, and finally to the House of the Bourbons, in Paris, where my own ancestorial roots can be traced," he told the silent room.

"So, isn't it fitting, that all of us, brothers and sisters in the Cause, and with deep roots stretching back as far as eye can see, should be gathered together, illegally, I must say, under this roof, to celebrate this fine occasion?"

Thunderous applause followed his second to last statement.

Dr. Jeremiah Hale, father of Aurora's Mardi Gras partner, Samuel, gave a final toast, and the music swelled to the rafters high overhead.

"This Mardi Gras night will go down as one of the most memorable of this here Confederate State, and many will hear how the South bit their thumbs at their Northern Oppressors while still dancing and singing this Mardi Gras night away!"

Aurora was soon lost in the splendor of the evening. As dusk turned to darkest night, she felt as if she floated her way through hours of small talk, a dinner repast, and finally, the dancing.

She was overwhelmed with the splendor, the lighting, the music and fine victuals, but even more, she was overwhelmed knowing all of this was soon to be hers, as she vowed to marry the man who didn't leave her side the whole evening through.

∞

Full of victuals and a small nip of deep, dark ruby red wine, and dizzy from dancing for hours with her new beau, Aurora Devereaux was flush all the way up to her red face. It was difficult to tell behind her dark satin mask, but she was flush all the same.

She knew she needed a break. Some fresh air, and probably something sweet to tamper the dizziness from the wine.

And so, she swept her date, her beau, her future husband out the double doors of the famed Ballroom, and found their way out through the bustling kitchen to the back porch, and out into the dazzling and over-ripe green grounds of the Hale House.

She could barely see the sliver of moon through the trees and hanging moss surrounding the back grounds space, but the heavy yet cooling air settled her soul, and allowed the sweat glistening on her chest above her breasts to dry somewhat.

Until she turned to see the look Samuel Hale was giving her, barely visible from the bright lights coming through the tall windows of the home behind them.

She couldn't help herself. She suddenly saw her entire future together with this man, and as if fate itself pushed the two of them together under the waning crescent moon high overhead, their lips met in the deep darkness and heavy air around.

Angels sang their sweet chorus around them, all was right and correct with Aurora's world, and as the kiss lengthened into something almost scandalous, she felt the heavens open up both figuratively and actually.

The raindrops were heavy, warm, and wet. Like a many-armed sea serpent, wet tentacles rained down on Aurora's flush shoulders and chest, and forced the young lovers back to the large mansion, and the gaiety within.

Laughing, she and Samuel Hale ran back through the bustling kitchen, through the throngs of bejeweled Southerners standing around enjoying the frivolities of the late evening, and into the darkly paneled ballroom to dance the final minutes of Mardi Gras night.

And as the clocks around the mansion struck the eleventh hour, loud thunder accompanied by dazzling lightning lit up the house brighter than the very middle of the unseen sun usually baking the land therearound.

Those enjoying the festivities, music loud in ears, spirits raised on spirits and bubbling concoctions, and full with the fat of the bountiful land around, had no idea that as the clock struck the eleventh hour, it would be the very last hour any of them had to live.

∞

The pattering rain created large puddles surrounding the grounds of the Hale House, but they were no hindrance to the dark blue-clad soldiers moving toward the gaily lit home in a pincing maneuver.

Enemy soldiers surrounded the home, and no one within knew that they were without.

Rifles held at the ready, bayonets fixed, and powder dry, soldiers moved toward the home to carry out the orders that had come down to decimate the local Confederate leadership in an Encirclement Manuever Ambush.

Hearing the loud music and raucous laughter coming from the rich, brightly lit mansion, many of the soldiers had thoughts of plunder, rape, murder, and theft on their minds as they moved swiftly through the wetlands and the mud.

The Union soldiers were wet, tired, angry, and ready to relieve all of those conditions posthaste.

They would move into the mansion, gathering up everyone attending the party into a central location, with no exits, and accomplish orders at the stroke of midnight, when the gaiety was at its climax.

Smiles and wet hot lusts reverberated through souls, warming them with the thoughts of what was to come.

Those in the large, well-lit mansion would have no idea what was about to happen.

∞

Aurora Deveraux smiled brightly at her best friend and constant companion as they both danced around the central area of the grand ballroom to music that reached their very hearts.

The strong arms of the men who moved them around the rich appointments and under the bright candlelight chandeliers held tight the very futures of both young women, and they had not a worry in the world.

Sweat dripped between Aurora's breasts, but she happily accepted it, as well as the soreness in her tired feet as she made faux love to her future groom with the decadent dance of the Virginia Waltz.

All of her thoughts were awaiting the next few days when her parents and Dr. Hale would solidify the union between their children with a dowry paid, and understandings reached.

The string and brass instruments rose to a crescendo as the final hour of Mardi Gras drew to a close with the playing of "Dixie," loudly and proudly, and crystal plates of King Cake were distributed around the room.

All in attendance, even the help, as well as the staff and drivers, entered the brightly lit Ball Room for the striking of the clock, and the end of Carnival. It was always Aurora's favorite time of the festivities.

Joshua Loyd Fox

As she indulged in the delicious cake, taking sips of champagne out of tall crystal flutes, her smile behind her mask couldn't have been brighter.

The noise and cacophony of the revels rose to a fever pitch, laughter and drunken exclamations of success and victory in the coming War of the States made this ending of Carnival even brighter than most, as was the strategy of the benefactors of the Ball.

And because the noise and exclamatory excitement rose loudly around the large room, not a single reveler noticed the wet, muddy boot prints of a squad of Union Soldiers sullying the expensive carpets of the first floor of the mansion, nor the quick movements of the squad outside the Ball Room.

As soon as the first bullets flew, though, the music cut off mid-note, and the screaming arose as loud as the celebrations only seconds before.

Blood splattered, screams rent the air, and the crowd was pressed toward the middle of the Ball Room into a tight ball of bright sequins, blacker-than-night tuxedos, colorful dresses, and even more colorful words being exchanged between the victims and those doing the victiming.

Aurora and Cassandra were in the very middle of the slowly dwindling group of revelers, and as their screams rose in staccato accompaniment to the shots from rifles surrounding the room, all of the merriment, the future fantasies, and the deep, easy confidence of a blessed future were suddenly cut off with the precision of eighteen-inch bayonet blades thrust into bosoms, and out the backs of pretty little shoulder blades, so gloriously dressed and jewel-covered only moments before.

Black felt feline masks fell from faces stuck in mortis, frozen screams on frozen faces the only death masks needed as the clocks around the Ball Room finished the twelfth peal, and silence found its home at the end of Carnival, finally.

The blood widening in a large pool under the bodies piled in the middle of the Ball Room would be the only testament that night of how Mardi Gras, 1862, would go down in history as the world's cruelest, and the Civil War's bloodiest, night.

∞

The morning of Wednesday, March the 5th, 1862 was bright as the sun, with crystal clear skies. Birdsong flew from tree to tree on the road from New

Orleans. A single open carriage, drawn by a single dapple mare, moved through the wheel ruts of the dirt road leading to Hale House.

In the carriage sat one Sally Hale, daughter-in-law of Dr. Jeremiah Hale, and wife of the son that the great doctor chose to never talk about again. Jack had left home late the year prior to fight for the North, and the abolishment of slavery in the United States.

Driving the carriage was the slave, Henry. The older man had taken Ms. Sally to her parents' home for the jubilee of Mardi Gras, so as not to ruin the festival for the good Dr. Hale, by seeing the wife of his treacherous son.

Driving the carriage into the grounds of Hale House, the spectacle awaiting the pair on the horse drawn carriage was confounding in the least, down right macabre and mysterious at the most.

Dozens of carriages, horses still in tracks, and with reins dragging the ground, took up most of the front lawn and carriage way leading to the entrance of the home.

As Henry pulled the carriage to the front of the home, scattering riderless horses and carriages about, he could see the concern on Ms. Sally's face at the sight of the wide open, yet deserted door.

"Miss Sally, you best stay with the horse, ma'am," Henry told the young woman.

"I'll go in the house and see what's about," he finished.

Sally was used to minding, so she didn't argue with the older man.

He climbed down from the large, spoke-wheeled carriage, handing the reins to Ms. Sally, and made his way slowly up the steps to the front door.

He could smell a sweet-sickly smell before he entered the dark interior of the mansion.

Henry couldn't open the door all the way, but he put his shoulder into the door, and pushed against something that whispered against the marble floor of the front hall.

And that's all Henry needed to do as he stepped into the shaded and smoky interior.

One look at bodies covered in expensive gowns and tuxedos, blood spilt and pooled everywhere, and he knew right away what had happened.

He ran back to the carriage as fast as his old, damaged legs and back would let him. The panic in his eyes and the sweat growing hot on his brow even made the normally gentle mare side step away from the traces of the carriage.

Sally saw the white of Henry's eyes as the man jumped back into the carriage and snapped the reins from her hands, hurting her slightly, and smacked them on the rump of the horse.

They left the grounds of the Hale House at a dead run, nearly killing them all. Sally couldn't utter a word as she listened to the deep, chest-rumbling keening coming from the mouth of a man who had seen atrocities enough for anyone.

Whatever the older ex-slave had seen in the house had spooked the man in ways he would never recover.

Sally chose not to ask, but knew she would soon be privy to whatever the old slave had seen, and that had scared him nearly senseless.

∞

Watching the black man run back out into the bright sunlight, and alight out of the grounds of the Hale House, the apparition still felt deep, vengeful wrath from the front windows of the Ball Room.

Aurora had not gone into the light as her lifeblood left her body from the deep bayonet wound she could still feel as a ghost.

This home was supposed to have become *her* home, as she was to marry the only remaining son of Dr. Hale.

And damn it, the ghost thought to herself as she looked back at the bodies strewn all about the bottom floor of the Hale House, and the destruction to the home, and the violation of the female bodies, *this home* would *be hers*.

It would be hers for the rest of time, even if she had to haunt the goddamn place forever.

Second Floor

Ah, yes, good to see you again.

Feeling alright? Heart rate steady?

Follow me up the main stairs.

Can you hear it? That's a bit of Bach floating on the air. Lovely, isn't it?

Our master bedroom is unusually spacious for a house of this age. Feel free to try out the bed, but keep an eye on your candle. Yours is white. Not red. Stay away from the red ones.

Take a peek at the nursery. Have a seat on the rug. Let your inner child out to play. There are plenty of toys. Just… steer clear of the knives.

Our bathroom is, admittedly, a bit outdated, but still fully functional. Observe the unique hooded bath. Ignore the claw marks.

In the trophy room, you will find Hale House's fine collection of taxidermy specimens. I must ask, however, that you look but *do not touch*. Under any circumstances. In fact, keep as much distance between yourself and the specimens as possible.

Perhaps it's best if you just stand in the doorway and glance around.

The music room is locked, but press your ear to the door. The Bach is louder there. If the notes begin to falter, step away… quickly.

And last, if you need a little time to catch your breath before we climb to the third floor, stop and sit awhile in the game room. Please, take full advantage of our selection of entertainments. Just know that here in Hale House… winning *is* everything.

∽

So, stop standing here listening to me.

Pick a door. Peer in.

Go on…

I'll be here, waiting in the dark.

Master Bedroom
2016

Roses and Worms
Joe DeRouen

"I get that it's probably going to be hard to sell," said Venessa, Arn's wife, over his iPhone, "but what's the use of bitching about it? Just do your job."

It was 4:30 in the afternoon and Arn Saxby stood before Hale House, the giant monstrosity he'd been tasked with selling. The mansion had been built sometime in the early 1800s, making it somewhere around two hundred years old.

Just about the entire town thought it was haunted. On a related note, just about the entire town were idiots. Truth be told, it was much more likely to be filled with termites than with spirits.

"*Probably* hard to sell? It's going to be impossible. And I'm not 'bitching,' I'm just not sure who I pissed off to get saddled with this."

"I think you're just scared of the ghosts."

He laughed, though he found her humor more annoying than funny. Arn didn't believe in ghosts, as Venessa well knew, but the rumors wouldn't make it easy to sell. Nor would the actual tragedy that had happened in the house.

About ten years ago, a couple apparently killed each other in the kitchen of Hale House while having sex. No one seemed sure of the details, but the whole town seemed convinced ghosts were somehow involved. More likely, they were probably on drugs or just plain psycho.

"Hardly," Arn finally said, biting his tongue.

"Well, babe, just do your best. That's all anyone can ask."

Arn sighed and shook his head. Pulling out the set of keys he'd been given by Carl, the assistant manager at Sanders Realty, he walked up the steps and unlocked the front door to Hale House.

"Okay, well, I'm about to go inside and get the lay of the land. Love you. Talk to you later."

"Love you, too, Arn," she responded, almost by rote, just before he thumbed off the phone.

Did she really love him, though? More importantly, did he really love her? They'd been married for nearly twenty years, and she'd become much more annoying than she ever was lovable. But that was a question for another day.

He held his breath and walked inside.

∾

Arn wasn't sure what he'd been expecting, but it definitely wasn't this. While incredibly musty, the house wasn't in bad shape at all. The plumbing seemed to be working, and the electricity was on.

Most of the furniture had stains and rips and smelled more than a little dank, but they'd haul all of that out to the dump. This might not be the train wreck he thought it was going to be, the house's reputation notwithstanding.

He'd spent a good thirty minutes exploring the first floor of the house and now stood at the top of the stairs on the second floor, just down the hall from the master bedroom. The first floor had been entirely ghost-free, and he didn't expect the second floor to be any different.

Something squeaked, and he jumped. He looked at the floor, where the sound had come from. It was only a little field mouse.

"Are you a ghost?" he asked, smiling, as the mouse skittered away.

Well, that was something. He made a mental note to make an appointment with Wallace Rodent and Pest Control. After all, it wouldn't do to have mice running all over the place while he was trying to sell it.

"He's not a ghost," said a voice from behind him, with just the hint of a southern drawl.

"but I am."

Twirling around, his heart thumping in his chest, he came face to face with the most beautiful woman he'd ever seen standing in the doorway to the master bedroom.

She was just about his height, maybe a little shorter, had long, jet black hair, and beautiful deep blue eyes. She wore an old-fashioned black and red polka-dotted dress that went down to her knees and accentuated her curves in all the right places.

Whoever she was, she was no ghost.

Arn shook his head. "You're no more of a ghost than I am. Who are you and what are you doing in here?"

"My name is Lillian, and as to what I'm doing here, I'm waiting for you, actually."

"For me?"

"Yes, silly. For you."

"You can't be waiting for me. This place isn't even listed yet. It won't go on the market until we can clean things up and make some much-needed repairs."

"Oh my. Apparently, I was given the wrong information. I'm so sorry for wasting your time." She swayed unsteadily, like she was about to faint.

"Are you okay?"

"I just think I just need to sit down. This place is big, and I've done a lot of walking for the last hour."

She turned and stumbled into the bedroom before glancing over her shoulder to look at him.

"Are you coming?"

He stared after her. Shrugging to himself, he stepped into the bedroom.

∞

The master bedroom was beautiful, by far the most luxurious room he'd seen so far in the house, and in perfect condition, too.

A huge four-poster bed with a cream-colored canopy occupied the north side of the room, while a stately oak dresser stood against the opposite wall. There were chairs and a small table beside the two huge windows looking out over the western half of the property.

The floor was made up of black and white pinwheel tiles, part of it covered by a large pink rug, and the walls were painted a creamy white that matched the bed.

One part of the wall seemed… different, somehow, like it was painted later than the rest of the wall or with a slightly different color. He couldn't quite put his finger on it, but it was something he'd have to investigate later. This place needed to be perfect if he were going to be able to sell it.

Atop the little table by the window sat a burning red candle, filling the room with an intoxicating scent he immediately fell in love with. At first it smelled like lavender, and then immediately shifted to roses, then cherry blossoms, followed by vanilla, marshmallows, freshly mowed grass, oranges, and… a smell he couldn't quite place, like a certain type of spice. Sage, maybe?

"The room is lovely, isn't it? So… I told you my name, could you please return the courtesy?"

Arn turned his attention to the woman now sitting on the edge of the bed with one leg crossed over the other. Lillian. He blinked. He'd become so lost looking at the bedroom, he hadn't even noticed her sitting down.

Had she brought the candle, or had it been here all along, waiting for someone to light it? He decided he didn't care as he noticed the candle switch to the smell of warm earth after a storm.

"I'm Arnold Saxby, but everyone calls me Arn. I work for Sanders Realty. Which you'd know if you had actually been waiting for me."

She looked at him, her beautiful eyes downcast.

"Oh, dear. I've been found out. Actually, the door was open, and I just came in. But I really am interested in buying Hale House."

If the door were open, why had he needed to use the key to gain access? Then again, had he tried to open the door before putting in the key? He couldn't remember, so he put that thought aside for now.

The candle changed to hot chocolate. It made him feel hungry.

"Well, I'd love to sell it to you, but we're just not to that stage yet. We need to get pest control out here, for one thing, and–"

"Come sit with me, Arn," she said, interrupting him, patting the bed beside her.

"Both parties should be sitting when discussing business, don't you think? Plus… I like you."

His cheeks colored. She liked him? What a strange thing to say. She barely knew him.

But he didn't mind keeping the conversation going a little while longer. Instead of sitting next to her, however, he walked over to the windows and picked up one of the chairs.

He glanced out the windows. Why was it so dark outside? It had been almost painfully sunny when he'd first walked into the house.

Was there a storm brewing, or maybe even an eclipse he hadn't read about?

"Are you coming?" she asked, and he shook his head, blinked, and the sky looked sunny again.

What the hell?

"There," he finally said, as he walked back toward her, put the chair beside the bed, and lowered himself onto the seat. "Now we're both sitting."

"How much are you asking for the house?"

She was leaning forward now, staring into his eyes. The candle smelled briefly of jasmine before switching to butterscotch and finally roses again.

"Well, $1,655,000. I know that's pricey, but it's really not that bad for a house this size, especially when it's on eighteen acres of land."

"Sold."

He looked at Lillian, waiting for her to laugh, but she just smiled.

"Seriously?"

"Seriously. I adore this house. And now that that's settled... tell me a little bit about yourself, won't you? Are you married?"

She was going to buy the house, without even negotiating? And why was she asking him if he was married?

He looked into her eyes. God, she was gorgeous. For a moment he wished he weren't married, but he was wearing his ring, so he couldn't very well lie about it.

Arn shook his head. What was he thinking? He was married and even if he and Venessa didn't get along like they used to, he'd never broken his wedding vows and wasn't about to start now. Especially not with someone he'd just met, and a potential client at that.

"Yes," he finally said, "I'm happily married, and have been for twenty years. How about you?"

"Happily single," she said, with a lopsided smile,

"for pretty much all my life. Too bad you aren't. We could've had some fun. Then again, maybe we still can."

The smell changed yet again, this time to a woodsy, musky smell. It reminded him of the first time he'd had sex, on a camping trip with his then-girlfriend when they were both seventeen.

"What's up with that candle?" he asked, but she ignored him and instead reached across the divide between them and caressed his knee.

Arn felt an electric thrill course through his body. He should stand up and leave, get the hell out of this strange situation entirely, but...

Did he want to? The scent of the candle grew stronger. It still smelled of musky wood but now with just a hint of roses.

"I think you like me, too," she said, ignoring his question about the candle. She slid her hand between his legs, slowly rubbing him.

"Hmm?"

Arn didn't know what to do. This was wrong. He was married, and he hardly knew this woman. But her hand on him felt so good. And then she was pulling him up from the chair, their lips meeting, and he knew he didn't want to stop.

Their tongues danced together as the kiss grew deeper, and then she pushed him onto the bed. She shrugged and her little black and red polka-dotted dress pooled at her bare feet.

She was completely naked underneath, no bra or panties, and soon his clothes joined hers beside the bed.

"Oh, Arn," she moaned, as she straddled him, taking him inside her, "this feels amazing."

His hands caressed her breasts as she moved up and down on him, faster, faster, until—

∞

Arn sat up in bed, slowly looking around. Where was Lillian? He blinked, remembering. They'd made love three times, each more passionate than the last.

After the third time, they'd lain there in each other's arms, spent. He'd only planned to close his eyes for a moment or two.

And what was that awful smell? The smell of roses, marshmallows, and freshly baked cake was gone, and instead it almost smelled like something had died in here.

He looked at his watch, and his heart raced. Jesus Christ! It was 5:36 in the morning.

Venessa must be out of her mind with worry.

Venessa. The guilt came crashing down then. He'd spent the night with another woman. He'd cheated on his wife, something he'd managed to avoid doing for nearly twenty years of marriage.

They'd never had children, despite years of trying. He was suddenly thankful for that. If he had kids waiting at home, he could only imagine how worried they'd be. Venessa was going to be bad enough.

"Lillian, I have to go," he called out, but there was no reply.

"Lillian?"

Had she gone home, wherever home was? He realized with a start that he had no idea where she lived, didn't even know her last name. How would he find her? Would he ever see her again? His heart sank at that thought.

He shook his head. None of that mattered right now. He snatched his cell phone from the bedside table, thankful it hadn't yet run out of power.

The iPhone had almost twenty missed calls, all from Venessa. There were five voicemails. With a shaky press of his forefinger, he forced himself to listen to them.

"Arn," said Venessa's voice in the first voicemail, recorded just after seven last night, "it's getting late. I'm worried. Are you okay? Call me."

It wasn't until the third voice mail, this one at 10:14 at night, that she started to sound angry.

"I can't think of a single good reason why you'd be out so late. Call me, God damn it."

The one at midnight said: "Okay, Arn, fuck you. This is ridiculous. Where the hell are you and who are you with? If you're cheating on me, I swear we're done."

And then the final voicemail, at just past four in the morning: "I'm so scared, Arn. Please, please call me… and if you're not dead, I'm going to kill you myself!"

He started to call her, then paused. What was he going to say? What excuse could he possibly give for staying out all night?

"Lillian," he yelled into the empty room, "where are you?"

There was no answer. He started to get out of bed and immediately felt dizzy. Had she drugged him? But no, he hadn't had anything to drink or eat since lunch yesterday, and his wallet wasn't missing.

Forcing himself to his feet, he dressed quickly, and it wasn't until he was finished that he noticed the room had changed from last night.

There was dirt and grime everywhere, just like the rest of the house. There were deep scratches on the walls, the stately canopy he'd stared at last night while Lillian was riding him was ripped and stained, and that awful smell made him feel like he might throw up.

How could this be? He shook his head, regretting the action when almost immediately a huge headache sprung raging into his forehead. He staggered a bit, blinking, and for a second the room looked and smelled like it did last night.

He blinked again and it was back to the state of disrepair he'd awoken to this morning. His eyes began to water from the disgusting odor that permeated the room. It smelled like dead worms.

Ignoring for now all the questions he had about Lillian and Hale House, as well as the growing headache, Arn forced himself to walk across the floor. What else could he do? He had to save his marriage. He stumbled to the door and left the bedroom.

∞

Arn Saxby sat in his Ford Flex outside Hale House, unsure of what to do next. He'd made up a stupid story that involved having a flat tire, his iPhone running out of juice, and him falling asleep in the car, but of course Venessa hadn't believed him.

She'd insisted he tell her the truth, but he'd stuck to his story. It was then that she'd taken off her wedding ring and thrown it in face before slamming the door behind her and driving off to God only knew where.

He was almost certain now that he'd been drugged, though how or for what reason he couldn't quite fathom. Nothing had been stolen, and an incredibly beautiful woman had sex with him.

None of it made any sense. Had he suffered a stroke?

He almost wished he'd found ghosts in Hale House rather than Lillian. He would have run screaming from the place, finally a believer, and he wouldn't have cheated on his wife.

His phone rang, and he jumped. Venessa? No, it was Carl, the assistant manager at Sanders Realty, probably wanting to know where he was and why he'd missed his 10:30 a.m. appointment to show a potential client a house on the other side of town.

Fuck Carl. After all, it had been Carl who'd sent him to Hale House yesterday afternoon. Carl had ruined his fucking life. He stared at the phone until it stopped ringing, then shoved it into his pocket.

Arn pressed the palms of his hands against his eyes, unsure whether to cry, scream, or do both. As much as he regretted cheating on Venessa, there was a part of him that absolutely didn't regret it at all.

He'd had sex with ten women in his lifetime, and not even one of those encounters were half as good as last night with Lillian. Not even close.

What if... what if he could divorce Venessa, find Lillian, and start his life anew? If Lillian actually did buy the house, he certainly wouldn't lose his job. In fact, he'd more than likely be promoted.

Hell, if she could afford to spend $1,655,000 on an old, run-down mansion without blinking an eye, she must be fabulously wealthy. Screw his job. He'd become a kept man.

He surprised himself by feeling no shame at those thoughts. Instead, he felt an almost manic glee. Was he going crazy? At this point, he wasn't sure he cared.

Arn got out of the car, slammed the door behind him, and marched toward Hale House.

∞

Was there a lady behind the door, a tiger, or something else entirely? It'd been ten minutes since Arn walked into the house, and yet he couldn't bring himself to open the bedroom door.

He knew the chance that Lillian was in there was almost nil, but much like Schrödinger's hypothetical cat in the hypothetical box, as long as the bedroom door remained closed, he couldn't know for sure, hypothetically or otherwise.

What was wrong with him? He'd never been one to hesitate when an opportunity came his way, even if he was unsure of what the ultimate outcome might be.

Either she was there, or she wasn't.

He opened the door.

∞

The bedroom was like it had been when he first entered it yesterday, and he could smell roses and sandalwood. A slow smile crept over his lips. Lillian was sitting on the bed, wearing that same red and black polka-dotted dress she'd had on yesterday.

"Arn!" she exclaimed, rising from the bed.

He quickly walked over to her, and she threw herself into his arms, kissing him deeply. He wanted nothing more than to be with this woman for the rest of his life, Venessa be damned.

When the kiss was over, he said, "Where were you this morning?"

"I had to visit the lady's room. When I got back here, you were gone. But you're here now, and that's all that matters."

Had she only been in the bathroom? So disoriented was he when he awoke this morning, he hadn't even bothered to search the house. He felt silly.

Arn hadn't wanted to admit it to himself, but it actually crossed his mind at some point that she might have been a ghost. Ghosts weren't real, of course, no matter what the simpletons in town believed, and Arn Saxby was no simpleton.

Joe DeRouen

His phone rang, and both he and Lillian jumped. Arn reached into his pocket for the iPhone. It was Venessa. So now she wanted to talk. *Sorry, dear, but it's much too late for talking.* He pressed a button, sending the call to voicemail, then muted the ringer.

"Sorry about that."

He looked at Lillian. Her eyes were wide, and she was staring at his phone. "What is that?"

"It's… it's just an iPhone. You've never seen an iPhone?"

"Oh. Well, of course I have. It just startled me, that's all. Who was calling you?"

"It was my wife. She… well, she left me," Arn said, surprised at the words coming out of his mouth, "and I don't care."

"Good."

Her arms encircled his neck again, and she flashed him that lopsided smile before going in for another kiss. Before he knew it, they were in bed again, making love. The smell of roses from the candle was so intoxicating it was almost overwhelming.

Just as he was about to release himself inside of her, she grabbed his hips to stop him from moving and looked deep into his eyes.

"Do you love me, Arn?"

He'd known her for less than twenty-four hours; how could he love her? But he realized with a start that he did. He was madly, truly, and deeply in love with this amazing, gorgeous woman, and he didn't even know her last name.

"Yes, I do. I do love you."

She started to move again, slowly thrusting her hips up against his.

"More than you love Venessa?"

"Yes," he whispered, pushing down into her. "So much more."

Her movements began to speed up a little.

"And do you give yourself to me, like you once gave yourself to her?"

He was about to say yes, and then something occurred to him. He couldn't remember ever telling her Venessa's name. He started to ask, and she sped up even more, bucking her hips against his.

"Do you, Arn? Do you give yourself to me? If you won't give yourself to me fully and completely, then this can't happen, and you'll never see me again."

The woodsy smell of roses and pine began to fade, and he knew he couldn't lose her.

"Yes. Yes. Yes! I give myself to you, all of me."

The smell was so strong now. Roses everywhere. She slammed her hips up into his hips, over and over, harder and faster, pulling him deep into her, and he finally exploded inside of her.

They both screamed in ecstasy.

Arn and Lillian lay together, out of breath, spent, and he felt almost blissful. But what was that awful smell? He wrinkled his nose. Gone was the smell of roses and chocolate, replaced by that rotting odor of dead worms he'd smelled this morning.

He stared up at the canopy. It was ripped and tattered, and he could see the ceiling through the cloth. He felt a shiver go up his spine as gooseflesh prickled his arms. Was he losing his mind?

"What's going on?" he finally asked out loud.

"I've been trapped here nearly eighty years," Lillian whispered.

"I could never move beyond the bedroom door."

Arn turned to look at her. "What are you talking about?"

She sighed.

"I like you, Arn, I really do, and I'm so sorry for this, but a girl's got to do what a girl's got to do."

He felt like he was going to throw up. "I don't understand."

"You will," she said, rolling away from him to get out of bed.

Lillian, his beautiful Lillian, didn't look right.

He blinked, shook his head, and looked again. She had a long, bloody gash running from her forehead to her chin. One of her eyes was missing, and she had a gaping hole in her ribcage, just under her left breast.

He screamed.

"I was murdered in this very room, forced to spend an eternity in Hale House. Or at least I thought so, before I met you."

Arn threw himself out of bed, naked, and ran for the door.

He grabbed at the doorknob, but his hand went through the metal. He tried again with the same result, and again. He finally threw his shoulder into the door, but he just bounced back, like a ping pong ball hurled against a mountain.

He turned to Lillian.

"What's happening to me?"

And then he noticed another Arn Saxby lying in the bed, his eyes open, staring straight up into the air.

"What the fuck is going on?"

"You're a ghost now, Arn," Lillian said, as she walked *through* the bed to touch the other Arn's forehead.

"Just like me."

"You told me you were a ghost, when we first met, but you were joking. Ghosts aren't real. They can't be real. They just can't."

She laughed, and then shrugged.

"Believe whatever you want. I'll come back from time to time, to check on you, and maybe we'll even have sex again. That part was really nice."

"But… how? How are you doing this?"

"You gave yourself to me, remember?" she said, slowly fading as she merged with the empty body on the bed.

"Which I really and truly appreciate, though being a man is going to be a bit of an adjustment."

She vanished completely, and then the other Arn lying on the bed sat up.

"But I'll get used to it," the other Arn said.

"You stole my body."

The other Arn shook his head.

"You gave it to me."

"But why me? Why target me."

"Because you could see me. You're the only one who's ever been able to see me."

He flashed back to when he was four, a memory long buried. He was playing with his best friend Johnny in the backyard, only his mother couldn't see Johnny.

She told him his friend wasn't real. "If I can't see this 'Johnny,' then he must be a ghost, and ghosts don't exist, and anyone who believes otherwise is a damned fool," she told him, over and over, spanking him every time he mentioned Johnny or any of the others that he saw but she couldn't.

After a while, he just stopped seeing them.

"No, no, no," he yelled, waving his arms, flinching as his left hand phased into the wall.

"All of it… everything, even the candle… was it all in my mind? This isn't real. This can't be real. It just can't."

The other Arn, Lillian now, put on his discarded clothes, walked through him, opened the bedroom door, and stepped across the threshold.

"Come back here," Arn yelled, reaching for her wrist, watching in horror as his hand vanished when it crossed the doorway.

He pulled his arm back, and his hand reappeared. He stumbled backward, staring at Lillian inside his body.

"Where are you going?"

Lillian looked back and smiled.

"I'm going to go make up with Venessa, and then I'll seduce her. I've never made love with a woman before, but it sounds fun. After that…the sky's the limit. Goodbye, lover."

The door closed as Arn screamed.

Nursery
1918

Bluebells in the Rug
Jo Kaplan

With the Spanish flu running rampant, we've had no choice but to isolate in our new estate – listen to me, estate! I can hardly believe Robert was able to purchase it, but then he has always kept the particulars of his finances – indeed, all such worldly worries – to himself. I suppose I should count myself grateful.

He wants only the best for me, you see.

My impression of Hale House – isn't it marvelous? A house with its own name! – was of some enormous shape lurking behind a curtain of Spanish moss, revealing itself by degrees through the choke of green tendrils, ornamented with all manner of gables and dormers.

When we stepped inside, I asked Robert what we should ever do with all this space, and he said, "I suppose we'd better fill it up with a whole brood."

Only if you make like a seahorse, I wanted to tell him, *and carry them all yourself!* Robert finds humor unbecoming a lady, so I have tried to temper my sarcastic nature. I did let on what an exhausting business it already is, though.

He brushed his lips over my cheek. "You wear it well. Lovelier than the day we met."

His flattery makes me blush! It's the way of newlyweds, I suppose. And I do think we ought to have more than one. A single child with no siblings can be such a lonesome thing. He might rely overmuch upon his own imagination, grow simultaneously too mistrustful and also too desperate for affection.

I should know; like Robert, I was an only child. What a delight it was, for the pair of us, then – two wind-tossed, wayward souls – to find each other!

This house makes me dizzy. I've never dreamed of having so much space! Yet despite all its furnishings, it feels somehow empty: the ceilings too high, the walls too pronounced. I've struggled even to find our servants as they scurry off into the cavernous reaches.

It *is* wonderful – marvelous! – but it's all a bit too much, you understand.

Robert saved a special surprise for me. He brought me to the second floor with my eyes closed (I stumbled and told him walking is a tad easier with my eyes open, but he only took me more firmly by the arms), then stood me in the hall while I heard the creak of a door swinging open, and finally he told me to look.

A room, shrouded and dim, with faded yellow walls the color of buttermilk and the ghost of a slatted crib stood on the other side of the doorway. He went ahead and threw open the curtains. Dust plumed into the air, whirling in jagged sunbeams. A peculiar smell – stale and sour, with a slight coppery edge – haunted the air.

"What do you think?" he asked me.

"Needs a bit of work."

"Exactly," he said.

"This will be the perfect project to occupy you! You can fix it up exactly to your liking."

The room *is* oddly charming, despite its disrepair. It will have to be aired out. I'll need to beat the curtains and the old sprawling rug. Blue flowers march along its edges, their vines weaving patterns that move inward, suffocating the center.

I told him my mother would know exactly what to do with the space.

"She has an eye for such things."

At this, Robert stiffened.

"We won't be having any visitors. It would be unwise, with this influenza. Don't forget, you are especially vulnerable, in your condition."

No visitors at all! Not even my mother! Even the prospect made me terribly lonesome. It's why I write this down, to feel as though I have someone to talk to, even if it is only paper. All this rambling space – yet with these walls separating us from society, it is almost like a tomb.

I would not tell Robert this, of course. After all, he has bought this impressive estate for me! I would hate for him to think me ungrateful.

At least I have the nursery to keep me occupied.

∞

A bright spot: I've discovered something in the nursery which has cheered me considerably.

As I was airing out the space, I found a trunk pushed into the corner. Thinking it had been misplaced when our things were brought to the house, I opened it to see what was inside, and do you know what I found?

A pile of children's toys!

Spinning tops, marbles, a set of building blocks, board games, a toy drum, a magic lantern, little wooden figurines. Another surprise of Robert's, no doubt.

These must be his old things from when he was a boy – though where he has been keeping them, I can't imagine. He must have wanted to pass them onto our son – at least, I feel it *must* be a boy, as my *linea nigra* begins above the belly button.

I have brought out the toys and arranged them around the nursery. I know I'll need to put them away when we repaint, but they make the room feel so much homier, as if there is already a child here.

∞

How are the days already such a listless drag? It has only been a week!

If only Abigail, or Cousin Bertie, or Mother could visit.

I could so well do with a bit of levity and gossip. Robert is away so much on business, and he doesn't even like me to leave the house. And why *should* I want to leave? Look at all this space!

"You have everything you need right here," he told me when I suggested a trip into town.

"Isn't this everything you've always wanted?"

Of course it is. I'm being silly.

I dared to ask him, yesterday, how he had come to afford this house.

"Don't concern yourself," he said, his voice clipped.

I could tell he felt insulted.

"You know I do whatever it takes to get what I want. What we *deserve*. And we deserve the very best of things, don't you think?"

He is right, of course. It's only that – I can hardly bring myself even to write it here – I think I may go mad here alone!

Each time I return to the nursery, I swear, I *swear* those little wooden soldiers are not quite where I left them. Has one of the servants been moving them? But I hardly ever see any of the servants anymore.

And yet, look! The soldiers stand in a kind of battle formation. I certainly *didn't* put them there, but Robert insists he hasn't been in the nursery, that he has left the room entirely to me.

Am I only imagining it? I admit, my thoughts have been scattered since I discovered I was with child. Sometimes I don't trust myself.

When I – now, I wouldn't dare breathe a word of this to Robert, but – when I found out, tears sprang to my eyes and a sob hardened to a ball in my chest.

I don't know why I should have reacted that way, for what greater blessing is there? And only three months after the wedding! Too much change all at once, my mother would say. That's all.

But I haven't – *perhaps* – been quite right since then, and so it's no wonder I'm misremembering where I laid the soldiers.

I will put them into a very specific shape that will be impossible to forget (a star) just to be sure.

∞

I thought I was alone in these endless halls, but of course I haven't been alone at all.

I am certain, now, that he is speaking to me!

If Robert would only listen – but he is busy, and he reminds me that the nursery is my own project. I've no one else to tell! I used to talk with Wilhelmina, but she is off in the servant quarters, and I never seem to cross paths with her. I've half a mind to tell her off for avoiding me.

The soldiers have taken leave of the star in which I placed them to march around the edges of the room. I did *not* put them there, I swear it!

When I found them, I cried out with surprise – and at once, the tops went spinning as if a great wind had blown them up to their points. They stood like tiny maelstroms, and after a moment they fell, clattering across the floor.

This was also when I first perceived the building blocks had been constructed into a shape I don't remember setting: I am sure they hadn't been set up at all, but I found them now in the shape of a pyramid.

Only a child, I knew, could be playing with these toys.

And so, my experiment: I took up the soldiers and carefully placed them to spell out "Hello." I took some longer pieces from the block set and used them to form lines. When I was satisfied, I deliberately left the room and went walking about the house – not outside, though the flowers beckoned from their sunlit garden.

The house echoed my steps, as if I were a lone creature in the timeless halls of eternity – no time but the clap of a footfall, no air but my own stale exhalations. I imagined what these halls would be like filled with visitors. The life that could brighten this space!

But Robert insists on precaution, and I cannot say I disagree. Loneliness is nothing to the agony and swiftness of death when the lungs fill with fluid and cyanosis turns the body blue. It is like drowning in fresh air, he has told me.

Of course, there are those who survive the flu with barely a cough, but one can never be sure.

One can never truly be sure.

When I returned to the nursery, that is when I knew!

So distinctly had I fashioned the toys into my message that it was clear I had received a response. Many of the soldiers had been scattered across the rug, with teeth-marks in them as if they had been chewed, while the ones still standing now spelled out the word: "Hi."

You see! He was talking to me, I know it – *my own son!*

I know it sounds absurd – yet somehow, my unborn child, but a few months into his gestation, has found a way to communicate with me. Who else could it be, playing with toys in the nursery that will become his room?

I still haven't done more than beat out the dust. Though the walls remain peeling and faded, I've yet to decide on a new paint color, and though the rug is shabby and worn, it too has maintained its place on the floor.

I only fear if I change things, perhaps my little one won't like it so much, won't talk to me – and I couldn't bear the thought of that!

It is more than just the soldiers, too. The building blocks have been reshaped again – two pyramids now, connected by a thin bridge between them.

I called out, "Hello?"

Two things happened at once: I felt a kick, deep in my abdomen, and the little toy drum I had nearly forgotten about gave several quick taps.

"It *is* you!" I said with delight. "You're there!"

My sweet, sweet boy. It's as if he is telling me: don't worry, Mother. You are not alone. I am here with you, and we will be together forever.

I could cry. In fact, my eyes are prickling. I'd think me a fool if I hadn't seen it myself!

∞

It came to me like a flash, so I asked Robert, as it only felt right: "What do you think of the name Theodore?"

He hasn't spelled it out for me, but the name arrived in my mind as we conversed in the nursery – playing with the soldiers and making battlements out of the wooden blocks.

As if from nowhere, the name *Theodore* appeared in my mind, and I simply couldn't shake it. I had the sense that is what our son would like to be called, when he enters this world.

I had expected Robert to tell me he liked the name – he has been amenable, thus far, to my suggestions – but his words were scathing and cold: "Where did you get that idea?"

"It just came to me," I told him. "You don't like it?"

"Out of the question," he said.

"Weren't we deciding between Adam and Jeremy? One of those will do, and I won't hear another word about it."

I nearly told him he certainly *would* hear more words about the important business of what we would name our son, but I managed to hold my tongue. Robert does *not* take well to quarreling or disagreement.

When he has made up his mind about something, that is that.

As we lay in bed, I traced my fingers gently along the scar down his abdomen: a white, knotty rope of hard flesh. We have hardly been intimate since we moved into the house, but still he pushed my hand away and turned over. I suppose it's because I am already with child, so what's the point?

Or perhaps it's only that he doesn't like me touching his scar. He never speaks of it. I think he's embarrassed. It was some childhood incident. If he managed to injure himself so seriously from child's play, I can only imagine he's ashamed.

Robert despises imperfection of any kind. He is an exceedingly scrupulous man who refuses an overdone roast and likes his gimlets just *so*.

I only wish he would talk to me, though. Was I foolish in assuming a husband would be a confidant – the one person you could tell everything to? And thus, that I, as wife would be the one he could tell *his* everything to? Our conversation, while he courted me, was of course polite, crowned with decorum. But is that all our conversation will ever be? Does he think that is all I am – decorous, polite, a womb for his child?

It is *too* quiet! I hear every creak the house makes, and I fear to so much as clear my throat lest it echo. I will go to the nursery awhile, where at least I have some company.

∾

It is only nerves; Robert would surely tell me. But I *cannot* seem to rid myself of that peculiar smell.

In the nursery, we played with the magic lantern, projecting phantasmagorical forms onto the dull yellow wall. Children cavorting, playing on a seesaw, dancing in a ring. Exotic animals one may find in a zoo – giraffes and elephants.

Then a shape loomed up the wall and seemed to emerge from *behind* it, a monstrous face with protuberant eyes and distended tongue. Even when I switched off the lantern, I felt I could still see the impression of eyes in the yellow paint, as if the gruesome visage had left a ghost of itself.

"I cannot imagine why Robert would keep such images in this toy," I told my child.

"I hope it didn't frighten you."

The drum offered a faint patter. I rubbed a hand over my belly and told him not to fret. "All will be better when you are truly here with me," I told him.

"And when the flu has passed, and we can welcome guests. And you will meet your father. I know Robert means well – he *does* want the very best for us!"

The words having left my lips, I clapped them shut – for the marbles, which had lain in a small pile, rose up as if thrown and clattered angrily to the floor, rolling every which way. My heart shook with each sharp clack.

When I bent to gather them again, I found myself unable to continue.

I was so distracted by the bluebells in the rug, which drooped and stared like strangled blue faces, heads lolling on crumpled necks. They were so like that awful face the lantern put onto the wall!

My breath left me. I stood and dropped the marbles, which scattered again, then rolled back toward me, collecting around my feet as if there were a dip in the floor. Though I am *sure* it is quite level.

I could hardly stand to look down at that rug again, because it made me feel like *I* was choking, too – as if the breath had gone from my lungs, leaving the rattle of a chest full of marbles.

And I was met, then, by a peculiar smell: the sweet sweat of unwashed boys, except copper and rancid, and the blooming of fungus on old bread.

I had to cover my nose it was so strong, and I haven't been back to the nursery since. I don't even like to *look* at the blue curtains anymore, afraid I will find those strangled heads in the patterns there, too!

I must lie down now. Theodore – or Adam, or Jeremy, or *whoever* he is – has been kicking most insistently. If only he would *stop!*

∞

I haven't been to the nursery. It feels like a betrayal, but I am afraid–
The walls seem to suffocate me so.
A disturbing thought has come to me over the last few days.
What if it *isn't* my child I've been speaking with?

∞

I can't remain any longer by myself in all this empty space, wandering from hall to hall, room to room, like a lonely phantom which hasn't realized it's dead.

Listen to me, talking of myself as a ghost! Robert certainly *would* think me mad, wouldn't he?

Hah!

I cannot stop thinking of the news he brings back each time he returns from his business: the horrors of the influenza, skin turning blue and black – I cannot *think* of it! And now when he comes home he doesn't even like to be near me, because he is afraid he might inadvertently pass on the contagion to our son.

But if *he* isn't near me, then no one is. No one but the faces in the rug, in the shadows of the halls, the faces I see everywhere now, like the faces of the dead.

If only I had known so much space could feel so like a mausoleum!

But none of that – I must not think so much. Robert would tell me I am allowing my imagination to get the better of me. It is the way of only children, isn't it? We are too much in our own minds.

Robert suspects I am unwell. I grow dizzy when I look too long at any rugs or curtains – any patterns at all. I hardly sleep, and sometimes I look out the window for hours, wondering what it might be like if I were to throw myself out into the bright clean air.

Where else am I to go?

There is *something* in the nursery – and I no longer believe it is my son!

∞

The smell follows me from room to room, offering whiffs of sweat and ammonia and something intangible, half-rotten. Sometimes it is an odor like a gymnasium, and other times, like rusty nails.

I try to perfume the air, instead, with flowers, green-floral, hyacinth, but that only seems to make it worse.

∞

I finally told Robert my suspicions.

"I didn't take you for the superstitious sort," he told me, amused.

"We mustn't use the nursery," I said. "There are plenty of other rooms in this house."

We were at supper – dining on a meal cooked by unseen servants – and Robert set down his knife with enough force to rattle the table. "Rooms have a specific purpose," he said.

"They were built for that purpose. You can't simply decide something is what it isn't."

"There is something *in* that room!"

"If you are ill, you must tell me. Have you a sore throat? Headache? Fever? Delirium is one of the symptoms, you know."

"How could I have possibly caught it?" I asked him.

"I haven't left the house!"

"They don't know how it travels," he said, and I nearly laughed.

A mysterious traveling illness! And he says *I* am the superstitious one?

"I don't feel ill," I told him, but even I could hear the doubt in my voice.

"The influenza can cause miscarriage," he said, and his voice had gone cold. Cold and angry – as if he were angry with *me!* As if I could control it!

He threw down his napkin and came around the table. Though I reared back from him, he placed the back of his hand on my forehead and sucked in a breath.

"You are burning with fever!"

He put me to bed, and thank goodness he doesn't know I've kept this diary in my nightstand drawer, for I fear he would disapprove of any sort of stimulation while he believes me ill. He is rather Victorian, in that way.

But you see, I do *not* believe I am ill!

When he first felt my head, I admit I felt a thrill of fear; I thought about drowning in my own rattling lungs, I imagined the deadly infection creeping through my body like the chill of a draft that creeps through an old house – but I have seen no other soul but him, and I have been nowhere save our own halls.

If this flu can penetrate even my own absolute isolation, we may as well call it the Red Death!

And if I *am* ill?

Then so is the child in the nursery.

Oh Theodore, I am so sorry. You must be so *lonely*. I have been such a coward, to leave him there. Whoever he is, there is a child in the nursery, and he is utterly alone, just like me.

I must set him free.

∞

I only thought Robert had to see for himself, or else how am I to help Theodore?

I convinced him, at last, to visit the nursery with me (I told him I wanted to show him how I have fixed it up, though in truth, I only wanted him to see what I have seen). He was irate, of course, to discover nothing had been fixed in all this time, and that the room had hardly even been cleaned – but he was astonished to discover his old childhood toys!

I had thought, all this time, it was his gift to our son, but it must have been a mistake after all, for he never intended the trunk to end up here. He demanded to know where I had got the toys, but I could only tell him they were in the trunk, which had been moved in with the rest of our things.

The look on his face – I have never seen it's like.

"I want them gone," he said.

We tarried there only long enough to see the scattered toys, the chewed-up soldiers.

I am exhausted, and perhaps – indeed, *perhaps* – I am ill. Perhaps the flu has colonized my lungs, has reached its tendrils into my brain, has made me believe things – impossible things–

That smell again!

It chokes me.

∞

I stood at the window, for it looked like such a lovely day, the sun as ripe as an apricot – and the breeze came in warm and smelling of magnolias, the first breath I have taken, I think, without that peculiar coppery smell, in some time – and I heard, from somewhere in the distance, the sound of children singing:

I had a little bird
And its name was Enza
I opened the window
And in-flew-Enza

It is me, I wanted to call out to them! I am Enza!

∾

Eventually, I went to gather the toys in the nursery, as Robert instructed, but I had no idea just *who* I had been communicating with over these last weeks, or what he might do, so I brought along with me a knife I found in the kitchen.

If Wilhelmina minds, she can very well come tell me.

It isn't that I don't trust Theodore, but that I do not *know* him. Who – or *what* – he is.

All was quiet when I entered the room. I set down the knife and began to gather the blocks and soldiers, which lay strewn about the floor. I tried very hard not to look at the strangled bluebells in the rug.

As I packed the toys back into the trunk, an overwhelming sadness came over me. *These poor toys*, I thought, *tucked away in the dark, as they had been these last twenty years!* To be lonesome and confined, as I have been – oh, but it is foolish to assign human feeling to inanimate objects.

When I overturned a board game to fit it atop the other toys, I discovered written on the bottom in childish handwriting the name: *Theodore*.

It *wasn't* only in my mind!

But these toys are two decades old!

"Who are you, Theodore?" I asked.

Some unseen force took up the knife I had left and threw it into the floor, where the handle wobbled. My heart went into my throat. I watched the knife go back and forth until it was still.

It is the *things*, you see – not the room!

I went to Robert at once and demanded he tell me who Theodore is.

At first, he refused. I thought of myself like the knife: though I may wobble back and forth, I remain firmly embedded in the floorboards, and it will take far more than *that* to yank me free!

"Haven't I given you everything?" Robert asked me, disappointed.

"Haven't I given us the best start in life?"

The one thing he hasn't given me, I told him, was the truth. I had lived in smaller spaces; I had gone without servants and gardens and beautiful halls in my youth. All I have ever wanted from him, I say, is the *truth*.

"The truth?" Robert spat, his voice rising to echo through the halls.

"What use is the truth? Theodore? He is *dead!* Why should you care who he was? Why do you insist on hearing about my twin? How could you even *know* about him?"

The air seemed to hush in my ears.

"You never told me you had a brother," I said. "What happened to him?"

Robert looked like a sheet hanging on a clothesline. At last he said, his voice gone low, "We were joined."

"I'm not sure I understand."

"Joined," he repeated. "Siamese." He pointed to his chest, to the place where his scar puckers the skin.

"We shared a liver."

It took me some time to get the rest out of him, as he tried to convince me it wasn't a story fit for my ears (I had half a mind to ask him if he was at all aware of what childbirth is like and whether he thinks earmuffs will protect me from its trouble), but eventually I learned it all.

When they were six years old, he and his brother – conjoined, as they had been all their lives – had been playing a game of mumblety-peg: a little folly whereby one throws a knife into the ground and the other must try to remove it with his teeth.

It was a game which suited them both equally, requiring no ambulatory coordination like most sports.

Only this time, there was an accident.

The knife slipped. Theodore got hurt. A physician had to separate them, but Theodore did not survive the surgery. There was only one liver between them, after all.

"Oh, Robert."

I took him into my arms, imagining the guilt he must feel. All this time, carrying the burden of his brother's death. No wonder he has not spoken of it! Yet the tears that spilled from my eyes were glad.

"Don't you see? Theodore doesn't want to hurt us. He is lonely, being apart from you all this time. We brought him here with us. He came along with your old toys, locked up in that trunk all these years. He is only looking for a playmate because he misses you!"

But Robert did not share my joy. In fact, he seemed angry! He put me to bed, told me this was preposterous, that ghosts were not real, that my imagination was running wild – that I was delirious with fever, riddled with flu.

Maybe I am!

Maybe in a short while, my skin will grow putrid red spots, and my face will turn blue, and I will drown where I stand! Maybe that is the fate we all face!

But I won't *stay* in this pattern any longer, and neither will Theodore!

We are getting *out* of this graveyard of bluebells!

∞

I told Robert to help me carry the trunk out of the nursery.

"Get the servants to do it," he said.

I didn't want to say I could not *find* them – for I haven't seen them in weeks! – so I told him I would only feel better if we got rid of the trunk together.

"Then we can put this whole business behind us and forget about Theodore."

This brightened him considerably, so he decided to humor me.

Only I didn't have any intention of removing that trunk!

When we arrived, the knife stood in the floor and Robert looked at me with a question, almost with recognition, at the way the knife's tip was embedded there. It must have been so familiar to him!

Well, it didn't take long for Theodore to realize his brother was here.

The knife pulled itself free and shot through the air straight for Robert, landing in the wall behind him. Poor Robert went as pale as a corpse.

I was shocked.

"Theodore!" I admonished. "You almost hurt him!"

"Of *course* he would want to hurt me," Robert snapped, and I had never heard his voice so filled with venom, never seen his eyes so wild.

"I *hated* him."

The confession ripped out of his chest as a growl. It frightened me.

I felt a kick and clutched my belly protectively.

"You don't mean that."

Robert laughed. The sight of the knife had loosened something inside him.

115

"You don't know what it's like, to share your body with someone else. You are never only *yourself*. You are never alone. And the way we were hid from society! My parents isolated us, they were so ashamed. What else was I to *do*?"

In my horror, I watched the knife behind him begin to wiggle back and forth.

"What *did* you do?"

Robert looked at the door, as if he thought about leaving. He was always leaving – for business, or just to get away. Leaving me in this big empty house all alone.

"Theodore is *here*," I told him, my throat closing.

"What did you *do*?"

The knife went back and forth, back and forth, inching its way out of the wall.

"It was him or me," he said.

"The game of mumblety-peg?" I asked. "The knife didn't slip."

Robert shook his head.

"After I stabbed him, do you know what it was like, being tethered to his dying body? My parents summoned a surgeon, but it was too late. They cut his body from mine, and for the first time in my life, I was *free*."

He was right. I could not imagine.

The magic lantern sprang to life, though I am *sure* I had put it back in the trunk with the rest of the toys. And there was that face – *his* face – wide-eyed and demonic, too large, creeping across the wall like the face of death itself!

I backed away, wondering how I had been so desperate for affection that I had *not* seen what he really was.

"Didn't I deserve my life?" he roared.

"An ordinary life? A *good* life? Not that of some sideshow attraction! We were monstrous. Don't tell me you could ever conceive of marrying the likes of that?"

I could not speak.

Marbles rolled across the floor like thunder; the trunk lurched and banged as it spilled its contents.

At last the knife came free from the wall.

As it did, I felt a sharp pain in my gut, like a series of frantic kicks.

Robert never made it out that door, of course!

The knife found a new home, but one which was softer than wood – and it went in and out, in and out, in a dozen frantic rounds of mumblety-peg, until its handle was riddled with teeth marks.

Until the bluebells had all gone red.

∽

Up until the very brink of nine months, I kept my new habit of walking all through town. Everyone I've met in my rambles has been so kind.

They call me a brave widow, after that thief in the night murdered my husband with my babe still in the womb.

The fresh air has done me much good. I have already invited them all to Hale House to come see the child when enough time has passed, as the flu recedes from us, though we may not be here for much longer; there is simply too much space.

Listen to me. I wrote *child!*

I should have written *children*.

For what a miracle it is! I'd thought I was only pregnant with one, but two have come out: perfectly joined at the chest so that I believe they might even share a heart – and one of them looks at me in such a peculiar way, as if he knows me already!

"Don't worry, Theodore," I tell him.

"You will never be alone again."

.

Bathroom
1995

Spiraling Upward
Gage Greenwood

Gretchen leaned heavily on the iron handrail as her feet brushed against the intricate swirls on the balusters. *She spiraled upwards.* The words made her laugh, a drunken, audible cackle that echoed through the cavernous space above and below her.

These were not spiral staircases, but with the alcohol swirling in her belly, pulsing through her bloodstream, throbbing in her brain, she felt like she was spiraling. Her body ping-ponged off the handrail to the wall on the opposite side of the stairs.

A hiccup escaped her, and again she fell into a fit of laughter.

Spiraling upwards.

What a way to describe her life. Six months ago, she was a hardcore punk kid, living in Rhode Island, selling shitty zines to kids at Club Babyhead, and now she owned a ridiculous house bigger than her home state. It would have been one thing to take the money and run. Who wouldn't?

But Gretchen went all in on her newfound bank account, trading in her JNCOs and labret piercing for long sun dresses and pearls. This wasn't upward mobility. It was spiraling upward.

Those X's she wore on her hands washed off quickly, too. She surely wouldn't slap a Bordeaux glass from her neighbor's hand and yell, "It's a crutch!" like the kids at Earth Crisis shows did.

Instead, she accepted Mrs. Thornton's drink offers until she'd had, jeez, she had no idea. Probably a thousand dollars' worth of wine.

No matter. Only one thing mattered right now.

Gretchen really had to fucking pee.

She loved the bathroom; it being the only room in the house where she didn't have to pretend, because even though she lived alone, she felt a need to play a part, to the walls, to the opulence, to the ghosts in the rusty pipes.

Her need to prove herself extended to even the vast emptiness of the house. She didn't just luck into power; she earned it. This place belonged to her, and her to it. Or so she tried to tell herself.

But the bathroom allowed the freedom to breathe easy. Like her, it was too small for the rest of the house. Sure, it had its gilded edging, and Victorian tiling, but it was also contained. Mold spots freckled the ceiling corners.

She could be herself in a place like this.

And the fucking bathtub.

The first time she walked in, she half-expected a clawfoot, but what she found was a monstrosity, a glorious beast resembling a casket. The realtor acted excited, calling it a "hooded bath." Shaped like an L, the end of the tub came up into a small…

Gretchen didn't know what to call it other than a room.

Three walls and a ceiling. It was like someone took a second bathtub, lifted it on its side, and left it there. She imagined Dracula standing in it, showering in a rainstorm of blood.

Gretchen sat on the toilet, which was like every other toilet in the world, and leaned her head against the wall next to it. The alcohol was really drenching her bloodstream now.

She recited the science.

"Alcohol, in. When the liver goes to filter the drink out, it becomes stressed, allowing the alcohol into the bloodstream, where it eventually crosses the blood-brain barrier. The alcohol targets brain cells by binding receptors. This really screws up the signaling. Neurotransmitters, have a good day. Glutamate. Haha. You're going to have a fun night."

The room spun.

She focused on the tomb-tub across from her, hoping that a focal point for her eyes would stop the room from acting like a merry-go-round.

"Alcohol releases dopamine. The neurotransmitters are combining to make this all enjoyable for me. Over time, tolerance will make it less likely to reach this point of enjoyment. If I continue to drink regularly, alcohol's interactions with my brain's stress systems will create a dependence."

Her chest felt heavy, like someone held her down and pressed hard on her ribs. Her legs, too. Heavy. All of it so heavy. Gosh, that hooded bathtub was ugly. She smiled and closed her eyes.

Spiraling upward.

"I don't feel the enjoyment, though. I feel sleepy."

Only she would buy herself an enormous house just to fall asleep on the toilet. But she didn't resist, either. It wouldn't take much to pull her fucking underwear up and stumble to the next door over, to her bedroom, but screw it. Punk rock and all that jazz.

Her first time drunk should have a fun story to it beyond "Miss Thornton showed me her petunias." When Derek or Megan called to ask about her adventures, she needed to have some kind of story to talk about.

I got so smashed; I fell asleep on the toilet. They'd bust her chops about losing her straight edge, but they'd be happy to see her living it up, too.

She fell into a dream world, thinking of her old friends, probably spending their weekend at Club Babyhead or the Strand, watching Kilgore Smudge, Times Expired, and a marathon of other local bands.

As she drifted between realms, the rapid banging of imaginary hardcore drums sent a calming chill down her spine. Weird how the intensity of the music always relaxed her, steadying her heartbeat.

With her eyes shut tight, head pressed hard on the wall, she envisioned a crowd of sweaty kids slamming into her as they danced to the music.

There was beauty in hardcore dancing.

It wasn't the infamous mosh pits MTV News warned about. This dancing had style. Sure, it was aggressive and bumpy, but it had substance.

Slowly, all the punk kids in her mind popped out of existence, and she was alone in the darkness. Floating. Until she felt something wet on her leg.

She woke with a start as an anomaly snaked around her ankle. Still partially drunk and rollercoastering from dreamland to the real world left her mind muddled. The room was misty, as if the dream came out with her.

And the thing around her ankle continued to squeeze. Worse, it squeezed and slithered up her leg.

She looked down, expecting a snake. What she found was more of the mist. "What the fuck?"

Maybe she wasn't awake enough yet. It had to be a snake. She could hear it hissing. And somehow a snake was a much better alternative to materialized mist.

Heart pounding in her temples, the drink still increasing the drumbeat within her, she stood, and instantly fell on her ass. The misty substance released its grip.

She couldn't see two inches in front of her. The fog had taken over. It was thin, but all over. She swatted at it, and the tendrils danced around her hands, spraying in all directions, but instantly filling back in.

The room smelled wet.

She stood up, panic setting in. What if it was smoke? Was she inhaling smoke? She didn't think so because she couldn't smell anything.
She swatted at the wall. Once her hands found purchase, she used it as a guide toward the door.

As she took slow step after slow step, she recited the science to herself, the same coping mechanism she'd used since she was thirteen. Whenever something upset her, she evaporated from her surroundings, and recited the biology.

After a Madball show a few years back, Gretchen witnessed a man getting curb stomped. While everyone around her ran away from the violent scene,

Gretchen stared as the man stood up, jaw hanging loose, teeth spilling from his bloody lip, and fought back. The dude actually kept fighting after a curb stomping.

While all of this happened, Gretchen told herself all about the man's adrenaline, about his injuries, about anything she could so she didn't have to accept that a few humans held a man down as their friend slammed the bottom of his boot onto the back of the man's skull.

The steam in the bathroom thickened.

"My fight-or-flight response is triggered, which will speed up my breathing. This will make me inhale more of whatever this shit is. A rapid release of hormones is entering my bloodstream. Mixing this with my already drunken state means my heart rate is blasting."

Her fingers struck hinges, making her gasp. She slid her hand to the doorknob and twisted. It spun, never hitting the stopping point where the bolt would remove from the strike plate. It just spun and spun.

Spiraling in place.

"Oh, fuck."

She inhaled deep. Her chest pressed in a little.

"Oh, fuck."

In her panic, something clicked in her brain. When she had foolishly thought a snake was on her, she had heard hissing, and that noise continued, but it wasn't hissing.

It was the shower.

Was that all this was? The shower? Had she drunkenly turned it on and forgotten about it? Was all of this just hot steam?

As she walked toward the shower, she chuckled. "Fucking idiot."

Each step sent wisps of steam scattering. She had her first drinking story for her friends.

I got so drunk I turned the shower on and fell asleep on the toilet, only to wake up thinking I was drenched in smoke, that was actually just shower steam.

Then her leg hit the tub, clearing enough mist to reveal a nightmare. She fell over and screamed.

The shower wasn't running, and the tub wasn't the hooded monstrosity her realtor showed her, the same one she had stared at just a few minutes earlier to stop the room from spinning.

Well, the room sure as fuck spun now.

But it wasn't the wine that caused it. It was the ghosts within that tub.

In place of the hooded structure was a lime green, ugly 1970s bathtub complete with white soap spots caked in the corner, and a tub full of pink swirls dancing within the bubbly water.

The same tub she grew up with. The same tub where at eight years old, she found her mother dead, wrists torn open and her blood pumping out in the water.

Gretchen screamed again.

"Mom!"

She crab walked backwards until her head hit the lip of the toilet.

The mist covered over the tub, shrouding it.

"What the fuck? What the fuck is happening to me? This is fucking nuts. I'm broken. I drank some wine. It's not like I took acid."

She gripped for the science but couldn't find it. She needed it so desperately, but it evaded her.

Four years.

That was how long she went without understanding. She had just been a kid, and no one tried to explain any of it. Her mother had loved her and loved their life. Gretchen had begged for answers, but none came. Not from her aunt, who adopted her. Not from the police, or the doctors.

The mist in front of her shifted, but she hadn't moved. Something else pushed through it.

A piece of her knew what it would be before it reared its horrid face.

The hyena.

Its snout poked through the mist, a snarl revealing its blackened gums and its bladed teeth.

"Am I having a psychotic break?"

The hyena barked so loud and shrill, Gretchen jolted up, slamming her shoulders into the toilet. Pain shot down her spine.

"This isn't real. It can't be real." But she knew it was.

She knew before something whispered in her ears. "*You've always known that was a lie.*"

The voice was thin, as wispy as the mist. She turned her head left and right, trying to see the source, but all she saw was more steam.
The hyena stepped forward, so close now she could smell rotten meat on its hot breath.

When the police had used the word "suicide," Gretchen insisted they were wrong. She was eight, but she understood the term, and it was an unfeasible, unwelcome beast in her life. Her mother LOVED her, would never intentionally abandon her.

When she first blamed it on a hyena, it was a blurted, rambling figment of her imagination, a desperate clutching for an answer. One she found when thinking of the Lion King. A hyena killed her mother, somehow found its way on the wrong fucking continent, snuck into her house, and killed her mother while the woman bathed.

But the more she blamed the hyena, the more she stepped into her own lie, not only working to convince the police and her family, but herself. She imagined the thing, creeping in on its mud-soaked paws, click-clacking its sharp nails against the white and black tiles, before jumping into the tub and slicing two perfect claw marks up her mother's forearm.

The delusion grew deeper as weeks became months, and months became years. The hyena was real. She'd *seen* it, watched from the keyhole in her bedroom door as the thing crept through the living room, dabbing bloody prints on the rug.

Never mind how the prints disappeared before the police arrived. They had been there.

Gretchen saw them. She woke from nightmares, picturing the beast rip into her sheets as she slept. She heard its shrill yelp. She felt its claws press on her flesh.

Fuck what they had told her. The hyena killed her mother and she'd never accept another answer.

Until she did.

The therapists drilled into her, and eventually she tired of telling the same story, knowing they were hunting for different answers. Just as the hyena slowly materialized from her repeated stories, the truth became palpable the more she told it.

Eventually, she didn't really care which story was telling. The end result was the same. Her mother died.

At thirteen, a year or so after pretending to come to terms with her mother's suicide, she asked her therapist, Dr. Renard, to explain it to her.

Dr. Renard scrunched her forehead. "What do you mean?"

"I understand how my mother died, but I want to know what happened."

The doctor shook her head. "I'm still not understanding."

"Like, what physically happens to someone when they die that way."

"I don't know if that's a good idea to talk about."

Gretchen shot forward. "I need to know. I'll just look it up when I leave."

Dr. Renard sighed. "The good news is the only pain she probably experienced was from the initial cuts. Eventually, she'd go into shock and wouldn't feel a thing."

Gretchen's eyes began to water. "You think you're helping by being vague, but you're hurting me."

Dr. Renard clapped her hands together, startling Gretchen.

"After a significant amount of blood left her body, she would get dizzy and sweaty. She'd feel very tired, and a headache might come on. As more blood entered the water, her skin would turn pale and cold. Her heart rate would speed up. Her breathing would grow shallow. She'd get confused until she finally lost consciousness."

A calmness swept over Gretchen, hearing the rhythmic way the doctor described the symptoms. It was the opposite of the hyena, buried deep in rationality. It was clear, not a jagged shard tossed on top of a nightmare, but little pieces clipped together in a perfect jigsaw.

"*It's hungry, girl. Needs feeding.*"

The voice whispered in her ear, and the hyena stepped closer yet again. The tips of its fur tickled against the bare flesh of her lower leg.

"What the fuck do you want?" Gretchen asked to nothing, to her crazed imagination, her nightmares come to flesh and bone.

"*You know. Don't you, girl?*"

She wept and hated herself for each tear. "I don't. I don't have a fucking clue what is happening."

She coughed, her throat dry again.

"*Who are you, girly?*"

"Please just leave me alone. Let this end."

"*Oh, it'll end. Now answer the question. Who are you?*"

Maybe if she gave it the answer, a key would twist in her brain, something to unlock her from the bathroom, from her mental break.

"Gretchen. Gretchen Casci."

The hyena snarled and leapt forward, slashing into her leg. A burning pain shot across her calf as the creature dug its claws in.

Screaming, Gretchen jumped up to her feet and charged forward, slamming into the door. She kicked at it with her good leg and punched with both fists.

"Get me the fuck out of here."

No longer soft, more like a lawnmower grinding in a chunky patch of grass, the voice spoke again. "*Who the fuck are you, girly? Why are you here? In this house?*"

Gretchen couldn't breathe, the air wrestling with her to stay deep within her throat.

"My friend's grandmother was selling it. She was the realtor. Said it was a score. Only half a million for a gorgeous house."

"*That didn't answer my question.*"

The clicking of the hyena's nails came closer.

"I wanted to move away. I love my friends and the hardcore scene in Rhode Island, but I needed to prove I was more than that. I wanted to start over and see if I had it in me to be whatever I wanted, that I wasn't stuck where I had planted myself."

"Shut up. Do better. Why are you here? A dirt-poor little asshole living in this house. THIS house."

"MTV!" She slammed the meat of her fists into the wooden door.

"MTV is trying to be hip. Trying to show they still have underground roots or something. They bought my shitty little serialized story I published in my zines so they could turn it into a television show. It's not even a fucking good story. It was just *My So-Called Life* set at hardcore shows."

The hyena lunged, slamming into her back. Her head slammed into the door and her ears rang. The thing's claws dragged down her back, leaving two burning gashes on each side of her spine. She turned to kick, but the hyena was gone before she could.

"One more chance. Why are you here?"

Tears twisted down her cheeks. "I don't know what you want. Please. Just let me go."

"Answer."

"I don't know what you want me to say!"

"Say the truth!" The voice echoed so loudly throughout the room; the tiles vibrated under Gretchen's feet.

"I told you already."

"Three. Two…"

"I'm here because I fucking belong here, you motherfucker. Because I want to be here. Fuck you."

Nothing happened.

The voice stopped yelling. The gentle clicking of nail on tile stopped. But the mist refused to clear. She reached for the doorknob, but it spun endlessly, keeping her trapped.

She felt the walls closing in around her, the oxygen leaving the place. It was all in her head, she knew, a symptom of her anxiety mixed with the actual, real horror she faced.

But that didn't make the suffocating nature of it any easier to swallow. Closing her eyes, she went back to the science of what happened in her body, but her mind was chasing ghosts and couldn't land on substantial ground.

The claw marks in her flesh ripped her from her focus, burning, throbbing, searing pain.

In the silence, she picked up a gentle dripping from the sink. *Drip. Drip. Drip.* She imagined it as the beginning of a song. The light tapping of a drum, building a rhythm, all leading up until a chaotic blasting of music that would set the crowd on fire.

Drip.

Drip.

Drip.

"You still have one more question to answer."

The voice had reverted to its whisper, but it still penetrated her bloodstream, fraying her nerves. A forceful tingle jolted up her spine, and her back muscles spasmed.

"I asked you why you're here, and I asked you WHO YOU ARE. You answered only one of those."

She bent down, placing her knees on the cold tile, and used her hands to swat the steam as she crawled forward. She didn't know what she searched for, but the door wasn't going to open, so she had to look for something else, a weapon against the hyena, anything.

She crawled away from the voice.

"Speak now. Tell me who you are."

She thought about her last answers. The thing seemed to accept it when she showed confidence, faith in herself. When she stood up for herself.

"I'm Gretchen. A kickass writer who just made two million dollars from MTV."

As her hands moved forward, they bumped into something. She looked up to see the hyena staring at her face-to-face. It showed its gums. Trickles of blood dripped from its incisors Gretchen's heart lost its punk rock rhythms.

Now it performed like a death metal drummer, banging so rapidly she couldn't tell when one beat ended and the next began. The rotten meat smell shot into her nostrils, causing her to gag.

Maybe it wouldn't do anything.

It just stared at her.

Then boom. It slashed its beefy paw across her cheek. She felt its claw tear through her flesh and enter her mouth. A blast of blood gushed down her throat. Gretchen fell over and screamed in agony.

"Who are you?" the voice asked.

She whimpered, barely able to form a word.

"WHO ARE YOU?"

Gretchen jumped to her feet.

"I'm scared. I just want to get the fuck out of here. I'm scared and I'm so fucking sick of being scared all the time."

She turned to run, but the hyena slammed into her back. She crashed forward, tripping over the edge of the tub, falling in. The water was freezing, as if it had stagnated there since she was eight.

Her face fell in, and in her startled state, she gulped a huge mouthful of bloody water. Soap and blood.

As the water hit her gashes, it doubled the pain radiating from the wounds. She lifted herself to the surface and coughed up water and blood.

The voice yelled at her. *"Who are you? Who are you? Who are you?"*

But even if she wanted to answer, she couldn't, too busy hacking up water from her lungs.

Her blood mixed into the water, swirling into pink spirals.

The hyena barked somewhere in the field of mist.

"WHO ARE YOU?"

The room spun again. Gretchen felt dizzy, short of breath. Despite the cold water, she felt sweaty, clammy. But also freezing cold. Her teeth chattered. Confusion set in, and worse because she *knew* she was confused.

It wasn't because of the hyena or the voice or the mist, it was more than that. She couldn't place what was happening. How did she get in this room? In this house? Nothing made sense.

"What's happening to me?"

"Who are you?"

"I don't know. I don't fucking know who I am."

The mist cleared. The hyena was nowhere within the four walls of the bathroom. Gretchen was alone in the bathroom.

"Where am I?" she asked the empty room.

She turned over, the water splashing as her body twisted. Little waves blipped over the edge onto the floor. Gretchen's finger traced a swirling pink mass.

"How did I get here?"

A tiredness washed over her, and she closed her eyes.

"She loved me."

Her finger left the water and traveled up her arm along the gashes the hyena had left. She remembered the slashes toward her legs, her back, and *dear lord her face*, but she didn't remember the hyena getting her arms.

But she had trouble remembering much right now, couldn't even place landing in the bathtub.

"She loved me."

Her head dropped hard on the slanted edge of the tub, resting against the cold porcelain. She turned toward the back wall where Dr. Renard sat, legs crossed on a chair.

"How are you feeling today, Gretchen?"

"I'm fine."

"That's good."

"My mom loved me, but she suffered from depression, which causes the hippocampus to pump out cortisol, messing up the development of neurons in the brain, which creates a disparity between excitatory and inhibitory transmitters."

The doctor smiled.

"Good. I mean, your science is all sorts of wrong, but you're trying. So, you understand your mother's suicide was not a reflection of how she felt about you. She loved you. She just suffered from a mental illness and hadn't received the help she needed."

Gretchen nodded.

"Yes. I understand."

She slid down, her chin hitting the water. The blood spiraled all around her, twisty little streams.

"My mother loved me, but she had a hyena."

The doctor cleared her throat. "You mean a metaphorical hyena, or do you mean the one you thought you saw as a child?"

Gretchen slid further down, her mouth going under.

"Gretchen? Can you answer me?"

No, she couldn't. Her mouth was under water.

Then her nose. She could hardly keep her eyes open.

She let out a small burst of air, creating a twister of bubbles.

"She loved me," Gretchen said into the water before inhaling deep.

She loved me.

Trophy Room
1910

Rug Burns
Clay McLeod Chapman

Inspired by the one act play "Animal Play"
by Josh Ben Friedman

Benjamin brought a bear back from Alaska just for me. Kodiak this time – its pelt already peeled, preserved for the journey home.

Another trophy for his trophy wife.

All the fat and excess flesh had been removed from its skin. My husband took great care not to tear the area around its face and claws. He preferred to do his tanning at home himself, rather than hire a taxidermist, personally turning the ears inside-out, folding over the lips and eyelids to prevent any spoilage along the trip back.

He would simply leave that dead bear's body behind, abandoning its corpse, nothing but a tender hemisphere of pink tissue now, still warm, the pared flesh steaming from the sudden exposure to the cold air. Benjamin had what he wanted. Let the birds peck at the rest.

Happy anniversary, dear, he said, wrapping me up inside its hide, as if it were another fur coat to add to the menagerie already cluttering up my closet.

The bear skin rug was nearly five times the size of me, swallowing my body whole. I could have lived inside its pelt had I wanted to.

Took two shots just to slow the damn thing down, Benjamin beamed.

He'd been hibernating, lowering his heart rate so much, he would barely even bleed for me. Had to use a higher caliber just to get him hemorrhaging.

The bear's head hung over mine, like an oversized Halloween costume, complete with mounted open mouth, its jaws locked into an eternal roar. Epoxy substituted all the soft tissues, molded to resemble flesh. Its tongue curled up in a permanent pink wave, now rendered in wax… while its eyes had been replaced with the blackest glass.

Plasticine teeth. False claws. Even its skull was a replica, now made of wood, hand-carved to duplicate the bone that had been below.

What little was left of the actual bear seemed so pale in comparison to its former self. So empty now. I couldn't help but imagine the body that had once been housed within this skin, towering at ten feet when the bear stood on its haunches.

It would have weighed over a thousand pounds when all of its organs were still intact. Now it was nothing more than a hot air balloon made of fur, deflating its way in for a crash-landing on our hallway floor.

And who other than my husband had been the one to shoot it down? Looking so proud of his prize.

Sewed its shoulder up with a bit of black felt just to hide the bullet-hole, he said. *Blasted Magnum always tears the flesh to shreds.*

… May I take it off now, please?

Don't you like it, darling?

There was a leathery scent inside its hide, still fresh from Benjamin's workshop. The curing chemicals burned at my nostrils the longer he insisted I wear the bearskin rug over my shoulders, as if this were all some sort of prehistoric rite of passage I had to endure for his sake, laughing at the very sight of me, while the tannin continued to singe the inside of my lungs.

It's getting heavy, Benjamin. Please...

I believe it fits you, he grinned. *Much better than those lemmings you wrap over your shoulders.*

For our fifth anniversary, Benjamin brought me home the head of a Siberian elk. Its neck is now mounted to our library wall. The tangle of its antlers branch up to the ceiling.

A red-necked falcon for our fourth.

A Tibetan snow leopard for our third.

Every year, it's another deer or a prong-horned antelope. An abundance of bearskin rugs splayed across every bedroom floor. Cougars preserved in a facsimile of their natural habitat, baring their teeth at our maid whenever she comes dusting.

Not to mention a couple caribou from Eastern Europe.

Mountain sheep from Mongolia.

Even a Persian sturgeon fished up from the Caspian Sea.

There isn't an inch of wall-space in our entire house that doesn't have one of Benjamin's gameheads mounted upon it, lining along his study, the library, the living room, as if an entire phylum of animals were now stampeding through our house, tearing our very home apart, room by room.

Let them have the house for all I care. I may as well be mounted on the wall myself, salted and cured, my head hanging alongside the rest of Benjamin's treasures.

I'm having an affair.

Benjamin snorted. *With whom? You never even leave the house…*

I could if I wanted to.

Of course, dear. Seek and ye shall find.

Benjamin begged to make love to me that evening wearing nothing but my sable sheared beaver coat that he had just brought back from Scandinavia.

Turn the lights right off and let him just run his fingers over the fur. Over the last year or so it has become increasingly more difficult for Benjamin to remain erect without the aid of me wearing one of my furs.

He'll ask to mix it up now and then. Wear one for a while before switching things up with another. White king fox one week, winter mink the next.

This is not a conversation topic that has ever been brought up outside of the trophy room before.

I've never complained, for Benjamin's sake, knowing quite well we would never get far without a little fur leading him along.

I've got you now, he always mutters under his breath. *You can't escape me…*

I could still smell the tannin in his hands. His skin has coarsened over from the constant exposure to his curing chemicals, hardening into this husk, all rough to the touch.

Benjamin once told me it took over twelve beavers just to make one jacket, a whole family hemmed together to comprise this single coat. And here were his fingers, rustling over my body, like the legs on one of those poor creatures.

A dozen of them, all scurrying across my skin. Up my arms, my waist. Over my breasts.

I merely closed my eyes, surrendering to the sensation of their paws pitter-pattering across my body. Benjamin himself had dematerialized, his presence in bed replaced with this pack of rodents ravishing me.

Caressing me in this orgy of taxidermy. Slapping me with the broadside of their flattened black tails.

Building a dam at the very precipice of my wetlands, the barrier erected from driftwood and mud, until the pressure mounted within my legs, nearly about to burst, the water level only rising higher, *higher*, reaching the very edge of the levee before… just before… yes… *yes*, a flood, *a flood*, a biblical flood rushing over everything.

Good God, Abigail, Benjamin said. *What on earth has come over you?*

I had absolutely no idea.

What came over me?

I had just turned nineteen when Benjamin first proposed. My family had held little hope of me marrying a man of much wealth – which was precisely why, when Benjamin began courting, my parents left me with little choice in the matter.

Never mind his hunting expeditions seemed to send him away every few weeks. What wife wouldn't want a little time away from her husband now and then?

The very next morning, Benjamin's travel bags were lined up beside the front door. Already packed.

Where are you heading off to now?

A quick trip to Colorado, he said. *Bison are running wild up there. There's a corner in the library still open that would be a perfect fit.*

But what about our anniversary?

We'll celebrate when I return, darling. These buffalo are about a generation away from becoming an endangered species. We need to act fast if we want one for ourselves!

The only thing endangered in this house was me.

Why not take me with you?

I highly doubt you'd enjoy yourself, dear. He shook his head, the tone in his voice bearing similarities to a parent patronizing their child. *I daresay you might find it all a bit too… grubby for your tastes.*

Upkeep was my responsibility when Benjamin was away. He didn't trust our maid to handle his trophies anymore, leaving the dusting up to me.

Benjamin's trophy room was sacred ground in our house.

I had to remove each mounted head from the wall, placing them gently on the ground in order for the feather-duster to reach the deeper crevices. Behind the ears.

Brushing away the cobwebs within their jaws.

Polish the eyes.

Always go with the grain of hair, Benjamin had meticulously instructed me. *Never against. Their fur becomes brittle over time, which can cause the hairs to break under unnecessary ruffling. You have to be gentle with them now. Gentle...*

Their silence was what was most frightening. That emptiness settled inside their mouths, hovering just above their tongues. When all they wanted was to roar.

Fill the hallways of this house with the sounds of their wrath. Let them reclaim their voices that Benjamin had taken away. Wild once more.

Hello, Mr. Bear, I said, running my fingers through its fur. *And how are we feeling today?*

I actually caught myself pausing, expecting the rug to respond.

Looks as if we need to clean you up a bit.

I wiped the dust from its glass eyes. Patted down its nose with a damp cloth. I held out my hand, waiting for it to lick my palm.

Nothing.

Its tongue remained rigid, refusing to move for me. I pinched the hair behind its neck, lifting the rug up and letting it go, watching its skin momentarily catch the air, taking shape for a brief instant before collapsing lifelessly onto to floor, empty all over again.

I pictured myself setting up tent under the rug whenever Benjamin chose to throw another one of his dull dinner parties, regaling our guests with tales of all his safaris.

Our company would suddenly wonder whatever had become of me, asking themselves – *Where has dear Abigail run off to now?* – while all the while, I'd be right here, burrowed beneath our brand-new bearskin rug.

Growling at our visitors in my best impression of this beast as they searched the house for me. Ready to pounce.

No imbibing allowed in the trophy room. Not anywhere near his rugs. That meant I had to hold my merlot out to one side, away from his gameheads.

Cleaning wine stains from their skin is practically impossible, Benjamin said. *Solvents will only dry the hide. Water only. Make sure to dab at the spill, rather than some reckless wipe.*

Wandering through the trophy room all by myself, I felt like a little girl lost at the zoo. Left with nothing but the animals to keep me company all day.

I was always a bit tipsy by the time I reached Benjamin's most prized possession – a Katanga lion, king of the jungle, shot in Zimbabwe mere seconds before it could maul Benjamin with its claws.

Its mane wrapped around its throat, thick as wheat.

Its jaw now hung sprung open like a steel trap, lips curled back, baring its teeth at me as if it were about to bite.

I ran my finger along the length of its teeth, *slowly*, ever so slowly, letting the tip of each tooth press against my skin, wondering if it might draw blood and revive this lion's hunger.

Aren't we a bit bashful today? I asked. *Cat got your tongue?*

Leaning in, I listened for the presence of breath as one holds a shell up to their ear, searching for sounds of the sea. Waiting for that tidal wave of an exhale to rush down my neck, all warm and sticky.

Benjamin would have a fit if he saw me now. The thought of him discovering me, some amateur lion tamer practicing with his most treasured trophy…

I couldn't help but giggle a bit, wishing he would.

Better keep this a secret, I whispered into the lion's ear. *Just between you and me.*

Bought your affection with another fur coat, has he?

I pulled my head back, finding the lion's eyes settled upon me. *I beg your pardon?*

Simply toss you another muff and everything's fine for one more year, eh?

But I like my fur coats!

Feeding a queen such measly beasts is a sin, it said. *You deserve… a much larger offering.*

Marching up to my menagerie, I could hear the slightest scratching against the inner panel of the closet door.

I went ahead and flung my wardrobe wide open, discovering all my fur coats dangling from their hangers, alive, writhing upon the wires.

A half-dozen different pelts. Mink stoles. Baby seal muffs. Sheared beaver shawls. All presents from Benjamin over the years, all of them wriggling in their prison.

All of you – run! Run as far away as you can!

I released each fur coat caged within my closet, watching them leap right off their hangers and onto the floor. Unleashed into the halls of our house.

You're free now! Go!

I spent the next hour before my boudoir mirror, applying eyeliner. Pooling the rouge upon my cheeks. Benjamin would come home and find me waiting for him on our bed. He'd see me as he had when we were first married, young and soft and supple.

I would be his prize again.

He could hunt me through our house, never leaving me behind. I wouldn't be abandoned with the rest of his assembly of heads, all their eyes falling upon me as if what had happened to them were my fault.

I sense their necks turning just behind my back, following me through the hallway whenever I wander by.

If I ever stop and glance over my shoulder, their heads snap back before I catch them, acting as if they hadn't moved a bit.

Stop looking at me like that! Don't blame me!

One look at my gaudy reflection sent me into a sobbing fit, crying until the eyeliner bled down my cheeks. I looked like a weeping raccoon now.

Benjamin said it's best not to walk on his bearskin rugs.

They're not toys, darling, he reprimanded me. I received a lecture after sauntering across his grizzly during one of our dinner parties, my heel accidentally piercing its hide. *It's not some stuffed animal, not a teddy bear that you can just pick up and play with whenever you want.*

You're the one who treats me like a child!

What do you expect from me when you can barely take care of yourself?

Now I went ahead and sprawled across our brand-new Kodiak, rolling over the furry surface as if I were lying in the grass.

I'll show him, I said to the bear. Its skin felt warm. So soft.

I closed my eyes and imagined myself in an open field, under the sun. I could have laid there for hours. Basking in the heat.

I'll teach him to leave me behind, I said to every animal in our house.

I dragged the bearskin upstairs into the bedroom with me, replacing our duvet. Snuggling inside its hide, I burrowed below its body as far as I could go.

Sleeping underneath the pelt felt warm, its skin generating a temperature that seemed nearly life-like to me. *Alive.*

The bear still smelled of leather, the odor all around me now. I took the musk of the tundra into my lungs, inhaling deeply.

The scent made for feral fantasies that night.

I found myself in the woods, surrounded by all the animals from our house, bodies intact, everything below their necks spoken for once more.

I recognized the panther from the trophy room, the lion from the library wall.

The falcon from the hall.

None of them said anything, simply staring at me. Watching on with those blank eyes, those marble eyes.

The Kodiak from the hallway floor stepped forward, lifting onto its haunches. I had to look up to find its eyes, staring down at me.

When I would wake from my hibernation, it said, and I could smell the lingering scent of carrion still on its breath, the flavor of past prey drifting out from its mouth, *my penis would be a bulging purple rod that defied all comprehension.*

What do you want from me?

You are our queen.

The bear leaned forward, pressing its lips to my mouth. I felt its wax tongue lap against mine. Felt myself melt. Every muscle relented. My own tongue branched out from my mouth until the two intertwined like ivy.

I closed my eyes and pushed my body against the bear's chest, plunging under the surface of its fur. Its arms wrapped around me, and I descended into that bear's embrace, diving in head-first and never coming back up for air ever again.

All the animals in the house watched on as we made love, practically attacking each other. Their heads turned within their mounts, craning their necks for the best perspective as we thrashed about the trophy room. Then the bedroom floor. The bathtub. The hallway. Baring our teeth at each other. Hissing. The steam from its nostrils swept over my face. It pawed at my body, claws raking across my skin, while I simply swam through that brown fur, mounting the bear's body to release a roar that filled up every room within this house.

Let it echo through the trophy room so that every animal could hear and know that their queen has finally arrived.

Time to kneel. Bow your heads and chant – *Hail. All hail the queen of the jungle.*

The very next morning, I discovered myself covered in claw marks. Pink abrasions ran the length of my back. My legs.

I could still smell the lingering hint of leather on my skin, all raw now.

What had I gotten myself into?

For the life of me I could barely remember. I had to cough up a hairball before brushing my teeth, spitting a tuft of brown fur into the bathroom sink.

My head was wrecked. I felt absolutely famished. I forgot to fix myself dinner the night before, my stomach now tightening itself into a knot.

If I was to eat, I needed to find food somewhere within this house.

Tugging the rug into the kitchen behind me like a child with its blankie, I accidentally knocked over the nightstand table. Shattered an antique ceramic vase. The shards spread over the floor, looking like an animal's teeth.

I stepped on a piece of pottery, the shard cutting the sole of my foot. Had to hop for a bit before pulling the splinter free. Blood now pooled up under my foot. Hurt like hell but I kept walking, leaving a trail of red left feet behind me. Let the maid clean it up for all I care.

There.

Hiding in the corner of the hallway.

A fox hide stole. It had a clasp attached inside the roof of its mouth, using its teeth as a fastener that snapped into place by biting its own tail.

I grabbed it with my bare hand before it could scurry away, quickly bringing it up to my mouth and sinking my teeth into its pelt.

A warm rush of blood ran down my throat, spilling over my cheeks.

I ripped a piece of flesh free.

The fox's skin dangled from my chin before chewing it through, flinging the rest of the carcass against the wall with a wet slap, knocking off a photograph of Benjamin kneeling next to a cougar he shot down in West Africa, sending the frame crashing to the floor.

Glass scattered everywhere.

There he was. Everywhere again. The hallway walls are all pockmarked with pictures of Benjamin's hunting expeditions. Rows of framed photographs where we see him proudly displaying his prey just before skinning them.

Here's Benjamin kneeling next to a wild boar shot down in the outback, wrapped in khaki from head to toe.

And here's Benjamin kneeling next to a moose he shot in Canada. Always smiling the same silly grin.

I followed the row of photographs while I finished eating my breakfast, until I came upon this one picture. There, hanging alongside a shot of Benjamin kneeling next to a panther he poached from Central America, was a picture of…

Me.

It's our wedding day. I'm wearing a white satin dress. Benjamin wears that very same smile lining the hallway wall, looking no different standing next to me than when he's kneeling next to any of these other animals.

Presenting his catch for the camera.

I remember following a gazelle, the lion sighed, turning his neck towards me.

It was drinking from a stream when I pounced upon it, tearing into its neck. I remember feeling its warm blood flood into my mouth. As I fed, I heard a twig snap from behind me. I heard a shot… then blackness. Now I am empty. Nothing but sawdust. Hollow on the wall.

What can I do?

There's a corner in the trophy room still open, the lion said. *Empty. Waiting for one last mount. A perfect fit.*

For what?

The lion went silent.

Tell me.

You know.

Suddenly the silence evaporated from our whole house. Sound seeped out from the open mouths of each animal, filling up the hallways with their voices all at once–

Hail. All hail the queen.

There.

A gazelle foraging in the library.

I hid myself just next to the bookshelf, watching it chew through our Chaucer. It suddenly looked up, freezing. I had less than a second before it would go bounding off – so I leaped, grabbing the gazelle by its antlers and ripping its head right off the wall, prying up plaster and wallpaper along with its mount.

Together, we tumbled onto the floor. The gazelle struggled under my grip as I bit into its throat, yanking off a thick strip of dried skin. It buckled beneath me as blood seeped freely from its tattered neck – but I wouldn't let it go, cradling the gamehead in my arms as it thrashed about the floor, slowly dwindling into death.

Leaving me to feed.

Taxidermy. Derived from the Greek. *Taxis* – meaning movement. *Derma* – meaning skin. Altogether translated, quite literally…

The movement of skin.

Once the taste of blood is on your tongue, you'll never hunger for another flavor for the rest of your life. Nothing else will satisfy.

I am queen. Queen of the jungle.

The front door wouldn't fully open when Benjamin first came home. He had to press his shoulder against the paneling and push hard, forcing the overturned nightstand table out of the way. Then step over the broken glass, the shattered fragments of the light fixtures. All the loose bits of plaster now scattered along the floor.

My God... Abigail? Abigail, are you alright?

His Katanga lion now lay on the floor, is flesh flayed free from its face, leaving behind nothing but the wooden skull resting in a mangy blanket of its own mane.

What on earth happened here? Abigail! Answer me!

Further down the hall, he saw the tatters of his grizzly skin rug. A few loose feathers from his falcon, drifting through the air.

Abigail – where are you?

Benjamin never sensed me. Not until I had closed the door behind him.

He spun around, eyes widening.

I actually heard him gasp.

The look on his face petrified in place, shock dropping his lower jaw at the sight of me, all of me, wearing nothing other than the remnant pelt of my fox stole draped over my shoulders, my waist wrapped in scraps of Kodiak, a branch of antlers gripped tightly in each hand, crookedly extending their way out from between my knuckles, along with a string of bear claws hanging from my neck.

I smiled for him; bits of leather still stuck between my teeth. My cheeks were now painted in thin rows of blood. Animal blood.

Happy anniversary, dear, I whispered.

I am at the top of the food chain in our house now.

Music Room
1902

Death in C Major
DE McCluskey

1

The soothing tones echoed throughout the house, wafting softly down the grand staircase, filling the hall with their beautiful simplicity. The music was in the key of C, and the easy, two-handed melody was both lulling and comforting in equal measures.

Johannes Sebastian Bach's simplistic descant, one that many a piano student held dear as their first ever piece, danced around the house, filling each room with its calm subtlety.

The music room had been designed for this very purpose. When music was played on the grand piano, it carried through a complex series of openings that allowed the whole house to enjoy it.

This was easily combated by the closing of two flaps; that way, when a student was practicing, the household needn't suffer their inconsistencies.

The flaps had been closed for some considerable time, yet the sweet music still flowed, filling each room with its dulcet tones.

Every night.

Every *single* night.

The impromptu concerts would usually begin about ten-thirty, and continue its tribute until late into the night, sometimes till three in the morning.

The residents once sought comfort in the delicate tinkling of the keys, but now the tune was akin to their jailor, locking them inside their lavish cells, keeping them docile with its delicate threats of malevolence.

The master of the house was Jeremy Nixon, a celebrated lawyer with ambition. He had his eyes set on congress, and who knew, perhaps one day, the White House itself.

He had only once braved the room himself and had been the person responsible for closing the flaps, doing so to stem the pollution of their home from the melodic tune.

It was always the same tune.

And it always began in the same manner.

2

"But their son is already giving recitals, Jeremy. He's two years younger than Edward, and they've invited us to his latest one. Two years younger. Do you hear me? The boy is just twelve."

Evelynne was in a state of near hysterics as she held a small card in her shaking hands. Her breakfast sat forgotten as she re-read the fancy wording for what must have been the fifth time.

Her husband was too busy tucking into his boiled eggs with toast to take much notice of the hysterical woman. He offered the odd noncommittal, noise of agreement every now and then, mostly just to keep her happy.

"So, you agree then? The boy must have a tutor. We really can't allow those Davies having one over on us. I mean, who do they think they are? They're from *Kentucky* of all places. Imagine those hillbillies having a child more talented than our own. It's… It's unheard of."

Evelynne looked at her husband, who was now spreading a fine layer of marmalade over a triangle of toast.

"Are you listening to me, Jeremy?"

"Yes dear," he lied, putting the delicious scrap of bread in his mouth.

"So, what do you propose to do about it?" she demanded.

Jeremy sighed as he chewed.

"Whatever you want me to do about it, dear," he mumbled between chews.

Evelynne sighed as Jeremy picked up the daily newspaper that the butler always left for him on a side table and exited the room without looking back toward her.

"Whatever I want to do about it, eh? Well, I'll tell you what I'm going to do it about it, dear Jeremy. I'll hire *the* most dedicated and *expensive* music teacher there is. So, you can stick that in your pipe and smoke it."

3

The music plays on, and on. It's always the same tune, always the same tempo, at first.

Prelude in C Major.

The opening notes repeating themselves over and over.

At first it comforted Evelynne and Jeremy. The lovely music piping through the house on warm and balmy evenings was like a gift. A very special gift, all things considered.

However, as some gifts are wont to do, it became an annoyance. It became a maddening distraction, and then it became something else entirely.

Now, whenever they hear the opening chords, they know it's time to lock the doors, to ask their guests to leave, and to barricade themselves into their bedroom.

The music *was* beautiful; it was haunting, and seductive. At first no one would notice it, as it hung in the background, filling the void of silence in the large house. The ripple of keys, perfectly in tune, and with perfect pitch and rhythm, would sail through the ether.

The master and his wife would find themselves absently whistling along, the maids and the butler tapping in rhythm with the notes which made up the background of their days.

It was beautiful and welcomed.

Until it wasn't!

4

"Marianne told me they tried to get him, but he was unavailable."

Evelynne was chatting excitedly while Jeremy sipped his fine whisky and puffed his cigar.

It had been a long day in court, lots of lawsuit-happy plaintiffs bringing ridiculous cases, and he was drained, in no mood to chat about damned music tutors.

"That's nice, dear. So, what do you propose?"

"Well," she said, sitting on the edge of the couch in the parlour.

The fire was blazing; the flickering orange light was dancing over her face. Her grin was strange to him, almost maniacal.

"I was thinking we offer him more money than they did. If we can persuade a man who is *simply the best* at what he does, then it stands to reason that Edward, a boy with such promise, will be performing his own recitals in no time."

She stopped talking and swallowed. Her eyes were wide; something akin to madness blazed within them.

Jeremy looked at her.

She was scaring him. Him, a man who'd stared down seasoned, grizzled lawyers and dangerous criminals, was feeling intimidated by his wife.

She needs a hobby, he thought. *If I give her this, then maybe the boy's welfare could be that.*

She had always been a woman with whims.

At first it had been him. She had pursued him with gusto, seducing him with lightly veiled, salacious promises – that, to be fair, she *had* fulfilled.

Then it had been the house, then the furniture, then her wardrobe, then the house staff.

After she had everything she wanted – position, wealth, stature – she focused on children.

God had only seen fit to bless them with the one.

Edward.

Edward was, if Jeremy was to be honest with himself, an odd child.

He was reclusive, short of friends, and with a very odd interest in the macabre. Jeremy had caught the child once in a field with a dead fox before him.

The poor animal had been cut open, and Edward was investigating the innards with a stick. Jeremy had scolded him, of course, but secretly he harboured hopes of the boy becoming a surgeon, or perhaps a vet.

Both very noble, very honourable professions.

But alas, to date Edward had shown no more interest in pursuing these pursuits, although on hunting trips Jeremy had stumbled upon many a discarded carcass within the trees.

The boy, too, needed a hobby. Maybe the music lessons would be exactly what was required to remove him from his bedroom, and maybe make some friends.

"Yes, yes, woman," he replied, looking at the glowing orange tip of his cigar.

"You have my blessing to approach this tutor if you must. What is his name?"

The smile on Evelynne's face was worth whatever fee any tutor commanded.

It was pure glee.

Jeremy could envision how she would gloat to Mrs. Davies when they met in church on Sunday. He could see the one-upmanship blazing in her eyes.

∞

Mr. Crabtree looked exactly as she thought he might. He was a short, crouched old man. His hair was unfashionably long at the back, and thin on the top; it stayed in the shape of his hat as he removed it upon entering the house. He stood with a stoop. The hunch of his back bent him in an eternal bow, and his fingers were gnarled, like the branches of an old oak tree.

It was these fingers that made her doubt her initial reaction. Maybe she'd made a mistake hiring this man.

"Mr. Crabtree?" she asked, her voice giving away her disappointment at the old man's dishevelled appearance.

"Yes," he snapped.

"It is I. Can I ask where the student is? I hate tardiness, and I will not be forgiving for it."

"I… erm," she stuttered as the withered old man blustered in, offering her his removed hat.

She took it, without thinking.

She accepted his cloak too once he'd struggled it off. She looked over at the maid, who was watching the troll shuffle into the house. The girl snapped into life at the glare of her mistress and accepted the man's outer garments.

"This is a pleasant environment," he growled.

He didn't sound angry; Evelynne suspected it was just the way he spoke.

"Where is the instrument?"

"It's in the… erm, the music room. Can I show…"

He was already walking off in the direction she was pointing, heading toward the grand staircase.

"Up here? Yes, yes… come along, young lady. My time is money, and the student is not going to benefit by us swapping niceties."

In a whirlwind of black jacket and a cane she hadn't noticed, Mr. Crabtree was already halfway up the stairs, and she had to rush to catch up with the spritely old man.

"Yes, it's just the first room directly to your…"

"Right. Yes, I can see it," he shouted back.

As she caught up, he was standing in the doorway, gawping at the baby grand that stood proudly in the center of the room.

"Lovely," he remarked.

She noted his voice was without his trademark snarl.

"This is an 1878 Stokes baby grand, is it not?"

Evelynne's brow creased. "I'm not sure," she replied, looking at the proud piano.

The old man turned his head and snapped. "It is. I was stating a fact."

She nodded and continued. "So, your fee…"

"I haven't decided if I'm taking the job yet," he snapped again.

"Oh," she replied, cowed by his aggressive nature.

"Would you like to meet Edward?"

"I suppose it would help. I won't be teaching the boy to play via correspondence, will I?"

Rude, she thought.

"I'll just get him," she said with a fake smile.

Just remember what it will be like at the recital, she told herself as she allowed the little man into the music room, while she ventured to fetch her son.

5

The maids refused to enter the room alone, especially when the music was filtering through the house.

The butler was forced to ignore his own duties for a time to accompany them. Thankfully, the music only came during the dark hours of the day, when there were minimal staff on rotation.

No one, not even the butler, would enter the room when the *other* music started to play.

One staff member did once, but she rushed out, less than two minutes later, down the stairs, and straight out of the front door. She never returned to the house again.

The music would always start in a good place. Slow, light, melodic. But it would eventually turn. The song remained the same, Prelude in C Major.

It had been remarked that when it turned, when the keys were being abused, it sounded like the Devil himself was torturing the ivories.

Anger, aggression, psychosis… these were just a few of the words used by the professionals in such matters, who had been called into the house by the family, after the *incident*.

The incident that occurred less than three weeks after the appointment of Mr. Crabtree.

6

Edward was a sullen child. His unruly black hair was unkempt, and his dark beady eyes were a contradiction to the pale, fish-belly flesh of his face. His looks could unnerve even the hardiest of staff.

"It's no wonder the boy has no friends," they would say.

"He's so creepy, so cold… and the way he looks at you!"

Whoever said this would inevitably shudder afterwards, and maybe, if they were overly dramatic, they might cross themselves.

But they were not wrong. The boy *was* cold. He was curt, he would grope the maids, and on more than one occasion he had lashed out and struck members of the staff.

"Edward, get up out of that bed at once," Evelynne shouted in a hushed tone.

"Mr. Crabtree is here, to give you your first lesson."

Edward poked his unruly head from beneath the blankets and glared at the woman hissing at him in the room.

"Who?" he croaked.

"Mr. Crabtree. Your piano tutor. He's the one who's going to transform you into a professional pianist, maybe even world-renowned."

"I told you, I don't want to play the piano," he groaned as he pulled his bedcovers back over his head.

"Well, that doesn't matter. Your father has already paid Mr. Crabtree for his services. So, do *you* want to explain to him why the money that has changed hands has been wasted?"

The boy sighed beneath the blankets before lifting them and looking up at his mother. He was shaking his head.

"You always get what you want, don't you?" he hissed, his dark eyes accusing her.

She smiled at him.

"Be ready in five minutes. Mr. Crabtree seems to be the sort of person who does not take kindly to waiting."

"Well, poor Mr. Crabtree," Edward hissed again as he swung his feet from the bed.

Evelynne grinned as he stretched and yawned.

"Do you mind?" the boy asked, glaring at her.

"If you want me to get ready for a stupid piano lesson, I'm going to need a little privacy."

"Of course," she replied before walking out of the bedroom with a smile, set deep on her face.

∞

Ten minutes later, Edward made his entrance into the music room where Mr. Crabtree sat at the piano, frowning at Evelynne.

"The boy is late. I do not take kindly to tardiness."

"I'm sorry, Mr. Crabtree, it won't happen again," Evelynne grovelled.

"I'll see to that. If he's late again, I will inform his father, and he'll be properly admonished."

"That is agreeable," the teacher snarled, before turning his attentions onto the boy.

"Get over here boy and sit next to me. I'm about to instil some discipline into you."

Edward looked at his mother. He had a grin on his face that said he didn't quite believe what was happening.

Evelynne glared at him and gestured to the stool.

The boy huffed, and dragged his heels to where the old man was waiting.

"Good," the tutor snapped.

"My name is Mr. Crabtree. You will call me Mr. Crabtree, and I will call you *boy*. I'm truly in Heaven when teaching new students, so *do not* disappoint me. Now we have the pleasantries over with, I want you to play me something."

Edward looked at his mother again, she was looking away. There was a flush to her face.

"I can't play anything," Edward mumbled, his head bowed, looking at the black and white keys before him.

"You what?" Mr. Crabtree ranted.

"You can't play *anything?*" he spat.

"You have an 1878 Stokes baby grand at your disposal, and you can't play a single note on it?"

Edward grinned and hit a key. The note rung through the air like an accusation.

"There, I've played a note. May I be excused now?"

"No, you may not, *boy*. Your mother is paying me a great expense…"

At these words Evelynne's head snapped toward the old man. The fee had not been discussed yet.

"… to teach you to play. And teach you to play I will. Mrs. Nixon, I'm going to ask you to kindly leave the room. I will not have you distracting the *boy* while I teach him."

He shooed her with both hands, from her own room.

"Go on now, run along," he said, turning his attentions back to Edward.

∾

As Evelynne was ushered from the room, her heart pounded. She worried now about her decision to bring in Mr. Crabtree for a few reasons. How expensive it was going to be, how he was going to treat Edward, and how rude he was to her just then.

She is the lady of the house, after all.

She was beginning to think the Davies' had sent this man to them on purpose, on hearing about Edward learning to play, in order to make Elijah look more talented than her Edward.

She turned, took a deep breath, and grabbed the handle of the door. She was ready to storm in, force the rude Mr. Crabtree to leave, and bring order back into the house.

But she stopped.

The most beautiful sound was ushered from the room. She'd never heard such a melodic tune, magical in its simplicity, yet lulling. She swallowed, a tear began to form in the corner of her eye, and her hand released its grip on the door handle.

She was not a musical connoisseur, not by any means, but she did know what she liked, and she liked this.

Then it stopped.

Her life seemed emptier somehow, like she had gotten just a small taste of something she had never had before, and she wanted – no, she *needed* – more.

"Now it's your turn," the old man snarled from behind the door.

Her heart beat rapidly, and she was a little dizzy, listening anxiously for Edward's version of what she had just heard.

The ugly sound jolted her away from the door. It almost stilled her racing heart. She cringed and skulked away, shaking her head as she went.

7

DE McCluskey

The music in the dead of the night soothed her the very first time she heard it. She had thought she was dreaming. It was a lovely dream, where they were all in the house. The whole family had gathered, along with friends and work colleagues of her husband. They were all seated in the music room, eagerly awaiting the recital from her talented and engaging son.

When the opening notes tickled the air, they were pleasing to everyone. The tempo and the cadence were perfect, and she, along with a few of the others, found themselves swinging with the rhythm, allowing it to carry them from the room, to float along with the beautiful notes, into warm spring fields, filled with singing birds and gambolling lambs.

It made her cry.

This wasn't just a forming of tears. It was thick, heavy tears coursing down her cheeks, accompanied by ugly sobs that wracked her body. The music was so lovely, it was so soothing, that it was a sin what it meant to her.

It was supposed to be an escape from the mundane parts of life into a different plane of existence, one where there were no worries, no regrets. One where there were no extravagant bouquets of flowers decorating the ground floor of her beautiful house.

Their overstated colours, that in any other time might have brought gaiety. However, now only reminding her of what she had done, what she had caused, and what she had lost.

That was when she woke from her dream.

Only the music didn't die with her fantasy.

It remained with her. It teased her. It accused her of things she had no control over.

As she brought blankets tighter to her face, as her sore, red eyes scanned the shadows of her room, paying special attention to the deep black silhouettes by the window, the music stopped.

It was a relief. She thought she might still be dreaming, that her overworked and racing imagination had formulated the music to help transition her from an old life into a new one.

Only it was not meant to be.

The crashing sound, the ugly sound, the parody of what she had just been listening to, raged around her room. She knew it would be resounding through every room in the house.

She knew everyone would hear the abhorrent cacophony of notes, mashed together to form the vilest of sounds.

There would be no one going to investigate. There were very few staff left, six out of the ten maids had quit; the butler remained, but refused to leave his quarters after ten at night.

Her husband was finding more and more excuses to work late in his office at the courthouse.

Evelynne was left on her own, alone to deal with the horrible sounds, and the vile memories the sounds conjured.

8

"How was your lesson today?" Evelynne asked her son as the family ate their evening meal together.

Edward looked sullener than ever as he spooned his soup.

His father was reading a large newspaper, and ignoring them both, lost in his own world of laws and politics.

"What did you do to your hands?" she asked as she noticed Edward's knuckles were red raw and bruised. In some places open cuts marred his skin.

Edward put his spoon down and thrust his hands beneath the table, hiding them.

"Nothing. I, erm, fell in the woods. I was chasing a fox, and the stupid thing dived into a hedgerow. I thought I could dive in after it, but I didn't fit. I hurt my hand."

Evelynne nodded, satisfied with his excuse, even though it didn't quite fit the narrative. "How are you getting on with Mr. Crabtree?"

At the mention of his name, the boy dropped his head. "Okay," he mumbled.

"I've listened to you. You're getting much better. I can't wait to be able to sit and watch you play. When is your next lesson?"

The boy shrugged.

Evelynne smiled a tight smile and returned to her soup.

"Mother, I hate it," the boy blurted, slamming his spoon onto the table.

The unexpected reaction caught the attention of his father, who peered around from behind his newspaper.

"What?" she asked.

"I hate it. I hate playing that damned piano. And I hate Mr. Crabtree. I am in *Hell* whenever I'm in there. It is the worst thing you have ever made me do. I hate it, I hate it, I *hate* it," he screamed before getting up from the table and running out of the dining room.

"I'm guessing your Mr. Crabtree isn't all that popular, after all," Jeremy said before putting his face back behind the paper.

Evelynne just looked at the newspaper covering his face.

∽

"Straighten your back. Eyes forward. If I see your shoulders slumping, it will be the cane for you, right across your back. Spare the rod and spoil the child, that's what I say."

Mr. Crabtree was in fine form – for an old, crouched over man, he was rather sprightly, and agile with his walking cane.

The metronome that had been placed on top of the piano, was ticking away, and the old man was pacing up and down, in perfect timing with the *tick, tick, tick*, of the swinging point.

"One, two, three, four. One, two, three, four. Come on *boy*, get playing."

The opening chords of Prelude to C Major were staggered, they were out of time, and there were some missed notes.

Edward screamed as the thin wooden cane came crashing down on his hands. The scream was one of pain, but it was also one of surprise too. The rounded wood hit him his knuckles, aggravating an already stinging injury from the day before.

"C, E, and G, *Boy.* C, E, and G," the teacher shouted. "You know the notes, now *play* them."

Edward had tears in his eyes as he rubbed his hands, trying to sooth his smarting fingers. He wanted to cry, he wanted to lash out and run away to somewhere else, anywhere other than here.

However, he knew if he did run, he would have to explain himself to his father later, and that was not going to happen. His father – or *Jeremy* as he liked to call him – would thrash him, would cut him off from his wealth, maybe he would even send him off to that boarding school he was always threatening him with.

The old man sneered as he tapped his cane, the source of Edward's pain, on the floor. He did it perfectly in time with the incessant *tick, tick, tick* of the metronome. Edward knew how to play this tune.

He *had* been practicing. He liked the music, but he had no interest in learning how to *play* it.

He hated this piano, he hated this music room, and he hated Mr. Crabtree more than anything. Or maybe not quite.

That damned metronome… I hate that the most.

He longed to knock it off the top of the piano. He ached to tear it open, to expose its workings, like he did with the animals. He wanted to smash it under his feet, to grind it into a thousand different pieces.

He could see the way Mr. Crabtree treasured the item, and he wanted nothing more than to see the old man's face as he destroyed his most cherished possession.

"Play it," Crabtree growled. "C, E, and G, play it now. If you don't, you'll get another rap on the knuckles. Back straight, and the correct notes… NOW!"

Edward cringed as the old man shouted, expecting the whack of the cane across his hands.

He played the notes. The key of C on his left hand, and the grace notes with his right. He played the tune again, and again, and again.

Three times Mr. Crabtree hit him with the cane that session, swelling his knuckles so much that it became difficult to even flex his fingers.

The blasted metronome was one step closer to getting what it deserved.

9

She knew what the horrible music meant. She also knew what the beautiful music meant, but she didn't want to think about either.

If she closed her eyes when the gentle music played, then she could imagine all the bad things that had never happened. She could imagine she had never even heard of Mr. Crabtree, and she had never had envious feelings about the Davies and their talented son.

She could see that talent now, not only could she see it, but she had another reason to be envious of it, too.

The Davies' family still *had* a son.

They had a functioning family life, a husband who loved and respected them, a son who lived for his family. All she, Evelynne Nixon, had now was a distant husband, silent meals, tears at bedtime, terrible memories, and ghostly music sending her a little closer to insanity every time she heard it.

The days were merging. Because of the lack of sleep, they were a blur, and her nights were terrifying.

When the music started, the night after the incident, they had both thought it was the wind, blowing through the eaves of the house, giving them a musical tilt.

Jeremy had locked up the music room, closing the flaps that allowed the music to filter through, coldly blocking all her memories.

She had cried the first night.

She had cried the second night.

She was comforted on the third night.

She was petrified on the fourth night.

10

Edward became more reserved and withdrawn with each piano lesson. Mr. Crabtree was more and more agitated.

The sounds from the room were not encouraging. They were so bad that after ten minutes, Jeremy would go in and close the flaps. He made the excuse that it stopped drafts around the house, but in reality, it was to stem the infernal racket.

It had been going on for three weeks now, and Edward was getting nowhere, fast.

"Are we just throwing good money after bad with this hairbrained scheme of yours?" Jeremy asked, on a rare expedition away from his newspaper.

"No," Evelynne replied, without even having to think about it. "Not at all."

Jeremy shrugged and returned to his pages.

Then it happened.

The commotion, shouting and screeching. There were bangs and smashes, and the sound of piano keys being mashed together.

There were raised voices and screaming.

The screaming was not the argumentative kind.

It was the agonizing kind.

There was a bang, as if something heavy had fallen to the floor, and a door slammed.

Jeremy looked over his newspaper again. "What in Heaven's name is happening up there? It sounds like all Hell is breaking loose."

Evelynne looked up at the ceiling, her brow creased.

A sound like someone rushing along the landing followed by a series of bangs as if someone was tumbling down the wooden staircase.

Then the whole house fell silent.

∞

"I'll not tell you again, *boy*. Play the notes in the *correct* order. It makes a difference," Mr. Crabtree snarled as Edward sat looking at his ruined hands.

There were tears in the boy's eyes, and a danger in his gait, that belied his doleful face.

"Fuck your notes," he mumbled beneath his breath.

"What did you say, *boy*?" The old man stared from the back of the piano, one hand on the metronome, the other gripping his cane.

"I said, *fuck your notes*," Edward replied, standing from the stool. He was breathing rapidly, all the while flexing his swollen, bruised fingers.

"How *dare* you curse in this music room. Have you no respect, *boy*?" The old man was heavily breathing himself.

"I'm not your boy," Edward hissed as he stepped over the stool, approaching the hateful old man with the hateful cane.

"Sit down and stretch your fingers, otherwise you'll be feeling the cane again," Crabtree hissed, taking a step away from the advancing boy. As he moved, he knocked the metronome, setting it to a rapid pace.

Tick tock, tick tock, tick tock, tick tock, tick…

"I will *not* sit back on the stool, you old fart," Edward whispered, as he hunched his shoulders and lowered his head. "You'll *not* use that cane on me again. Do you hear me?"

"Mr. Nixon," Crabtree shouted. "Would you be so kind as come up here, please?"

"No one can hear you, old man. The flaps have been closed. Don't you remember?"

Crabtree raised the cane, holding it above his head, threatening the boy who was still advancing.

"Sit back down, *boy,* or I'll thrash you within an inch of your life. Do you hear me?"

Edward bared his teeth. "I'd like to see you try," he hissed.

Mr. Crabtree snarled and lunged at the insolent *boy*. He swished his cane. It was not his first time, and he expertly caught the boy full in the face.

Edward screamed and fell backward, onto the piano. The sound emanating from the instrument was atrocious.

As he fell, Edward reached out to grab something, anything, to break his fall. All he could reach was the damnable metronome, the one that was *tick-tocking* its way through this escalation, keeping it in time and in perfect rhythm. It came with him, before dropping to the floor.

Crabtree looked at it, as did Edward.

Crabtree's eyes narrowed, and he raised the cane again.

Edward combatted this by raising his foot over the still-ticking instrument.

"You wouldn't," Crabtree whispered.

"Why not? You did…" Edward replied before bringing the raised foot down and stomping the instrument into the carpet.

Crabtree gasped. He looked up from the broken device to the boy.

With his cane still raised, he advanced, quicker than Edward would have thought possible. The cane was brought down upon him, again, and then again.

Edward howled as the thick wood striped him multiple times. He fell, tripping over the stool he had been sitting on only moments earlier. The old man continued raining down blow after blow.

His head, his back, his legs, and arms were all targeted by the tyrant.

Edward raised a hand to protect his face; with the other, he reached out, searching for something to protect himself with.

His hand found the broken metronome. His fingers scrabbled around it, eventually wrapping themselves around the metal pendulum.

The old man continued his attack, swinging with abandon at the fallen youth. His breath was short, and his swings were becoming weaker.

Eventually they stopped, and he looked at the bruised and bloodied child on the floor. A line of drool hung from his lower lip as his mouth turned down in a breathless grimace.

"You… will… do as you're… told," the old man panted, as he raised the cane one more time.

Edward saw his chance.

With what little energy he had left, he thrust upward, the pendulum of the metronome in his painful grip. He thrust the makeshift weapon with all of his strength, piercing the old man beneath his chin.

The metal shaft entered the old man, as Edward continued to push. He pushed until there was nothing left of the metal shaft except the small part he had been grasping, protruding from Mr. Crabtree.

The cane slipped from Crabtree's grasp as he fell to his knees.

He landed, thick blood was bubbling from his mouth and streaming from both nostrils, as if someone had opened a faucet. His eyes were a deep red. They were staring at Edward, accusing him.

Edward watched as the pink bubbles popped from the old man's mouth as he breathed his last. He swallowed, then turned. He threw the door to the music room open, slamming it closed behind him. He dashed along the corridor, wanting to get as far away from the hateful old goat as possible.

As he headed toward the stairs, his momentum was too fast, and the slick blood on the soles of his shoes allow him no grip.

He continued.

Hurtling toward the dark wooden staircase.

He tipped over the first step and tumbled down, hitting every single one on the way down.

Bones snapped, flesh was split, organs that were designed to stay inside his body leaked from the many lacerations. Finally, as he hit the last unforgiving step, his neck snapped, turning his head to an impossible angle.

Edward's lifeless eyes stared into the lobby of the Nixon family home.

They didn't see the staff running toward the clatter. His ears didn't hear the screaming of the maids, or the wailing of his mother as she dashed to see what the fuss was all about.

Edward Nixon was dead.

11

Music poured through the house. Horrible, rushed notes. Wrong notes in the wrong order, bashed out against a keyboard that didn't deserve the violence it was being subjected to.

The cacophony was interjected with a perfect rendition of the same tune.

The combination was atrocious.

As were the screams, the thuds, and the other noises heard filtering through it.

The music and the noises were not the worst part of what occurred in the aftermath of the *incident*. The worst parts were the sightings of an old, gnarled man.

Blood bubbling from his mouth, with a shard of metal jutting from his chin as he played the piano.

There were also sightings of a boy, his head lolling at an impossible angle, while thick gore oozed from the ugly split in his head. He was also sat at the piano, banging out the hideous notes.

∾

The gruesome sightings, and the continuous, unnerving music was enough to drive a grieving mother into a fugue state of mind where anything was possible, including lacing her husband's food, now that there was no longer a maid to cook for them, with lashings of arsenic, before slipping her head through a thick rope loop, and dropping herself from the landing rail.

Her body swinging like a metronome pendulum.

Tick tock, tick tock, tick tock.

It was all she could do to escape the vile, repetitive music, and the continued sightings of her son, and his tutor, trapped within the personal Hell of their own making.

Game Room
2014

Opening Move
J-F Dubeau

The house is horrid.

Though the website did not promise much beyond what's in sight, it managed to leave room for disappointment.

Light scrutiny is enough to see how uneven the upkeep of the Georgian mansion has been through the decades. The eastern walls are clean, with new windows and lush vines creeping up the bricks. That's the side featured in most photos I saw.

The front porch offers a less inviting view. Paint on the door and windowpanes looks cracked and peeling, even from the parking lot.

If there's one redeeming quality, it's the cupola atop the roof. The expected color of aged verdigris, it has an aesthetic all its own.

A large weathervane, adorned with a brass duck, looks down at us as we drag luggage from our cars up to the estate.

There is no way a stay here is worth the ticket price. Even with meals included.

Emmy would have adored it. She had a love of the ugly and the broken. Anything and anyone in need of a fresh coat of paint, or with flaws that begged to be ignored, she would cherish.

I packed light, but the luggage remains heavy. Small wheels drag through the gravel, scraping along rather than rolling.

Our guide, a pale and tall man named 'Patton' unlocks the door for us, reciting a litany of historical facts about the estate.

Like reading through a catalog, only a few items are worth the attention. Call me morbid, but the date on which they broke ground blurs when compared the three fires that ravaged the structure through the ages. Patton makes no mention of it, but it is tempting to ask about casualties.

On an average day, my thoughts wouldn't be so dark, but this is no average day.

Like ants in a line, we walk through the foyer, a parlor, and then a dining room. There's a large library, which looked amazing on the website, but is currently half-gutted and undergoing renovations. All the while, we pull our luggage and carry our bags.

Nine of us all told. Ten if we count Patton. Everyone is paired. Each couple has an obvious whisperer and listener. One who points and comments on everything they see. While the other listens patiently, nodding and raising eyebrows.

If Emmy was here, she'd be the one yapping my ear off. She'd marvel at the threadbare carpeting on the stairs. She'd ask pertinent question about the scratches on the wood paneling near the kitchen door. The uneven floors would be enchanting to Emmy. And she'd somehow find excitement in the musty smell of ash pervading the estate.

There was a time when I would have loved her for it, but that time is gone.

Now, I listen to Patton explain how we all have access to whatever is in the refrigerator, and if we can figure out the machine, as much coffee as we want. But we should stay away from the cold room, pantries, and authentic gas stove. He puts special emphasis on the word 'authentic', which reminds me of the fires.

Before long, I despair that we'll be going through the entire manor before we get an opportunity to rest. My luggage seems to grow heavier, as if weight were being added with each new moment. I'm reminded this trip was Emmy's idea.

We get no reprieve, even after our tour of the first floor. The two couples lucky enough to have their rooms here are triple blessed. They are closest to the kitchen and dining room, with easy access to food and drink at all hours, day and night. Theirs are the most recent and modern rooms, having been converted from the old ballroom. Best of all, they get to abandon their luggage before we move on upstairs.

While Emmy would have gushed over the first floor and all its creepy little hints of a rich and storied past, the second flood is far more my speed. The view from the old nursery, where I'll be sleeping, is magnificent. Most the estate is visible from here, and it seems the perfect place to look out the window and feel sorry for myself.

There's a music room that feels more like a museum, though Patton assures us the piano is in tune should anyone wish to tickle its keys. Though not before ten in the morning, nor after eleven at night.

Then, there's the game room.

Of all the places, this is the one of least importance. After all, there's a nearby lake with kayaks and paddle boats to enjoy. A pool on the grounds for those less adventurous. Long trails through the garden and surrounding forest await the would-be athlete. And there's a glorious terrace with long chairs on which to relax.

What use will they have for a game room?

To me, it might as well be an oasis.

A small room compared to the rest of the estate; it's made even smaller by the dark oak shelving that crowds the walls. Two tall windows allow the fading sunlight to pour in from the front of the estate. Craning my neck, I'm even able to see my car from here.

There's even a fireplace which would be wonderful on a cold winter night.

To my delight, this is no modern game room. There are no arcade or video games here. Not even a television on which to watch movies.

Instead, the shelves are stacked with books, refuges from the library on the first floor. They tower over two lush leather chairs begging to be read in. There's a massive pool table, and Patton explains how we can install a top on which to play ping-pong. Though he calls it 'table tennis'.

One wall has a dart board cabinet that looks stolen from an Irish pub, and there's a shelf bending under the weight of a dozen board games. Again, these aren't the games of today's youth, or even that of my childhood.

There are names I recognize, like Clue and Monopoly, but they are ancient editions in tattered old boxes. I would be shocked if they weren't all missing crucial pieces. There's also some backgammon and rummy, and an impressive collection of playing cards.

A leather-bound case contains poker chips, but there are no tables suitable for the game here.

Sovereign amongst all these features rests the true king of games. Between two unassuming wooden chairs, sitting on a round table almost dead center of the room, is a chess set. Humble and unassuming, it is a simple yet pristine specimen.

The board looks made of painstakingly lacquered wood, mixing half a dozen essences. The pieces are carved of soap stone and quartz.

As beautiful as it is, the real miracle lies in how complete the set remains. No pawn is replaced by an empty saltshaker, and there's no square missing on the board. Everything is laid out with obsessive precision, waiting for someone to sit down and play the first move.

This is where Emmy and I would have spent our evenings.

The tour advances while I linger. Luggage still in tow, I drink it all in, finding at last some morsel of melancholic joy in the estate.

Patton has moved on. He's showing the other guests the trophy room, another vestige of the estate's past life. I'll have to go look for myself whether these are the grisly trophies of the hunter, or the brass plaques and statues of the sportsman.

Once the tour is done, he invites everyone to settle in and get comfortable. Dinner is at seven, but drinks are available at six-thirty.

All the while I listen from a distance, lingering in the game room.

The load of the journey presses on me, and the lure of lying down for an hour or two is too much to resist. I pull at my suitcase again, but not before succumbing to the temptation.

Looking first to my left, then to my right, like a kid about to steal from a jar of cookies, I move a piece.

Always the same overture when Emmy let me have the white side of the board, I push a pawn from king-two to king-four.

∞

Dinner is an unremarkable affair.

The food is good and the wine fantastic, but the ambience is one that caters to a different person. Even with Emmy, I would have been the odd duck in the pond, but at least she would have been here to anchor me.

Instead, all I can do is eat in silence while every couple exchange tales of how they met and what their plans are for the weekend.

Some woman – Kaleigh I think her name is – even has the gall to show off her engagement ring.

Between the appetizers and entrees, there's a half-hearted attempt to drag me into the conversation.

"What about you, Nadine?" some large, bearded man named Martin asks.

"What do you do for a living?"

I recite my platitudes, but there isn't much meat to my career. 'Accounts receivable' isn't the spark that ignites dialogue. Once the veal in port sauce and caramelized onions arrive on the table, I am once again relegated to the shadows.

All-you-can-drink wine and grieving loneliness are some of the worst dance partners. They step on each other's shoes, stumble and trip, but refuse to let go.

I listen to my new roommates, each of their tales a sprinkling of salt on my open wounds. Martin and Lucy laughing in unison at a boring joke rips at my flesh.

Gordon and Hank hold hands, letting go only to cut meat, each dig of their knives felt in my heart.

A masochist starved for sensation, I stay seated for too long. In this, wine is my ally. It isn't difficult to claim too much drink as an excuse to remove myself from the table. Leaving the raucous meet-and-greet behind, I half walk, half stumble out of the dining room.

It's only once I've stepped into the foyer that I realize I have nowhere to go.

My small room, which is cozy on my own but would have been crowded with Emmy, offers no entertainment. There is no television, books, or even anything to see out the window. Night has fallen, and apart from letting an hour or two drain while I sit on the porch, there's nothing to pass the time.

There was a point where I could have driven to the nearest town, but I've crossed the wine Rubicon where that's concerned.

Like a confused fool, lost on the streets of a small town, I stand at the foot of the stairs, contemplating my limited options.

Books. That's it.

While Martin, Kaleigh and the others have moved the drinking to the remains of the library, I can go to the games room. Perhaps there's something simple enough for my fogged-up brain to enjoy.

Nothing about this estate speaks to me. This was Emmy's idea, from the social aspect to the old creepy vibes of a forgotten mansion.

When I step into the games room though, all this foreign discomfort lifts.

The warm oak and the plush leather chairs reach out like open arms, offering refuge from all the awkwardness.

In less of a rush, I can enjoy the feeling of old carpeting through my socks and the smell of ancient wood in the air. Even the old fireplace has its own kind words for me, spoken as a scratching that I attribute to the age of the construction.

I run my finger over the spines of library escapees. Mary Shelley, Agatha Christie, Jules Verne, and so many other classic names.

It's only once I've almost selected an old Mark Twain – *The Gilded Age* – that I remember the chessboard.

Lacking an opponent, there's no entertainment to be had there. I am curious if someone, Patton perhaps, has moved the piece back from my opener.

Quite the opposite, I see. I've been offered a riposte. Whether it's the caretaker or another guest, I can only imagine they did it as a joke. But I can't help analyzing the move.

Pawn from queen-bishop seven to queen-bishop five.

I'm not enough of a connoisseur to call a move interesting at this stage of the game. I recognize the response as something Emmy has used a handful of times in the past. I simply must remember what I did next and whether or not it got me victory.

After a moment of chin-scratching, I settle on pushing a pawn from queen-bishop two, to queen-bishop three.

Allowing for a little smile, I grab *The Gilded Age* from the shelves and settle into one of the leather chairs, allowing the old cushioning to swallow me whole.

The plan was to read a few pages before retiring to my room. Between wine, food, and the long trek to the estate, I barely make it beyond a few pages before falling asleep.

The night still lingers when I drop Mark Twain's work, waking myself up in the process.

I can't tell what time it is, but there's no sunlight coming from the tall windows. The sound of animated conversation has faded from the dining room. I can hear the plumbing struggle as a toilet flushes upstairs.

Otherwise, the mansion is as quiet as the dead.

This is my cue to go to bed. After pushing off from the chair, I put the book away, making a note of my selection for later. A yawn stretching my jaw, I'm about to walk out of the games room when I notice the chessboard.

Someone is playing with me. Either at my expense, or as a challenge to my modest skills, but they've moved another piece.

Knight from king-knight eight to king-bishop six.

I wish I had the memory that locks away the full range of moves from a game. There's something familiar about this one, but tired, still tipsy, and frustrated at being here, my mind is not up to the task.

With the strange bed calling me from upstairs, I don't want to waste more time on this phantom game with an anonymous stranger. On my second attempt to leave, my foot passes the threshold and *The Gilded Age* falls from its shelf.

The book hits the carpet on the corner of its spine, and I hiss thinking of the damage it must have suffered.

A quick inspection confirms my fears, but exhaustion keeps me from worrying too much about it. I slip the book back on the shelf, careful to make sure it cannot fall again.

I pass the chessboard again on the way out, but this time I stop.

There's no logical reason to think that the book and the game are related, but the old estate and late hour beg that superstition be obeyed.

Better safe than another bump on the book's cover.

I move a pawn from queen-two to queen-three, then make my way up to my room.

∾

There is no formal meal the next morning. We're offered a continental breakfast – muffins and Danishes with orange juice, coffee, and tea – and invited to meet Patton for a tour of the grounds. I expect a safety briefing for the pool and further explorations of the grounds.

Not wanting to subject myself to more forced socializing, I take my coffee and Danish to the game room.

There's no sense pretending that I'm going there to read. Aside from the isolation, there's only one reason I want to go back.

Since finally dragging myself to bed, finding easy sleep under my covers, there's been plenty of time for my opponent to play the next move.

Queen-knight eight to queen-bishop six.

My adversary is showing teeth.

For the first time in too long, I feel a sense of excitement. The unfamiliar feeling of looking forward to the next moment, not as more grief, but rather a place to explore.

I have no care for who is responding to my moves on the chessboard. This isn't a dialogue where the participants matter, only the conversation.

I make a move, showing teeth of my own.

Queen-bishop one to king-knight five.

Hopefully, this gives my mysterious opponent pause.

Settling into the leather chair, I keep my ears peeled as to not miss Patton when the tour begins.

I've little interest in the gardens on chapel, or even the many paths to hike. But the sooner I leave, the sooner I can come back, and hopefully give a window for my opponent to make his next move.

But I don't have to wait that long.

Either *The Gilded Life* has taken a larger bite of my attention than anticipated, or something else far more remarkable is going on.

Whatever the case, sometime between the flipping of pages, a black pawn is moved.

My tea is still steaming, too hot to sip, and the conversation from the kitchen keeps going, uninterrupted. There's no evidence that I blinked and fell asleep. No time for someone to have snuck in to play.

Stranger still, I keep getting this vague sense of familiarity in how the game is played.

Emmy always had this detached playfulness in how she approached chess. Better than I, she was prone to toying with me. Never to the point of patronizing, but enough to keep things interesting.

Of course, through the filter of grief, everything reminds me of Emmy.

Placing a finger on the head of a bishop, I think again how she planned this trip. The choice of this county, the estate, even the dates, were picked out by Emmy.

At the time, I resented how this was her vacation and I was little more than an accessory to it.

Today, contemplating if I should move the piece or go home, I question how big a bite of my sanity was taken by losing her.

A nervous laugh escapes me. Could I be playing against myself, or my own memories, without even realizing?

My therapist would have a field day.

She would also recommend that I don't feed the delusion any further. Which would mean abandoning the game.

I rub the bishop's head between my thumb and index finger, hoping to draw my course of action out of the piece.

This wouldn't even be a good move anyway.

Realizing that, I decide.

I want to see this through, if only to justify my presence at the estate.

So, on impulse, I reach for another piece and forge ahead.

King-knight five to king-bishop six. Bishop takes knight.

No sooner do I let go of the piece that my tea and Danish fall to the floor. No. They didn't 'fall.' They were thrown.

The sudden violence shatters both my mood and the idyllic calm of the estate.

"Sorry," I cry out, kneeling to pick up the mess. "Just being clumsy."

My quick thinking is fueled by a fear of having to explain what happened. Fear brought on by a lack of explanation. Do I tell them that I might be going crazy and hallucinating a game of chess against myself?

That would make an already uncomfortable stay far worse.

The tea is drunk by the carpeting, nibbling on sodden crumbs of Danish at the same time. The pastry has split into a few flaky pieces.

Neither cup, saucer, nor plate broke in the incident.

The vestiges of my breakfast in hand, I stand and look at the chessboard.

My bishop has moved back to its original position, the knight returned to where it was. Then it hits me.

The touch-move rule.

Toying around with that original pawn meant that I have to move it, not the bishop.

Astounding how much of a stickler my broken subconscious can be.

Exasperated, tired, and more than a little frustrated, I perform the original move I had in mind: Pawn from king-rook two, to king-rook four.

Satisfied, my thoughts turn to ways of quieting my mind. A few hours wading in the pool might not be such a bad idea. A sane activity to distract myself from insane delusions.

I'm about to make my escape from the gaming room, almost eager to get into the water, when I hear a weak scraping.

Hands shaking and dishes rattling, I watch as a black bishop moves to an adjacent square. King-bishop eight, to king-bishop seven.

My move again.

∞

J-F Dubeau

Cheers and cries of excitement carry over the water, bouncing off the shallow waves to reach me.

I struggled to escape the splash zone of my fellow guests, wading into the deep end of the pool on my ratty inflatable raft.

Torrid heat scared most of them away from trails and forest, enticing them instead into the cool waters.

They push each other off dive board, swimming and drinking in the shallow are near the steps. I think I would have enjoyed this. Not on my own, of course, but Emmy and I were always playing. This, more than last night's dinner, or any meet-and-greet, would have been the icebreaker for me.

Instead, without her to buffer my anxieties, I've taken to my own corner of the pool where I let my hand drag through the refreshing waters.

Like a fever, my thoughts boil. Sifting through my memories, I look for the exact moment where I moved the black pieces, or the trigger that started the hallucinations. Because that's what they have to be.

My eyes drill into the back of the estate from afar. Anchored to the back windows as if I could see through bricks and masonry and into the game room.

I left without putting in my next move. Like a child quitting a game out of anger, I walked away from the board vowing not to go back. Best I forget the incident until I talk to my therapist and get his opinion on the matter.

More than likely, he'll put my mind at ease with reassurances that this sort of thing happens to everyone. I have a vivid imagination and a robust inner life. Telling myself stories as a coping mechanism wouldn't be out of character.

Already, I'm starting to feel better. My demeanor softens and the muscles in my face lose their tension. Have I been frowning at the mansion this whole time? I can't blame the estate for my burgeoning delusions, but the alternative is to take responsibility. Who wants to do that?

A woman screams, then melts into laughter met with more splashing. What am I doing here?

If I can acknowledge that this is all in my head, why am I apart from everyone else while they all have fun?

The mansion – the whole estate – couldn't look more normal. Bathed in the sun, flowers and topiaries at its feet, it doesn't look like the kind of place to be haunted. As old and decrepit as it might be in places, it looks more like an heirloom than a cursed artifact.

Angry at myself and my childish fears, I wade through the water again. The smell of chlorine and old plastic scratch at the surface of my concerns. I barely notice them, the same way I barely notice as I swim past Martin and Kaleigh and exit the pool.

I nod at the subdued greetings and ignore invitations to join in. Possessed by an urge to see things through, I picture the chessboard in my mind, planning what I should do next.

Mostly, I struggle to decide what this game means to me. Am I staring down the face of catharsis? One last game with the remains of a relationship that lingers unresolved. Is this but a crack in the ongoing shattering of my psyche?

Is it a ghost?

Fists clenched; I walk barefoot up the stone steps leading to the mansion. If anyone asks about my welfare, I don't notice or acknowledge them. All I want is to feel that odd proximity to Emmy that I get from the game.

The room is as I left it, which seems off somehow. I expected my opponent's impatience to have translated into sort of damage. Books thrown to the floor and the perfectly arranged billiard balls scattered around.

Instead, a touch of the outside splashes through the window. Sunlight beaming directly onto the chessboard, making the white pieces – my pieces – glow with a beatific halo.

Motes of dust float gently down then scatter as I take a seat in front of the board. Here we go, subconscious, show me what you've got.

King-knight one to king-bishop three.

Gooseflesh rises on my arms. I can feel every grain of sand between my toes as I wait to see if the black pieces will move on their own again.

When observed, delusion tends to shy from the light. It's far easier to trick myself into seeing things if I'm not expecting them. Even more so if I'm not staring directly at the object of my delusion.

Seconds tick into minutes as I wait. Even a fraction of a second would be enough for the hallucination to kick in. Only the utmost vigilance can–

Laughter interrupts my train of thought, breaking my concentration in the bargain. Crystal, one of the other guests, has barged into the estate. She's laughing at something that was said or happened outside. Not at me as paranoia would have me believe.

She barely glances in my direction before making her way to the washroom, smiling a pitying smile in my direction.

But that's enough.

As soon as I turn back to the board, I can see a pawn has moved. Queen-seven to queen-six.

The experiment begins anew.

More aggressive, I move my king to queen-knight three.

Crystal passes again as I wait, but I ignore her this time. However, as she rushes by, the wind pulls the games room door closed, attracting my attention once more.

Frustrating, but it's for the best. This way, I don't have to deal with any further distraction.

My opponent has reacted in kind while I was distracted. The black queen has moved to queen-knight six.

Either I can't remember how Emmy played, or this isn't my subconscious I'm facing after all. She would never have made this aggressive a move. I could trade my queen for hers in that instant, but instead, I move mine back to queen-bishop two.

Again, I wait. I blink my eyes one at a time, preventing either from drying out, but without ever letting the board out of my sight.

More laughter outside tries to pull my attention, but I refuse the bait.

Even when a book falls off its shelf, slamming with a loud thud on the used carpet, I manage to keep my eye on the board.

I become hyper-aware of every noise in the estate. Someone running water, punishing the old plumbing in the process. Billiards balls knocking against each other on the pool table. The unlikely sound of a car engine going down the road. Through a herculean effort on my part, none distract me.

At long last, it happens. Hallucination or supernatural entity, my opponent moves a piece before my very eyes.

A black bishop slides over next to its twin on king-seven.

With all this waiting, I've had plenty of time to ponder my next move. Knight from king-knight one to king-two.

My opponent doesn't waste any time in countering. They move a rook, and I move one of my own in response.

They move a pawn; I move a bishop again.

The more the game plays, the more certain I am that this isn't Emmy I'm up against. Not her memory, nor some cathartic incarnation that lives in the back of my mind.

I feel almost played with through this game. Like Emmy, my opponent is toying with me. But this isn't to give me a chance. It's to prolong the pleasure.

A black pawn moves; I respond with a bishop again.

Why am I doing this? I need my therapist, or a psychiatrist. Not to be playing against myself while on a couple's retreat.

Angry, frustrated and a little bit scared, I decide to end it. The game, the trip, everything.

I swipe the pieces off the board with a dramatic wave of my arm, making sure the game is truly and completely irretrievable.

Standing over the ruined chessboard, I enjoy the lifting of a weight on my shoulders. The need to be here, to see this through, is gone. Whether I was looking for petty revenge or some strange closure, it's not here that I'll find any of it.

With a deep sigh, the kind that feels like surfacing from under water, I walk to the door.

But before I can touch the handle, before I can pull it open and get on my way, the lock turns.

The metallic click of the bolt echoes through the games room.

No sooner do I process the event that the curtains of both windows fall closed, plunging the room into darkness. Enough light filters through cracks between the fabric that I can still see, but it's like twilight fell over the room. This place that I found inviting and comforting upon my arrival is now hostile and claustrophobic.

The dust that was so charming while dancing in the sunbeam feels like that which you would find in a tomb.

I turn from the door only to see a deluge of books. They rain from the shelves in a steady cascade. Each volume only falling once its neighbor is already on its way to the ground. Like a choreography, the walls vomit volumes.

In the middle of it all, immune to the chaos, there's the chessboard. And as I suspected, the pieces are back on the board. Not only is the game restored, but it is brought back to the exact moment at which I quit.

In disbelief I stare, eyes wide as the chorus of thudding books calls for me to sit back down and finish the game.

Only now that my attention is back, that I'm retracing my steps to the small table, do black pieces move again.

My opponent, who I no longer suspect is imaginary, is castling.

Too stunned to think straight, and barely aware enough to sit without falling over, I mirror the move and castle too.

I play through the game. Each time my attention is pulled from the board, as when I stare at the door, or scan the room for another exit, something happens.

A board game will spill its contents, dice and pieces, like an eviscerated animal spilling its guts. A billiards ball will fly across the room, punching a hole through a wall, or bouncing off a brass fixture.

Play the game, the room insists with all its might.

But I can't decide on the desired result.

Emmy loved to win, and she was good enough that it was the expected outcome.

But this isn't Emmy. Whatever this entity wants, I can't fathom. Am I supposed to best it and win my freedom? Will a victory only serve to frustrate it further? Could I even beat it if I wanted to?

The black bishop trades its life for my knight, falling to my own bishop.

With each move, my fingers shake more and more. The warmth that drove all the guests to the lake no longer penetrates the estate. The mansion feels as cold as it has become dark, having far more in common with the depth of the lake than the sunlit pier.

I lose a pawn. Not a big deal considering the state of the game. But I have no answer to the loss, no black piece I can take in revenge. A sob escapes my throat, the weight of this imbalance far heavier than it should be.

Back and forth we play. There's a building playfulness to the movement of black pieces, a joy in the game that increases with my commitment to see it through.

The more eager my opponent, the more afraid of losing I become. I keep thinking that if Emmy was here, she'd know how to play this. But she isn't, and all I have of her is the memory of when we were happy. When we would go to the park, sneaking a bottle of rosé in a thermos, and play under the summer sun.

And this is where the Emmy of my memory, the one that resides in my subconscious, decides to manifest. Worry over the lost pawn vanishes. Instead, I start to build my own trap, mimicking the trickery my favorite opponent was always so fond of.

Pieces move back and forth until finally, with a smile, it's my turn to disturb the silence.

"Check," I say with confidence.

I know it's not checkmate. My opponent, after a moment, moves the black king out of harm's way, but it's the shakeup I was hoping for. I take a pawn, tilting the balance in my favor. Then I take another pawn, further thinning my opponent's ranks.

For the first time, I wish I could see the face of who I'm against. Emmy always said she could read the next three moves in my face. That's a trick I never got a hang of myself, but any hint of the state of mind of this presence would be welcome.

My pawn takes a knight, but the satisfaction is short lived. Something in my plans went askew and I lose my queen. I can steal another pawn in response, but I can see it now, the walls closing in.

The black queen moves with purpose. There's something I missed. Something more important than losing my own queen to lack of attention.

My king isn't exposed, but he's trapped, walled tight in his keep.

I bring out a rook, trying to counter the queen, but that's not what I should be worried about.

No sooner have my fingers let go of the white rook than the black queen slides across the board, slamming my knight off the square to sit in front of my king.

Check.

The memory of my hand pulling at the locked door rushes back and I feel trapped anew. My teeth draw blood biting at my lip while I struggle to find an escape, a chance at victory, or at least some reprieve.

The room is buzzing with the black player's excitement. Books flip through their pages on the floor. Billiards balls roll languidly on the green felt, clacking as they brush against each other. The whole game room is alive with anticipation.

Terrified of the consequences, fingers trembling, I reach over to the board. With a slow, controlled motion that belies my inner panic, I tip the white king over to his side.

Checkmate.

I pause, and the whole world seems to pause with me. The cavernous halls no longer carry the creaking of the floors and the settling of the structure. The ventilation doesn't whisper into the room, and the usually vocal plumbing keeps to itself.

The reprieve lasts but a second. A timely lapse in activity to punctuate my defeat. Laughter and splashing interrupts the moment, and with it the singing of the natural world returns.

What now?

The pieces remain still on the chessboard. The pages of the many spilled books stay where they were last turned. The billiards table is dead.

Is that it? All my opponent wanted was this victory? To humble me after I played that first move?

A nervous chuckle escapes my throat as I back toward the game room's door. The only question that bounces around my head is whether I should run directly to my car, or if I should do some hasty packing first. The truth between these two options is that I don't want to spend another hour, let alone another night in this place.

I turn away from the chessboard, putting my hand over the handle.

Already I can feel my brain rationalizing what just happened. An episode is what I'll call it. And surely there will be more tests and many more questions to diagnose what it is, but in the end, an episode is all it will be.

I push the handle and pull at the door, but it won't budge. The lock is just as stubborn when I try to twist it.

Kicking and punching at the oak won't do the trick either, and none of my screaming seems to make it out of the game room. The only response I get is the screams and laughs of my fellow guests, still splashing in the lake.

Keeping my hand on the door, I twist my body around to look behind me. The room remains a mess, with empty shelves and littered floors. Even the small coffee table between the two leather chairs has been knocked down.

The only piece of furniture that remains untouched is the one with the chessboard.

No, not untouched. While I was fighting a losing battle against the door, all the pieces had gone back to their original places. Everything was set up for the next game.

Then, as if in quiet invitation, a white pawn pushes forward.

King-two to king-four.

Third Floor

Hello again! I'm so glad you're still here.

Oh. Your hand is trembling.

Take a deep breath.

Careful with that candle.

These next stairs are a bit narrow. And more than a bit dusty. But worth the climb.

Welcome to the attic. I apologize for the clutter. Not to worry, nothing here will hurt you. Just avoid the blankets in the corner. And don't mind Inez. She's harmless. Mostly.

Over here are the servants' quarters. Sad places where people led sad lives. Keep a tight hold on your own candle. Stay away from the silver one. If you feel a bit of hanging rope brush your face, just back away slowly. You should be safe. I think.

Yes, that wall is a little off. The third floor should be bigger. I feel like you're trustworthy enough to know: Hale House has a secret room. The entrance is downstairs, in the main bedroom, but it's been blocked off for years. If you press your ear against the wall, though, just there… you never know what you might hear. Tortured moans. A woman weeping. Maniacal laughter. But never fear. It's just the wind.

If you're not afraid of heights, you can climb the stairs in the corner there and check out the widow's walk. Hold on tight. It's windy up there. But… steer clear of the chimneys.

∾

Take your time. Explore.

I'll be here.

I'm always here.

Attic
2019

Inez
Jennifer Anne Gordon

1
Inez

I was never a sex mannequin. I was, when David was still alive, a silent companion.

Watching but not creeping.

A voyeur.

I was somewhere between a sentient being and a house plant. I was not haunted; I did not haunt.

Not yet.

I was made of plaster and had painted fingernails. There were no splinters under my nails when I lived with David. Were no shavings of haunted wood. My body had not started to warm… not yet.

David would change my clothes; not often, but on a regular basis. That summer I wore a glittery silver dress that bled sparkles on his floor when he tried to arrange my unmoving body.

Where should I be? What did he want me to see?

My jewelry was vintage. I was adorned with Edwardian costume pieces that made my neck and face seem elegant, like pieces of a broken heart.

Where did he get these things? Where did he get the clothing he dressed me in? Did he shop for me? Were they left by the woman who used to live here with him so many years ago?

Time is funny.

Time is dusty.

I could not ask questions. My mouth never worked. Questions formed but they never came out. They felt like lumps. Tumors. They were shadows with long fingers.

My questions turned into cancer.

I always waited for him to say something. I wanted his voice to cut through the dark silence that pressed against both of our bodies. He rarely spoke on the phone, and the silence in his house, our house, felt like the air before it rained. It was thick and moved over me the way I imagined a lover's hands would.

But I was not a sex mannequin. I could only imagine. I could only wait.

For years he would leave the house, and come back mumbling about dance steps, and singing bits of Moon River.

These were the days before my unasked questions turned to cancer and carved holes into his bones. This was back when he could still take large strides across his kitchen and dining room. He practiced what I would eventually understand to be a foxtrot.

He was happier then.

I was aware of a change in the air around me during what turned out to be his last days. Instead of spending time making pencils dull as he filled notebook after notebook with his poetry, he just stared out the window.

His breath sounded like bare branches against a tin roof.

His breath.

Lonely.

Pained.

Sick.

I have never been sick. I have never *been*, not really.

When he picked up a pencil again, he wrote only on small yellow Post-it notes. When those ran out, he used pink, and then eventually a garish blue. He labeled everything. His art collection went to his granddaughters, galleries, and known collectors.

I did not get a Post-it note on my chest until the third day.

I was the last thing he labeled before he went into the garden and put a gun into his mouth. His tea roses and Swiss chard were painted in his blood and bone.

The garish blue sticky note on my chest said: "for Gwen (last I heard; she is still at Hale House looking for ghosts"

I had not been haunted, I did not haunt, but soon I realized, I would have to.

For him.
For her.
For me.

2
Gwen

Gwen always wanted to live in a haunted house, in theory that is.

When she heard that Hale House was being rented out, she and Jason joked that it would be the perfect place to ride out the end of the world. If this virus that was killing everyone *was* in fact the end of the world.

They talked about Hale House; they circled it in their travel books. For the first month of the lockdown, they spoke of it like a lover they both missed.

Twice, they packed a picnic lunch and drove the three hours to it.

They would sit on the trunk of their car and stare up at the house, its windows like eyes with half plucked lashes staring out at them.

"Can you imagine the view from the attic windows?" Gwen's voice was barely above a whisper and had the quality of old letters being pulled from a drawer.

"The view from the widow's walk would be even better." Jason gave a playful – but still a little painful – finger jab just between two of her left ribs.

"I couldn't ever go out there, my intrusive thoughts would get the better of me and I would throw myself off the roof." Gwen laughed, and then stopped herself.

"Maybe they'll lower the rental price, it's been empty for months."

"Maybe…" There was that ephemeral sound again, her voice and her breath. They leaned against each other.

"Or maybe my mom will die, and we can use her life insurance to cover the rent in full for the first year." The words danced over their skin like they were walking through sticky cobwebs.

They laughed, but it sounded forced, like a high school production of Arsenic and Old Lace.

After they returned home, she made chicken broth and toast for her mother's dinner. Gwen gave her a sponge bath and put her to bed.

It was the ghosts of their laughter – dry and biting – that she heard in the night. It was that laughter in her head that played in a loop and prevented her from falling back to sleep. It was that laughter that made her legs twitchy and uncomfortable.

It was that laughter that sent her on a whim to her mother's bedroom, just to check on her – it was that laughter that erupted again from deep in her throat when she saw her mother's neck bent at such a strange angle, her head dangling off the bed.

This is death.

Beautiful and awful. This is what Gwen wanted, but what she… what she…

My mother is… my mother was…

She looked just like a mannequin.

It was the only thing that Gwen thought as her laughter turned into something else. Her voice seemed to catch on something and tear. There was a hitching noise – her mouth opened but if she screamed, she didn't know – the room smelled like lemons, it was coming from inside of her. It reminded her of disinfectant and childhood.

All that was left was all of her yesterdays.

3

Gwen

The life insurance, though not yet in their bank account, was the deciding factor when they called the real estate agent for Hale House. They did not know what to expect from such a house but thought that they would both find that it would inspire them.

Their life before the pandemic had consisted of being professional dancers and performers. But now, Gwen and Jason both longed for something – a home – they had never really known. In Welsh the word for that is *hireath*.

That first day during the first walkthrough of the house, Gwen expected to have an immediate sensation of connection. It didn't happen. They walked through the rooms, which had tall cobwebby ceilings and large windows that instead of letting light in only seemed to create shadows.

The corners of each room were dark and inky like water damage – the shadows crawled up the walls as if they were living things. Long fingers, with fingernails ripped down to the quick…

"I'm sorry, what were you saying?"

"I was saying that your husband mentioned you were a painter, I think the third floor, the attic especially, could make a lovely art studio for you."

Gwen gave Jason a wink, the attic, yes.

She remembered their lukewarm cheese sandwiches; she remembered staring up into the attic windows. She remembered that she wanted to look out those windows from the inside. From the outside they had looked like dead doll eyes.

Like a mannequin.

When they climbed the steep staircase to the top floor, Gwen thought she felt Jason's fingers on the base of her spine, walking their way up her back. Yet, when she turned around to give him a *cut the shit* look, she saw that he was still on the second-floor landing.

"Are you coming?"

Jason looked feverish and confused for a moment. But before Gwen could ask him if anything was wrong, the light was back in his eyes.

"No, no… you see it without me. It will be your space if you love it. You can tell me about it." His voice wavered a little. It shook.

But then Jason forced a smile and said, "I'm going to look at the ballroom again, I think the acoustics there are the best."

Gwen did not think Hale House felt like home until she got to the top floor. The attic had light. The inky fingers that crawled up the walls downstairs were replaced with sunlight, dust motes danced in the air like glitter… *like a dress that bleeds sparkles…*

Wait. What? She didn't know what she was thinking but she had a sense of knowing, not really déjà vu, but more of a remembering of something that was just about to happen. It did not make sense, but it felt important.

"My only request would be for you and your husband to never move the blankets that are in the corner—it may sound silly but as far as I know those blankets have been here almost as long as the house has. So, maybe it's superstition or sentimentality, but…don't move them."

4
Hale House

Hale House seemed to take in a breath when Gwen and Jason moved in. They did not feel it exhale, not exactly.

Jennifer Anne Gordon

There were days, and nights especially, that they felt the house's breath seem to almost give. They felt the house's body waver, but then it would steel itself again.

The house was not breathing. The house was not alive.

"Living in a haunted house is boring as shit," Gwen laughed, as she tossed back her fourth shot of the dusty whiskey they found in the back of a cabinet.

Yes, haunted house life was boring. Sure, there were shadows, whispers that ached out of laundry chutes, flowers in the garden that seemed to turn their stalks and watch when they fought about groceries and laundry.

But the house was sleeping, the house was not the noisy hopefulness that Gwen had wanted. She wanted her grief, and her guilt about her mother to come alive. She wanted the shadows in the house to do what they needed to.

To blame Gwen, to punish her – but instead – the house slept. It quavered. It did not make noise but still, somehow, its silence made Gwen's blood hum with anticipation.

She had not finished a painting since they arrived. The light, or lack of, outside the attic was smoky and fetid, and every time Gwen put paint to canvas or pencil to paper, she could only create one image. Her mother's neck – not her mother, no – but yes. A neck. An unnatural neck. A head not exactly twisted the entire way – but close to it.

Charcoal drawings.

Breathy summertime watercolors.

Hale House slept. Gwen did not paint. She could not create. Her mother, dead now almost six months, still held her in a schedule that she could not get rid of.

Medicines, sponge baths, nighttime stories – keeping the shadow man out of her mother's dreams.

Maybe Hale House should sleep.

But underneath that dark murky nap, Gwen did feel an energy. A restlessness. Hale House did not want to sleep, but it did. Grief and guilt are both sweeter and more awful than morphine. Hale House waited.

Gwen wanted it to wake up.

She cut herself, in thin, bitter, shallow lines.

Did the house want blood?

Gwen hated her mother but wanted her back. She knew that Hale House could – if it wanted to – give this to her.

Just for a moment.

184

Just for a goodbye.

Just for a… "Why mom? Why did you let…?"

The house slept.

Gwen grieved.

Jason wrote songs that ached up to the Gwen's space just outside the attic. He spent his days in the ballroom. He was not looking for ghosts. His music was never better. She could hear it echoing up the stairwell. It was beautiful and painful.

Grief. She knew it might kill her.

But still Hale House slept, until the phone rang.

5
Gwen

Gwen didn't move the musty corner blankets; she did not know what might be hidden in their folds for safekeeping.

They had been living in Hale House for almost five months, and Gwen had not yet moved her art studio into the attic. Instead, she set up her art table and easel in the little hallway in front of the attic door. Sandwiched in an almost unlit nook.

It was terrible for painting.

Servants' quarters in front of her. Rooms to which she never had a key. She didn't know why she could not bring herself to inhabit the space she was in love with – maybe it was the blankets; she had elaborate daydreams, they were always the same.

The blankets had a virus of some kind, and when she tried to move them to fit her easel into that corner with the best light – something *happened*. In the dreams she felt herself turning into something else. Her skin, not skin, but hard, almost porcelain but not quite.

She felt herself turn from a woman into a… doll, no… *a mannequin*… her eyes still seeing, still waiting, still longing for sound, still longing for a home, still longing…

Hireath.

Gwen would wake up each morning, her sheets damp and tangled around her legs like swamp grass. Was this the feeling of a sleeping house?

Yearning.

Jason was still in bed with her, but he seemed a million miles away. The house, their lives – an illusion. "Just breathe. Just breathe." She would whisper the words into the crook of her arm. She spoke to herself, and to the house.

Just breathe.

Every moment leading to this was both smaller and bigger than she could have imagined.

Her mother was dead.

Her mother was dead.

Gwen wanted to live in a haunted house, but now, with her mother's hair and fingernails still growing in the ground, she was not sure she wanted to live in a haunted house anymore, but maybe she needed it more than ever.

Why was Hale House not giving her mother back to her?

Gwen did not move into the attic, and Jason, loyal to his word, never went to the top floor. He mentioned Virginia Woolf and in a manic way talked about *A Room of One's Own*. He wanted to understand her. He wanted to give her space, not just for her art but also for her grief.

He was such a good man.

But still, Gwen waited in her dark hallway. She wondered if Jason was waiting for the house to breathe as well. She wanted to ask but couldn't. Her questions were unasked. They felt like… *lumps… tumors… cancer…*

No. Not that. She didn't know why she was thinking these things.

What would happen after Gwen's grief did not fill the house? What would happen when those feelings finally shrank enough to allow the house to reclaim what belonged to it?

All of the feelings.

All of the memories.

All of the blood and bone.

Jason had never seen the attic. Jason had heard of, but never set eyes on, the blankets. He didn't know she was not painting. He didn't know that sometimes Gwen would open the door to the attic and just stare inside, feeling the dry heat rush at her like a wave.

He did not know that after that heat would come a cold gust of wind.

He didn't know that sometimes Gwen would hear what sounded like fingers trying to pry the door open from the inside.

He was a good husband. He let Gwen have the attic.

Somehow, he knew she would *need it*.

6
Gwen

Gwen's back was resting against the attic door when her cell phone rang. A phone that she knew was always on silent. Her phone decided to scream. It was her first incoming call since they moved in. The phone lit up, like an explosion in a mineshaft.

Gwen was not the kind of narcissist that thought her ringer should be on all the time… but still, even with the ringer off – it rang.

The house took a shallow but very deliberate breath. Before Gwen could answer, the room went dark around the edges and a hand coming from nowhere reached its thin fingers out and slid them around her throat. Her heart skipped a beat.

She coughed, and the room – or hallway really – went back to normal.

Dim light.

Blank canvas.

Liam's name popped up on her screen. Her jaw ached, her back molars thrummed as she forced her mouth to stay closed, as she forced this scream inside her to not be born.

She had not even answered the phone, had not even really contemplated it, but still… her jaw locked. The back of her throat burned. Liam had never called her, would never call her. Liam calling meant…

David.

It meant David was–

It meant David *was*–

Gwen had, in her depression, stopped responding to David's emails. She stopped responding to poems about dead flowers, train rides with old lovers, fairy rings, and bone cancer. She read everything he sent her. She liked most of them, loved a few—but she could not respond.

There was no room in her life for anything else besides her mother and the frayed fabric of her life being put back together – not with careful stitching but with tape, and glue. Her life was messy, and ramshackle.

There was no time for someone else's pain or poetry.

When her mother died, she was afraid the best of her died with her. She was afraid she was turning into something – something dead, something – *a mannequin.*

She closed her eyes, and images of her mother's bent neck flooded over her. "Liam. Hi."

"Hi." He paused, and the silence felt like a pin pulled in a grenade.

Gwen's back was to the attic door, her art palette was dry. Her paints unopened. She had been in the unlit hallway for almost five hours today alone.

She thought she heard a simple *knock knock* on the door behind her.

A knock that sounded like blankets. A knock that sounded like her mother's bent neck. A knock that sounded like…

"He's dead isn't he, your father?"

Hale House exhaled.

Hale House allowed itself to give Gwen more room for this—pain. The house felt the pain from her mother ebb, and before the crushing guilt of David rushed in… Hale House pushed back a little.

It made room for itself.

Gwen had known David was sick, since the first time they danced together. Each foxtrot, each tango, they were all tangled up in his – sickness, all tangled up in his sadness.

She knew.

Last year he took her to the ballet and held her hand as he wept. They would never see each other again.

Gwen knew that bones were hard to kill; even cancer was slow and awful. She knew that David was sick – but not that sick, she knew–

"So, did you finally murder him? With a wrench in the parlor?" Her voice was jokey and affected like an Agatha Christie sleuth.

Didn't Hale House have a parlor?

"Unfortunately…" Liam used a faux British accent "It was a gunshot to the mouth in the garden."

"Fuck. Sorry. Jesus. Sorry, sorry, sorry…"

"Well, yeah, but it's what he wanted."

Liam's voice sounded like old oil paint being squeezed out of a tube. Strained and a little bit poisonous.

"We can go back home, obviously, is there a funeral? Or is there…"

"You need to take Inez, she… she had a note. He gave her to you." Liam paused and in the silence, there was dry awful laughter from inside the walls.

No one could hear it, but Gwen could feel it.

Hale House was breathing now.

"You need to take her, we can't have her here, she was the last one to see him, I guess. I know she's not alive, but it's how it feels. I don't know, I just look at her and I blame her. It's dumb—We can't let her watch us clear out the house."

"I can take her."

Hale House took another breath. It wound its way around every tumor, crime, and ghost that lived in the walls here. It was meaningful and painful. A breath.

"David told me about Inez. He told me about how he loved her... Um, sorry, not in a sex way, but she was... *It* was – she was important to him."

Gwen felt like an idiot but still she said, "She listened to him."

"We can have one of the girls drive her out to you, but it might be better if you come back, he labeled some other things for you, mostly poetry books, some cookbooks, though they seem to be mostly meat related. My father could be an asshole; he was probably being passive aggressive. He also labeled his old army coat for you. The note said, "Gwen said this made me look *'suicide by cop hot.'* So, I guess he wanted you to have it."

"I, I didn't... I think I said something dumb as a joke... I'm sorry Liam, I did... I loved your father, he was–"

"And he was *in love* with you, but those are very different things." He paused. "He wanted to die, and he did, on his terms, it's... better."

"Is it?"

"It's better for him Gwen, maybe not for the rest of us."

There was a definite knock from the attic. Gwent felt it against her kidneys.

"We all know you have a lot going on; my dad – he was in love with you – he hated that you were young enough to be his daughter, he hated that you were married. He hated that you had your own pain. He wanted it to be him..."

"I mean, I..."

"Just take Inez, as soon as you can."

Gwen had bitten into her hand, right over the knuckles. Her teeth, never corrected by orthodontics, left little frowning half-moons across her hand.

"I can talk to Jason, and we can go get Inez, and whatever..."

"Inez might like Hale House. Dad... David said you wanted to be haunted. He told me that. He said that he had never known someone as much like him; someone who just wanted ghosts instead of life."

There was silence.

Hale House waited. Hale House wanted.

Gwen's skin felt sticky. Her chest had a blotchy rash as if Post-it notes were being peeled and pulled from her skin.

"Just text me when you're coming to get her. I don't want to leave her outside, but I can't have her here with us."

7
Gwen

The nightmares started after she had received the phone call. They felt like a mold allergy, a scratchy throat, must, her clothes were damp. These dreams lingered after dawn, and she knew that they would rot her from within.

This is what she had been telling herself. They did not start after her mother had died. No, after her mother died, Gwen had stopped dreaming entirely.

Gwen had stopped hearing the rhythm of music.

Gwen had stopped seeing colors.

Gwen had stopped tasting food.

So, no, Gwen had not been dreaming. Her first dream was the night she found out that she would have Inez. When she slept it was hot and too cold. She woke with wet sheets and chafed legs.

She smelled like a teenager; she smelled like sweat and anger. She had not had an orgasm since her mother died.

Did that have a smell? Was that what Gwen smelled like when she sat in her unlit hall…waiting and wanting to open the attic door?

She dreamt of Inez. She was unruly. A thing forced into sitting position for her entire life. A vintage glitter purse balanced against her wrist. Inez had perfect fingernails.

But – there were mornings that Gwen would wake, feeling splinters deep under her own fingernails. Her fingers throbbed, off-rhythm heart beats. Her fingers were not a waltz. Her fingers were not a foxtrot.

Gwen woke up with copper pennies and gristle in her mouth. Her left-hand ring finger was missing a nail. Her finger was scabbed up. Gwen spit fragments of her fingernail onto the floor. Little bits of it stuck in her teeth like popcorn kernels.

In her dreams, Inez had the eyes of a con artist and the slender fingers of a pianist or a creeping shadow.

When Gwen woke, the room smelled like her mother's perfume, it smelled like her sour old lady skin, it smelled like yesterday, and tomorrow. There were echoes from the dreams. Words. Her mother's words, half French and half hate.

When Gwen woke up, she would tell herself over and over – Inez is a con artist, Inez is not real, Inez is just a shadow in this house.

Inez is a ghost, just looking to haunt.

Inez is just a mannequin.

8
Inez

I have only ever been dressed in vintage glamour clothing. Cocktail dresses, with vintage mink stoles draped across my shoulders lest I catch a chill.

This was before the Post-it notes and the gunshot. I wore a sliver sparkle dress and strappy black shoes that a *decent* woman would never be able to walk in.

My dress bleeds glitter. She bleeds glitter when I am picked up from where I lived before.

Picked up from the spot near the bookcase with the view of the garden. With a view of the blood and bone. The view of the time my world exploded, and I became an object to be gifted.

He thought I was just plaster and put a sticky note on my chest. Property of a name I had never even heard.

We were in the car for hours. The roads were winding, and the sun never hit my eyes.

My legs were taken off and put into the trunk of the car. My wig hung over one of my eyes. I could not see where we were going, but I felt like I was going home. My legs were not attached to me, but I could almost feel my toes wiggle.

The leather strap near my littlest toe broke on each foot.

I was no longer just inanimate limbs.

The woman whose name I was labeled with stared at me from the mirror in front of her in the car. She stared at me as if she knew me. She stared at me as if she was looking at an eclipse.

"Jason?" the woman, who I now know is named Gwen, whispered to the man driving the car. She talked to him, but her eyes didn't leave me. I could my feel fingers start to bend a little.

"She looks like my mother, right?"

Jennifer Anne Gordon

The man used the mirror to look back at me. He did not make eye contact. His eyes danced over my wig, and he did not linger over the shoulder strap of my dress. It had slipped down to my elbow.

It was the sweat.

I tried to move my hands when he looked at me. I thought I had been able to, I thought he had seen it. I heard his voice catch in his throat–

"She's a mannequin Gwen, she… no, she doesn't look like your mom."

Gwen pulled a phone out of her bag and stared at it, scrolling and scrolling. She undid her seat belt and turned around. She leaned into the back seat. She adjusted my wig and held a photo next to my face. Her eyes darted from the photo and back to me.

"They could be twins," she whispered. "Jason, seriously."

She turned back around just as my elbow straightened. Now she was trying to get Jason to look at the photo as well.

"Look at this."

"Gwen…" He swatted the phone away from his face, and tried to concentrate on the road, but not before he took a look at the photo.

"No, I don't see it. Sorry."

He looked up into the rearview mirror and glared at me once before adjusting the mirror so he could no longer see my eye, my shoulder, my strap, my now straightened elbow.

I was not a sex mannequin, but I might be alive. I felt like I was going home.

<h1 style="text-align:center">9</h1>
<h2 style="text-align:center">Hale House</h2>

She wanted to live inside me, that is what she thought. I know that I was made for ruin.

I ruined the earth underneath me. I was made to exist; to feel, to create… I was made to infect, and to destroy, to inspire. I was your words unsaid, your paintings that were not there. I was your cancer. I was all cancer, before and after.

I was rotted bones and hair falling out in clumps.

I was waking up in her bed after the shadows ruined her.

I was the shadows; the shadows in your unlit hall, the shadows between the blankets that she was too scared to move.

I wanted to haunt her.

192

I wanted to be her dead mother.

I wanted to be her dead father – she never thinks of him – but sometimes her sheets smell like him when she wakes up in the morning.

Gwen wanted to be haunted. She tried everything, but her house was inside of her – her pussy, her gut, her mommy, mommy, mommy mommy…

I wanted to get in.

I wanted to be her mother – who screamed in the night, shadows that became alive. I wanted to be shadows that had fingers that would tickle you and go inside you when she slept.

Shadows that open… shadows that…

I wanted to be her mother.

I *could* be her mother.

Gwen. My Gwen.

She wanted me to haunt her.

Little girl.

Little sad girl.

When Gwen gave me sponge baths… it never felt right.

It never felt like… home.

Hale House.

I was the shadows in her throat while Gwen slept; I think she recognized me; I think she knew how I felt. She may have always known me. My fingers. My shadows. My walls.

I was Hale House.

Her haunted house.

I was the time when she should have loved her mother more. I was the times she should have loved–

Her husband thought I was just a house. He was wrong.

I wanted to haunt her. I wanted her to give in and live in the walls…I did not know how to haunt her until *she* came here, with me, Inez.

I was her blank canvas.

I was…her. I was… *Inez*… I was her *mom*… I was Hale House. I am Hale House.

I took a breath.

In.

Out.

I breathe. The walls breathe. Vines and mold grow. Every ghost started to scream.

Gwen.

Gwen.

Gwennie, baby girl…

She was haunted now.

I made sure that there was skin and wood under Inez's fingernails.

Gwen did not notice it, but she could have, and eventually she will.

10
Inez in pieces

Jason wanted to leave Inez in the parlor.

He dropped her torso and legs, without being told – her plaster skin cracked and healed itself without anyone knowing.

When he took a last glance at her, her dead eyes were a cunning green fire that made his fingers cramp and burn.

"Where do you want her?"

His voice, thin and squeezed between memory and guilt. His words traveled down one of Hale House's long narrow corridors, and then faded into the walls.

This is where Inez simmered and laughed.

Inez was home, she wanted to be everywhere. She wanted to be everyone.

"Here's good."

"Do you know where you are going to put *it,* Gwen?"

Gwen did not answer, she did not seem to even hear Jason, she just stared at Inez; her face softened, became almost childlike. Inez's mouth relaxed a little, her lips parted, as if to let out a silent sigh.

"Did you say something?" Her eyes did not leave Inez's face.

"I wondered where you were going to put it."

He gestured towards Inez but now refused to look in the mannequin's direction.

"Well, I think I need to put her upstairs with me."

"In the attic?"

"Yes. She can help me work. She might be my muse."

Gwen said it as a joke but realized when she was done that she just might have meant it.

"Do you need help getting her up there?"

"No, it's fine, I'll take her apart and it will be easy. Her legs are already off." Gwen felt guilty about this suddenly, yet still she took Inez's arm's off.

She thought that Inez felt warm, and nimbler than she had when she was being loaded in the car, but that couldn't be – she must have been in the sunlight on the drive here, this was – of course – why she was warm.

Gwen let the silver dress fall to the floor. The glitter made the parlor look like it was filled with shattered glass.

Gwen wrapped her arms around Inez's torso, she thought she felt Inez lean into her hands, as if she were bracing herself for the journey upstairs.

It took three trips, the torso, then the legs, and then the arms. As they were about to get to the attic, one of Inez's hands fell off, her fingers bent a little, as if the hand were trying to hold onto the stairs to keep from falling.

Inez's painted nails had been perfect before, but now her left hand had chips on her nails, and just like Gwen, the fingernail of her left ring finger had been ripped off. Gwen had sworn that the fingernails were just painted on, but she must have been wrong.

She rested the pieces of Inez against the attic door and went down the stairs to retrieve the hand that was now resting on the landing in just the spot that Jason had stood in, when he told Gwen he wouldn't go up to the attic.

The hand was warm, even warmer now than it was a few minutes before. The hand rested in Gwen's, and before she could think better of it, Gwen went to the master bedroom and closed the door behind her. In the bottom drawer of her bureau was her mother's robe.

Gwen remembered her mother wearing this when she was a child, and she was wearing it the night Gwen heard the bitter laughter that woke her in the night.

She was wearing it the night Gwen found her, with her neck bent at such a strange angle, the night she had looked so much like—a *mannequin.*

Gwen did feel Inez's hand hold hers as she went back up the stairs; her skin was warm, and she felt what could have been a slow pulse. Inez's fingers curled into Gwen's palm, she felt the remaining nails dig into her flesh, the same way her mother's had when Gwen was a child misbehaving in public.

Gwen had always wanted to live in a haunted house. She was not scared to feel this hand come alive while she held it. She was not scared when she went up to the landing in front of the attic door to find it empty.

Inez who had been in pieces was gone.

The door to the attic was open. The wave of heat that came from that room had come and gone.

The cold was there now; Gwen could not see her breath, but she could feel the chill in her knees and hips. It was an ache that wanted to thrum but instead was silent.

The hand dug its nails a little deeper into Gwen's palm. She felt her skin give way. Small streams of blood trickled the length of Gwen's arms.

"Mom. Mommy?"

Inez's remaining nails dug a little deeper in.

The door to the attic seemed to breathe. It had not been closed all the way. Gwen looked at her blank canvas and saw a painting of her mother – of Inez.

"Mom. I brought your robe." Gwen placed Inez's hand on the attic door. She gave it a quiet *knock knock.*

She – no – *they* pushed the attic door open. The light was beautiful, and the forbidden blankets were rumpled, and Inez was no longer in pieces.

Only her left hand was missing. Her ring finger missing its nail bled into Gwen's palm. The blood felt like nightly sponge baths and shadow men.

Shadow men that Gwen tried to keep away, shadow men that were there, shadow men that made her mother's neck break, shadow men that turned her into a – *mannequin…*

"I brought your robe." Gwen saw it. She saw it all.

"Mom, those blankets…we're not supposed to move them."

Gwen entered the attic. Yes, she remembered now, why she wanted this, why she wanted this to be her home.

The attic

Dead eyes

Looking out

Being haunted

"I can put your robe on, Mom, if you need me to. Do you need me?"

Gwen stood in the attic now, and she did not notice when the door closed behind her.

"Mom?"

Inez smiled, her face was in shadows, a blurry memory. Inez was somewhere between a mannequin and a mother. She sat in the far corner with the blankets.

The hand Gwen held twitched and bled a little more.

Gwen forgot about Jason, her paintings, her life before – Gwen knew she wanted to live in a haunted house. Gwen knew she should have been a better daughter, Gwen knew that she should have been a better friend, Gwen knew she should have…

She knew she should have…

Gwen knew she wanted to be haunted…

"Mommy…?"

11
Hale House

"Yes, Gwen. I'm here."

Servant Quarters
1895

A Flicker of Candlelight
Simon Bleaken

Hannah sighed wearily as she closed the bedroom door; a thin barrier between her and the world beyond.

It was the end of a tiring day. But then, all the days at Hale House were long and strictly regimented, the work exhausting. She looked forward to making her way upstairs each evening, usually around eleven, to retreat into the seclusion of her room.

It was narrow and simply furnished. Besides a bed, it contained only a dresser for her few clothes, a bedside table, and a chair. But the bed at least was soft and welcoming.

She had been employed there for a little over three weeks. Her previous job had ended abruptly with the passing of the elderly homeowner and the decision of his son to sell the property.

So, she had come to Hale House, to a whole new set of faces and personalities. But the work was familiar at least, even if the other servants were distant and unwelcoming, watching her as though sizing her up, and whispering to each other behind her back when they thought she couldn't hear them.

She ignored it as much as possible. She needed this job, however lonely and isolated she felt, so she simply had to make the best of it.

But in truth, she was troubled by more than just the other servants. The house felt oddly unwelcoming. The rooms held an unsettling quality, a subtle but creeping sense that you were never truly alone, that someone was always watching.

Sometimes, it would be an unexpected noise from an empty hallway–a half-heard whisper, a footfall, or a sly creak of a door or floorboard–other times a fleeting glimpse of shadowy movement past a window or doorway.

She told herself it was just her imagination, but knew in her heart it was something more. Some houses collected secrets the way others gathered dust, and the shadows in Hale House felt far deeper than most.

She did her best not to notice, throwing herself into work that was as grueling as it was repetitive: cleaning, washing, folding sheets, making beds, helping in the kitchen, and dusting. She flitted like a ghost herself through the rooms of that house, voiceless and unseen, working in the background from dawn until dusk to keep the pulse of the home beating.

But that was all over for another day.

Tonight was a new moon and, while the sky was ablaze with stars, the grounds around the house were darkly tranquil. Hannah left the window open in the futile hope of a cool breeze to break the lingering summer heat, changed into her nightclothes, knelt to say a quick prayer, and slipped into bed before blowing out the bedside candle.

It was a curious flicker of light from the far end of the room that awoke her around an hour later. It was accompanied by a steady creaking from overhead, like a rope, or an old tree limb flexing in a breeze.

Just audible behind it was the faint sound of a woman sobbing.

Hannah blinked, stirred from deep slumber. The haze of sleep clung to her like cobwebs, and it took a moment for her mind to separate dreams from reality.

The light grew brighter, a spark of silver-white fire, a tiny beacon in the blackness. It bobbed and guttered, swaying to that eerie creaking, and she realized a strange tall candle was resting on the wooden window stool, its unearthly glow spreading outward like moonlight, though its illumination never broke the deep shadows in the farthest corner at the window's edge.

Slipping out of bed, Hannah was unable to pull her gaze from that curious dance of light, drawn to it as if in a trance. It was strangely alluring, mesmerizing, and as she drew closer, she discovered she could see the glass of the window through the candle itself, as though it possessed no physical substance. It also gave off no heat. Instead, an icy coldness emanated from its heart.

Confused, she reached for it, curious as to whether she could actually touch that spectral wax, only to snatch her hand back with a startled gasp.

A woman was watching from the corner of the room, her features just visible in the shroud of shadows on the edge of the light, and her cheeks wet with tears. She couldn't have been much older than Hannah, but her expression was twisted into a savage mask of pain and rage, the dark eyes glaring accusingly.

For a moment, Hannah could only stare back.

In the next instant, a wave of anger and grief crashed into Hannah like a storm wave breaking against the shore. It staggered her, sent her physically reeling, and she toppled against the wall, too shocked to cry out. The emotions were alien to her, but they pulsed through her body as though they were her own; a maddened fury and a sense of hollow loss so deep it left her unable to breathe, unable to think.

It lasted only a second. Before she could process anything of what was happening, it was already ebbing like a retreating tide, leaving an indescribable loneliness in its wake; despair so heavy the weight of it dragged her to her knees.

Through vision blurred by tears, she realized the woman was emerging from the shadows. Her neck was bent at an odd angle, the flesh around her throat broken and raw. With each jarring step the woman took, the shadows around the room shifted wildly, impossibly; a band of darkness cutting momentarily through that silver light, each accompanied by another ominous creak from overhead.

Choking back a terrified cry, Hannah scrabbled to her feet and stumbled to the door. She wrestled with the tarnished handle, but it refused to turn no matter how hard she twisted or wrenched.

"Help!" She pounded desperately with one hand while fighting the handle with the other. "*Please!*"

A floorboard groaned behind her. She glanced back in alarm.

The woman was halfway across the room, her ghoulish form lit from behind by the flickering candlelight, and her head lolling hideously. She dragged a length of old rope that hissed roughly across the bare boards.

Now Hannah screamed, as did the strange woman with the broken neck, their voices rising as one to the rafters.

There was a final sharp snap of rope as another shadow swept the room, this time casting the stark and unmistakable outline of a hanging body against the far wall in defiance of the silvery light.

Hannah was still screaming when the bedroom door opened quickly inward and Fannie Crane, one of the older servants, came bustling in, her face lit by the warm glow of a candle in a brass holder.

"Whatever is going on, child? You'll wake the household!"

Hannah fell into the older woman's arms.

"Steady now!" Fannie urged, holding the flame away from the trembling woman. "You'll set yourself alight."

When Hannah chanced a fearful glance over her shoulder, there was no sign of the strange light in the window or the mysterious woman with the broken neck.

"Hush, now." Fannie cast her own wary eye around the room. "What's happened?"

Hannah tried to speak, but her voice failed her. She could hear the other servants creeping from their rooms, whispering as they tried to see what was going on. The older woman shooed them away.

"Go on!" she chided. "This poor girl's been through enough tonight."

Putting an arm around Hannah's shoulder, Fannie guided her out of the door. "Come on, that's it. Come sit with me for a spell. You've had a bad shock."

Fannie's room was next door, equally small and spartan, but although it was only a few feet from Hannah's own room, and separated by nothing but a thin wall, it felt worlds apart.

Hannah perched numbly on the edge of the bed, her mind struggling to make sense of everything that had happened, while Fannie set her candle on the bedside table and settled into a chair in the corner, watching with an almost maternal look of concern.

Gradually, carefully, the older woman coaxed Hannah's story from her lips, past fear and self-doubt, and when it was told, Fannie nodded grimly.

"You're not going mad," Fannie assured her, reading her expression.

"That room's been vacant for a while. Nobody's been able to stay there."

Hannah shivered despite the heat of the night. She wrapped her arms tightly around her body, as though hugging herself.

"I'm not the only one to see something in there?"

"Far from it," Fannie sighed. "We've had dozens come and go."

"And nobody said anything to me?"

"Oh, it wasn't personal, child. We don't ever really talk about it. We all do our best not to see or hear anything that goes on here. But I've heard the sobbing at night through the walls, even when the room's empty, always around the new moon."

"What *is* it?" Hannah asked. She still felt dazed, but the fingers of fear were starting to ease their grip in the comforting presence of the older woman.

"Not what, child. *Who*."

Fannie settled back into the chair.

"You know, I'm probably the only one here who still remembers. I've lived at Hale House my whole life. I've seen a lot of good and a lot of bad here."

"A *lot* of bad?"

"When I was twelve, my father and I were away for the night. What we found in the ballroom the next morning when we came home will haunt me forever. But, that's a story for another time," Frannie said.

"What you need to know about is the girl who started here around '69. Her name was Mary, Mary Evans. I've never forgotten her, even after all these years. That room you're staying in was hers."

"Was she your friend?" Hannah asked.

"Oh, heavens no. I tried, but she wouldn't let anyone get close enough for that. She had a defiant streak in her. If she could find a way to bend the rules, she would. She was always courting trouble, and I worried for her. I feared things would end badly. Turns out, toward the end of '71, things did."

Hannah leaned forward. "What happened?"

Fannie paused before answering, her gaze settling on the brightly burning candle on the bedside table. "Well, I think it's enough to say she took her own life; hanged herself with a rope from one of the storerooms. It was a new moon then too, as I recall."

"But, *why*?"

"Honestly, the less you know the better. Her spirit's reaching out to you, and no good can come of getting involved. Her light brings only sorrow to those who see it."

There was silence for a moment, and the lingering unease crept back in to fill the void. Hannah felt terror and hopelessness blossom like a flower inside her.

"What am I supposed to do? I need this job. But I can't stay in that room."

"Whatever is left of her fades as the moon waxes. In just a few days it'll be gone, until the next new moon at least. You have to avoid looking at that candle, just shut your eyes tight and pray until it goes away."

"You think I can do that? Could *you*? She was in that room with me–*is* in that room! Am I supposed to shut out her cries too?"

"I'm sorry, I don't have any answers. But listen, if it all gets too much, you're welcome to the floor in here. I can put some blankets down for you. Or you can sleep in this chair. I'm sorry, I really am. I wish I could do more."

Hannah closed her eyes, taking a slow breath. The world felt wildly out of kilter, spinning sickeningly sideways. "I can't go back in there tonight."

"Stay here then," Fannie said softly. "You can take my bed for now. I can cope with this old chair for a few hours at least. Tomorrow, we'll work something better out."

"Thank you," Hannah said.

But, even as she settled back against the unfamiliar sheets, she knew that sleep was unlikely to return for the rest of that night. She lay there for hours after Fannie put out the candle, listening over the older woman's breathing to the faint snatches of sobbing from beyond the wall, and to the unmistakable sounds of restless pacing from within that other room.

By the time the sky was tinged pink-gold by the creeping approach of the dawn, all the sounds had ceased. Hannah finally felt the call of sleep tugging at her exhausted body, but even as she closed her eyes she heard Fannie stir and rise from the chair.

"Come on, child," the older woman said. "Time to get this day started."

That day felt longer and slower than any Hannah had known. The constant pull of fatigue on her weary mind and the concentration needed to battle it was arduous. She found herself forgetting simple things and making foolish mistakes.

Luckily, Fannie was on hand to assist and helped her put right the worst of them before anyone noticed. The slow, sticky heat of the afternoon sapped her energy too.

As the day wore on, her anxiety increased. Her little sanctuary upstairs was gone, and the thought of what she might have to face later brought a deep, brooding horror.

The character of Hale House felt transformed too; no longer simply odd and unusual, it now felt actively threatening, haunted by the secrets of its past, of the suffering and loneliness that had played out there.

"You just give the word if you want to stay with me tonight," Fannie whispered late in the afternoon. "I'll get some blankets ready for you."

"Yes," Hannah said quickly.

As unappealing as sleeping in a chair was, it was far preferable to facing another night in that room. "I'd like that."

Despite that reassurance, when the day finally drew to a close Hannah was unable to shake the feelings of dread flooding her heart.

Fannie was waiting for her as she made her way up the stairs.

"Don't look so worried," she said kindly. "You'll sleep soundly tonight."

And, as Hannah settled into the chair, cloaked in the shadows of that other room, she wanted desperately to believe those words. Instead, she sat there in the dark, trying to get comfortable and listening nervously to every little sound as the house settled around her.

But despite her fears, sleep must have stolen over her at some point, for her next awareness was of opening her eyes to the silvery-white light of that flickering spectral candle. She was standing in the middle of her own room once more, the window before her, as if she had been sleepwalking.

Her first reaction was panic, a burst of terror that rushed up from within her and clamped icy fingers around her heart. She went to flee–or rather, she *wanted* to–but the soft allure of that ethereal candle had snared her once more, and she couldn't turn her gaze from the silver flame swaying on the window stool.

It beckoned to her, and she answered without hesitation. Her bare feet cringed as they crossed that frozen floor, and she could feel the cold radiating outward from it, sharp as a frost on a winter's morning.

As she drew nearer, she lifted her gaze at last and stared out through the window. The stars beckoned in the night sky and the grounds below it were again an inky void in which nothing was visible, as if the world had fallen into a black abyss.

A faint sound from overhead, the song of old rope swaying and twisting, caused her body to stiffen involuntarily. She knew what it heralded.

Slowly, Hannah turned her head. That simple act took a monumental effort.

Mary waited on the edge of the candlelight, the shadows behind her impossibly deep. She clutched a length of rope that trailed off into that darkness and her eyes sparkled with tears of rage and sorrow. As she stepped forward, the noise of creaking rope mirrored her movements, shadows once more shifting, cutting through the silver light as they cast odd lines of darkness across the walls, such as might be made by a swaying rope.

"Please… *no!*" Hannah tried to shrink away, but again her body refused her commands.

Mary reached out, holding the rope toward Hannah as if offering or commanding. Her lips were moving, but no sound escaped her ravaged throat.

"I don't understand!" Hannah protested.

She was once more caught in the shifting pull of invisible tides of emotion, powerful waves of anguish, grief, and intense loneliness that flowed through her.

Simon Bleaken

She wanted to squeeze her eyes shut, to stop looking, but even that was denied to her.

Mary turned her twisted neck and gazed out of the window.

Hannah found herself turning to look too, though she had no conscious control over it.

Below them, something was moving, a dim haze out in the expansive blackness of the grounds. It was silver-white like the spectral candlelight, but far fainter, almost like a fading echo. It was hard to make out, but appeared to be approaching the house.

At the sight of it, the waves of anguish currently flooding the room elevated into a swelling crescendo of unendurable despair. Hannah gasped under the onslaught and turned dizzily, white lights erupting in her field of vision and one trembling hand reaching blindly for the door.

Then she collapsed to her knees, gasping for breath, as the whole room went black.

∞

"What are you *doing*, child!"

Fannie's startled cry cut through the darkness.

Hannah's eyes snapped open.

She was standing on a chair in the center of her room. There was no sign of the spectral candle or the spirit of Mary Evans.

Hannah's nightclothes, hands, and feet were filthy, and she held a length of old rope from one of the dusty storerooms. She had been looping one end over one of the larger beams in the ceiling.

Startled, Hannah dropped the rope and clambered down in distressed confusion.

"What's going on?" Fannie asked again.

"I-I don't know!" Hannah swayed almost drunkenly for a moment, and then Fannie bustled into the room to catch her before she fell.

Carefully, the older woman helped her back into the safety of the neighboring room. With the door closed and Hannah safely settled into the chair, the hold of the spirit of Mary Evans diminished once more; though, the thought of what she had been doing–and of what might have happened if she had not been interrupted–left a shocked, nauseating dread in its wake.

"How do you feel now?" Fannie asked quietly.

"A little better, I think. My head feels clearer."

"I was worried when I woke and found you gone. Why would you go back in there?"

"I didn't mean to. I was asleep in here… and then I was there."

"And the rope?"

"I don't remember getting it." Hannah shivered.

"I was afraid of this. She's forged a link with you; a kindred lonely soul."

"Why did she kill herself? You have to tell me."

"Oh no, child." Fannie shook her head sternly. "We need to separate you, not get you closer."

"She's in so much pain."

"You have to walk away, lest she drag you down into death with her, like she almost did tonight."

"Please," Hannah implored. "If I know, maybe I can do something."

Fannie looked skeptical, her brow knitted in a frown, but gradually she relented with an uneasy sigh.

"Very well, since neither of us is going to get much sleep tonight, I'll tell you. It was around the summer of '71 that a new gardener started over in the neighboring Westerman House."

She gestured toward the window.

"I forget his name – was it George? No, Jim. That's it. Well, anyway, Mary became smitten with him, in the kind of way that's hard to hide, though I imagine she *thought* she was more careful about it than she actually was," Fannie told her.

"She'd watch him working when she believed nobody was looking. And she'd signal to him with a candle in the window when the rest of the house was asleep, so they could meet in secret."

"But you knew?" Hannah asked.

"Oh, of course I knew, child. I knew everything going on here."

"Did they get caught?"

"No, nothing like that," Fannie said sadly. "The old tree out on the border of the Westerman property was struck by lightning, and Jim was told to remove it. While they were getting ready to bring it down, a large branch fell and killed him instantly.

"Mary took it hard. His death broke her heart, and her spirit. She faded away before that window, just staring out, night after night, as if hoping to see him again," Frannie explained.

"She still lit her candle each and every evening. But, where it had once been a beacon of hope and love, it now became a beacon of grief and loss, lit in the hopes of guiding his dead spirit back to her; her last desperate hope of being with him one more time," Frannie went on.

"Finally, consumed by loneliness, she took her own life, though in truth, she had become a ghost long before she died."

"That's awful." Hannah shivered, chilled despite the warmth of the night.

She thought again of that phantom face, the pain and torment that had been trapped in those eyes.

"That's why we have to break this link, before it takes you too."

"You really think she's dangerous?"

"That much grief and rage, it eats away at you, goes deep. It'll twist anyone into a monster, and it's been trapped here a long time without release."

"There was something else too, last night," Hannah remembered. "Out in the garden, a faint light, but it was moving around."

"I've seen it too, from time to time," Fannie confessed.

"I think that's him, or what's left of him. She drew him back with that candle, that's what I believe, anyway. But I reckon they both got stuck; him out there, her in here."

"You've never tried to talk to her?"

"I've been too afraid to."

"Must be nice to have that choice," Hannah mused grimly.

∾

The next day, as soon as she had the first opportunity, Hannah ventured out to the edge of the property, where it bordered the grounds of the Westerman House and where she had seen the strange haze during the night.

She was operating purely on gut instinct, playing a hunch, and she didn't dare tell Fannie or anyone else what she was doing. She could well imagine the disapproving look she would get, and she already feared she might be playing with fire.

It took less than ten minutes before she located the weathered old stump poking from a tuft of overgrown vegetation, all that now remained of the tree that had taken the life of Mary Evans's secret lover.

After checking that nobody was watching, she hitched up her skirt and waded through the tangle of undergrowth. She worked a tiny piece of the old bark free from the side of the stump before making her way gingerly back, avoiding the clustered thorns and nettles as best she could.

That afternoon she hurried upstairs and placed the fragment of bark on the window stool, before dragging her chair into the center of the room. She had noticed something the night before, when Fannie had come bursting into the room, and now, examining the beam in the middle of the space, her questing fingers discovered a few fragments of old rope fiber still clinging to the wood.

She couldn't say for certain these were left over from the same rope that had ended the life of the tragic young servant, but she quickly retrieved them before returning downstairs to resume her duties.

As the sun began its descent below the horizon that evening, she took two candles and some matches and went to her room, setting them in the window. She placed the rope fibers next to one, and the fragment of bark next to the other.

She had never tried anything like this before, though she had heard about spirits and magic, root work and conjure, from her grandmother. Time had broken those memories into fragmented and half-recollected shards, and she wished she had paid better attention.

There was a gentle knock on her door, and Hannah turned as it opened, trying to block the candles from sight.

"Everything all right, child?" Fannie asked, her face lined with gentle concern.

"Fine." Hannah tried to remain calm, praying that Fannie would mistake her nervous trepidation for fear of the night ahead.

"You want me to get the blankets ready?"

"No, I… I thought I'd stay here tonight."

"Here?" Fannie's brow furrowed. She took two steps into the room, looking around cautiously. "What's going on?"

Please don't let her see. Hannah edged closer to the window. *Don't let her suspect what I'm trying to do.*

But she did suspect. Hannah could plainly see that in the older woman's eyes.

"I can't sleep in your chair every month," Hannah said hurriedly.

"You were right. I need to close my eyes tight and wait for Mary to go away, to let her know I won't be driven out. Maybe that's all it will take."

"You sure you're up to that?" Fannie asked. "There's sanctuary next door if you change your mind."

"I know. I'm grateful."

"All right, child," she said reluctantly. "May the Lord watch over you tonight."

Hannah waited until the door had closed and she heard Fannie go into her own room, then she turned and moved the two candles about a foot apart, before retreating to the end of her bed, where she sat and waited as the hour slowly edged toward midnight.

Outside, the stars were the only sources of light, and the still darkness of that narrow room was almost absolute. Hannah sat motionless, hands resting in her lap on top of the matches and a small, folded cloth she had collected earlier.

Time seemed to slow to an impossible crawl, though her heart was racing, and a nervous energy was building in her body like a spring desperate to uncoil.

She tensed as a tiny pinprick of silver-white fire flared to spectral life in the window, quickly growing stronger and brighter. As its light spread outward, the candle itself appeared beneath it, as if that flame were calling it into existence.

Hannah gripped the matches in one hand, the folded cloth in the other, then stood and stepped into the expanding pool of illumination. She could feel the icy cold and see her breath pluming in the air before her.

A faint creak came from overhead.

Tucking the folded cloth under one arm, she lit a match with shaking fingers and touched it to the wick of her first candle. The warm yellow-gold flame it nurtured was so different to the icy silver one that burned beside it.

"I light this for Mary Evans," she said, taking the tiny fragment of old rope and letting it burn up, releasing any energy still bound to it.

"May it be a beacon to her spirit."

Her words were answered by another ominous creak.

Taking a deep breath, Hannah went to light the second match.

It was a raw howl of anguish that stopped her, a desolate and terrible cry from the corner of the room, and as Hannah turned in surprise, Mary stepped out of the darkness. Her lip was curled in fury, tears raced down her face, and she had an old rope twisted tightly in her hands.

"I'm trying to help!" Hannah said quickly. "Please, let me…"

Mary lunged at her, and an invisible wave of pressure struck Hannah, driving her backward as though forcefully shoved. She fell heavily, crying out as her head struck the floor. The match flew from her fingers.

Hannah sat up amid a dance of shadows. Her skull throbbed and the coppery taste of blood was on her tongue. She was aware of two things: the handle to her door rattling as someone tried to get in, and Mary looming over her, gripping a noose.

"Child, what's going on!" Fannie's voice was muffled by the door. "Are you all right?"

Hannah knew the door wasn't locked, but she also doubted Fannie would be able to open it. She remembered how it had refused to open for her on that first night. In this room, Mary was in control.

Acting fast, Hannah lunged for the small, folded cloth that had tumbled to the floor during her fall.

She grabbed one end and flicked it upward, scattering a fine spray of powder into the air as the cloth flew open, up into the face of the enraged spirit standing over her.

That powder – a mix of ground angelica root, basil, mullein, salt, black pepper and agrimony – that she had secretly prepared that afternoon in a quiet corner of the kitchen was one of the few things she still, mostly, remembered from her grandmother's teachings.

It may have been missing a few ingredients, but Mary recoiled from it all the same.

Seizing her chance, Hannah scrabbled for the second match and darted to the window.

A fierce draft howled around the room, rattling the glass in the window frame and matching the rage of the spirit that was now turning toward Hannah once more, drawing the heat from the summer night as she tightened her grasp on the noose.

Striking the second match, Hannah lit the other candle and held the fragment of tree stump to the flame. It must have been damp, for it smoldered rather than burned, but she hoped that would be enough.

"I light this for Jim, killed by the falling branch," she said quickly.

"May it be a beacon to his spirit."

With the two candles lit, she slid them both closer together, pressing them in on either side of the spectral flame that burned in that window, uniting them around that unearthly silver light.

"Child!" Fannie hammered against the door. "Let me in!"

But Hannah was staring through the window, her eyes widening at the sight of the faint haze drifting through the garden below. It was coming from the direction of the old tree stump, following the light of the candles she had lit.

Then Hannah froze as something else moved next to her. She turned in surprise to find Mary at her side, staring forlornly out of the window. The spirit lifted a hand toward the glass, but instead of the joy Hannah had expected, there were only fresh tears.

"You're stuck here, aren't you?" Hannah whispered, but the spirit gave no acknowledgement.

Instead, Mary's whole focus was on that hazy shape now standing directly below the window.

"He's out there, and you're in here, and neither of you can get to the other."

Mary closed her eyes, as if the sight before her was too much to bear. She began to sob.

"Let me help you," Hannah urged.

If she could have taken the other woman into her arms, she would have.

"I've guided you back together. Maybe I can take you the rest of the way."

Mary turned, as if seeing her for the first time.

"I can go out there," Hannah continued. "I may be able to carry you."

There was something in Mary's eyes now that Hannah had never seen before: a flicker of hope. It was faint, timid – as if Mary were afraid of daring to nurture such a thing after decades of relentless torment.

"Promise me you'll leave me in peace after this," Hannah said. "This room is *mine* now."

Again there was no acknowledgement, not in words at least, but Mary stepped forward, pressing close as if to embrace the other woman. Hannah felt the shock of sudden coldness infusing her whole body, like plunging into an icy pool.

There was a tingling through every limb and nerve ending, like pins and needles, and a moment of giddy lightheadedness. She braced herself against the wall until it passed.

When she opened her eyes, she could feel Mary *within* her body, like a whisper or a half-remembered melody; a living echo in the back of her mind, peering through her eyes and drinking in the world through her senses.

"Please, God," Hannah prayed as she walked toward the door. "Let this work. Set them both free."

The door opened easily. She stepped out, past Fannie and the other servants who all stood in the hallway like startled statues. She could see the unspoken questions clearly enough in their expressions, but Fannie's face held a glimmer of understanding, as if the older woman realized what was happening.

Mary and Hannah went together down the staircase, past empty rooms where whispering shadows watched them. Finally, they stepped out into a warm night alive with the song of crickets.

As she passed through the door, Hannah inhaled deeply, sucking in the fresh air as if it was her first breath in decades.

Another strange, cold tingle passed across her flesh as Mary left her body, marveling at the night and rejoicing at her newfound liberation.

Their eyes met only once, a brief glance of surprise and gratitude.

Then Mary turned, and Jim was standing there.

Hannah felt rage and pain transform into relief and joy as the spirits embraced beneath the glittering panoply of stars.

They moved as though dancing to music that only they could hear, turning in a slow waltz in the summer night. Their bodies seemed to mingle and merge as they twirled, from solid forms into phantom haze.

Hannah could hear their laughter, the faint joyful echo of voices.

Then, still wrapped in each other's arms, they faded into the night like smoke dissipating on a breeze.

Upstairs, in the window of Hannah's room, the spectral candle also vanished.

For a heartbeat there was an unbroken silence, as though the world were holding its breath. And then the crickets resumed their chirping, and everything continued on once more.

For a while, Hannah simply stood and stared at the stars, her tired mind and aching body readjusting to being solely hers once more. Eventually, she turned and made her way slowly back inside, feeling curiously alone, as if some part of her had forever been left behind in that garden.

Fannie was waiting for her just inside the door. "Is it all over?"

"I think so," Hannah said hopefully. "It feels different now."

"You gave us all quite a fright back there," Fannie admitted. "You're damn lucky the master of the house is away tonight; means we can keep this just between us."

"It all feels so strange now that she's gone," Hannah whispered.

"It sounds like the link between you is broken."

"I never thought I'd feel this way. I was so afraid of her, but in the end, she just needed a way out."

"I doubted that anyone could reach that girl."

Fannie gave Hannah a long, appraising look. "It's been quite a night. Now, shall we go get some sleep?"

Hannah nodded wearily. "I could sleep for days."

"Well, you've got four hours, child, give or take," Fannie chuckled.

"Better make the most of them."

Hannah let a smile cross her lips as the two women made their way quietly back up to the servants' quarters.

That curious sense of being watched continued to linger over the other rooms and hallways of Hale House for all the years that Hannah remained there.

Whatever secrets those walls held were as deeply imbued as the mortar and bricks that comprised the physical shell. But Hannah noted a distinct lightness within her little room from that day onward, as if a weight had been lifted from the atmosphere in that one spot.

The candle never returned while she continued to work there.

Nor did she think it ever would again.

Secret Room
1865

The Cursed Coin of Hale House
Jay Bower

With anticipation and an inkling of trepidation, Jack stood before Hale House, his family home.

A massive house built for his grandparents on the outskirts of New Orleans, it now belonged to him and his wife Sally after his parents were brutally murdered inside the old home.

He longed to wrap Sally in his arms, to find solace and comfort in her presence. It had been two and a half years since he had last seen her, since they shared their hopes and dreams for a future together.

The war had finally come to an end, and the Union emerged victorious, but at what cost? The thought of killing his brethren and spilling their blood on American soil twisted his sense of victory into a macabre dance of guilt and remorse, its horrors etched deep into his soul.

He had seen the darkest side of humanity, committed acts that haunted his every waking moment. The blood of countless soldiers stained his hands, and the atrocities he had witnessed haunted his dreams. No man should bear witness to such brutality.

But through it all, one thought kept him going: his unwavering desire to return to Hale House and his beloved Sally.

Months had passed since he last received a letter from her. At first, he dismissed it as a mere disruption in the delivery service, a consequence of the chaos of war.

But as time went on and the silence persisted, a gnawing worry settled in his heart. It clawed at his thoughts, whispering of unspeakable possibilities. The others in his regiment shared the same fate, their letters lost in the void of war. He'd received such terrible news in those letters and their sudden silence filled him with a chilling dread.

Now standing on the steps leading into his house, he could put all those fears away as his reunion with Sally awaited.

As Jack pushed open the heavy wooden door, he called out for Sally, his voice echoing through the empty halls.

Instead of the soft patter of her footsteps and the warm embrace he anticipated, he was greeted by Henry, the former slave turned caretaker he had entrusted to look after the house during his absence.

The man's presence brought a fleeting sense of relief, a familiar face in a world turned upside down.

"Jack? Sir, is that you? It's good to see you!" Henry's voice was filled with joy as he enveloped Jack in a bear hug.

But beneath his friendly demeanor, Jack sensed an undercurrent of unease.

Henry's solid frame had grown frail, and his bald head glistened with sweat. His eyes, once full of life, now held a hint of sorrow and fear, like when Jack's father, Dr. Jeremiah Hale, first rescued him from his pursuers.

"Henry, where's Sally?" Jack's voice trembled with anticipation, his heart pounding in his chest. He searched Henry's face for any sign, any glimpse of the truth he feared to hear.

Henry's gaze dropped, and he fidgeted nervously with his weathered hands. "Somethin' done happened to Ms. Sally," he muttered, the words barely audible.

Panic gripped Jack's chest, his breath caught in his throat. The world around him seemed to blur as he desperately clung to the hope that his worst fears were unfounded.

"The Confederates? Did those son-of-a-bitches hurt my Sally?"

His voice quivered with a mix of rage and fear, his mind conjuring images of unspeakable horrors inflicted upon his beloved.

"No, sir. None of those soldiers ever came up near here. Not like…not like them Union boys."

Jack dismissed the anger bubbling within. There was nothing he could do to change the awful past, the tragic massacre conducted in ignorance by those he fought alongside of.

"It's not good," Henry said, interrupting his thoughts.

"Please, sir, come with me, and I'll explain everything." Henry's voice was laden with sorrow, his brown eyes filled with unspoken truths.

A cold shiver ran down Jack's spine, a creeping sense of dread settling in. "Where is she?" he managed to choke out, his voice barely a whisper.

"Please, sir, come with me. I'll explain it all." Henry turned and headed toward the dining room, leaving Jack to grapple with the growing knot of fear in his gut.

The older man pulled a bottle of whiskey from the side table and set two cloudy glasses on the table. He filled both to the top and gestured for Jack to sit.

"I don't like all this subterfuge. Tell me where my wife is."

Jack's voice trembled as he lifted the whiskey to his lips, his hand shaking uncontrollably. The amber liquid burned its way down his throat, an unpleasant sensation that mirrored the emptiness inside.

"I really hate to be the one to tell you this. Sally…" Henry began, pausing to take a swig from his glass, downing half of it in one gulp. "Sally is gone, sir."

"Gone? Where'd she go?" Jack's voice cracked with desperation, his eyes pleading for an answer.

Henry waved his hand dismissively. "Go? It's... how do I say this delicately... she's gone, sir. She passed on."

The glass slipped from Jack's grasp, crashing onto the wooden table, the whiskey spilling in all directions. His hands clenched into fists as if to hold back the crushing weight of the news.

"Passed?" he whispered.

He closed his eyes, desperately trying to conjure an image of Sally in his mind. The last memory he had of her was the day he left for the war, her standing at the door in a white cotton dress and a matching hat with a green ribbon. She had dusted on some powder and added a touch of rouge that morning, a rarity reserved for special occasions.

Throughout his time in the war, the thought of returning to her was his sole motivation, his beacon of hope amid darkness. Leaving Sally had been the hardest thing he had ever done, and the longing to see her again had fueled his every action, keeping him alive.

Jack sat in silence, the weight of Henry's words echoing in his mind, amplifying his grief with each passing second.

Henry rushed to the kitchen, grabbing a towel to clean up the spilled whiskey. When he returned, he stroked his beard and winced, the words he was about to speak causing him obvious discomfort.

"I'm not sure how to put this," Henry hesitated, his voice strained.

"Just speak!" Jack's anguished cry filled the room. The torment of uncertainty twisted his insides, the burning whiskey doing little to quell his

Jay Bower

mounting anxiety.

Henry clasped his hands together, his eyes filled with sorrowful empathy. "Well, sir, she took her own life. Upstairs." His eyes darted upwards.

"What? No, that can't be," Jack whispered, his mind struggling to comprehend the unimaginable. Sally had her moments of emotional outbursts, like when the crows ravaged their sunflower garden, but the depths of despair required to take one's own life seemed inconceivable.

That wasn't the Sally he knew.

Henry pressed on; his voice laced with a heavy sigh. "When I couldn't find her anywhere in the house, I remembered the secret room upstairs. You know, the one that leads off the bedroom? I don't know why I hadn't thought of it before. But the moment I opened the door, the odor overwhelmed me, and I knew what I'd find would not be pleasant."

Jack's head shook in disbelief. Why would she do such a thing? None of her letters had indicated any unusual melancholy. He knew she was lonely and burdened by the absence caused by the war, but he had always believed their love could endure. The trials of battle were expected, and he had convinced himself that Sally would wait patiently, anchoring herself to the hope of their reunion. Jack's voice wavered as he spoke in a soft tone, his words a plea for understanding.

"How did you know she took her own life?"

Henry wiped his hands on his pants, the act an attempt to regain composure. He took a deep, steadying breath before replying. "The noose around her neck was tied to the rafters. She was a-swaying from it."

Jack hung his head, his sorrow deepening. The weight of his absence from home, the shattered dreams of starting a family and opening a general store with Sally, now suffocated him. The war had torn him away, forging a wedge between them that he couldn't bear. The words from her last letter echoed in his mind, a chilling refrain that took on a newfound significance: "I can't stand your absence. It's driving me mad."

At the time, amidst the imminent danger on the battlefield, he hadn't dwelled on it. He had believed she was safe, sheltered from the horrors he faced.

Henry stood up and placed a consoling hand on Jack's shoulder.

"She's buried out back if you want to say your goodbyes."

In a haze of grief, Jack grabbed the bottle of whiskey, sloshed its contents into his mouth, and drank deeply, seeking solace in its burn. With a nod, he acknowledged Henry's suggestion and carried the bottle with him, a companion in his darkest hours.

As they walked toward the back of the property where his family had erected a small graveyard, Jack's eyes caught sight of a newly placed gravestone, a cross made of granite. Its presence sent a shiver down his spine.

Henry gestured toward the marker with a gentle wave of his hand and stepped back, leaving Jack alone in the company of the pitted gray cross.

Jack's trembling lip quivered, his grip tightening on the bottle as he took another swig, seeking courage from the numbing effects of the whiskey. But the burn only dulled the edges of his pain; it couldn't erase the profound loss that engulfed him.

"Oh, my love. I'm so sorry," Jack choked out between sips, his words a lament whispered into the wind.

"I thought about you every day."

He dropped to his knees, clutching the cross adorning the grave. His body convulsed with raw anguish, the sorrow unleashed and unrestrained.

Sally, his love, his everything, now lay buried beneath the ground, forever lost to him.

Jack remained by the grave until the sun retreated, swallowed by the encroaching darkness, the bottle he clung to now empty. It was then that footsteps interrupted his solitary vigil, jolting him back to the harrowing memories of war. His heart raced, his body poised for combat, until he recognized the familiar presence of Henry.

"Dinner is almost ready," Henry offered, extending a hand to pull Jack up. Jack left the empty bottle leaning against Sally's grave and allowed himself to be led inside, a mere shell of a man.

Seated at the dining room table, Jack's stomach rumbled, yet the anticipation of a home-cooked meal was tinged with a melancholic unease.

Henry reappeared, his hands laden with dishes, and spoke with a quiet resolve.

"You need to eat. It will help you feel better."

He placed a plate of roast chicken, potatoes, and warm bread before Jack. The aroma tantalized his senses, a reminder of the nourishment he had long been denied.

Summoning every ounce of strength, Jack took a hesitant bite of the bread, its warmth providing a fleeting respite. Bite after bite, he consumed the sustenance before him, each morsel tinged with guilt and grief.

As Henry remained silent, Jack's mind wandered to Sally, contemplating the unbearable weight she must have carried in her final days. The loneliness and the agonizing fear of never seeing him again were the only explanation for the unthinkable act she committed.

Guilt wrapped around Jack's heart like a suffocating vine, pulling him deeper into the abyss of sorrow. The weight of his absence gnawed at his conscience, tormenting him with relentless whispers of what might have been. If only he had been there, the love of his life would still be alive, and the darkness that consumed her would have been vanquished.

After dinner, Jack ascended the creaking stairs to his bedroom, his weary body succumbing to exhaustion amid an uncontrollable outpouring of tears.

He collapsed onto the bed, his sobs mingling with the haunting echoes of his grief. Sleep found him, offering a temporary respite from his mental torment, but it was a slumber veiled in darkness.

In the middle of the night, he was rudely tormented by a powerful dream.

Sally materialized in his dream, her delicate form suspended from a noose, her tear-streaked face contorted in agony.

She reached out for him, her desperate cries piercing the air, but no matter how he strained, he was always too far away, forever out of reach.

The visceral horror of the nightmare shook him awake, leaving him gasping for breath, his heart pounding.

His trembling hands wiped the cold sweat from his brow, leaving a clammy residue on his skin. The room felt stifling, each corner holding secrets that churned his stomach with unease.

His gaze involuntarily shifted toward the concealed entrance to the secret room upstairs, a place shrouded in darkness and hidden histories.

The room had been a surprise revelation, a discovery born from childhood innocence.

Jack and his brother stumbled upon it during a playful exploration of the house, only to be met with his father's stern reproach for delving into forbidden territories.

It wasn't until later, when he had grown older, that the truth unraveled before him like a tapestry of horrors.

His father had utilized the secret room to inflict unspeakable torture in the name of medicine upon runaway slaves – like Henry, a man Jack took pity on and offered the position of caretaker after Dr. Hale's death.

The knowledge settled uneasily within Jack's mind, intertwining with the chilling visions that plagued his sleep.

The grim past of that hidden space resonated with the haunting fate of Sally, as if the room itself had absorbed the anguish of those who suffered within its walls.

A shudder coursed through Jack's weary frame as he contemplated the darkness that lay beyond the concealed passage. It was as if the room beckoned to him, whispering secrets too terrible to comprehend.

For close to an hour, Jack remained seated on the edge of the bed, his thoughts engulfed in a maelstrom of torment and trepidation. Sleep eluded him. Fear had made a home within his soul.

The room held a different memory now, one that pierced through Jack's sorrow like a dagger.

The image of Sally's lifeless body, swaying from the rafters, haunted his thoughts.

What demons had pushed her to such depths of despair? He couldn't bear the thought that his prolonged absence had driven her to this unimaginable act.

Driven by a mixture of grief, guilt, and a desperate need for answers, Jack rose from the bed, his legs trembling with each step towards the hidden passageway.

Grabbing a tallow candle from his dresser, Jack lit the wick.

A chill permeated the air as he reached the entrance, the musty scent of secrecy mingling with the anguish that filled his heart.

With a trembling hand, he pushed aside the false wall, revealing the narrow stairway that led to the hidden room upstairs.

As he ascended the staircase, the dim light of his candle illuminated the room's haunting relics above. The remnants of his family's dark past mingled with the fresh memory of Sally's tragic end.

Jack's mind was a battleground of emotions, his steps faltering as he approached the top of the stairs. He hesitated, afraid of what he might find.

Summoning every ounce of courage he had left, Jack stepped out on the landing and a wave of stale air engulfed him.

The room stood before him, silent and foreboding, like a vault of secrets refusing to be forgotten.

His eyes were drawn to the spot where Sally's life had been extinguished, the noose still hanging from the wooden beam and the vivid dream etched into his mind forever.

"Oh, Sally," Jack said, his voice choked with anguish.

A wave of agony crashed over him, tears streaming down his face like a ceaseless river. His trembling steps carried him toward the noose, each creak of the wooden floor echoing the weight of his despair.

He reached out, his fingers grazing the thick rope that had claimed the life of his beloved.

The haunting nightmare that had jolted him awake resurfaced in his mind, causing him to recoil. His hand trembled, and he pulled it back, a mixture of fear and grief coursing through his veins.

Jack stood frozen, half-expecting the silhouette of Sally's lifeless form to sway from the noose, but only the flickering candle and a biting draft greeted him.

In the dimness, a glimmer caught his attention. Jack's heart raced, pounding against his chest at the sight, fearing it might be some lurking creature of the night.

Lowering the candle, he realized the truth, and grief surged within him like a relentless tide.

It was the wedding coin he had bestowed upon Sally during their sacred union, a cherished symbol of their love given to him by his father to pass on as was the family tradition.

Now it lay abandoned, a silent testament to the irrevocable loss he had suffered.

With trembling hands, he wiped away his tears and gently retrieved the coin, holding it close to his heart.

The weight of the coin seemed to magnify the burden that had settled upon him. It felt as though an oppressive force had taken hold of him, suffocating him in its grip.

The need for fresh air consumed him, an urgent desire to escape the confines of the room and the lingering presence of grief.

Leaving the room behind, Jack hurriedly made his way to his bedroom, closing the door to his grief. The darkness enveloped him, offering little respite from the weight of his sorrow.

The candle sputtered and he set it back down on the dresser. He collapsed onto the bed, clutching the coin tightly against his chest.

The flickering candle beside him cast dancing shadows, only to extinguish with a final, fleeting breath. In the ensuing darkness, grief pressed down upon his soul like a leaden shroud. Exhaustion overtook him, and he surrendered to the abyss of unconsciousness once again.

A sudden clatter echoed through the room, jolting Jack awake from his fitful slumber. His wide eyes strained to make sense of his surroundings, a sense of disorientation clouding his thoughts.

"Where am I?" he murmured. The memory of the house and its secrets momentarily eluded him, shrouded in a haze of uncertainty.

"Who's on watch?" he instinctively wondered, the remnants of war etched deeply within his consciousness.

As his heartbeat thundered in his ears, clarity pierced through the fog of his confusion. Home. He was home. The battles were over, but the absence of Sally left the once-familiar manor now hollow and desolate.

Gradually, Jack's eyes adjusted to the darkness, and he noticed the door to the secret room open, a silent invitation into the depths of its forbidden secrets. His father had always insisted on its closure, for secret rooms maintained their power only when hidden from prying eyes.

Memories of the atrocities committed within those walls returned, a chilling reminder of the horrors that had transpired in that hidden space.

The air grew heavy with a foreboding presence, and Jack couldn't shake the feeling that something sinister lingered beyond that threshold, waiting to ensnare him in its clutches.

He quietly closed the door.

Moments later, heavy thuds reverberated through the house as Henry trudged up the stairs. The weight of his steps echoed with an unsettling cadence, amplifying the growing sense of unease.

From the hallway, his concerned voice pierced the silence, seeping into Jack's troubled mind.

"Sir? Jack? Are you okay? Is there something wrong?" Henry's words hung in the air. Jack crossed the room, his hand instinctively retrieving the wedding coin before he opened the door.

"I thought I heard a noise. I fear memories from the battlefield returned in the night," Jack admitted.

"Aye," Henry replied.

The candle in his hand flickered, casting an eerie glow on the man's face.

"In time, I expect the horrors will release you from their grip. Time has a way of healing things."

Jack held up the coin, twirling it in his fingers.

"I don't know if it will heal what ails me."

Henry gazed at the coin for a moment, his expression solemn. "I'm here for whatever you need, sir."

"Thank you."

Waiting for Henry's departing footsteps to fade down the stairs, Jack closed the door and returned to his bed. With great care, he placed the coin beneath his pillow, seeking solace in its proximity. The loss of that connection to Sally was a wound too deep to bear.

As the morning light seeped through the slit in the heavy curtains, gradually illuminating the room, Jack reluctantly joined the realm of the waking.

The tantalizing scent of bacon drifted in, teasing his senses, but his appetite waned beneath the weight of his sorrow.

Reaching under his pillow, Jack's heart skipped a beat as he realized the wedding coin was gone. Panic coursed through his veins, his throat constricting in dry disbelief. Frantically, he tossed the pillow aside, tearing up the sheets and flinging the blanket aside in a desperate search.

But the coin was nowhere to be found.

A dark, suffocating pit grew in Jack's stomach, its tendrils of despair wrapping around his very being. His knees weakened beneath him, threatening to give way. No, this couldn't be happening. Where had it gone?

And then his eyes fell upon the open door to the secret room, a sinister invitation lurking in the shadows. A shiver of dread raced up his spine.

"I closed this," he whispered, a tremor of fear lacing his voice.

The stolen coin and the mysteriously opened secret room converged in his mind. A sickening sensation settled in, suspicions taking root. Had Henry snuck into his room, seized the coin, and stolen the precious token of his love for Sally?

Jack bounded down the stairs, anger pulsating within him. "What games are you playing with me? Hand it over!" he demanded as he entered the kitchen, his voice quivering with a mix of accusation and desperation.

Henry turned from the stove, wooden spoon in hand, his face etched with confusion. The sizzling of bacon and the aroma of eggs permeated the air. "I don't know nothin' about what you're askin', sir," Henry replied, his voice soft but genuine.

"The coin! Hand it over. It doesn't belong to you," Jack seethed, his finger jabbing accusingly in Henry's chest.

"I promise you, I didn't take a thing."

Jack didn't know what to do. Where had it gone and why was the door opened?

Jack spent the rest of the day consumed by his desperate search for the coin. It was the last remaining thread connecting him to Sally, and the thought of losing it felt like a second death, an unbearable anguish. He had to find it, for his own sanity and for the preservation of their love.

As the sun dipped beneath the horizon, casting its final rays of light, Henry lit the tallow candles, casting eerie shadows that danced along the walls. The nocturnal symphony of owls and coyotes echoed through the darkness, a haunting chorus that mirrored Jack's growing dread. Still, despite his relentless efforts, the coin eluded him.

The loss carved a deeper pit in Jack's stomach with each passing moment. It was a void that threatened to swallow him whole, for nothing could replace Sally, but the tangible symbol of their love held immeasurable significance. Late into the night, long after Henry had retired to bed, Jack ascended the stairs to his room.

When he opened the door, a sudden, powerful thump reverberated against the secret door, causing Jack to stumble backward. A lump formed in his throat, his voice quivering as he summoned the courage to speak.

"Who... who's there?" he managed to utter, his heart pounding in his chest. Another thump sounded, jolting him to the core. Slowly, he moved toward the door.

With trembling hands, he reached for the secret lever. He swallowed hard, steeling himself. Hesitation gave way to curiosity, and with a deep breath, Jack pulled the lever, the false wall shifting and the door creaking open to reveal an otherworldly glow pulsing in the room above.

Creeping up the creaky stairs, Jack's senses heightened, his heart pounding like the rhythmic strikes of a blacksmith's hammer. "Hello?" he called out, his voice laced with trepidation. A faint blue glow shimmered in response, sending a trickle of sweat cascading down his spine. "Who's here?" he dared to ask.

"Release me," a disembodied female voice echoed back, its ethereal quality sending a chill down Jack's spine.

Sally? he thought. He stumbled back, his arms flailing before finding support on a wooden post, preventing him from tumbling down the stairs.

"Release me," the voice repeated, each syllable slow and hauntingly breathy.

Jack's eyes darted around the secret room, scanning every inch for his beloved, yet there was no physical presence save for the enigmatic glow emanating from the far corner.

"I must be hearing things. This isn't real," Jack whispered to himself, trying to anchor his fraying sanity. Determined to unravel the mysterious phenomenon, he ventured toward the ethereal blue glow, step by cautious step, careful to avoid the noose hanging from the beam overhead.

When he finally reached the far end of the room, his breath caught in his throat, his hand instinctively covering his mouth to stifle a gasp.

There, lying on the floor next to a wooden box of tools, bathed in a smoky luminescence, was the wedding coin. Its surface danced with an otherworldly light, evoking a primal fear within Jack. He longed to grasp it, to reclaim what he'd lost.

Then, from behind him, the sound of creaking wood filled the air. Jack's heart raced as he spun around, only to be met with a chilling sight. Before him floated an apparition resembling Sally. She hovered off the floor, her form bathed in the same eerie glow as the coin. Jack yelped.

"You must release me," she pleaded, her voice tinged with panic and her face etched with fear. A tremor ran through Jack's body as he observed her raised hand, from which long, ethereal ribbons like strips of flesh floated.

"It's awful here," her voice, a distorted echo of what it once was, filled the air, sending a chill down Jack's spine. Her hair flowed as if submerged in water, defying gravity.

"What do you want? What can I do?" Jack managed to utter.

"The coin," she pleaded, pointing behind him. "Please, you have to release me. Before it's too late."

His gaze shifted between the ethereal Sally and the coin, uncertainty clouding his mind. "What happened?" he stammered, trying to grasp the incomprehensible.

Then another spirit emerged from the shadows, making Jack quake. It was his father, Dr. Jeremiah Hale.

"Hand it over," his father said.

The disembodied voice of the dead man echoed through the room, his spectral form hovering just inches above the floor.

Jack hesitated, his hand trembling as he held the coin up, its weight and significance now more bewildering than ever. The sight of his father, transformed and menacing, sent a surge of dread coursing through Jack's veins.

"This is madness. It can't be real," Jack muttered, his voice barely audible.

A sinister smile spread across Dr. Hale's face. "It's as real as it gets. Now hand over that coin, and all will be well."

Jack's mind raced, desperately trying to make sense of the unfolding nightmare. Why did the spirits of the dead crave the coin? Couldn't they have just taken it before? How could a mere piece of metal hold such significance?

"You killed her, didn't you?" Jack asked, the thought surfacing in his mind.

Dr. Hale smiled wider. "How do you suppose a spirit can tie a noose around the neck of the living?"

Henry! Jack thought, growling. His father must have put Henry up to it. Even in death he held sway over the man.

Reluctantly, Jack clutched the coin tightly, his fingers trembling with uncertainty. "What will happen if I destroy it?" he asked.

Dr. Hale's gaze locked onto Jack, his eyes burning with an intensity that made Jack's blood run cold.

"No son of mine would dare defy me."

Sally's voice resonated in Jack's ears, urging him on. "Don't listen to him, Jack. Break the curse. Save me. If you give it to him, I am his forever."

Jack stood there, caught between the twisted desires of his father and the desperate pleas of his beloved Sally. The sense of dread intensified, permeating the air as the room seemed to shrink around him.

"Don't give it to him! If you do, all is lost. If you don't give him the coin, there is hope for me." Sally's voice cried out.

Dr. Hale's face contorted with rage, his eyes blazing crimson. "Shut up, girl!" he screamed, his voice reverberating with an otherworldly resonance. "This is between family. Keep your harlot's mouth shut."

Jack's heart pounded in his chest. Memories flickered through his mind, the realization dawning upon him that he had unwittingly played a part in binding Sally to this cursed existence when he willingly accepted the coin and gave it to her. How could he have known then what he was doing?

"Why do you want this so bad?" Jack's voice trembled as he dared to confront his father, his eyes locked onto the twisted figure before him.

"Don't question me, son," Dr. Hale sneered, his features contorting into a sinister grin. "Give it over and you can live. Forget her," he said with his gaze locked onto Sally.

"Leave her to me."

Sally's voice echoed in the room, her words filled with urgency and desperation. "It's an evil trick! It's what keeps me here. If he has it, I can never find peace."

A surge of realization washed over Jack as he recalled the moment he had presented the coin to Sally, his father's gleeful celebration ringing in his ears. The pieces of the puzzle fell into place, revealing the dark truth behind his father's intentions.

"What is this?" Jack's hand trembled as he held the coin up. "What did you make me do?"

Dr. Logan's laughter cut through the air, a chilling sound that sent shivers down Jack's spine. "I preserved her for myself for all time. It's an ancient family rite," he hissed.

Jack's mind reeled, struggling to comprehend the depth of his father's depravity. The coin, a symbol of love and commitment, had become a vessel for an unholy bond, a curse trapping Sally's spirit in this nightmarish existence.

A sudden commotion erupted as Henry, fueled by his master's command, lunged at Jack.

The two collided, crashing to the floor in a whirlwind of desperate struggle. Pain surged through Jack's body, and the battlefield memories that haunted his past resurfaced, intertwining with the present.

Dr. Hale's cruel laughter pierced through the chaos, driving Jack to fight with renewed vigor. Memories of survival and valor surged through his veins, lending him strength.

With a surge of determination, he managed to free himself from Henry's grasp.

Gasping for breath, Jack rose to his feet, his gaze locked on his father's twisted face. The coin lay on the floor near Sally's ethereal form.

"Please, let me go," Sally pleaded.

Dr. Hale's features contorted and transformed, his monstrous nature revealing itself fully. His elongated face bore rows of needle-like teeth, and his eyes burned with an insatiable hunger.

In a voice that resonated with malevolence, he bellowed, "Give me the coin! She belongs to me now!"

Jack's heart raced, but a newfound resolve coursed through his veins. With trembling hands, he reached for the wedding coin, the symbol of their love turned instrument of torment. He held it out before him, its radiant glow casting an eerie light on the room.

"Is this what both of you want?" Jack's voice quivered with a mix of desperation and determination.

"Release me, my dear. Let me rest in peace," Sally implored.

"Give me the coin and walk away. Leave here and never come back." Dr. Hale's voice dripped with venom. "Find another whore to bed. Leave this one to me."

Those words hung in the air like a curse, shattering the remnants of Jack's reality. The love he had fought for, the dreams they had shared, all twisted into a grotesque nightmare. Dread seeped into his bones, chilling him to the core. Nothing was as it should have been.

Tears welled in Jack's eyes as he gazed upon Sally's transformed spirit.

"Sally," Jack's voice quivered, his heart aching with a bittersweet farewell. "I love you."

With a deep breath, Jack made his decision.

Gripping the coin tightly, he raised it above his head, his gaze unwavering as he stared at his father's spectral figure.

"If this will truly end this torment, then so be it," he declared, his voice filled with a newfound resolve.

In an instant, the air around him grew heavy, a palpable tension enveloping the room. The ethereal glow intensified, casting an eerie light on Jack's determined face. He clutched the coin, his heart pounding in his chest.

He lunged past Sally and grabbed a hammer that had poked out of the toolbox. And then, with a mighty force, Jack smashed the coin with the hammer, unleashing a wave of energy that reverberated through the room. Jack pounded the coin, each strike creating a brilliant flash of light. Then a sound like a cannon forced him to stop.

Dr. Hale's screams echoed in the room. Sally's ethereal form contorted and shifted, her fragmented existence reclaiming its lost harmony.

The strips of flesh retreated, her features reconstructed. Her wild cry pierced the air as she glowed with an intensity that defied the mortal realm.

Dr. Hale's wails transformed into a string of curses, his malevolent power shattered by the force of Sally's liberation.

"Goodbye, my love." Jack slammed the hammer down on the coin.

In a blinding burst of brilliance, Sally exploded into a radiant sphere of light.

Jack's father yelled, then fell silent.

As the light subsided, Jack's surroundings became hazy, his vision blurred. He blinked, attempting to clear his sight. When it returned, he realized his father was gone, vanished like a ghostly specter. Only Jack and Henry remained, locked in a chilling confrontation.

"You," Jack snarled. "You did this!" He stepped toward the man, anger boiling within at his betrayal.

Henry's eyes widened with a mix of fear and guilt. "He made me! I had no choice," he said as he retreated. Reaching the top of the stairs, he spun around and raced down as he made his escape.

Jack trembled, his mind reeling from the intensity of the supernatural encounter. Was it over? Had he succeeded in breaking the curse? The absence of the spirits seemed to suggest so, yet a lingering unease persisted within him.

His eyes drifted to the spot on the floor where he had smashed the coin. It lay charred and mangled, remnants of the powerful release of energy that had just transpired. The significance of the coin, its connection to the spirits, remained shrouded in mystery.

A profound stillness settled on Jack as he stood amidst the remnants of his shattered world.

The weight of betrayal and loss bore heavily on his soul. The significance of what had transpired eluded him, the true meaning buried beneath layers of pain and confusion.

With a heavy sigh, Jack raised the now disfigured coin to his weary eyes, whispering a farewell to his lost love.

Tenderly, he tucked the coin into his pocket, sealing away the remnants of their entwined fate.

"I hope you're free. I will always love you." Jack's thoughts echoed in the empty room. With a solemn determination, he closed the door to the secret chamber, leaving behind the haunting memories.

As he descended downstairs, an uncertain path lay before him.

Whatever awaited him in the unknown, he would face it alone, his heart forever imprinted with the memory of Sally's love.

The wounds inflicted by his father's betrayal ran deep, leaving scars that time alone could attempt to heal.

The world outside beckoned, and Jack stepped forward, his spirit forged by sorrow, yet strengthened by the enduring power of love.

There was still one task left undone, Henry's fate forever sealed for his part in the terrible deed.

Widow's Walk
1955

The House Takes
Marie Lanza

Victoria's heart pounded in her chest as she stared into one of the two chimneys that bracketed the widow's walk of her house. When she stepped up on the ornate ledge that ran around the chimney, she could lean over the edge and stare down into the bowels of the home.

Her eyes were swollen red, and tears streamed down her cheeks. The night draped itself in a cloak of darkness, swallowing the moon and the stars, leaving Victoria in a realm devoid of light and hope. A cold wind whispered, carrying with it an icy touch that sent shivers down her spine.

As she peered down into the gaping maw of the chimney, a suffocating silence fell over the night, as if the world held its breath waiting for unspeakable horrors. The void within the chimney seemed to pulse with an otherworldly energy, beckoning her closer, an invitation Victoria struggled to resist as raw fear gnawed at her soul.

Her trembling hand traveled over her pregnant belly, then extended toward the void, the chilling air tugging at her fingers, as if a sinister force yearned to claim her. The darkness within the chimney grew deeper, only promising despair and dread – and ending it all.

"Victoriaaaaa…" A whisper from the abyss.

Victoria sobbed, terrified this evil would take her, but also wanting it to.

Her heart hammered against her ribs, its rhythm echoing in her ears, drowning out rational thought.

"Victoria!"

Victoria's breath caught in her throat and her eyes shot open, her body drenched in a cold sweat. She clutched her belly, looked up to her husband's face painted with concern. They were lying in bed.

"Another nightmare?" he asked.

"Yes," she whispered.

Eric gently touched her belly. "The doctor said this was pretty normal in the later stages." He kissed her cheek and got out of bed. "I'll go get you some water."

The doctor did say that, but Victoria had only been having these nightmares since they moved into the house – Hale House, it was called. Not that she hated it, she loved it, but there was just something… From the outside it was an imposing figure that whispered of stories untold, secrets locked within its timeworn walls.

When they first arrived, she couldn't explain the peculiar sensation that settled on her as she approached the estate. It was as if invisible tendrils reached out and gently guided her in. After being here for a few weeks it was like the house embraced her and wanted to keep her – she felt – safe, but trapped in a way she could not describe.

But the doctor explained those feelings away too.

"Lots of new parents have worries, fears, when they're expecting. And those worries get translated differently in our minds. To some, marriage makes people feel tied down. Some might say, babies bring the same feelings," he said simply.

Victoria walked over to her window. The sun was beginning to rise, bringing with it pastels of pinks and purples. She loved this view, an eternal landscape like a painting of a perfect moment.

She cradled her belly, though it was more of a habit than a connection. Victoria didn't know why it wasn't there; she and Eric had been looking forward to the arrival of their boy or girl—they didn't have a preference.

Though, after years of trying, Victoria had started to give up hope. Maybe she was guarding her heart from the previous losses. *Maybe she was resentful*, she thought.

The door creaked open. Startled, Victoria turned around, not expecting Eric back so quickly –but there was nothing.

"Eric?" she said without raising her voice.

"Victoriaaaaa…" A whisper from the fireplace.

Victoria's eyes shot over to the sound, feeling pulled by the same dread she had in her nightmare. The fireplace loomed like a shadowy keeper of secrets.

"Honey?"

Victoria gasped.

"Are you alright?" Eric asked as he crossed the room and handed her a glass of water.

Victoria took a sip. "I'm fine…" she lied.

"That nightmare really got to you." He gently rubbed her back.

"I think it's just a mix of everything… baby coming, new house. We're barely unpacked."

Eric kissed her forehead. "You sure you'll be okay today? I can stay home and…"

Victoria knew he didn't really want to stay. It felt more of an action, his duty. "No, no, I'm fine."

"Alright." He kissed her again. "I'm gonna go get dressed and head out."

As Eric left the bedroom, Victoria's eyes remained on the fireplace.

∞

Victoria's brush moved with graceful precision as she worked, filling in the details of the landscape below onto her canvas. She was wearing a tan-colored smock, her long, dark hair pulled back from her face. The sun set in the distant sky, silhouetting the house and Victoria in a warm, golden light.

They bought the house as a fixer upper. Eric was so thrilled when he found it – a new project he could dive into. Victoria had been hesitant, unsure if it was the right thing for them, maybe even intimidated by the size of it. Being pregnant, she couldn't imagine adding this on top of getting ready for the baby's arrival.

Once Victoria did look at the house, she instantly fell in love with what she assumed was an extra porch – the widow's walk, the realtor had called it. At first she thought, what a dreadful name. When she commented to the realtor, she explained why they had been popular in coastal communities. It was said to have come from the wives of sailors who would watch and wait for their husbands to return, but most never did – making them widows. The space was beautiful, perched atop the home, stretching across the roof, and reaching the chimneys on opposite sides of the house. The iron railings twisted and curled around as if they were alive. The perfect place to take in the view, breathe in the fresh air, and enjoy the quiet serenity overlooking the estate.

Eric climbed up to the widow's walk. His eyes caught the canvas placed on the easel standing alone on the center of the roof. Then he laid eyes on Victoria; she was near the chimney looking into it, her paintbrush in hand gently rocking back and forth. "Honey?"

Victoria, startled. "Oh… I didn't see you come home." Confusion draped over her. "I don't think I even heard you pull in."

Eric looked at the canvas; a beautiful view from the walk overlooking the landscape was coming together. He stood next to Victoria. "Whatcha looking at?" he asked as he looked down into the chimney and gently rubbed her back. When he touched her, he could feel her body stiffen slightly.

"I hear something… something struggling, scratches maybe? Do you think an animal could be stuck down there?"

Eric nodded his head as he thought about it. "Maybe. I hope not because if it dies it's going to smell," he chuckled at himself.

Victoria heard it again. "Do you hear that?" she asked.

Eric listened. "Sorry honey, I don't hear anything."

Victoria scoffed and looked at him, then back into the chimney. "You don't hear it?"

Eric shrugged it off and dismissed her concern. "I'll check it out a bit later. Dinner?" he asked as he made his way to the stairs.

"I'll be down in a bit," she said without looking at him.

"You sure you're alright?" Eric asked. "You should eat something."

Victoria's face fell. She didn't know if she was alright. She didn't even know how long she had been standing by the chimney before Eric came home. How long had she been standing there? Last she remembered she was painting but she didn't feel she could tell Eric this. He would think she was being hysterical.

Her mind raced around and suddenly went blank… then she bent over. "No…"

"No?" questioned Eric absently as he started down the stairs. Then he realized Victoria was holding her belly. "Baby? Already?"

"Oh my God, Eric, the baby!"

∞

Victoria lay on her back in the hospital bed screaming to the heavens as her body felt like it was splitting open. She gave a final push with all the energy she had left. Eric stood by her side, holding her hand and giving her words of encouragement.

"It's a girl!" the doctor shared.

But she never heard the baby cry. "Is she okay?" Victoria asked breathlessly.

Eric kissed Victoria on the forehead and praised what a great job she did. The doctor stepped to the bedside and laid the baby girl on Victoria's chest.

"What are we naming her?" Eric asked with a smile, and Victoria noticed tears in his eyes.

They hadn't landed on a name yet, thinking something would stick as they got closer to delivery, but nothing had. "Haley." Victoria said. It hit her suddenly at that moment. Victoria thought about the house. Hale House. It wanted her and so she should honor it, honor the future they would have in their new house.

"Haley. Beautiful, just like her mother." Eric kissed Victoria again.

∞

When they arrived home, the weight of everything that needed to get done grew heavy on Victoria. The nursery still had so much work, but she tried to remind herself Haley would spend most of her time in their bedroom in a bassinet anyway, so they had plenty of time.

Plenty of time, Victoria repeated to herself. *It'll all come together. It doesn't have to be perfect.*

"I have a caregiver starting tomorrow," Eric said as he watched Victoria meander around the room putting things away. "Someone to help."

"On such short notice?" Victoria was surprised but grateful.

"With me going back to work, I didn't want you to be alone. She'll just stay during the day, help with whatever you need to get back on your feet."

"Where did you find her? Shouldn't this have been something we discussed?"

"I'm sorry, honey. I thought I was being helpful. I've been working so much, and we weren't expecting Haley... so soon." He paused, then said, "Of course, what was I thinking? You're right, we should have discussed it. I was just trying to..."

"Be helpful," Victoria said.

"Yes, be helpful. While we were at the hospital, I made some phone calls, and this agency came recommended by one of my colleagues. Said to have the best homecare in the area."

"Okay, we can try them out," Victoria said.

The next morning, when Victoria woke, Eric was already gone. She was a bit taken aback that Haley hadn't woken her. Victoria popped up to look in the bassinet – Haley wasn't there.

Victoria made her way downstairs when she heard the humming of a woman. In the living room, the caregiver – Victoria assumed – was cleaning the kitchen.

"Good morning, ma'am. I'm Rebecca. Eric said he didn't want to wake you."

"Please, call me Victoria. I'm going to go get some things done upstairs in the nursery," Victoria said, and before Rebecca could respond she was already making her way back up the stairs.

Marie Lanza

Victoria spent several hours in the nursery, unpacking boxes, putting away the tiny clothes and diapers. She sat down in the rocking chair next to the crib and gazed in.

"Ma'am..." Rebecca gently knocked on the door.

"Come in. And please, call me Victoria." She gave a forced smile.

"Of course."

"Is there something particular you'd like me to focus on? I can help you with this room if you'd like or…" Rebecca asked.

Victoria gave another forced smile. "You're doing it, you being here is helpful. I'd like to do this room myself."

"Of course." Rebecca gave a gentle smile and she looked at the crib. I'll leave you to it. Please let me know when you need me." Rebecca left the room without waiting for Victoria to respond.

Victoria leaned back in the rocking chair and longingly looked at the crib. She felt like the weight of the world was on her shoulders with everything motherhood brought. To make a child feel loved, and to keep them safe. All the things a mother instinctively does.

The problem was, Victoria hadn't felt those instincts yet and she wondered when they'd hit her. *Maybe they come later for some women*, she thought. Maybe they don't come at all. But she pushed that worry down. *Maybe they will come later.*

A creak from the floor in the hallway brought Victoria back from her thoughts. Her eyes caught a shadow cross by the bottom of the door. Victoria figured Rebecca was quietly checking to see if she needed anything, and maybe Rebecca didn't want to bother her while she was with Haley. Victoria hadn't realized how long she'd been sitting in the nursery. Haley was such a quiet baby, and easy, she thought.

As Victoria crossed the room to leave, a shadow passed the door again, another creak came with the steps. She opened the door and said, "I'm finished Rebecca..." The hallway was empty. She stood there, listening for the sound, but was only met with silence.

Victoria walked downstairs to find Rebecca in the library. "Rebecca, were you just upstairs?" she asked.

Rebecca shook her head no, and said, "I've just been straightening up a bit. I'm sorry if I didn't hear you call."

"I didn't. Is there someone else here?"

"No one. Are you expecting a visitor?

"No…"

238

"Is everything okay?" Rebecca asked.

Victoria looked around. "Yes, it's fine. I just thought I heard someone."

"Old houses." Rebecca smiled.

Old houses, Victoria thought. "I'm going upstairs."

It was a beautiful afternoon and Victoria was happy to have a few hours to herself to paint. She sat on her stool in front of her canvas, soaking in the warmth of the sun, and took in a deep breath of the fresh air. Victoria gave her painting a long look to decide where she wanted to continue; she was half finished with this piece.

"Victoriaaaaa…" A whisper from the chimney.

Victoria froze and listened, but nothing came after. She stood up and slowly approached the chimney.

"Victoria?"

She turned around quickly to find Eric, and then she noticed the sun had gone down. Her eyes searched around the evening sky and confusion fell over her.

Worry came over Eric. "Are you alright?"

"What time is it?" she asked.

"It's past seven."

"Is Rebecca still here? I'm surprised she didn't need me."

"Rebecca said she did come up here. Honey, are you sure you're alright?"

"She never came up here. Is she still here?" Victoria's tone grew agitated.

"No, I dismissed her for the day. Don't stay outside too long. It's getting cold." Eric headed down the stairs, back inside the house.

Victoria felt lost on the day. She knew she had come up to the walk and started to paint, but everything else was like a dream she couldn't remember. She looked over to the chimney, and then her eyes caught a light flickering in the window of a tiny chapel set on the back of the property.

Someone had lit a candle.

Victoria thought about the creak in the floorboards and the shadow that crossed the door. Was there someone in the house? She knew what she saw but couldn't explain it. Then, a shadow crossed the window of the chapel. Determined to confront whoever was on the property, she left the widow's walk and made her way through the house. As she passed the kitchen, Eric called out, "Victoria?" but she didn't stop. Victoria stepped out the back door, fully focused on the chapel.

The little chapel past the small cemetery came into view. A shadow crossed the window again, stopping Victoria in her tracks. She waited. Victoria didn't know what she would even say when she ran into this person on their property. Maybe the usual *what are you doing here? Are you lost?*

As she pushed forward again, a hand grabbed her shoulder from behind. She screamed.

"Victoria, it's me!" Eric stood there as shocked as she was by her reaction. He was holding a flashlight. "What on earth are you doing?"

"Look!" Victoria said in a loud whisper and pointed to the chapel. "The light!"

Eric didn't have anything to say on it. The property was so large, they hadn't fully explored everything since they moved in. The pool house, tree house, greenhouse, then there was the graveyard and mausoleum and this chapel along with the gardens. "I'm sure it's one of the groundskeepers. Maybe they forgot to blow it out?"

Eric seemed to have an explanation for everything which only bothered Victoria more. "I saw someone inside. Are you coming with me or am I going alone?"

"Don't be silly, of course I'm coming with you." Eric didn't wait for her to respond. He stepped forward and made his way to the chapel entrance. He paused to let Victoria catch up and threw open the door as if he were going to catch someone off-guard.

The chapel was empty except for a single candle burning. It was a small space with only the one door they entered.

Victoria looked around, frustrated. "But I saw someone in the window."

Eric put his hand on her shoulder, almost in a condescending manner, "Honey…"

"No!" She pulled away. "I saw someone in here, Eric."

"Okay. But no one is here now. Can we go inside?"

Victoria didn't answer and watched Eric turn and walk away. As he disappeared, she walked up to the candle burning near the window and blew it out. She lingered a moment watching the smoke curl and rise like ghostly apparitions, then turned her attention back to the room.

Walking back to the house, Victoria took in the beautiful night. The moon was full, shining down on the estate. Shadows stretched long across the yard like the trees were reaching for the house – guiding her to where she should be – back in the house. She tried to think back to the lost hours when she was on the widow's walk and recall any details to develop a connection to her day. She thought about Rebecca claiming they had spoken earlier and tried to remember if she even spoke to Rebecca at all.

Victoria stopped and her breath stuck. On the widow's walk a woman with her hands clasped together, in a plain black dress, her hair pulled up in a bun, stood, looking down, staring at her. She couldn't believe her eyes. Victoria looked away for just the briefest moment to see if Eric had already made it inside, then back up to the roof. The woman was gone.

Eric was back in the kitchen when Victoria entered. "Hungry? Probably too late to cook anything but we always have leftovers."

Victoria decided not to tell him about the woman on the roof. He wouldn't believe her anyway. She would figure this out on her own. "I'm not hungry," she said plainly and made her way upstairs. Victoria sighed. "I'm tired. I just want to go lay down."

Eric approached the stairs. "Hey, I'm sorry, okay? I'm sure you saw someone. It's a big property, probably fascinating to people with its history. I don't know. I love you, okay?"

∞

Victoria walked up the stairs to the widow's walk. Standing there, she found herself unable to breathe, her heart racing.

Unnaturally thin hands with bony, claw-like fingers and razor-sharp nails gripped the chimney's edge and slowly pulled a body cloaked in darkness up, as if the figure was being conjured from the bowels of hell. The figure revealed itself— a woman, the woman she saw before, with movements that were unnatural, disjointed. Shadows seemed to meld and disintegrate around its form, an ever-shifting embodiment of nightmares. The breeze grew colder, stinging Victoria's skin, as sickening anticipation filled the air.

With each step the figure took, the world distorted and warped, reality fragmenting like shards of broken glass. Time itself seemed to bend and contort, playing tricks on Victoria's senses, heightening her terror. She wanted to run, but an invisible force held her captive, preventing escape.

Just as the figure loomed mere inches away, its grotesque features contorted with malevolence and with a raspy, wet voice said, "It takessssssss…"

Victoria's eyes shot open, her body drenched in a cold sweat. It was dark, and she could feel Eric was asleep next to her. The lingering imprint of the dread-filled vision remained etched in her mind.

Its voice… a message that felt like a warning. But what did it mean? Victoria laid back down, stared at the ceiling, and tried to calm her nerves. She had only just begun to relax, lulled by the quiet darkness, when the echoing of sound of her own name shattered in.

Eric's voice sliced through, "Victoria! Victoria!" He shouted as he rushed out of the bedroom.

Victoria's heart leapt and her eyes flew open, but the room remained cloaked in darkness, the edges of reality and dreaming blurred together in a disorienting haze. In an instant, she was on her feet; her nightgown clung to her clammy skin as she stumbled toward the window. Her eyes grew wide with fear as she stared out. Panic seized in her chest – the chapel was on fire.

Victoria ran outside and a gust of wind whipped her hair and carried with it the acrid scent of smoke. She took the scene in – smoke billowed up from the chapel and flames danced wildly against the dark sky. Eric was fighting the flames with a garden hose, his silhouette illuminated by the fire's fiery glow. There were sirens in the distance. *Eric must have already called the fire department*, Victoria thought.

Victoria watched as he wrestled with the hose. Eric moved with desperate determination and charged towards the inferno. He wasn't thinking, his urgency defied reasoning.

"Eric, no!" Victoria shouted and she ran across the yard.

The sirens were growing louder.

In his fight, Eric moved closer and closer to the burning structure. The heat scorched his skin, his hands brushed against the blazing wall, and a pained cry tore from his lips.

"Eric!" Victoria cried out.

"Don't get too close!" He held his hand out signaling her to stop.

The fire department arrived, and everything began to move in slow motion as Victoria watched them gear up, arming themselves with hoses and extinguishers. She watched a man pull Eric away and take him to a waiting ambulance. She watched as they tirelessly fought against the fire.

As the smoke cleared, the extent of the damage became apparent – one wall of the chapel had been consumed, leaving a charred void in its wake.

Victoria's gaze fixed on the ruin, her thoughts drifted back to that candle – the candle she blew out herself. Her mind went back to her dream; now she was sure it was a warning.

Eric was checked over by the medics; his burns were luckily mild and quickly tended to. As he walked across the yard, he held eye contact with Victoria, only her gaze was blank, like she was looking right through him. He stopped in front of her and that grabbed her attention.

"Are you alright?" she asked.

"I'm fine." He looked back at the chapel. "Most of it can be saved. There's nothing we can do at this point."

"I blew out that candle," Victoria whispered.

"Let's get back inside, get some sleep."

"You believe me... right, Eric?"

"I'm tired," he said as he walked back to the house."

"Eric..." Victoria said. "You believe me, right?"

Eric turned around for a brief moment. "If you say you blew it out, honey... then yes." he said with a sigh, then he headed back inside the house.

∾

The next morning, when Victoria woke, Eric was gone. She took her time getting ready for the day, although she didn't plan to do much. Unpacking was still priority one, but she also wanted to have some downtime and paint. Most of the day, Victoria avoided all the responsibilities she should have focused on, including things for Haley; she would let Rebecca do that. Rebecca seemed good at it, a natural, and Victoria didn't feel like a natural at being a mother yet. *That's why Rebecca should take care of Haley*, she told herself.

Victoria spent her time on the widow's walk to get some fresh air and paint instead.

It was after dinner when Eric returned home. He had been so caught up in his work, he lost track of time. The house was quiet. Eric hung his coat and set his briefcase down along with his car keys. "Honey? I'm home…" he called out.

The silence was pierced by the sharp sound of a crash coming from upstairs. Eric rushed up the stairs towards the noise. "Victoria!" he called out. He checked the nursery and found Rebecca working through some boxes.

"I'm so sorry, I didn't hear you come home..." Rebecca said.

"Did you hear that? The glass break?" Eric asked.

"Yes, it came from the roof. I was just headed to see if Victoria needed my help."

"How long has she been up there today?"

"All day, sir."

"Stay here. I'll help her." Eric left and went up the stairs and outside. A rush of cold air hit his face. Victoria was standing near her canvas that had been knocked down along with her table of brushes and jars of water. Glass had shattered all around.

Victoria's face was ashen, eyes wide with fear. "Did you hear it too?" she asked, her voice shaky.

"Hear what, honey?" Eric's gaze darted between her panicked face and the broken jars.

"A whisper. A woman's whisper," she stuttered, her eyes welling up with tears. "In my ear… so close, yet it seemed like it was carried by the wind."

Eric stared at her, the eerie atmosphere prickling at his own fears of what might be happening to his wife. Not that he believed she heard a woman talking to her— that wasn't rational. What scared him was his wife's mental health had seemed to quickly deteriorate since they moved into this house and since Haley…

The thought also crossed his mind that this was her way of punishing him for something, maybe working too much, he didn't know. He tried to laugh it off, hoping to lighten the mood, but what he really wanted to do was throw his hands up, let his anger out. "A whisper? Victoria, it's just the wind."

Victoria glared at him, frustration replacing fear. "It's not just the wind, Eric! I'm not imagining this!"

Silence fell between them, fraught with tension. "Alright, honey," Eric said, then cleared his throat. He kneeled down to pick up the remnants of the broken jars, trying to ignore the chill creeping up his spine – because… it wasn't rational.

∞

It was a stormy night; the house was filled with the roar of thunder, accompanied by the ceaseless lashing of rain against the windowpanes.

Eric was in the kitchen putting dishes away. It had been months since they'd moved in, and it was time he started at least trying to help chip in and keeping some type of order. He had been so busy at the office and since Haley… He realized he had been working a lot since Haley. Eric had a small moment of guilt; he knew Victoria needed him around and instead he had retreated in a way.

Eric paused when he heard crying and just listened. His eyes followed the footsteps pacing above. It was a few seconds later when the crying stopped, and he continued what he was doing. The crying started again; Eric let out a long sigh. He wondered if he should go up to help but only a moment later, Victoria came walking down the stairs.

Turning around, Eric found her standing in the doorway, her face pale, her eyes glassy with unshed tears.

"Victoria, what's wrong?" Eric asked, his heart pounding in his chest as he looked at his wife. Her frail figure seemed to be swallowed by the darkness around her. He could see her hands wringing nervously.

"Do you think she hates me? I think our baby hates me…"

"Haley doesn't hate you, honey. Rebecca says…" he paused when he saw Victoria's body tense.

"Rebecca says what?"

Eric swallowed hard. "Nothing, we just need to talk more, okay… spend more time…"

"Is that what Rebecca says? I'm not spending enough time talking? To who?"

"That's not…"

"Maybe you could spend more time at home. You made a lot of promises when we bought this place and so far, since Haley came… Well, you've stayed as far away as possible."

Eric stood, frozen. He wasn't really sure how to respond. Victoria was being hysterical, and he wasn't good in these moments. So, he stayed quiet.

"You're always out…" she spat out. "Always busy with work. You barely spend time with us! Are you having an affair?"

Eric took a step toward her, attempting to reach out, but she recoiled, her eyes flashing with anger.

"Honey, stop! I've been working hard for us."

A bitter laugh escaped Victoria's lips. "For us? As much as you've been away you must have gone off and had another family. As soon as we moved in, I became a prisoner and you… well, you get to come and go as you please, don't you?"

"Victoria, there's no one else." Eric's voice was steady despite his racing heart. "You're imagining things. Where's this even coming from?"

"Am I?" Victoria's voice was shrill. "Just like I'm imagining the whispers, the shadows?"

Eric felt a shiver run down his spine at her words. He watched in silence as Victoria turned on her heels and stormed out of the room, leaving him alone with his thoughts and a feeling of despair creeping over him.

The storm outside mirrored the storm inside the mansion. Eric's mind swarmed with worry – for his wife and for the unexplained occurrences that seemed to be driving her mad.

∾

Eric finished the last of the boxes; feeling proud of his accomplishment, he went upstairs to tell Victoria. He figured she'd been up on the widow's walk painting, but he heard the bedroom door close. Eric followed, opened the door, and said, "Victoria?"

He called out, but she wasn't there. Eric noticed papers laying on the bed, maybe stuff Victoria found and was going through. He picked the first few pages up—property papers from previous owners. Delmare, he read. He didn't know the name.

As he read, the slightest movement caught Eric's eye. Wallpaper had come loose and was flapping just slightly due to the invisible hand of a soft breeze.

He hadn't noticed until this moment that part of the wall seemed different, an uneven patch beneath the peeling paper. Eric crossed the room to investigate; he began to peel away the layers of wallpaper.

To his astonishment, he uncovered a hidden door, its entrance cleverly concealed within the ornate patterns of the wallpaper.

As he stood there in the empty bedroom, staring at this door, he heard footsteps walking across the ceiling. Eric pushed the door open. It creaked ominously, revealing a staircase shrouded in darkness. He stepped inside, the dust-laden air filling his lungs. Eric entered the room at the top of the stairs. It was a time capsule, untouched and hidden away. Antique furniture was covered with sheets, and portraits on the wall were faded, but the eyes seemed to follow him around the room. It felt as though he had stepped into a world that had been intentionally forgotten.

Eric found a collection of articles and personal letters bundled together. The letters told the tragic tale of Margaret Delmare. Her life had dwindled into a long wait, walking the widow's walk, her gaze forever fixed on the horizon, hoping for a return that never came. A husband lost, no children, her soul trapped in endless longing – she had gone mad.

A door slamming pulled him from the letters. Eric retreated from the secret room.

He headed upstairs to the attic. Canvases were spread out over the floor. Eric noticed some of the canvases were damaged, like someone had torn at them with a knife. He picked one up, noticing it was the one Victoria had been working on, of the estate.

He took in the scene of the unfinished painting. Then, he turned over the other canvases one by one. They were a stark contrast to Victoria's usual work. The vibrant colors were replaced by somber hues, figures distorted, and the scenes chaotic. Figures – he thought.

After flipping over the last canvas, he stood in the center of all the pieces. His heart pounded in his chest looking over them. All of them were the widow's walk, the estate below it, under a stormy sky.

Eric was able to discern a clear pattern; Victoria's work was getting measurably darker. He was able to arrange the paintings and observe the light drain from them over the series. As the tone darkened, he noticed a rise in the prominence of an eerie, shadowy figure near the chimney, faceless, yet emanating an inexplicable sense of dread. In every painting, on the other side of the chimney, Victoria stood just like he'd found her there before. In each progressive canvas, that eerie figure grew closer to Victoria.

Eric thought the only rational explanation was that Victoria read about Margaret Delmare, sympathized with her, related to her loss, and now this tragic past was casting a shadow over their lives.

Eric made his way to the widow's walk, knowing that's where he'd find Victoria.

First he saw a canvas had fallen, then Victoria, standing near the chimney, looking down into the darkness, swaying back and forth. Eric didn't call her name, he simply watched for a moment. He picked up the painting and fear consumed his mind.

It was another piece like those downstairs, a depiction of the widow's walk with the shadowy figure lurking near the chimney, only this one no longer had his wife standing next to it. His eyes pulled away to look over at Victoria, swaying, staring down into the chimney. It all made his blood run cold. "Victoria?" He set the canvas down on the easel.

It wasn't just a tragic past casting a shadow over their lives, it was a past now entwined with their present. Victoria had become a twisted mirror of this Margaret Delmare. All the time Victoria spent up here seemed more sinister now. She had been dwelling in a mausoleum of unending sorrow.

As Eric approached, Victoria didn't even acknowledge his presence. He joined her at the chimney, gently placed his hand on her lower back.

"Honey?"

Her body stiffened when he touched her. "Do you hear it… the scratches?"

Eric looked down into the dark abyss of the chimney, then to his wife.

"Victoria…" Eric began, uncertainty straining his voice.

Victoria's once vibrant eyes were now dull, an edge of hysteria simmering beneath their surface.

"I'm sorry, I haven't had a chance to check what it could be." The truth was, he had no intention of checking because he didn't hear anything.

"Victoria, can you look at me?" She didn't. "Honey, I know neither of us have really faced our reality, and I'll take some of the blame here…"

"Did Haley wake up? She's been sleeping for a while now…"

"Honey…" he whispered.

Whispers slithered up through the chimney, their words indecipherable but laced with malice. They burrowed deep into Victoria's mind, planting seeds of madness, twisting her thoughts and emotions, unraveling her sanity. "Do you hear them? The whispers…" she interrupted.

Eric swallowed hard as he looked back into the darkness. He didn't see or hear anything and didn't want to pretend he did. He just wanted in some way to help Victoria.

"Victoria, both of us need time to grieve. I'm sorry I haven't been here for you. Losing Haley…" He wiped a tear from his face. "I can't imagine how hard this has been for you…"

When he looked up, Victoria was no longer standing next to him. He turned around and found her behind him. But it wasn't his Victoria, the woman he knew.

"Honey?"

Victoria slammed both hands into Eric's chest, shoving him backward and into the chimney. He didn't even have time to scream. The first cruel impact met his head, a searing pain exploded across his skull with a *crack!* His body folded in an unnatural way as he fell, bouncing against the harsh unyielding bricks until he was wedged, the cold walls pressing viciously against his bruised and shredded flesh.

His head was spinning, vision blurry. Eric's fingers scraped against the bricks to free himself, the desperation ripped his nails back, leaving bloody marks on the wall. With every moment of struggle, Eric's body felt strangled, his breath came in short, shallow gasps, and as he went to call out for Victoria to help, his lungs tightened in his chest.

His body screamed in protest, each rasping breath a strangled struggle as soot filled his lungs, choking him, smothering him. Panic bubbled within Eric like a nightmarish brew, its potent taste worse than the ashen residue coating his tongue.

Victoria walked to the edge of the chimney and looked into the darkness. She could hear Eric struggling, could hear his scratching.

"I was just trying to do my best. I really did want to be a good mom… a good wife."

Victoria stood up straight, looked out over the estate from the widow's walk of her mansion, hands clasped together in front of her.

She was dressed in a simple black dress, hair pulled up in a bun, and her feet bare against the weathered wood of the walkway. She was deep in thought, her eyes distant and sad, and her forehead creased with worry.

The widow's walk is where she'd long for her loves that were no more.

∞

The Grounds

Goodness. You look like you've seen a… well, like you could use some fresh air. Let's head outside. Follow me. Through the kitchen. Out the back door.

That's better, isn't it? A brisk breeze. A bit of moonlight. You'll have a nice chance to stretch your legs here.

Visit the garage first. It's every man's dream. And every woman's worst nightmare. It's…well, you'll see.

Then take a stroll across to the pool house. You might want to find a way to block the doors from closing behind you. And don't breathe too deeply.
After that you can stop by the treehouse. Climb up if you're into that kind of thing. Careful on the way back down, though. People fall from treehouses all the time, you know.

Next you should visit our beautiful greenhouse. All kinds of things grow there. Flowers. Ferns. Poisons. Evil. You'll be fine. Just keep your hands to yourself.

Just outside the greenhouse are the gardens, and hidden behind some vines you'll discover the entrance to our special, *secret* garden. If it looks a bit neglected… count yourself lucky.

When you've finished with all of those places, you might feel the need for a bit of peaceful rest. Hale House's chapel is just the place. Feel free to leave your candle there. She'll appreciate that.

And, finally, no visit to Hale House would be complete without a nice walk through the private graveyard and a stop at the crumbling, moss-covered mausoleum of the great family patriarch, Josiah Hale. If you would be so kind, could you whisper a little message to old Josiah for me while you're there? Here's the message: "Go to hell."

∽

Ahem. Thanks. I'll just wait here.

Garage
1997

My FairLady
Brooklyn Ann

Hale House was full of ghosts, if the stories were anything to go by, but it was hard for Audrey Martell to worry about that when she felt like a ghost herself.

She haunted the hallways, grandiose library, and parlor with only two staff members who were here from ten to six every day, wondering how in the hell she could have made the same mistake for the third time.

Like Audrey's previous husbands, Ben had only married her for her money.

They'd been married for less than a year before he was cheating on her with another rich woman – Lana Renault, an actress half Audrey's age. The same day the divorce was finalized, Audrey read in the latest issue of the *National Enquirer* that Ben and Lana had announced their engagement.

Audrey supposed she should at least be happy Ben hadn't been able to fleece her in the divorce. Since he was at fault – Audrey learned from her first marriage to be sure to *get* proof of fault – he received no alimony.

But she'd assumed he'd have fought to keep Hale House. *He* was the one who chose the grand old mansion with its vast grounds, luxurious rooms, and especially the enormous six-car garage and adjoined shop.

Ben idolized the late-night talk show host, Jay Leno, who had an infamous car collection, and had aspirations of restoring classic cars to add to his own growing collection.

When they first moved into Hale House six months ago, Ben had filled the garage with project cars. But he'd barely spent the first week tinkering with a '65 Mustang before giving up and sending the car off to a professional restoration shop.

He tried again on another car, only to come back inside, cursing and bleeding from cuts he said came from slipping tools, or parts falling on him. By the third week, all four cars went off to be restored by another's hands.

If Ben had been new to working on cars, Audrey wouldn't have thought anything about him giving up so early. But he wasn't. One of the first things he'd shown her when they'd started dating were restoration projects.

Audrey remembered seeing the three he had then: a '63 Dodge Challenger that was done, aside from the paint job; a '72 Chevy Nova that was complete mechanically and now needed bodywork and upholstery; and a clunker of a '69 El Camino that he'd just started.

How many hours had she spent in his garage, watching him work on those cars?

Watching how capable Ben was with his hands and the gradual transformation of the El Camino from an eyesore into a shiny classic was a huge part of why Audrey had fallen in love with him.

She'd also assumed since Ben was well-off from his family's trust fund, had a hobby he was passionate about, and didn't seem to care too much about whether it was profitable, that he wasn't like her two ex-husbands and wanted to be with Audrey for herself, and not her inheritance.

But she'd been wrong, yet again. Three strikes, she was out.

The signs had been there from day one. She'd justified his indifference with the house he'd been so insistent they buy – with *her* money – as his single-minded enthusiasm about the garage and his project cars.

To distract herself, Audrey had tried to throw herself into decorating her new home, but she was never able to muster an ounce of passion for making her living space suitable for magazine spreads and episodes of *Lifestyles of the Rich and Famous*.

Besides, Audrey was an unlikely subject for any of those puff pieces. She wasn't an actress, or a model, or a businesswoman. She hadn't done *anything* to earn her millions. More and more, that was starting to bother her.

Therefore, after the third interior decorator fled the property in fear of the ghosts, Audrey set aside the wallpaper and paint samples and turned to trying to be a model wife for Ben.

At first, she thought everything was going great. Ben was spending less time in the garage and more time in the house, inviting his friends over for game nights, and having Audrey host dinner parties.

Then everything went wrong. Game nights were a disaster because the TV went on the fritz the first time, and the second time, one of the guys had a heart attack. The dinner parties were even more cataclysmic. Half the guests left early with rambled excuses that belied the terror in their eyes. The other half were drunken fools that Audrey and the hired caterers had to wrangle like feral cats to keep them from destroying her carefully decorated dining room and parlor. And Audrey's husband was nowhere to be found.

A month later, she'd found out that Ben had been making out with Catherine Hayward in the trophy room. Catherine was another heiress, there because Ben handled her ancient father's investments. *New money*, Audrey's father would have sneered.

By then, Ben was working late nearly every night, and going away on business trips every month.

When Audrey served divorce papers, Ben blustered with outrage, but she could see the relief in his eyes. The only real hostility from him came during the settlement, when their prenup prevented him from taking any part of her fortune. She also got to keep Hale House, but Audrey felt that was more of a curse than a blessing.

By then, there was no denying that the house was haunted. Every room made her feel uncomfortable, like she was being watched with hostile eyes. Whispers echoed in dark rooms and phantom winds blew through the corridors.

On the night Audrey decided to sell the house and get out, she poured herself a second glass of Moscato and went into the garage. She wanted to find some proof, some reason as to why everything went wrong.

After all, the first cracks in their marriage came when Ben had given up on his dream of restoring a collection of classic cars.

When she walked into the vast space and turned on the overhead fluorescent lights, Audrey felt like she was noticing the garage for the first time. Half of the building was old and desiccated, smelling of dust, rotting rubber, and old motor oil. An oddly comforting scent.

The other half, furthest from the side door, was newer. She remembered Ben joyously talking about the expansion that had been done in the seventies. He'd seemed so happy then, before they bought this house. Before the garage seemed to change him.

"Over here," a voice whispered.

Audrey jumped, even though it wasn't the first disembodied voice she'd heard in this house. Yet something felt different about this whisper.

For the first time, she whispered back. "Where?"

Something rustled in the newer half of the garage. The light she'd turned on only lit the old half, casting the new in ominous darkness, where shadowy shapes crouched like monsters waiting to pounce.

Every cell of Audrey's being screamed at her not to approach that area, but her legs carried her forward.

From the dim light coming through the small, dirty windows, Audrey found a grimy light switch. For one heart-stopping moment, it seemed that the lights on this side of the garage were broken or burnt out. Then she heard a series of familiar electrical clicks before old overhead fluorescents buzzed to life.

Audrey didn't let out a breath until her eyes scanned the area, making sure there were no monsters lurking. All she could see was a car-shaped lump under a tan canvas tarp, some workbenches, a come-along hanging from the rafters, and a toolbox.

As for what she couldn't see… Audrey licked dried lips and whispered, "Here?"

The canvas tarp rustled in answer. Audrey suddenly remembered what was under it.

Ben had cleared out all his project cars, except one. This car had been in the garage when they'd moved in.

Unable to decide if she preferred the rustling to be from a ghost or an animal, Audrey lifted the tarp, coughing as dust flew up in a thick cloud.

The rusted silver convertible looked like the car James Bond drove in the old movies.

She remembered Ben's excitement when he found the car, thinking it was an Aston Martin. And his disappointed tone when he found out what it was.

∾

"A '67 Datsun Fairlady. I don't like imports unless it's a Mercedes or a Maserati, but I wouldn't mind fixing this up and selling it to someone who likes these things."

"Or maybe you could restore it for me," Audrey had said, threading her arm around his bicep and looking up at him with adoration. "I think it's beautiful."

There'd been a slight frown and a pause before he bent down to kiss her nose. "Nah. You deserve something better than a Jap novelty. Maybe I'll get you a Porsche, or an Audi."

Aren't those also imports? She'd almost said, then broke off, reminding herself that she'd be grateful if he gifted her with any car he'd lovingly restored.

Had Ben left the Fairlady because she'd admired it or because he wanted to avoid fighting in court? Or had he left the car because he'd never liked it in the first place?

In those early days when he'd still been in here working on his projects, Audrey had brought him pitchers of lemonade in the afternoons and a cold beer in the evenings.

She'd never seen him go near the Datsun. The tarp remained over the little car from that first day when he'd replaced the old rotting one.

Now, standing over the car, Audrey admired the Fairlady's sleek curves, chrome grille, and black leather seats. It *was* a cute car. Anyone could see that past the rust spots on the silver body, wear on the convertible top, and faded black interior.

Maybe she should pay to have it restored and take it with her when she sold the house.

"Yes," the voice whispered. Or maybe that was wishful thinking.

Or maybe... She sucked in a breath at the boldness of the next thought.

Maybe *she* could restore it!

As Ben said, as long as one had the right tools, any job could be done. And she was in dire need of a new hobby. Why not use the knowledge she'd gained from him, so their short marriage wasn't a total loss?

Heart pounding with more excitement than she'd felt in years, Audrey looked around and spotted a rusty Craftsman toolbox.

Ben probably sneered at it. Snap-on was his brand.

Her hands shook as she opened the drawers, one by one. She found a set of metric wrenches, sockets, and countless other tools whose names she didn't know.

Foreign cars had metric nuts and bolts; Audrey remembered Ben complaining. Most of the tools were Craftsman, so if Ben had looked inside the toolbox, he would have left them.

She returned to the car and opened the driver's side door, wincing at the rusty squeal of protest. Audrey added Liquid Wrench to her inner shopping list.

The interior looked better than she'd feared; sun-faded plastic dash and leather seats, worn, stained carpet, and a slight musty smell that could probably be banished with a good cleaning and some fresh air.

The keys were tucked in the cracked sun visor. She reached under the steering column and pulled a lever. The hood opened with a satisfying *pop*.

Crossing back to the front, she lifted the unlatched hood and inserted the prop rod. With the overhead lighting she was able to take inventory of some of the car's problems.

The first one was apparent.

The oval air filter was shredded, and held the corpses of four partially mummified mice. She also spotted rotted belts and hoses, a *very* corroded battery, a few wires that looked chewed up, and a puddle of oil on the cement floor.

Audrey resumed adding items to her list. "Air filter, battery, belts and hoses… and a repair manual."

A tremor of nervousness crawled up her neck and tried to crawl into her head and scream that she couldn't restore a car, that she was crazy to try, but Audrey refused to be dissuaded.

"It's not like Ben was all that smart. If he could do it, I can do it."

"*Yes*," the ghost whispered again.

Audrey smiled and tilted her head in the direction the voice came from.

"I think you and I are going to get along. Now I'm going to head to bed, then go the closest auto parts store in the morning."

In response, the car shook, filling the garage with creaks and squeaks of old rubber tires and dormant metal. Audrey's smile faded. Was that a happy response, or was the ghost angry she was leaving it alone for the night?

If it could make things move, she wasn't ready to find out. She took her half-finished glass of wine and fled the garage.

If the other Hale House ghosts were out and about, Audrey was too tired to notice. She finished her wine in the library and transcribed her list for the Fairlady on a monogrammed notepad.

Then, after a soak in a hot Calgon bath, she went straight to bed.

The next afternoon, Audrey returned to the garage with her arms full of parts and supplies to tackle her project.

Pete, one of the weekday staff members, grunted as he carried in a heavier load of items.

As soon as Pete left, Audrey spoke to the ghost.

"They *laughed* at me at the parts store. Tried to convince me to take the car to a shop that 'specializes in import restorations,'" – she made air quotes at the last.

"Well, I'll show them. The manual for this specific car is on special order, and will take a month or so to get here, but there's a copy in the reference section of the library and I made enough photocopies to get me started."

The car shook again, squeaking and rattling.

"I hope that means you're excited about me bringing this car back to life."

Because if the ghost was angry, she'd abandon the project in a heartbeat. Audrey may not know the details of Hale House's ghosts, but she knew the place had claimed its share of lives.

The hood lifted on its own.

"I'll take that as a yes."

Audrey steadied the hood and inserted the support rod.

She started with the grossest part first, cleaning those poor dead mice out of the shredded air filter. Audrey gagged a few times, but once she'd removed the old air filter and put the shiny new red one in, a surge of triumph rushed through her being.

It felt so good to accomplish something with her bare hands.

Next, she removed the corroded battery and installed the replacement cables. The battery itself could wait until she knew it would power functioning parts.

Hours passed as she familiarized herself with turning wrenches and using a ratchet while following the directions on the photocopied pages from the manual.

Sometimes, it felt like someone was standing behind her, but it was a comforting presence that radiated approval and matched her excitement.

"I wish I knew who you were," Audrey murmured, after draining the radiator into an aluminum pan she'd found.

"Find me," the ghost whispered.

Its voice was stronger than yesterday, and sounded feminine.

But what would a woman ghost be doing in the garage? Audrey's nose wrinkled as she scolded herself for the thought. She was being just like those snide men at the parts store.

"I will find you," Audrey promised before heading back into the house for a long overdue meal, shower, and bed.

Her days settled into a busy routine that Audrey previously would have found grueling, but now she found fulfilling.

Mornings at the library, weekly stops at the parts store to pick up orders and place more, then long afternoons that often bled into evenings, slowly bringing the car back to life.

Her nails broke when replacing the battery, so she cut them short. Her designer clothes quickly got stained with old oil and gunk after changing the belts and hoses, so she bought jeans, off-the-rack T-shirts, work boots, and even two pairs of coveralls.

After performing her first oil change, she made good friends with borax and degreaser soaps.

Her carefully styled blonde tresses were now relegated to messy buns, so her hair wouldn't get caught in the creeper when working underneath the car. She abandoned her makeup.

The ghost – who was *definitely* a woman – grew stronger on pace with the Fairlady.

Between photocopying pages of the car's repair manual, Audrey began to research the many tragedies that had occurred at Hale House, hoping to find her ghost.

The newspaper articles were numerous, and included many details in the last decade that the real estate agent should have disclosed. No wonder the parlor was always so creepy! And that one bathroom, the dining room, the ballroom…

Holy hell, was *every* room in the house haunted? And she hadn't even gone back twenty years yet!

But none of those stories felt like the ghost in the garage.

So, Audrey continued going back, reading through papers transferred to microfiche and microfilm. After a month of weekly library visits, her eyes landed on a headline that made the back of her neck prickle:

November 20th, 1981
Evelyn Horne, Missing for Seven Years, Declared Dead.

Windom Horne, still mourning, has had his wife, Evelyn Horne, née Palmer, declared dead after an unsuccessful search of seven years.

"It kills me to give up on her, but it's time for me to move on and make better memories," Horne said, wiping a tear from his eyes.

The real estate tycoon has put his own house, the infamous Hale House, back on the market.

Other community members, who asked for their names to be withheld, commented: "It's the house that killed her. We all know it."

Another concerned citizen said, "I think it's morbid that Horne had her declared dead in the first place. He has more money than God, so it's not like he needed access to her bank account, or wanted that adorable little convertible she'd brought home shortly before disappearing."

The article went on to give a cold, brief list of the deaths and disappearances that had occurred at Hale House. But Audrey was pretty sure she'd found her lead. The Fairlady belonged to Evelyn.

"Find me," the ghost had pleaded.

If she'd been a ghost of one of the multiple people who'd died in the house, her body would have been found. Otherwise, there wouldn't have been a newspaper article about it.

But a missing woman? That was indeed likely.

Audrey jotted down notes of years to check tomorrow and drove back to Hale House, getting a burger and fries on the way.

Yet again, she shook her head in wonder. The old Audrey wouldn't dream of eating fast food. But a nice, juicy cheeseburger and hot, greasy fries gave her the calories she needed for the hours she spent working on the Fairlady.

Besides, she hated eating in the house.

She'd gone through five cooks before giving up and fending for herself. Not that she blamed them. The damned ghosts in the kitchen and dining room rarely gave her peace.

After she donned her coveralls and tied her hair up in a messy bun, Audrey returned to the garage.

"Is your name Evelyn?" she called out.

A sudden breeze blew through Audrey's hair before the dim shape of a woman appeared beside the Fairlady. The woman grinned and nodded before fading away.

"I found you, then!" Audrey said, both excited and a little scared of her first visual confirmation of the ghost's presence.

The toolbox rattled. Audrey approached it and saw two letters form in the dust on the red-painted top.

NO

Then a drawer slid open, revealing her ratchets and wrenches – both old ones she'd cleaned and new ones she'd bought. The 3/8 ratchet she used most often – a 12mm socket still attached – raised up until it stood on end.

"I need to fix the car to find you?" That didn't make any sense.

The ratchet rose higher, then floated toward her.

Audrey took the ratchet. "Okay. I'll fix it. I want to, anyway. It's a beautiful car. If you picked it out yourself, you have great taste."

The horn honked once for yes. Two was no.

The sound echoed off the concrete in the large space, but the horn system was better than shaking the car, which was now propped up on jackstands. Audrey approached the open hood and got back to work.

Sometimes, a phantom hand would pass her wrenches, sockets, and the photocopies from the Fairlady's repair manual.

As she worked, Audrey chatted to Evelyn about her day, about the ghosts in the house, and about her life with Ben and her previous two husbands.

Curiosity about Evelyn's life and husband burned in her mind, but she didn't quite have the nerve to ask the ghost. Not when she was lying on a creeper underneath the car so she could get at the sway bar bushings.

Still, Audrey couldn't help wondering how Evelyn had died. *Had* the house killed her? Or was it her husband? Or the butler with the candlestick?

Once she had all the new hoses, filters, and wires where they were supposed to be, Audrey got in the driver's seat. For a moment, she was surprised that she didn't need to move the seat back or forward.

Evelyn had been her height.

Heart pounding with excitement, she turned the key in the ignition.

The starter cranked with a metallic scream, then the engine spluttered to life. But it was an unhealthy spluttering. A cloud of blue smoke blatted out of the tailpipe, filling the garage with the stench of burnt oil.

Audrey cut the engine and pulled out the keys. She remembered some things Ben said about that sound when he fired up one of his project cars. "It's not getting enough compression," or "Maybe a blown head gasket."

Audrey sighed and leaned her head on the steering wheel.

"I'm sorry, Evelyn. I'm going to have to take the engine apart. I don't know if I can do it."

A soft, cool hand settled over hers on the gearshift knob.

"You can do it."

Resisting the urge to jump and pull her hand away, Audrey lifted her head from the wheel and looked over.

A pale brunette woman in blue denim bell bottoms, a purple paisley top, and a fringed brown suede jacket sat in the passenger seat.

"E-Evelyn?" Audrey stammered.

The ghost was so vivid that she looked like she was alive.

The ghost nodded. *"Please, help me get out of here."*

Then she vanished.

Audrey nodded shakily and reached for the glovebox. She could kick herself for not looking in there. All those hours at the library, only to find a pair of women's sunglasses, and a registration made out to Evelyn Horne, dated November 1974.

"You bought the car right before you died."

Audrey's heart clenched with pity.

"I'm so sorry you didn't get to enjoy it more."

The glovebox also held the used car dealership receipt for a down payment of five hundred dollars, with an accompanying check stub paper clipped to the edge. Audrey noticed another pertinent detail.

"You paid for it with your own bank account."

Not the joint one that would have been more usual back in those days. And Evelyn's own loan… an odd one for a woman who should have had access to a fortune.

Half a down payment for a thousand-dollar car, with fifty-seven-dollars-a-month-payments, and an interest rate that was absurd for the '70s.

Something from a class way back in her college days in the '80s whispered at the fringes of her memory, but Audrey was too exhausted to grasp it.

"I *will* pull that engine and get it fixed," she promised before leaving the garage for her nightcap, shower, and list-making routine before bed.

∞

The engine rebuild adventure took months.

There were gaskets and more tools to order, a machinist to hire to hone the cylinders, polish the crankshaft, and do a valve job on the head.

Instead of attending some glitzy party to ring in the New Year, Audrey spent the first hours of 1998 installing new piston rings and the rear main seal. The backordered manual finally arrived, but Audrey continued to visit the library and read up on Evelyn Horne.

The articles revealed the story in reverse.

> *May 25th, 1975:*
>
> **Evelyn Horne Still Missing. Distraught Husband Insists the Search Continue.**
>
> *Evelyn Horne, former New York Socialite, and wife of millionaire, Windom Horne, has now been missing for six months...*

> *December 14th, 1974:*
>
> **Evelyn Horne Still Missing**
>
> *The search continues for Evelyn Horne, former New York Socialite and second wife of Windom Horne, millionaire real estate mogul.*

> *November 29th, 1974:*
>
> **Former New York Socialite and Wife of Local Millionaire Reported Missing.**
>
> *Evelyn Horne left her home at Hale House on a shopping trip last Tuesday, but she never came home.*
>
> *"She told me she wanted to find a new dress for our annual Thanksgiving Gala," her frantic husband said. "But she never came home. Then, the next afternoon, the police found our Mercedes in the ditch out by the woods."*
>
> *The search began on Thanksgiving and has been going on since...*

Between the three articles, Audrey pieced together what happened.

The official story was that Evelyn had gone out shopping and had never returned.

But Audrey knew that both Evelyn and her car – her *real* car and not Windom's Mercedes that had been found in a ditch near the woods – had never left the garage.

"It *was* the husband," Audrey murmured, rubbing her eyes.

"How long had they been married?"

It took seven more years of historical microfilm to sort through, to finally get the answer.

After skimming countless articles about Windom Horne's parties, fundraisers, comments at political rallies, and other mundane things Audrey had also done but was rarely publicly lauded for, she finally found a reference to their wedding date.

March 1967:

Real Estate Tycoon Marries New York Socialite

Windom Horne, millionaire real estate broker, has claimed his second bride, celebrated New York beauty, Evelyn Palmer.

After an eight-month honeymoon in Europe, the couple plans to move into the infamous Hale House.

When questioned about the house's reputation, where many people have reported seeing ghosts on the front porch, Mr. Horne said, "We don't believe in ghosts."

"I'm sure *that* went well," Audrey muttered.

"And I wonder what happened to the first wife?"

But she didn't have time to read up on that today. The library was closing in an hour, and she still needed to pick up the cylinder head from the machinist.

When she got back to the garage, Audrey laid the cylinder head beside the new gasket on the now-clean workbench.

The work on the engine block was completed, and once she put the head back on, she could use her new hoist to put the engine back in the Fairlady, right on its shiny new motor mounts.

But she had other things on her mind.

"I read more articles about your disappearance." Audrey walked around the garage, searching for Evelyn.

"Windom killed you, didn't he?"

The toolbox rattled and the car's horn honked once.

A faint outline of a woman appeared in the passenger seat of the car.

Evelyn nodded.

"Why did he kill you?"

The toolbox rattled again, and shelves creaked as if in indecision. Fog formed on the Fairlady's windshield, then lines and curves appeared, forming a date.

"You want me to check that date at the library tomorrow?"

One honk. *Yes.*

"Ok. I'll look. But first, let's get this engine back together. The new carburetor should be arriving tomorrow too."

Evelyn's form appeared beside the car. She gave Audrey a thumbs-up and smiled.

Audrey put the head gasket on the block with minimal sealant as advised, then bolted the head on with the correct amount of torque. The transmission was bolted back to the engine, ready to go in just as it had come out.

Just like when she'd hoisted the engine out of the car, Evelyn helped. Though the ghost couldn't do any of the mechanical work, she was there to steady the powertrain and make sure everything lined up.

Once everything was bolted in place, Audrey celebrated with a beer.

Evelyn stood beside her. Her smile was radiant. *"I knew you could do it."*

"Thank you." Audrey lifted her beer in a toast.

"But it's not done yet. I still need to put the carb, belts, hoses, and everything else back together."

"And you will." Evelyn reached out and squeezed Audrey's shoulder.

∽

The next morning, Audrey went straight to the library and requested the microfilm reel for 1974 again.

She wound it to October 28th and read the front-page headline.

Women Score Another Breakthrough Against Credit Bias.

"Oh my God," Audrey whispered. "The Equal Credit Opportunity Act."

That was the thing that whispered in her mind and took her back to college when she looked at Evelyn's check stub.

Evelyn had *just* been granted the right to have a bank account separate from her husband's, to get a credit card... or take out an auto loan.

But the last had probably been difficult. That's why a woman with her wealth had to resort to some shady used car dealership to get her own car.

She'd been trying to leave her husband, had been given the keys to freedom, but had been caught and killed for it.

Windom Horne had been fundraising and hobnobbing with politicians, according to the articles Audrey read. He was probably against the ECOA.

But Evelyn not only supported it, she'd prepared for it.

The car itself probably would have been disposed of if it didn't have a paper trail and witnesses like the one quoted in the newspaper.

Audrey left the library for the last time and drove to the parts store to pick up her latest order.

Without the library research to distract her, Audrey dedicated more time to putting Evelyn's Fairlady back together.

Evelyn passed her tools and held the shop light for her when necessary.

The day Audrey fired up the Fairlady and the engine roared to life with a smooth purr, she screamed with triumph and Evelyn screamed with her.

She backed the convertible out of the garage and took it on a short drive around the neighborhood, not yet daring to break in the engine, which would require her to "drive like you stole it," according to the machinist.

But soon, Audrey would be ready. Her heart soared with every push on the clutch and shift to the five gears.

"Get the title in your name." Evelyn's voice was stronger than before. *"Now."*

A trip to the DMV revealed that Windom had never bothered to change the title to his name. He'd always intended to leave the car in the garage to rot.

But why? And why leave it in the newer addition to the garage?

Then it hit her.

Audrey filled out the Lost Title form and rushed back to Hale House, only making one stop on the way.

She couldn't call the police yet. Not when all she had was a bill of sale, a check stub, and knowledge of women's history.

The moment she got back to Hale House, Audrey parked the Fairlady in the older part of the garage.

Then she went to the spot where the convertible had sat for the last twenty-four years.

With the sledgehammer she got from the hardware store, Audrey broke up the concrete, working outward from the round oil-stain from the Fairlady's previously leaking gaskets.

She used a pry-bar to free the concrete chunks, then got to digging with the shovel.

Eventually, the shovel struck bone. Audrey dug a little more, biting back a whimper as Evelyn's skull was revealed.

"I found you," she whispered.

Now it was time to call the police.

When asked what prompted her to tear up the concrete, Audrey said a ghost had told her to do it. Let the papers have their fun with that.

The media circus that followed exhausted her to the point that she collapsed in bed, still filthy from digging up Evelyn.

The next morning, Audrey awoke aching and still tired, but determined to leave Hale House. Evelyn was at peace.

Yes, there was more to do with the car, but she could finish it in another garage. The paint and interior could get done at a shop.

After showering, she went down to the garage, ready to do the engine break-in before more reporters arrived.

Evelyn stood in the garage, next to the Fairlady.

Audrey's heart surged with mingled joy and worry. Yesterday she'd hadn't gotten a chance to say goodbye to her spectral friend, but now she didn't want the poor spirit to be stuck here. "I thought you'd moved on."

"Take me out of here," Evelyn pleaded.

Audrey's heart clenched with sympathy for the poor woman. Even in death, she still wanted to escape.

"Can I *do* that?"

The ghost smiled.

"You helped me bind myself to the car. Wherever the car goes, I go. Until I'm ready to move on. For now, I want to stay with you. It's been good to have a friend."

"It has, hasn't it?" Audrey smiled and opened the passenger door of the Fairlady, even though Evelyn didn't need her to.

"Let's go break this engine in."

But when Audrey backed out of the garage, she spotted a black car in the driveway. She turned off the ignition with a groan.

"I'll try to get rid of them."

Two men stood on the wide covered porch. From their buzzcuts and auras of authority, Audrey knew they were plainclothes detectives.

"Mrs. Martell?" the first man inquired in an uncertain voice when she approached them.

Both men eyed her stained jeans and t-shirt, messy ponytail, and makeup-free face with curiosity.

"Yes?"

"I'm Detective Briggs, and this is Detective Milford. Your ex-husband asked for a wellness check on you."

From the partner's snort, Audrey could tell that Ben hadn't really wanted to make sure she was okay.

"What's *really* going on?"

Detective Milford spoke first.

"Your ex has been arrested for murdering his third wife."

"Excuse me?" Audrey blinked at him.

"Did you say *third*?"

Ben claimed he'd never been married before. Then the rest of what Milford said sank in.

"He murdered that actress?"

"He did indeed." Detective Briggs said.

"Confessed to it earlier this afternoon. As well as the murder of his first wife, previously assumed to have gone missing."

"Oh my God."

Audrey sank down on the porch swing, dizzy as it all came together. A spectral hand patted her shoulder, oddly comforting.

She blinked and looked past the ghost of an old woman leaning over her.

"Ben was planning to murder me too, wasn't he? It wasn't the garage he wanted. I could have paid for a new house with a big garage. He wanted to use this house's reputation for cover."

Milford nodded.

"Only now he thinks all the stories about this place are true and that the house killed you," the detective said.

"He asked for you to be checked on. Somehow, I don't believe he'll be relieved at the news that you're safe and sound, while he got so scared of this place that he abandoned his plans of playing Black Widower and had to start all over with courting his next victim."

Audrey remembered Ben coming in from the garage, pale and bloody from trying to work on one of his cars. Evelyn had given him hell.

Maybe she even knew what he'd planned for Audrey.

She saved my life.

"That's enough, Milford," Detective Briggs's voice brought Audrey back to the present.

"She could be called in to testify at the trial. We don't need to be accused of witness-tampering." His gaze shifted back to Audrey.

"Now, Ms. Martell, I think you should consider selling Hale House. Not that I believe in ghosts or anything, but I do believe you may have used up all your good luck in a place with such an unlucky history."

Audrey smiled.

"I already plan on leaving tonight and putting the place on the market. I just needed to finish work on my car," she said.

The detectives turned to look at the gorgeous silver convertible.

"What kind of car is that?"

"A '67 Datsun Fairlady."

Audrey smiled at the transparent shape of Evelyn in the passenger seat.

"*My* Fairlady."

Pool House
2006

I Can't Miss You if You Never Leave
Caitlin Marceau

Brianna rolls her eyes as she drags her thumb around the wheel of her pink iPod mini, enjoying the soft clicking it makes as she scrolls through what feels like an endless number of songs.

When the MP3 player first came out, her parents had refused to buy her one thanks to its steep price point. But after breaking the news to her that they'd be leaving her childhood home in Kamloops for Middle-Of-Nowhere, USA, they'd been quick to get her one in an attempt to soften the blow.

It hadn't.

Once she finds the song she's looking for, she pushes play, sets it to repeat, and takes a seat in front of her computer. She pushes the power button on the tower and then turns on the monitor, the black screen first turning slate grey and then bright blue as it comes to life.

She selects her name from the Windows XP user menu, bobbing her head in time with the music as she waits for her desktop to load. Once it's done, she logs into MSN Messenger and crosses her fingers that her friends are online.

They're not.

She closes her eyes and exhales slowly, trying to calm herself down. Although the time difference between her new home and her old friends was only three hours, it had thrown her social life entirely out of whack.

Her friends were never awake when she logged on in the morning and she was always heading off to bed when they came online at night.

She missed getting to talk to them about new music, arguing about which video *really* deserved the top spot on the Much Music Top 20 Countdown, crushing on Pete Wentz, and complaining about her family.

271

Caitlin Marceau

She opens her eyes and leans forward in her chair as she clicks on her display name to change it. Her fingers hover above the keyboard, unsure which song to quote, before deciding on one of her favorite tracks.

♀ ~~ </3 *im NOT okay (i promise)* 😨 </3 ~~ ♀

With a sigh, she logs off MSN and is about to open her email when her headphones are roughly yanked off.

"Ow!" she shouts, spinning around in her seat as she rubs her ears.

"I've been trying to get a hold of you for almost ten minutes!" her mom shouts at her.

"How was I supposed to know? I had my music on!"

She picks her iPod up off the desk and presses pause, her brain still singing along with "Helena" even though the music has stopped.

"What are you doing?" her mom asks, pointing to the monitor.

"Building a steam engine. What do you think?"

"I don't appreciate the attitude."

Brianna rolls her eyes.

"I asked you a question."

"I was online. Why?"

Her mom crosses her arms in front of her chest and frowns.

"How many times do I need to tell you that I'm painting your bedroom today? I've been asking you for *days* to make sure everything was moved away from the walls and covered with the plastic sheets I gave you. But instead, you've been wasting your time talking to strangers on the internet."

"I'm not talking to strangers! They're my friends! And I've told you like a *million* times that I don't want you to paint my room unless you're going to paint it—"

Her mom grabs one of the plastic sheets off her dresser and begins to unfold it as she cuts her daughter off.

"For Christ's sake, Brianna. I'm not painting your room red, black, or purple."

"Mauve. I wanted it mauve."

"I'm not painting your room *mauve*, Brianna. Do you know how hard that's going to be to repaint when we eventually sell this house? Or when you want to redecorate because you're done pretending to be a vampire? Or, fingers crossed, you decide to stop being an angry teen?"

"Oh my God, I'm *not* pretending to be a vampire, Mom. You don't… Whatever."

"I don't *what*?"

"You just don't get it," Brianna says, frustrated. She turns her attention back to her monitor.

"Well, what I *am* about to get is annoyed if you don't turn your computer off and do as I asked."

"I'll do it later! I'm in the middle of–"

"Now, Brianna," her mom orders, draping the plastic sheet over Brianna's bed. "Or I'll cancel the broadband until you go back to school in September."

Brianna clenches her fists, watching as her mom exits the room and heads downstairs, shouting something to one of the repairmen hired to renovate the home. After a few minutes, she puts her headphones back on, playing the music even louder as she wraps the monitor—and the rest of her belongings – in plastic.

∾

"Brianna, can you come here please?" her mother calls loudly from upstairs. "I want your opinion on which color you like more, cloud or morning mist."

"I don't care!" she shouts back. The paint swatches looked identical when her mom brought them back from the hardware store and she's sure they look the same on her bedroom wall.

"Get up here, please!"

Brianna gets up off of the sofa in the messy library – frowning at the scorch marks sprawling across the floor, half hidden by moldy debris and piled of yellowed paper – but can't bring herself to go upstairs. She doesn't want to see what kind of damage her mom has started doing to *her* room or help her ruin what was supposed to be her space.

And, if she's being honest with herself, she doesn't want to see her mom at all. It's a feeling she's grown more familiar with the older she's gotten. Although she'd never felt as close to her mom as her friends had felt to theirs, the last few years have especially strained their relationship.

While her mom still blames Brianna's friends for being a bad influence, Brianna's convinced she's just better at seeing through her mom's bullshit.

For a long time, she wished she could have a close relationship with her family.

Now, she just wishes she'd been born to different parents.

"Can you bring me another one of those paint sticks on your way up too?" her mom asks.

Brianna rolls her eyes and makes her way across the living room, through the house, and out the back door, making sure to close it quietly behind her. She knows her mom's going to get angry at being ignored, but she doesn't care. She just wants to be alone right now.

As she approaches the gardens, she realizes that time to herself might be a steeper ask than she realized. Although the idea of admiring rows of flowers and lying on the grass appeals to her, dealing with the trio of talkative gardeners currently working on the flowerbeds doesn't.

They talk loud and make noise as they mow, cut, and prune the overgrown garden that's been left to run wild since Hale House was abandoned and put up for public auction by the city a few years ago.

She debates going back to the house and accepting defeat when she spots the faded white bars of a short wrought-iron fence in the distance.

Oh yeah! I totally forgot!

She smiles and makes her way over to the large kidney bean-shaped pool and its adjoining house. Like the fence along its perimeter, the white paint of the pool house is faded and worn from years of neglect.

The windowless shack is fairly small, just big enough to store pool supplies and provide guests with somewhere private to change. The roof is large and extends beyond the house where it rests on two wooden support pillars, the grey shingles dirty and sun-bleached.

The overhang provides sizable space and shade for patio furniture or a massive dining set, but Brianna knows her parents won't put anything useful there.

Instead, she imagines her mom will convert the space into a small bar that she'll use to make her friends back home jealous or use to get day drunk at, before losing interest in the space entirely.

As Brianna opens the gate to the pool, a man in a white uniform exits the pool house. She groans to herself and is about to turn back toward the house when the man smiles at her.

"Hey there! Do you know if Mrs. Mueller is still at the house?" the man asks her.

"Yeah, but I think my mom's painting right now."

He frowns, clicking his tongue against the back of his teeth as he looks down at his clipboard. "Hmmm, okay."

"Is there something I can help you with?" she offers, willing to do anything if it means getting to be left alone.

"Yes," he says.

He pulls a stack of papers off his clipboard and shoves them into her hands along with the key to the pool house's padlock.

"Would you be able to give her this invoice and let her know that the boxes of chlorine she ordered are inside the pool shed against the back wall? They're right next to the strainer and vacuum, so they should be easy to see. Make sure she knows to keep them stored away from other chemicals and acids."

"Yeah, sure. Anything else?"

"Stay out of the water until tomorrow morning so the treatment has time to settle. Everything is on the pool maintenance plan and care guide I've given you, but she can call me if she has any other questions. She should already have my information, but my number is on the invoice if anything."

"Sounds good."

"Thanks! Have a wonderful day and please give Mrs. Mueller my best!"

The man gives her one last smile before he heads back toward the house. Brianna folds the papers up, shoving them in her back pocket before putting the padlock key in her front one so she doesn't forget it.

She approaches the water and looks into it, enjoying the way the sun overhead and the cerulean tiles at the bottom of the pool make it shimmer blue. Despite the chemical smell that burns her nose and the back of her throat, she's tempted to go for a swim.

Between the blazingly hot sun and the air thick with humidity, a day by the pool sounds like heaven.

"Brianna!" her mom calls loudly from the house. "Brianna, where the hell are you?"

Her eyes widen in surprise and she panics as she looks around the pool for somewhere to hide. She knew her mother would go looking for her eventually, but she'd hoped that she'd have a bit more time to herself before being dragged back to the house to help paint her room a boring shade of greige.

Deciding the pool house is her only real choice, she quickly makes her way to the small hut, opens the door – the stiff hinges squeaking loudly and threatening to give away her position – and slams it closed behind her.

Caitlin Marceau

She leans against the door, grateful that the pool service technician hadn't bothered to shut the padlock behind him, and is relieved when her mom's voice gets fainter instead of louder.

The hut is dark, the only light coming from the small gap under the door, and Brianna feels along the wall next to her looking for a switch. Once she finds it, she flicks it up, turning the small overhead light on. The inside of the pool house is small and cramped.

Boxes of chlorine tablets rest against the back wall next to some pool toys and accessories. There's a small screen that sections off the left side of the room as a changing area, and a few shelves and cubbies built into the wall for fresh towels and spare clothes.

In the back corner is a small fridge that looks like it's been there since the '60s with a young woman leaning against it.
Brianna gasps, suddenly realizing she's not alone in the pool house.

"Who the hell are you?" Brianna shouts, pushing her back hard against the door.

The girl in the corner smiles uncomfortably, the strap of her orange paisley bathing suit visible through the collar of her terrycloth cover-up. She wears a pair of strappy brown sandals and her braided pigtails are half hidden beneath a wide-brimmed straw hat.

"My name's Susan," she says with a wave.

"What the fuck are you doing here, Susan?"

"Uh, so this is kind of embarrassing," she says, going red, "but I used to be friends with the last owner. She'd let me use her pool whenever she wanted. And then after she, well," Susan makes a face and runs a thumb across her throat, "I just kind of figured I could keep using the place until someone moved in."

"Oh, okay, but like, we moved in. So…"

"Yeah, I didn't realize that until I was getting changed back here and had the pool guy walk in on me. He didn't notice me though, so I was going to sneak out when he left, but then you came in here and didn't see me right away and now it's just super awkward."

Brianna laughs but stops when she hears her mom's voice again.

"Brianna Mueller! Where are you?" her mom screams from the house.

"I'm not fucking kidding, Brianna! Now!"

They wait for Brianna's mom to shout again, but she doesn't.

"I take it you're Brianna?"

"Yeah."

"Yikes. Your mom sounds *really* angry."

"Yeah, but she always sounds like that."

"I think all moms do."

The two girls laugh, trying to keep their voices down.

"I guess you live around here?" Brianna asks.

Susan nods her head, looking anywhere but at Brianna.

"Have you been here a while?"

"Yeah, forever," Susan says. "What about you? Like, are you from the area or–"

"No, not at all," Brianna interrupts.

"I'm from Canada, but my parents moved me here because of my dad's work. The university offered him a tenured associate position and he couldn't say no. I wish he did, though," she mutters to herself.

"Then I wouldn't be stuck with my mom and no friends for an entire summer."

"Sounds like a real bummer."

"Totally."

"But, on the plus side, you don't have to be *totally* friendless. I mean, unless you have a rule about staying away from strangers who hide in your pool house," Susan says as she looks mortified, hiding her face in her hands as Brianna chuckles at her.

"Normally, I would. But desperate times call for desperate measures."

Susan pantomimes wiping sweat off her forehead and gives an exaggerated sigh of relief.

"Phew."

"Brianna, you get over here this *instant*!" her mother shouts, her voice louder and closer than before.

"Ugh, I should probably go."

"Yeah, she kind of sounds like she's going to murder you if you don't. Is it cool if I wait here for a bit and then sneak out once nobody's around?"

"Sure. And, uh, if you want to use the pool tomorrow, you're welcome to swing by," Brianna tells her.

"I'd *love* that."

"Cool, see you then!"

"Brianna! This is your last chance, missy!" her mom howls from somewhere outside.

"Good luck!" Susan calls after her.

Brianna closes the door to the shack behind her and makes her way over to the wrought-iron fence. Her mom is standing in the gardens, her back to the pool, as she screams for Brianna.

"Hey, sorry," Brianna calls out, slowly making her way over to her mom.

"I had my headphones on. Did you say something?"

∞

"It's not like I *meant* to ignore her," Brianna says, pushing a string bean across her plate and into a pile of mashed potatoes.

"I told you; I was listening to music."

Brianna's mother shakes her head and grabs the bottle of white wine from the ice bin. She pours the last of it into her glass and takes a swig before putting it down onto the dining room table and crossing her arms in front of her chest.

"I'm not mad that you couldn't hear me. I'm mad at the shitty attitude you've had since we got here. I don't appreciate the disrespect."

"Seriously?" Brianna says, her voice raised and her eyes hot at the corners.

"*You're* disrespecting *me*! How many times did I ask you not to paint my room that ugly beige color? How many times did I say that I didn't want to move here? I was one year away from graduation – *One*! – and you move me away from my friends and the rest of our family because you're too selfish to–"

"Now that's enough!" her dad yells, finally tearing his eyes away from his lesson plan.

"You know this was a difficult decision for us to make. Don't pretend it wasn't. I'm sorry you're unhappy, but you'll get over it. As for your room, what's done is done. When you buy your own house, you can paint it whatever color you want. Until then, your mother has the final say when it comes to how she wants the place painted. Got it?"

"Whatever."

Brianna slams her fork down onto her plate and stands up, the chair scraping loudly against the hardwood.

"Easy! We just had the floors re-done!" her mom says, shaking her head.

Brianna storms out of the dining room and heads toward the stairs but stops as the smell of fresh paint gets thicker. She grumbles to herself before turning back around, cutting through the ground floor, and heading out into the backyard to get to the pool.

In the short time that it takes her to get to the water, her face is pinched together and turning red as she tries not to cry. She hates how angry she gets at her parents and how everything they say gets under her skin.

She knows she's overreacting, but that only makes her feel worse. She doesn't want to seem childish or like she's constantly throwing a tantrum, but sometimes she feels like it's the only way to get her parents to notice her.

She takes a seat on one of the old loungers, grabbing onto the armrests with her hands when one of the chair legs sinks a little more than it should.

Like the paint on the pool house, the plastic has faded from years under the harsh Southern sun, patches of dirt and grime staining the white loungers.

"I'd be careful on that," Susan says from a nearby seat.

"Those chairs have been here since the '70s. Like, they've been around since before the previous owner moved in."

Brianna is surprised to see the young teenager still at the pool and raises an eyebrow at her. "I thought you said you were leaving a while ago."

"*Technically*, I said I was going to stay for a 'bit' and leave when no one was around."

"So… ?"

"So a 'bit' turned out to be a lot longer than I'd planned. Can you blame me though? On a day like today, it's practically a crime not to spend it by the water."

"Why don't you want to go home?" Brianna asks bluntly.

"Like, why are you still hanging around here?"

Susan flinches at the questions. Normally Brianna would feel guilty for being this rude, but she's too tired from arguing with her parents to exert the energy needed to deal with Susan tactfully right now.

"I don't know…"

Brianna crosses her arms over her chest, waiting for the girl to give a better answer than that. After a moment of heavy silence, she does.

"I just… I don't have a lot of friends. And, I don't know, you looked kind of lonely too, you know?" she says quietly.

"I can go away if you want though. I don't want to—"

"No, it's fine," Brianna sighs. "I… I get it."

She doesn't want to admit that Susan's right about her. It's one thing for her to cry about being lonely on Livejournal, but another to confess it to a girl she hardly knows.

"So why are *you* out here?" the girl asks. "I mean, you're not wearing a swimsuit so…"

"Because my mom likes to throw her weight around and my dad's too busy with work to realize she's being a bitch. They're such assholes."

Susan frowns at Brianna. "You shouldn't say that about your parents."

"I wouldn't if it wasn't true."

"Still."

"Oh, come *on,*" she says, rolling her eyes and looking at Susan. "You're telling me you don't think *your* parents are assholes?"

Susan looks horrified at the thought.

"God, no. My parents were wonderful. My mom and I were close and used to do things together all the time. My dad was usually away on work, but it was like Christmas when he came home. He'd always bring me and my mom gifts. Sometimes, if he was away for a long time, I'd get to take a few days off school and we'd go to the movies and the beach and…" she sighs, smiling.

"It was pretty amazing."

Brianna raises an eyebrow. "So what happened to them?"

"What do you mean?"

"Well, you said they *were* wonderful. Did something happen?"

Susan purses her mouth and looks away. "No, nothing happened. I just… I misspoke, sorry."

Brianna is unconvinced but doesn't push the issue further.

"Well, *your* parents might be incredible, but mine suck. They don't respect me enough to let me live *my* life. Like, my mom especially feels this need to control every little thing about me and just… I don't know. Sometimes, I think I'd do anything to get away from her. You know?"

Susan nods her head.

Brianna gets up off the lounge chair and takes a seat on the soapstone tiles by the edge of the pool. She knows she's not supposed to go swimming while the chemicals settle, but the technician never said anything about her not being able to hang her legs in the water for a bit.

She puts her flip-flops on the ground next to her and dips her legs into the pool, making a face and gasping at how cold the water is despite how warm it is outside.

"Having fun?" Susan laughs.

"God, no. But also, yes," Brianna chuckles, submerging herself up to her knees.

As the two girls talk, Brianna hears the back door to the house slamming closed in the distance and she rolls her eyes.

"Incoming," she tells her friend.

Susan watches as Brianna's mom stomps across the backyard toward the pool. She has a frown plastered across her face, but it quickly changes into a polite smile when she sees that her daughter isn't alone.

"Brianna, who's this?" she asks, voice uncomfortably stiff.

"I'm Susan," the girl says pleasantly, waving hello. "I live nearby. You must be Brianna's mom. It's nice to meet you."

"You, too. Do your parents know you're out so late?"

Susan nods, looking at the ground instead of Mrs. Mueller's eyes. "I was just heading home."

The woman nods. "That's good because it's time for Brianna to come inside and get ready for bed."

"Mom," Brianna whines, "it's not even late! Like–"

"I need your help setting up the guest bedroom while the paint in your room dries. I don't want you breathing in chemicals all night. And get out of the water. You said the technician told you not to use it until tomorrow."

Brianna rolls her eyes and shoots her mom a glare. "It's just my legs."

"Are they in the water?"

"Yeah, but–"

"Then get them out until tomorrow," her mom hisses.

"*Fine.*"

Her mom flashes Susan another smile.

"It was nice meeting you, Susan. Please feel free to come back during the day to enjoy the pool. Brianna, hop to it."

Mrs. Mueller waves goodbye to Susan and frowns once more at her daughter before heading back to the house.

Once she's out of earshot, Brianna speaks. "I told you she was a bitch."

"She's not a *bitch*. She was fine to me," Susan giggles as she watches Mrs. Mueller walk away.

"That's because she likes you," Brianna sighs, leaning forward to splash a bit of water at Susan.

Caitlin Marceau

Her blood runs cold as she watches the water pass through Susan to land on the furniture beneath her. Although she doesn't see the water pooling on the plastic recliner, she sees it slowly dripping onto the tile below.

Brianna places a hand against her chest and stares at her friend, who's too distracted by the house to notice the sudden panic on her face. Brianna's heart pounds fast and she's surprised it's not banging against her ribs loud enough for Susan to hear.

She cups a bit more of the water in her hand and tosses it at the girl again, her chest tightening as it passes through Susan once more. She stares at her friend, breath stuck in the back of her throat, as Susan finally turns around to look at her.

"Are you okay?" she asks, raising an eyebrow.

"Yeah. Yes. I'm fine," Brianna eventually says, the words heavy on her tongue. "Just… distracted."

She gets out of the water and grabs her sandals as she stands back up. "I have to go."

"I know," Susan laughs. "I'll catch you later?"

"Tomorrow," Brianna says, her mouth suddenly too dry and her body tense.

"Cool. Later!"

Brianna waves a stiff goodbye and heads back to the house, trying not to sprint for the door.

∞

Brianna looks out into the yard, trying to catch a glimpse of Susan without being seen through the window. She hasn't been to the pool in a few days. Although it's been lonely only spending time with her mom, she's been too nervous to speak with her friend.

She stares at the wrought-iron fence, keeping herself hidden by the drapes as she waits for Susan to appear like she does every day. While Brianna has yet to return to the water, she's seen the girl waiting for her by the pool house or sitting patiently on a lounger on more than one occasion.

While she looked happy—even excited—for the first couple of days, by the end of the week she looked like she'd given up hope of ever seeing Brianna again.

Brianna looks over at the clock on the wall and frowns to herself, realizing that she's been waiting for almost ten minutes, before turning her attention back to the pool. She can't help the gasp that escapes her as she sees Susan materialize out of thin air.

The girl leans against the door of the poolhouse, kicking the toe of her sandal against the stone tiles as she waits.

Brianna ducks behind the curtain, rubbing her arm as goosebumps make their way across her skin. Her heart is beating fast again, and she wants nothing more than to go back up to her room, but she knows she can only avoid Susan for so long. It is her house, after all.

She lets out a shaky exhale and exits through the back door, her towel and sunscreen gripped tight to her chest as she makes her way across the backyard.

Susan notices her approaching and a wide grin spreads across her face.

"Hey!" she calls, waving happily. "I hope you don't mind that I let myself in."

"Not at all," Brianna answers, her smile not reaching her eyes and her voice unsteady.

"Have you been waiting a long time?"

"No, no. I just got here. I was actually here a few days ago, but I must have just missed you. So, I thought I'd see if you were here today, and you are!"

Brianna nods at the lie. She knows Susan has been here every day since last week, but she doesn't want to call the girl – the *ghost*? – out like that. At least, not yet. She takes a good look at Susan, squinting from the sun overhead as she takes her in.

Like the first time she met the girl, Susan is wearing an oversized terrycloth coverup with an orange – no, rust-colored – paisley bathing suit underneath. Her hair is in braided pigtails, but Brianna doesn't think she's trying to pay an ironic homage to Britney Spears like she originally thought.

Instead, she wonders if Susan's hair and retro accessories – like her old-fashioned sunhat – aren't fun fashion choices but a marker of when she was alive.

"Yeah, I've been pretty busy. My mom keeps getting me to help her with house stuff. I'm so over it, honestly."

"Over house stuff or your mom?"

Brianna can't help but laugh at the question. As nervous as she is, she'd be lying if she said she hadn't missed Susan's company.

"Both," she admits. "Not that you can relate. You said you were close with your mom, didn't you?"

"Yeah. We've always been a really close family."

"I wish I knew what that was like."

"It's amazing, honestly. It's reassuring to know that there are people out there who just *get* you. You know? And who will always be there for you, no matter what," Susan says, looking off into the distance.

"And where's your family now?"

"I told you, I live nearby," she says quickly, not meeting Brianna's gaze.

"I know where *you* live, but where does your *family* live?" Brianna pries.

Susan frowns at her. "What are you getting at?"

Brianna looks at Susan sadly, trying to find a delicate way to phrase things as her heart beats faster. She's nervous to confront Susan about the water, about the way she saw the girl materialize out of nothingness. What if she's a violent spirit? What if she doesn't *know* she's a spirit? What if she's not a specter but something else entirely?

Brianna's legs shake at the thought, and she suddenly feels too cold and too hot at the same time. She looks back at the house and debates running back to it like a coward but forces herself to stay.

"I don't know, you just… you seem so sad when you talk about them. Or like, bittersweet, I guess. I don't know, you don't talk about them like someone who sees them every day," Brianna admits.

"You talk about them like someone who has, I don't know, maybe unfinished business with them?"

Susan throws her head back and laughs. "Oh man, you sound like one of those cheesy psychics my mom hired after I died," she finally says, gasping for air as she continues to laugh.

Brianna freezes, her breath catching in her throat. She's not sure what she was expecting the other girl to say, but it wasn't this. She looks at Susan, unsure if she should laugh too, play dumb, or stay quiet. Eventually, she settles on asking her a question.

"How did you figure out that I knew?"

"Suggesting I have unfinished business is kind of a dead giveaway, pun intended. And, sorry, it's not like you were subtle about it. I mean, you practically *sprinted* back to your house the other night. I figured something was wrong and then saw the water under my chair so…"

"Oh." She knows it's not an adequate reply, so she pushes herself to say more. "I'm sorry I ran away like that."

"It's okay. I'm sorry I freaked you out," Susan says, playing with one of her braids.

"Don't be," she says a little too quickly. She wants to say more but isn't sure what, before settling for asking a question. "How did you... you *know*?"

"Die?" Susan offers.

Brianna winces at the word. She wonders if it's gauche to ask about a person's passing and regrets the question. "Sorry, that was rude to ask. You don't have to tell me or anything."

"It's fine. I was playing in the water and ran into the pool house to get a drink from the fridge and slipped on the wet floor. I cracked my head open pretty badly and was dead before I even knew something was wrong."

"I'm sorry."

"Don't be. My parents warned me over and over again about running when wet. I just never took them seriously. And, you know, it was almost thirty years ago so…"

Brianna nods her head, surprised by how open and unbothered her friend is about something so serious.

"If it was that long ago, then I guess your family must have moved or passed aw—" she stops when she notices Susan's expression change to a more somber one.

"Then they must have moved a while ago," she finishes awkwardly.

"It was a long time ago," she confesses. "It wasn't *right* after I died, but it wasn't exactly long afterward, either."

"Why did they leave? Like, why didn't your parents stay?"

"Because of me," Susan says quietly. "It was too much for them."

"Did they know you were…?" She's unsure how to finish the question without sounding rude, so she doesn't.

"Still here?"

"Yeah."

"Yeah, they knew. They couldn't stand to see me stuck here—stuck like *this*. And when nobody could do anything to help me, I think it started driving my mom nuts. She used to say, 'I can't miss you if you never leave.' So, they left instead," she tells Brianna sadly, gesturing to the clothes she died in.

"Which, in hindsight, is pretty funny."

"Why's that?"

"I didn't cross over because I hated the thought of abandoning my family. And once they left and I *wanted* to move on, I couldn't."

"That's messed up."

285

Caitlin Marceau

Susan nods in agreement. Her eyes look glossy, her face is red, and her lip quivers as she tries not to burst into tears. Brianna finds herself torn between feeling sorry for her friend and being fascinated that the spirit can cry.

"I miss them so much," she whispers. Brianna wonders if the girl is speaking to her or herself and decides that keeping quiet is best. "I'm really lonely," Susan confesses.

"I'm lonely too."

Susan smiles sadly. "At least you have your parents."

"I think they're *why* I'm so lonely. Like, they don't understand me. They don't *want* to understand me. It sucks."

"I'm sorry you're stuck with your family."

"I'm sorry you're stuck *without* one."

∾

Brianna grips her fork tightly in her hand, the metal digging into her skin. She stares at her mom in disbelief and waits for her dad to intervene, but he doesn't.

"This is a joke, right?"

"Do you always have to be this oppositional?" her mom asks, taking another sip of her wine. "I thought you'd be happy to get a chance to make some new friends ahead of the school year."

"Mom, nobody my age goes to a day camp! *Nobody*! Now I'm going to be the freak who went to camp with a bunch of six-year-olds! It's like you're actively trying to ruin my life!" she shouts, hands shaking with anger.

"Don't be ridiculous! The day camp is meant for teenagers!"

"Yeah, for teenagers who've been *homeschooled*, Mom! It's meant for religious freaks whose parents don't let them go to public school! It's not meant for–"

"I don't know why you have to make everything so difficult. I really don't. I did something nice for you and *this* is the thanks I get?" her mom asks.

"I appreciate you *trying* to do something nice, but I don't want to go. You're literally taking me away from the one friend I've made here and sticking me at a civic center with a bunch of social rejects. I don't want to go. *Please* don't make me go!"

"You're so dramatic!" her mom says, shaking her head. "You're going, Brianna."

"Dad, come *on*! You can't let her send me to–"

"Sweetie, this is a good opportunity to meet more kids your own age. You've been glued to your computer or in the backyard with that one neighbour girl, Sarah–"

"Susan," Mrs. Mueller corrects.

"–since we moved here. We know you miss your friends back home, but your mom is giving you a great opportunity to socialize with other kids your age," he says between bites of his dinner.

"But dad, I don't want to–"

"Look, I've had a long day," he tells her, pushing his glasses further up his nose with the tip of his pinky.

"It's camp, Brianna, not hard labour. Try it out for a few days and if you still hate it, we'll revisit your options. Okay?"

"I think that's pretty fair," her mom adds with a smile. "If you're unhappy, you don't have to stick it out. But just *try* it. You might be surprised to find you actually enjoy it."

Brianna clenches her jaw, wanting to scream in frustration. She puts her fork down on the table and gets up from her seat.

"Sweetie, you've hardly touched your meal," her mom says, pointing at the remaining pork roast. "Sit down and–"

"I'm not hungry," she says, storming out of the dining room.

She debates going upstairs and locking herself in her room but knows she'll just end up in a fight with them if her mom comes up to talk. Instead, she runs through the house and out the back door, making her way across the lawn, past the iron fence, over the hard tile, and into the pool house.

She shuts the door behind her and sits on the ground, crying to herself.

"What's wrong?" Susan asks, materializing out of thin air.

"I hate them so much," Brianna hisses as she hides her face in her knees.

"Who?"

"Who do you think?"

Susan frowns and sits on the floor next to Brianna. "What happened?"

"They're forcing me to go to this weird day camp thing and like… I *know* it's not a big deal. I *knooooow* it's not. But like, I just wish they'd let me have a say in my own life. Like, just *once* I wish they'd give me the freedom to make my own choices. But why let me do anything that *I* want to do when they can smother me instead, you know?"

Susan smiles sadly at her. "I know you don't believe me, but try not to be too mad at them. I promise you, there's going to be a day when you miss being smothered. I know I do."

Brianna laughs. "Then I hope that day gets here quickly because right now, honestly, I just wish you and I could switch places."

"I do too."

∽

"Wait, so you've *never* heard anything from Panic! At The Disco?"

"Never. But I enjoyed that last album! I mean, they're no ABBA, but they're good!"

"Ew!"

"What?"

"My grandmother listens to ABBA, and I can't stand them," Brianna says, side-eyeing Susan with a horrified expression on her face.

"Then your grandma has great taste."

The two girls laugh, and Brianna pulls her iPod back out of the front pocket of her low-rise jeans. She tries to pass Susan one of the earphones, but the white plastic passes through her hand and lands on the pool house floor.

"Oh, sorry, I totally forgot," Brianna says, embarrassed.

"It's fine! Honestly, I sometimes forget I can't hold solid objects too."

She picks it back up and cups the two earphones in her hand before selecting the next album on her device, Paramore's *All We Know Is Falling*, and pressing play. She turns the volume up and looks at Susan expectantly.

"Okay, what about this one?" she asks.

"What *about* this one?"

"Have you ever heard–"

Brianna stops mid-sentence as the door to the pool house opens. Her mom stands in the doorway, arms crossed over her chest, looking furious. She looks like she's about to shout but stops herself as she notices that her daughter isn't alone.

"Susan, do your parents know you're here?"

"They do," she admits sadly.

"Are they home?"

"Yes," she lies.

"Good. I'm sorry to be so rude, but I'm afraid I need you to leave now. My daughter is grounded, and she's not allowed to have company over."

"Oh, sorry," Susan says.

"What? What are you talking about?" Brianna shouts angrily.

"I will deal with *you* in a minute," her mom tells her, voice raised.

Susan gets up off the floor, shooting Brianna an apologetic look, before heading toward the door of the pool house. Mrs. Mueller moves to the side, giving the girl room to pass. Susan carefully squeezes through, making sure not to touch the woman or accidentally phase through the door frame as she exits the shed.

"Sorry about that, Susan. Please tell your parents I say hello."

"Sure thing, Mrs. Mueller. Bye, Bri!"

"Bye."

Good luck, Susan mouths to her friend. She heads towards the wrought-iron gate. She checks over her shoulder to make sure Brianna's mom isn't watching and disappears out of sight.

"What do you mean I'm grounded?" Brianna asks her mom, getting to her feet. "I didn't do anything!"

"Your father and I told you to give camp a try, to give it just one day! *One day*!" she shouts, stomping out of the pool house and through the backyard as Brianna quickly walks after her.

"I did! I—"

"You did?" her mom asks, spinning around on her heel. "Really?"

"I did," Brianna lies. "I went there this morning and they let us out early, so now I'm home."

"Are you sure that's the lie you want to stick to?"

"It's not a lie."

Brianna's mom stares at her. She knows her mom wants her to say more, but she doesn't. After a few minutes, Mrs. Mueller continues her warpath to the house. She opens the back door and stomps into the kitchen as Brianna follows behind her. She stops in front of the answering machine on the kitchen counter and hits play.

There's a small beep followed by static, and then the voice starts to play.

"Hello, Mrs. Mueller," the reedy voice says, "I just wanted to check in and see if Brianna was going to be joining us today. In future, if your daughter is going to be absent or late, we ask that you please call us ahead of time and leave us a voicemail. Thanks, and have a great day!"

There's a long silence, followed by a soft click as the message ends.

Brianna opens her mouth to say something, anything, but her mom is already making her way to the staircase, her feet loud on the steps as she marches up to her daughter's room.

"I told you that I didn't want to go!" Brianna says, following her mom up the stairs. "But you didn't listen to me! So, what was I supposed to do?"

"You were supposed to *go*!" her mom screams, throwing open the door to Brianna's room.

"What are you doing?" she calls after her mom. "Get out of my room."

Her mom doesn't listen. Instead, she makes a beeline for the computer and begins yanking wires out of the tower.

"Stop!" Brianna shouts. "What the fuck are you doing?"

Her mom doesn't answer. Instead, she continues to disconnect the tower from the monitor, unplugs it from the wall, and heaves as she picks it up off Brianna's desk.

"Mom, what the fuck?" she shouts. "Stop! That's my computer!"

Her mom carries the tower down the hall and into the master bedroom, putting it down a little too roughly in the corner of the room.

"Mom! I said–"

"I don't give a *fuck* what you said!" her mom shouts, face red and eyes wild. "I'm *sick* of the attitude. I'm tired of you being so disrespectful, argumentative, and *rude*. I've had it up to here," she yells, throwing a hand over her head, "with your bullshit. I know you didn't want to move. None of us did! But it was the right choice for your father's career and he *deserves* to pursue this opportunity. And instead of being supportive, giving this place a chance, or even trying to meet us halfway, you've been a miserable little *bitch* about it!"

Brianna takes a step back, her body flinching like she's been slapped.

"You're grounded. You're *beyond* grounded. You'll be lucky to see this computer or your friend between now and the end of the year. Do you understand me?"

"That's not fair! You can't–"

"Don't tell *me* what I can and can't do," she shouts back.

"Is it fun constantly trying to ruin my life? Do you, like, get some kind of sick joy knowing I'm miserable being your daughter?"

Her mom shakes her head and points to the hallway. "Go to your room, Brianna. I don't even want to look at you right now."

"Whatever."

Brianna exits the bedroom and starts making her way back down the hall.

"Why can't you be like Susan?" her mom asks. "Why can't you be polite and respectful and just… *good*? What happened to the kid you used to be?"

Before Brianna can reply, her mom shuts the bedroom door in her face.

∞

Brianna stays awake long after her parents are asleep. She goes over the plan a few times in her head, hoping that Susan will agree to it, before quietly opening the door to her bedroom, her mom's discarded painting mask around her neck.

She stands at the end of the hallway, listening to her parents' snores, before carefully creeping down the staircase. She stops at the bottom, making sure they're both still asleep before she makes her way into the kitchen.

She looks around the room, not sure where her mother stores the vinegar, and quietly checks the cupboards under the sink before looking in the pantry. Her heart pounds when the hinges squeak, and she waits for her mom to wake up.

When she doesn't, Brianna opens the door the rest of the way and smiles, spotting the bulk-sized jug of vinegar. She quietly lifts it out of the cupboard, the five-litre bottle heavier than she expected, and heads for the back door.

She opens it quietly, holding her breath as she steps into the backyard, and closes it gently behind her. She waits a second more before sprinting to the pool area.

∞

Brianna lets out a shaky breath as she dumps the last box of chlorine onto the floor of the pool house, the skin on her hands starting to burn and itch.

"Do you think this is enough?"

"I don't know," Susan admits. "It's not like I've ever done this before."

"No, I know, I just… I might hate them, but I still want it to be quick, you know?"

Susan nods. "Yeah, quick is good. Mine was quick."

"Yeah."

Brianna makes sure everything is in place – she double-checks that the towels are on the ground outside the pool house, that the silver key to the padlock is in her pocket, and that her mom's painter's mask is properly secured to her face – before nodding to Susan.

"Okay, let's do it."

"You're sure you want to go through with this?" Susan asks one last time.

"I'd rather be alone than trapped like I am," Brianna mutters. "I'd do *anything* to swap places with you, Susan. I really would. Plus, we both get what we want, right?"

"Right."

Brianna picks up the plastic jug of vinegar and dumps it onto the first pile of chlorine tablets, hoping the mask is enough to keep her safe from the fumes as she works.

"Then I am."

∽

"Mom! Dad!" Brianna shouts, running through the living room of the big house. "Where are you?" she screams.

"Up here," her dad calls down, voice thick with sleep.

"What's wrong?"

"Come down here, quickly!" she screams.

She listens to her parents' unsteady footsteps as they get out of bed and make their way to the top of the staircase.

"What? What is it?" her mom asks, annoyed.

"Susan's hurt!" Brianna shouts, hands shaking with nerves, as she looks up at her mom.

"What?" Mrs. Mueller asks, quickly descending the staircase with her husband in tow. "What happened?"

"I was mad at you and needed to vent, so I called her, and we snuck out to the pool. We were playing and she started running around and she slipped and… She won't get up. She's bleeding pretty bad–"

Before she can finish her sentence, her parents have descended the staircase and are running to the back door.

"Get the phone," her dad calls to Brianna, "and call 9-1-1!"

Brianna runs into the kitchen and grabs the portable phone off the hook, taking it with her as she follows them through the house, the backyard, and past the iron fence.

"Where is she?" her mom asks, not seeing Susan on the tiled ground around the pool.

"She's–" Her voice is shaky and her words catch in her throat. For a moment, she's not sure she can go through with things.

"Damn it, Brianna! Where is she? And I thought your father told you to call 9-1-1! Don't be so useless!"

"She slipped in the pool house," she says quietly.

As her mom heads to the door and throws it open, Mr. Mueller following closely behind, Brianna grabs the painter's mask out from under one of the recliners and straps it to her face.

Inside the shed, Susan lies face up on the floor, a puddle of blood growing on the wood around her, her mouth open in surprise and her eyes wide and unfocused as she looks up at the ceiling.

"What the fuck is that smell?" her mom asks, running over to the girl's side.

"Brianna, did you call the ambulance yet?" her dad shouts, his eyes widening in confusion when he spots her mask.

She only catches a glimpse of her mom's surprised face as she slams the pool house door shut and snaps the padlock into place. She hears her mom gasp in surprise as Susan – no longer bloody – materializes next to Brianna from the other side of the door.

"I never thought being able to relive my death would come in handy like that," Susan admits to her.

Brianna nods, grabbing one of the towels off a chair and pushing it under the pool house door, trying to block the chlorine gas from escaping through the small gap. On the other side of the door, she can hear her parents start to cough.

"What the hell? What's going on?" her mom asks, her voice high with fear.

"Just try to relax," she tells her mom, voice quivering. "It's going to be over soon and then you'll have Susan as your new kid. You'll finally have the daughter you've always wanted."

"What are you talking about?" her dad shouts.

"Brianna!" her mom screams, pounding on the door. "Let us out!"

"It'll be better this way, Mrs. Mueller," Susan says, smiling. "I promise."

Brianna hopes her friend is right.

As her parents beg for help and bang on the door, Brianna takes a seat on one of the recliners across from the pool house, closing her eyes and covering her ears.

∞

Brianna stands at the gate of the pool but doesn't open it. Instead, she stands behind it and looks at her feet, adjusting her backpack on her shoulder.

"Do you think you'll be gone for long?" Susan asks on the other side of the iron border.

"I don't think so," she lies, the plane ticket bringing her home suddenly heavy in her pocket.

If she has it her way, she'll never come back to this state, this town, this house. But she knows it won't be long until someone finds her family in the pool house.

If it's not one of the technicians or repairmen looking to get paid, then it'll be her school asking where she is or the university trying to find her dad. She knows she'll face the consequences of her actions sooner than later, but she tries not to think about it for now.

"Oh, awesome! I was worried I'd be alone with them for – I mean, it's not like I don't *like* talking to them or anything! Your family's great. It's just…"

It's not your *family*, Brianna thinks.

"Yeah," she says out loud. "I get it."

"I mean, I'm grateful to have parents again. It's just… I don't know," Susan admits, still looking lonely as she smiles to herself.

"Yeah."

"Are you going to tell them goodbye?"

Brianna can't help but look over at the pool house. Although the door is closed, she can imagine her parents' bodies inside, slowly rotting from the heat and the chemical mess left behind.

She looks away; her eyes find their spirits sitting on chairs by the pool. They stare into the water, unable to look at the daughter that killed them, and she feels her face growing hot with shame.

"No. There's no need for goodbyes," she says sadly.

"Besides, I can't miss them if they never leave."

Treehouse
1993

Inherited
Christy Aldridge

"You know you can stay here longer than you planned. We don't plan to sell the house for another couple of months. There's more than enough room for you and Jack in this big house. I wouldn't mind… Cynthia? Cynthia?"

The lady in question looked away from the window and toward the other woman in the room. She was staring at Cynthia, a small smile inching across her face as she stirred her cup of tea, amused at Cynthia's detachment.

"Where did your mind wander off to?" she asked.

"Jack is in the treehouse again," Cynthia answered.

Her friend, the owner of said treehouse, was Emily Hale. She looked out the same window Cynthia was staring at moments before and then forced another smile.

"He's a kid. You know how cool a treehouse looks to a kid," she told her, trying to sound nonchalant about the ordeal, but Cynthia knew her feelings were the same.

"I don't like it. I wish he'd stay away from it," Cynthia said, looking at her own cup of tea. She hadn't touched it since Emily poured it for her. Too many things on her mind.

"I know. I don't think I've been back inside since…" Emily stopped and looked at Cynthia.

"About as long as you, I'd imagine. I'd like to tear it down, but I feel a little superstitious."

"Why?" Cynthia asked, trying not to look too startled by this.

"That treehouse is as old as Hale House itself. I feel like my great-great-great-grandfather would probably come back from the dead and haunt me the rest of my life if I tore it down, even with its… *history,*" Emily said.

Cynthia didn't want to discuss any history. She just wanted her son with her now. Out of that treehouse and inside with her.

"But you know, I'd hate to ruin his fun during a time like this. Lord knows the kid needs something to distract him right now," Emily said, hitting the nail on the head for the reason Cynthia wasn't stopping him.

"How has he been handling it? I know it's only been a few days, but he's so young."

Cynthia shrugged, finally sipping at her tea. "I don't know. He's barely spoken a word to me since we got here. I was hoping that getting him away from the house while we dealt with everything would help him through it," Cynthia said, rubbing her hand over her face.

"Besides that, he didn't need to see the huge FORECLOSED sign in the yard. I'm sure he'd be able to read it, even if he didn't understand what it meant."

"I still don't know why you didn't say something about how bad things were getting," Emily told her, reaching out across the dining table to touch her hand.

"If you and Hugh were having money troubles, you could have said something. I would have helped."

"You were having your own issues. I mean, you're selling your family home," Cynthia reminded her.

"Would be the first time a Hale has sold the place," Emily answered with a smile.

"My parents sold it back in the seventies to that Windom Horne and I know they made a huge profit from that. But I told my mother that I would buy it back some day. A Hale deserves Hale House, but a Hale also deserves a house better than Hale House, so, we sell."

Emily shrugged this off like it was easy enough to do, but Cynthia wasn't sure if she would have been so easy to buy back the family home just to sell it a few years later. Then again, she wasn't born with an established name like her friend.

"Even so, you could have told me. We could have helped," Emily said, coming back to Cynthia's troubles.

"Hugh wouldn't have heard of that," Cynthia said. "He was too proud to reach out for help. He always carried the burdens himself, tried to handle it all alone."

"Do you think the stress is what caused the heart attack?"

"That's what the doctors think. He was younger than typical for heart attack risk, but he hadn't been taking care of himself for a long time," Cynthia said.

"His doctor had even explained that he had a few heart problems to keep an eye on, but Hugh stayed so busy, he barely gave his health any thought."

"It's such a shame though," Emily said. "Hugh was so young. Barely into his forties. It's awful for you and Jack. And then all of the problems you mentioned financially."

"Hugh was under a lot of pressure after losing those big accounts. The house being foreclosed on, his business slowly going under, he was stretched thin. I wish he would have told me more. Maybe I could have alleviated the stress. Gotten a job, something."

"You can't blame yourself," Emily told her. "And besides, he probably would be happy right now knowing that you won't have to endure that. That Jack won't. His love for you will still go on, even in death. And with the reading of the will tomorrow, I'm sure everything will turn out okay."

Cynthia slowly nodded, blotting her eyes. "I miss him so much though. I'd rather be penniless and have my husband. I'd rather Jack have his father," she told Emily.

Emily smiled softly, patting her hand. "I know you would. Jack knows that too. He'll be coming in soon, won't he?"

Cynthia glanced at the clock. It was nearing half past five. "I've told him he has to come in when it starts turning dark. So, he'll come in soon," she said.

"Good, I've ordered out tonight, so maybe you two can spend a little time together, talk about it," Emily suggested.

It wasn't entirely Jack's fault when it came to their lack of quality time. Taking care of her late husband's funeral and affairs had kept Cynthia relatively busy.

But they had come to stay at Hale House because Cynthia worried about Jack's wellbeing. What seven-year-old would want to stay in the home his dad passed away in?

She couldn't imagine him asking what a foreclosure was or messing with his dad's things. Hale House was the best option.

And Hale House was even nicer than their home. Not that it was their home now.

But Hale House wasn't a house. It was a mansion. Much nicer than any house Cynthia had ever lived in. As a child, she remembered wanting so desperately to own a home as grand as the sprawling estate of Hale House.

She never wanted to own Hale House. She didn't want to even stay within its walls, but this was temporary. Emily Hale was her closest friend and her husband was the family attorney. It seemed best to just stay here where she could finish off these affairs as quickly as they'd allow.

As a child, she had envied her friend. Her mother was also best friends with Emily's mother, and Cynthia spent much of her prepubescent years at the mansion before Emily's mother sold it off in 1973.

She would pretend, as a child, that it was hers. That she was rich enough to live here. That she was as fancy and poised as the Hale family.

She wasn't, as evidenced by Emily leaving to get 'dressed for dinner.' Cynthia wasn't a slob, but she didn't dress in certain clothes to have dinner with her family.

Jack came in before the pizza arrived and they ate with Emily and her husband, Carl. Emily and Carl talked, Cynthia chimed in every so often, but Jack stayed silent.

It worried Cynthia. She had always worried about her son, but even more so now. She expected questions, tears, something. Instead, he was withdrawn.

And sucked up by that godforsaken treehouse.

After dinner, Emily and Carl retired to their room, but Cynthia knew it was mostly to allow Cynthia some time alone with her son. Something she planned to take advantage of.

She poured herself a cup of tea and gave Jack a glass of chocolate milk. He didn't ask for it, but he sipped at it with her.

He didn't look depressed or upset. He still looked like her Jack, but she worried.

"How are you feeling, sweetie?"

"I'm okay," he answered. It was quick, even a little cheerful, but not enough to ease Cynthia's anxiety.

"You know we can talk about things. You don't have to stay in the treehouse all day. I'm not too busy to talk to you," she told him. "We could even put a puzzle together or play on the computer, if you'd like."

"I'd rather play in the treehouse," he told her. He tipped his cup to her, showing her the empty contents. "I drank my milk, Mommy. Can I go to bed now?"

Cynthia smiled softly. "Sure, sweetie. Want me to read a book to you?"

"No, I'm tired," he said, standing up and kissing her cheek. "Goodnight, Mommy. I love you."

"I love you too," she told him and watched him leave the room. She watched until his shadow disappeared, then her gaze went back to the window, back to the treehouse.

She hated it. Hated that treehouse with every fiber of her being. It was stealing time away from her with her son. It had too many memories. Too many *bad* memories.

And it followed her into her dreams. In her dreams, she was back in the treehouse. Those bad memories followed her as she danced around, not a care in the world.

Until she was falling, staring up at the treehouse, watching it watch her fall until she hit the ground.

Little dreams like that had plagued her every night since they had come to stay in Hale House. Closing her eyes only to find herself being pushed from the treehouse. Waking up to find a place on the cold floor of her temporary room.

And then spending the day watching her son stay cooped up in the treehouse, only coming out for lunch and bedtime.

"Jack really loves that old treehouse, huh?" Carl said, scaring her.

When she turned, he smiled apologetically at her and held up a folder.

"Sorry. I have the will and insurance papers here if you want to go over them."

Cynthia nodded. "I do. I'm going to go check on Jack first though," she told him.

He nodded. "Sure, I'll set up in the library. Just come in whenever you're ready," he told her.

Cynthia was more than ready to finish with all of the legalities. She wanted to be done with discussing all of the things she was now responsible for since her husband's passing.

She wanted to be able to move on, to comfort her son. Jack was the most important thing to her. She wanted to help him through this time, to make sure he was fine and not slowly drowning while she was tied up with paperwork.

She didn't think that was going to happen until they were both gone and far away from Hale House.

She walked outside to the treehouse and stared up the steps. She didn't want to go inside. She had vowed never to step inside. She had never liked the treehouse and it bothered her that Jack liked it so much.

"Jack?" she called out.

Jack stuck his head out the door and smiled. "Hi, Mommy!" he called out.

Her dreams came back as she moved closer to the ladder. "Please be careful!" she warned him. "You could easily fall out that door."

"I'm being careful," he said.

His tone implied that he also rolled his eyes, but Cynthia couldn't see him doing it. He had retreated back into the treehouse.

She could hear him though. He was speaking. She was used to Jack talking to himself as he played with his toys. All of his action figures regularly talked to one another during his games. They were all voiced by Jack, but this was different.

This wasn't her son making voices for different characters. It was his voice and when he said something, he paused as if listening to someone else speak to him. Like he was having a conversation.

"Who's up there with you?" she asked.

"A friend. She lives in the treehouse," Jack answered.

Great, Cynthia thought glumly. *The last thing he needs is another invisible friend.*

"What's their name?" Cynthia asked, but she knew Jack would answer with something off the wall.

All of his imaginary friends had wacky names like Bubble Boots or Catty Whack. Her husband said that it was Jack's way of asking for a sibling, but Cynthia refused to get pregnant again. She hated being pregnant and loved being able to spoil Jack.

But Jack didn't give a funny name this time. Instead, he didn't give one at all.

"She doesn't want me to tell you," he said.

A girl? That was strange. All of Jack's friends were normally of the male variety. Which made sense to her since Jack had affectionately reached the age of claiming that girls were gross and had cooties.

But this was a strange time in his life. He was bound to do things that didn't seem right. Things that were unlike the Jack she knew. He was just a little kid dealing with the massive weight of losing his dad.

Once this was all over, once they were on their own and didn't have to deal with these after-death rituals, she'd make sure he was okay, make sure that nothing had a lasting effect on him and that he could have the chance to grow up and be normal.

"Why doesn't she want me to know? Does she not like me?" Cynthia asked, laughing slightly.

There was a pause from her son. Then, she heard, "She wants you to leave. She really doesn't like you. She says you're bad."

"That's incredibly rude, Jack," Cynthia said, not feeling the laughter now. In fact, she was a little upset that her son would say such a thing to her. She hadn't raised him that way, not to speak out to his parents like that.

"I didn't say it, Mommy. She did," Jack reminded her.

Cynthia knew she could berate him for acting out and lying. She could banish him from the treehouse and let him think on it for a while, but she decided not to.

He had enough to think about and she decided to offer that instead.

"You know, you can talk to me, Jack. We can talk about your dad. I know that this has been hard on you, losing him, but you don't have to…"

"Mom?" Jack interrupted, his voice a little higher. "She's getting really upset right now. Can I just play instead?"

Cynthia sighed.

She didn't have to be a psychologist to know Jack was saying the girl was upset so he didn't have to discuss something that bothered him. She resolved to just leave him be.

She would talk to him again after the reading of the will and when he was out of the treehouse, she supposed. It was nearing dinner time already and he would be coming in once it started to get dark.

"Okay. When it gets dark, come in and I'll fix you something to eat," she told him.

"Okay!"

He began to giggle and talk again, resuming whatever conversation he had before with this 'friend' of his. She had to expect things like this. It was going to be hard. Things were going to be rough for a while. She had to prepare herself for this.

She walked back into Hale House and walked into the office. She knew this mansion like it was her own. She'd spent enough time here as a child, running the halls with Emily, playing dolls in the empty rooms, hide and seek along the grounds, she knew it, but it was just memories.

Ever since she was eleven, she'd tried to avoid most of Hale House. Despite her love for the grand home, she never wanted to be here longer than necessary.

When she opened the doors to the office, Carl was inside. He smiled at her.

"I have all of the paperwork now. Are we waiting for anyone else to read it?" he asked.

"No, just me. Hugh's parents passed away and he was an only child. I was all he had besides Jack," she told him.

"Can we go ahead and get it over with? Jack should be coming inside soon, and I want to get packed tonight. Our plane leaves tomorrow morning."

"Of course, I have it ready," he told her. "You're planning to go west, right? Emily mentioned your family was out that way."

"I think, for the time being, it'll do Jack and I some good to be with my family. Maybe we'll come back some day, but this place holds too many memories for now," Cynthia told her.

"Good job, really. With us selling, I doubt there's much reason to stick around. Maybe we'll also go west!" he said with a slight laugh.

Truthfully, Cynthia never planned to return. She was ready to move on. To move forward, and to never think of this place again. She was ready to put it all behind her and start a new chapter with Jack.

"How about we start with the will then?" Carl answered.

Cynthia nodded and made herself comfortable as she listened to what was now to become of her life. She was nervous. She'd been nervous for days, afraid of what would become of them, but hopeful.

Carl's eyes looked over the will as he spoke.

"Hugh left everything to you, just as we discussed when we created the will before. He's made no changes over the years. The house, the cars, all of his assets still go to you to be kept or sold off," he said.

"The life insurance policy he had will go into full effect and after paying off his outstanding debt, it looks like you'll still have over a half million dollars if the amount your accountant and I figured is right. This is before you decide whether to sell off his business as well," Carl said.

"I still plan to sell it to you if you still want it. As struggling as it's been, I still think the name should hold some merit and I trust whatever price you offer," she told him.

Carl nodded. "Good. You should be set for a long time, Cynthia. Hugh's passing gives you a chance to start over. I'd invest wisely, and you should be financially set."

A huge weight seemed to lift from her chest as he told her this. Knowing she would be fine, Jack would be fine, because of Hugh's passing. They would be taken care of. Despite the cost it took to happen, Cynthia felt relieved to know she wouldn't be broke.

A tear fell from her face, and she wiped it away. "Sorry, I just don't know how to handle it," she told Carl.

He smiled diplomatically. "Obviously, Hugh being gone is awful, but this is best case scenario in case of death. Hugh was looking out for you without even realizing it. No need to feel guilty about it. Hugh would want the two of you to go on and be happy," he told her.

Cynthia smiled, wiping her eyes. "I know. I just miss him," she said, sniffling.

"I'm going to go to my room and compose myself before I get Jack ready for dinner. He'll be coming in soon."

"Okay. Emily wanted to take the two of you to that new Italian place in town. She hates that you're leaving, you know? We'll have a few drinks and get out of here for a while," Carl told her.

Cynthia smiled. "That sounds good. We'll be ready in a bit," she told him.

Cynthia stood and left the room. She walked into the nursery, wiping the tears from her eyes as she closed the door.

Once it was closed, she took a deep breath and then released it with a shaky laugh. She then smiled, wiping the rest of the tears from her cheeks and walking into the bathroom.

She stared at her face in the mirror. It was a convincing face. Red cheeks, slightly puffy eyes, she'd been doing such a good job as crying at the appropriate times. No one suspected a thing.

She'd done it.

She'd gotten away with murder and a large sum of money. After she got settled, she'd invest the money and she'd set Jack and herself up to not have to work if she didn't want to. She didn't have to deal with her name being dragged into the mud as Hugh pulled them all under.

No more debts, as well as a new chance to meet any man she wanted.

And this time, she wouldn't let 'love' blind her. She'd get what she wanted from them and then move along if necessary. None of this *marriage and till death do us part* nonsense.

She'd take care of herself this time. No more dutiful wife. No more standing by her man as he stepped out on her marriage, and *she* was the one that had to keep it a secret.

No more.

He was dead. She was free.

There was some guilt that came with this, but it would pass over time. She felt even less now than she did when she slipped the belladonna into his coffee. She'd worried that someone would find it, someone would notice, but no autopsy was done. Maybe she'd been convincing enough as the grieving wife, all she knew was that she had to be the luckiest woman in the world.

She'd double checked all of her plans. She'd gotten the belladonna from here, from Hale House. There wasn't a single trace of it left at their home. Nor in his cup. Nothing to link her unless they had checked his bloodstream.

She looked out the window and saw the outline of her son still in the treehouse. Jack was the only one who had to deal with the aftermath. This would bother him because he loved his dad. But he was still young. He'd eventually move on, and she'd never tell him what she did. He'd grow up and she'd raise him right. Everything would be fine.

But first, she'd get him out of that stupid treehouse.

She left the room and walked outside. When she got the base of the treehouse, she called out to Jack and asked him to come down.

"No," was his reply.

His cattiness irked her. She tried to remain calm and patient though. It was her own fault that he was going through this, she knew it. They just had to adjust. Eventually, her baby would come back.

"Jack, please come down. Emily is going to take us out tonight and you need a bath," she told him, but was met with silence. He was doing a good job of irritating her, but worse, she knew she only had one option.

She was going to have to go up into the treehouse.

Cynthia didn't want to. More than anything, she wanted to avoid ever stepping foot inside the treehouse again, but she had to. She knew she could yell at him till she turned blue in the face or beg him until the sun was coming up, but he wasn't going to come down until she was there to force him.

She began climbing up the ladder. Her heart hammered in her chest as she did. Not only did she not like the treehouse, but she also didn't like heights. She tried not to look down, to focus on her mission, but she hated it.

"I'm coming up, Jack," she told him.

Jack said nothing, and didn't even look her way as she got to the top. When she crawled inside, she looked around.

Nothing had changed. It was the same as before, from her childhood and her dreams. It was older, probably less safe now than when she was a kid, but still the same. She didn't like how much it looked the same and it flooded her head with memories she tried desperately to push away.

The only way she could do that was by looking at Jack. Her precious son. He looked so much like her, and she appreciated that now. Living every day with her husband's replica could have been awful, but Jack looked more like her and her side of the family. She doubted that would change much as he grew older.

He was coloring by the other wall. Going mad at it, it seemed. So focused. She'd never seen him concentrate so much on something before. He was dialed in, nothing hitting his radar as he scribbled on the page.

She looked at the drawing, and her heart stopped. She quickly snatched the drawing from him and stared over it, her eyes widening at what her seven-year-old had done.

"My friend says the flowers killed Daddy," he told her. "She said the flowers will kill anyone."

Cynthia stared at the belladonna he had drawn. So detailed, he'd even drawn the exact location she'd gotten them from. It was as clear as a photograph, and it was hitting Cynthia like a pile of bricks to stare at it.

"Your daddy died of a heart attack," Cynthia said, but she wouldn't meet his eyes. She couldn't. Of all the things she couldn't do, she couldn't bear to look at him while she lied straight to his face. As she told him the same veiled lie she'd told everyone else.

"No, my friend wouldn't lie about it. She said she saw you pick them from the greenhouse. She said you killed him, just like you killed her," Jack said.

Cynthia finally looked up at her son. Her blood ran cold. Jack was staring at her, unblinking, seemingly possessed. She didn't want to recognize him now, didn't want him to look so much like her. His face was a mirror now and it reflected her sins.

"She says you pushed her out of the treehouse when she was little. She broke her neck and died on the ground, and you just stared at her. She said you didn't even cry and told everyone she fell out. But you pushed her," he told her.

"It's not true," Cynthia said, but her voice cracked as she did.

"It is. She says she was your sister," he said.

"My sister died a long time ago."

"She said her name is Candace. She looks like the picture at Grandma's, except her face is bloody and bruised now. But that's because of the fall," Jack said.

Cynthia felt the guilt come washing over her. The memories. She remembered the summer her little sister died. She remembered playing in the treehouse, angry that Candace wouldn't leave her alone. Candace would never leave her alone.

She always had to be there, trying to ruin her games with Emily. Trying to play with them, but she was annoying. She was loud and cried about everything. She ruined her time with her friends.

And that day, something in Cynthia had simply snapped.

When she pushed her out of the treehouse door, she had felt the flood of guilt. She stared down at her dead sister and fear washed over her. Fear of getting in trouble, fear of people knowing what she did, fear of living with the guilt every day.

But it didn't happen. No one suspected that Cynthia did anything to her sister. Instead, they consoled her, comforted her, told her how brave she was. She was seen with sympathy. And eventually, any guilt she had fell away as she distanced herself from the place of the crime and the memory of her sister. At some point in her life, it simply felt like she didn't even have one.

"That never happened," Cynthia told him.

"Candace says you lie a lot. She doesn't like you very much," Jack said.

"She's not real, Jack," Cynthia told her son. "Now come on. Let's get out of here. I still need to get you ready and get a bath."

"No," Jack said.

"Jack. . ."

"Candace said I have to tell the police what you did. She says I have to tell them that you killed Daddy because you're a bad person. Bad people have to go to jail," Jack said, putting away his crayons.

Cynthia stared at her son. Her sweet baby. He would tell and people would listen. He'd do the right thing because she had raised him that way. There was a part of her that felt good about that. A part that felt like she had accomplished something. That she was a good mom.

But him telling would hurt her. If they ran a blood test, if they started digging, all of her hard work would have been for nothing. She didn't want to lose that. She didn't want to lose her baby. The life she had in mind for them was so close, so good, and he didn't know how it would ruin that.

"Jack, you can't tell anyone. Don't you know Mommy could get in trouble if you tell? Do you want Mommy to go to jail and be away from you forever?" she asked him, her last plea to her baby.

"No."

"Then you can't say anything. Daddy died of a heart attack. Okay?"

Jack shook his head. "You killed Daddy. You killed Candace. That's bad and you have to get punished," he said, starting out the treehouse.

Cynthia looked out the treehouse window. She looked out the door. No one was there. Not Emily or Carl, not even her little sister. This treehouse, it was her prison. Nothing good happened here. She'd always known it. Always known that behind the beauty and richness of Hale House, nothing good lived here.

Nothing good ever could.

She looked at Jack. He was good. Pure. Innocent. A sweet little boy that she would love forever. She'd be sure to tell anyone who asked that Jack was the love of her life. She'd never be the same without him. She'd tell them she told him to stay out of the treehouse. She'd tell them she would never be the same after finding his body.

After all, kids fell out of treehouses all the time.

Greenhouse
1942

A Tree and a Life
Joe Scipione

"I wanted to show you this place last, Emily," Margaret said to her thirteen-year-old daughter as they walked from Hale House across the grass to the conservatory.

It was a large building made mostly of glass, set off the side of the main house. Margaret had marveled at it the first and only time she'd seen it. Even from outside the building, the bright green trees and shrubs could be seen through the windows.

"What is it, Mom?" Emily skipped across the grass a few steps behind her mother.

"The building?" Margaret replied.

"It's called a conservatory. Only very nice homes like this one have them. We're lucky your aunt and uncle are allowing us to stay here while your father is away. We'd never experience anything like this otherwise."

"So, it's like a big greenhouse?" Emily asked as Margaret reached for the door of the building and slowly pulled it open.

"Yes, sort of," Margaret tugged on the heavy door and the clean, fresh air from inside filled her nostrils. "But much more fancy."

The pair walked into the wide-open space inside. The sun shone in through the windows on the ceiling and through the ones that lined both walls.

The building appeared large on the outside but was even bigger inside.

Large trees climbed up to the ceiling at the far end while the sides were littered with smaller shrubs and bushes of various sizes.

There were some ferns and even a Belladonna plant, though Margaret wasn't sure which one that was. Emily knew better than to eat something without asking first. The predominant color was green, but reds and oranges and even a few blues were also mixed in at seemingly random intervals.

"Oh my gosh, Mom." Emily entered behind Margaret and then skirted around in front of her. Through the center of the massive room was a gravel path. The girl looked back at her mother, a wide, toothy grin on her face.

"This is amazing."

Margaret returned the smile and nodded. It *was* amazing, but her daughter's joy was what brought the smile to Margaret's face. She'd been down ever since Dale left for Europe. They both were.

Emily was talking less and less, spending more time in her room alone. At first, she was reading or listening to the radio. Then, even that stopped, and she slept more.

It had only been a few months since Dale had left, but the change in Emily was drastic. Margaret understood how Emily felt. Emily was smart and read the newspaper, she knew what was happening in Europe and understood there was a good chance she'd never see her father again.

Margaret knew it too, but tried her best to remain positive. She hoped moving to the Hale House and being closer to family while Dale was away would keep Emily's mind off it. It appeared as though the conservatory of this beautiful mansion did the trick, at least for the short term.

Emily skipped down the path and disappeared behind one of the taller plants. Margaret strolled along, looking at the green leaves and branches around her. At the far end, Emily walked across the path, gravel crunching under her feet.

Eventually, the girl got more adventurous and went off the path, slipping between the plants. Even when Margaret couldn't see her, she could hear the giggles and watch the branches rustle when Emily moved past them.

Maybe, Margaret hoped, this was the change they needed.

"Mom," Emily's voice emanated from behind one of the larger bushes. Margaret couldn't see her, but could tell exactly where she was.

"Do you hear that?"

Margaret, who was walking down the gravel path, stopped her forward movement and stood still.

"No, I don't hear anything," Margaret said. "What is it?"

"Sounds like voices. Singing, maybe. Or someone talking. I'm not certain," Emily said.

Margaret didn't hear anything. There wasn't much around them but empty land so she didn't think it was from any of the neighbors, but it was their first day here. It could have been a normal thing.

"I can't hear it at all," Margaret said. "Must be my old ears, hunny."

"It's strange. Different." Emily's voice was distant. Like she was focused only on the sound.

"Maybe it will be louder outside." Margaret said. "Come on. We have a lot to do in the house."

When they walked out and opened the door, Margaret still couldn't hear anything.

"It's gone now," Emily said.

The pair walked back up to the house, Emily in the lead and her mother behind. A few steps away, Emily stopped to look back one last time at the conservatory and then continued on to the house.

∞

Margaret had enrolled Emily in school but kept her home for the first week to get settled in the house. It was a beautiful place and Margaret's Aunt Lillith and Uncle James said they could stay as long as they needed. The first week allowed them to think of the place as home.

If Margaret had sent Emily to school right away, the house would still have felt foreign to her and it would have taken that much longer for her to be comfortable there.

The move did wonders for Emily's mood. She'd seemed perked up ever since they arrived. And she'd started a new routine as well.

She would help Margaret around the house during the day and then spend about an hour in the conservatory each night before they ate dinner and got ready for bed.

Margaret hoped it would continue once school started.

Then one night, about six days after they first arrived at Hale House, Margaret's sleep was interrupted by a sound outside her window. She rose from bed, threw on a robe and went to the window. It was too dark to see anything but as she looked, there was second metallic bang.

Margaret sighed. This was something Dale would have done if he'd been here. Without him, the responsibility fell to her. She dressed and went out to the yard. Nothing appeared out of order. Maybe just the wind, she thought.

She turned to go back into the house when the door of the conservatory caught her eye. It was open and shouldn't have been. Again, Margaret blamed it on the wind. If the door had been left even slightly ajar, a hard breeze could have pushed it open.

That would explain the loud clang she heard. She strode to the door with the intention of closing it and returning to bed, but when she got closer, she could hear the familiar crunching of feet on the path inside.

Was it an animal? An intruder? Would Dale have just closed the door and left after hearing those noises? No. He would have investigated the sound, he'd do it to make sure she and Emily were safe. So, Margaret would check out the sound to keep Emily safe. This was her job now.

The door squeaked when she pulled it open. The crunching further down the path stopped.

"Hello?" Margaret called out. She took a few steps into the conservatory and wished she'd brought a weapon with her. Too late now.

A faint green glow emanated from the far end of the building, but she couldn't see what was glowing. Margaret tensed. Her hands shook and her heart beat faster. A sheen of sweat formed on her forehead and across the small of her back.

The conservatory was noticeably quiet. Silent. The only sounds were the crickets and June bugs whose songs crept in through the open door.

She shuffled down the path, slow and cautious, her neck craning to the right in a futile attempt to see the source of the green glow. Her head tried its best to convince her that it was nothing: a rabbit snuck in through the open door; moonlight reflected off a leaf, creating a glow, it was nothing. It *had* to be nothing.

Even when she repeated this mantra in her head, Margaret knew it wasn't true. There was something more going on.

She went around the last slight bend in the gravel path and stopped when the source of the green glow came into view.

"Emily?" Margaret said.

Her daughter stood in the far corner of the conservatory. Her back was to Margaret, her hand outstretched, touching one of the taller trees along the back wall. A single leaf of the tree she was touching glowed in her hand.

Emily didn't respond to her name.

"Emily, what are you doing? Come on. I want to go to bed."

Emily still didn't respond or even move.

Margaret went to her, put her hand on the girl's shoulder, and tried to turn her away from the tree.

Emily didn't move, her body held firmly in place.

"What are you doing, young lady?" Margaret said. There was anger in her voice, but she wasn't mad; she was scared and uncertain. "Come on."

Margaret shook her daughter this time and then pushed some the branches out of the way to get a better look at her. Emily's eyes were wide open, unblinking, staring off into distance through the window on the other side of the tree.

More unsettling than her far-off stare was the fact that Emily's mouth was moving. It wasn't like when she would mumble to herself in her sleep, either.

Her mouth was moving as if she was talking or repeating the same words.

Yet there was no sound coming from her. The conservatory itself was silent.

Margaret's stomach dropped. It was the same feeling as when she found out Dale would be leaving for war. Fear, and the knowledge there was nothing she could do.

"Em, come on."

Margaret shook the girl and pulled at her with more force this time.

Emily still didn't move.

The uncertainty of the situation made her feel helpless; Margaret started crying. She pulled harder, begging Emily to stop what she was doing, but her mouth continued moving; her body remained stiff and immovable.

Margaret was losing control of the situation. She needed to regain her composure so she could think. She had to figure out a solution. Dale was already gone. He might not make it home. She needed Emily. She couldn't be on her own. She couldn't lose her whole family.

Margaret took a deep breath.

Even though it was difficult, she pulled her gaze from Emily's face. The wide-open eyes and fast-moving mouth were horrific and too much for her mind to take. If she was going to free the girl from this situation, she needed to avert her eyes and focus on the task at hand. Not looking at Emily's face let her do that.

The green glow was not coming from Emily but instead from the leaf in her hand. *Maybe,* Margaret thought, *if she could get Emily to break contact with the leaf, it would also break the trance.*

"Let's try this," Margaret said to Emily even though she was certain the girl couldn't hear her.

Emily's fingers were as stoic and unmoving as the rest of her; they felt almost like the fingers of a statue—cold, solid rock under her touch.

Emily held the leaf between her thumb and the index and middle fingers of her right hand. With the gentleness only a mother could use, Margaret held Emily's index finger with one hand and the leaf with the other. She slowly slid the leaf from between the two.

The leaf still glowed, Emily was still locked in her trance, but she was also still holding the leaf, now only between her thumb and middle finger.

Margaret took a moment. Then she went back to work. She took hold of the leaf and Emily's finger again—this time the middle one—and slid the leaf out from between them.

As soon as the leaf was no longer making contact with Emily, the glow stopped.

Emily rocked back as if slapped in the face and Margaret was able to catch her with a hand behind her back, stopping her from falling onto the dirt.

"Whoa, Mom," Emily said. She blinked and shook her head.

"Are you okay?" Margaret asked.

"Yes. Of course, why wouldn't I be..." Emily trailed off and looked at her surroundings. "What happened?"

"You must have been sleepwalking," Margaret said. The lie came out of her mouth so fast she didn't even have time to think about it. She'd apparently already made the decision to keep exactly what happened in the conservatory to herself.

"I heard a noise, came out to see what it was, and found you back here."

They walked down the path as they talked; Margaret kept a hand on Emily's shoulder making sure she didn't turn back. She didn't, and they left the conservatory and returned to the house.

It wasn't long before Emily was back to sleep. Margaret, however, didn't sleep the rest of the night.

∞

The next few days passed without incident and Margaret was even able to get some sleep, though not much.

After those few days, Margaret built up the courage to go back into the conservatory. She'd kept her distance since that night and made certain Emily stayed away as well, but now that she was alone at the house and had enough mental fortitude to enter the place, she needed to act before she lost the nerve.

The door squeaked when she pulled it open. Margaret tightened her lips together, thought about the sight of Emily, unmoving, and steeled herself. She stepped inside with no idea what to expect. The odor of the place hit her first.

It still smelled fresh and alive like the first time entered. Even with her fear of it, she couldn't help but admire its beauty as the morning sun streamed in the massive windows.

Margaret hadn't even stepped foot on the gravel walkway yet. Her eyes went to the tree at the back of the conservatory. The tree with the glowing leaves that had taken her daughter hostage.

"Come on, Margaret, you've got this," she said.

Then she walked down the path. Slow at first, but picking up speed until she was walking at a normal pace. Her eyes remained forward, looking at the plants, shrubs, and bushes surrounding her, but each time her eyes scanned to the right or left, she always made sure to bring them back to the tree.

The walk took only a few seconds, half a minute at most, but it felt longer. When she reached the end of the path, she looked up to her left. The leaves all looked the same, but the events of that night with Emily were burned in her brain. She knew which leaf it was right away.

It had been glowing then; now it looked no different than the rest, a deep, dark green, broad and flat. She examined the tree, something she hadn't done that night. It was tall with a thick trunk that split about two feet off the ground.

It seemed as if the tree was too large to fit in the space, but somehow it was there.

Margaret hadn't known what she would do when she got here, only that she needed to confront the tree. Now that she was here, she knew what she needed to do.

The tree had tried to hurt Emily, so Margaret would hurt the tree. She would tear the leaves from it, pull the branches off and break them until the tree was bare, as close to dead as she could make it. She had second thoughts but knew she couldn't shirk her responsibly.

Dale wasn't here; this was her job now. This was about protecting her family. This was for Emily.

Margaret reached up and wrapped her hands around the branch as far up as she could. She pulled as hard as she could, hoping the branch would break off the tree, but expecting at least all of the leaves to come off in her hands.

When she pulled, her hands slipped over the leaves, but none of them came off; her momentum carried her backward and she fell away from the tree empty-handed.

"Shit," Margaret said when she hit the hard gravel.

As she turned to get up, a weight pressed against her and forced her back down to the ground. It was like getting hit by a bag of rocks. Margaret's breath was forced from her lungs.

She struggled against the weight and pushed back against it. At first there was no movement. She wouldn't let herself be pressed back to the ground, but the unseen force wouldn't let her get up.

"What do you want?" Margaret said without thinking.

She strained in an attempt to get up. At first, she made no headway in the effort, then, all at once, the weight against her was gone. She was out of breath, sucking at the air to fill her lungs once again.

Margaret looked around. The tree towered above her.

She ran from the conservatory.

Once outside, Margaret gathered her thoughts. It was obvious something was wrong. Margaret didn't understand it. The tree should not have been able to fit inside that building. Yet somehow, it was there. It came for Emily, and it came for her. Dale wasn't here.

This was her job now.

There was no hesitation the second time around. Margaret marched into the conservatory, down the gravel and right up to the tree.

She wasn't going to allow any more attacks on her, or her daughter. First, she was going to rip the leaves off the tree, tear them into small pieces and get rid of them.

Then she'd come back with a can of kerosene she kept in case of emergency. She'd drench the tree and light it up. If all the other plants inside that place went up with it, so be it.

Margaret was determined, but something had changed. The air inside the conservatory was dense, thick and cold. It was still late summer. The warm sun combined with the countless windows should have made it warm and humid.

But it wasn't, at least not at this far end. The air was freezing. A chill jolted her body. Something was here with her. She hesitated and reached for the branch.

Before her hand could touch any part of the tree, there was a rustling as if a breeze had come through the building. Margaret looked back at the door. It was closed.

And the air was still. The rustling grew louder – the sound of wind through a forest.

The leaves on the tree moved, swaying back and forth in a breeze that didn't exist.

The leaf in front of her swayed on its own, first left and then right. It moved independent of the other leaves on the tree, as if it was different from the rest. It was strange and it gave her a moment's pause, but Margaret would not be deterred. She reached out to grab the single moving leaf.

It was not to be.

The leaf moved to the side, deliberately dodging her grasp. Then it moved toward her and touched the back of her hand. The cold feeling that had filled the air migrated to her hand. Cold surrounded her hand, like plunging it into a pile of snow.

Margaret tried to pull away from the leaf, but it was stuck to her. A second leaf came toward her; this one attached itself to her upper arm, bringing with it the cold.

The limbs of the tree swayed, still caught in a phantom wind. Margaret brushed the second leaf, but it wouldn't budge. A third leaf came at her, this one attaching to her cheek, followed by a fourth and a fifth sticking to her clothes as she fought and twisted, trying to get away.

But the leaves and the tree wouldn't let her go. Their grip on her tightened and solidified. She wasn't going to be able to get away.

Cold enveloped her entire body. The chill worked its way inside her. She could feel it, not just on her skin, but cooling her to the core. Her bones, her muscles, her brain all falling victim to the sudden chill.

∾

Noises surrounded her.

She didn't recognize them initially. The sudden change was disorienting. Margaret wasn't dreaming and she wasn't unconscious. She could feel everything around her.

The cold that had accompanied the touch of the leaves was gone.

As she grew accustomed to the differences around her, she was able to place the sounds. It was the sounds of night. Crickets and June bugs, like when she'd left the house to get Emily.

Margaret's body was tensed, trying to get away from the tree's grasp, but once everything changed, she was able to relax. As she did, she heard another sound, a low, almost inaudible chanting.

It was still totally black. Margaret could see nothing, but as the chanting continued toward a crescendo, a warm, orange glow appeared off to her right.

She was no longer attached to the tree; she was free to move her body and look around as she wished. However, she had no idea where she was.

Margaret watched as a fire came into focus and the ominous, strange chanting grew louder. She still couldn't see who was chanting but she was able to walk toward the fire.

She had control of her body once again, though she was certain the control was only in this place and not in the world she knew. Still, she moved forward, walking across soft ground toward the fire.

It crackled and popped but was soon drowned out by the chanting. Margaret stopped a few feet from the orange flames when, in between the chants she did not understand, she heard movement behind her.

She whipped her head around and held her hands up, expecting an attack.

A group of six people approached the dim firelight. Margaret backed away but the people either didn't see her or didn't care she was there. When they got closer, Margaret could tell that there were three men and three women, all six of them naked head to toe.

There were strange symbols painted on their chests. Margaret wanted a better look at the symbols but wasn't going to get closer.

The group walked right past her, the shoulder of one of the men almost brushing up against her, yet there was no indication they saw her. The chants continued and were as foreign to Margaret as the symbols on their chests.

As they chanted, she recalled seeing Emily's mouth in silent movement that night. The movements were the same. Emily had been chanting. But why? What was the purpose of any of this?

The group marched to the other side of the fire and knelt down into the darkness. For a moment they were gone. When they rose up, they had something in their arms.

It was large and seemed to be moving back and forth in their grasp though wrapped in canvas or some other thick cloth.

Margaret's stomach dropped. Whatever it was, it was alive. They hoisted the thing – body? – up on their shoulders and marched back the way they had come. Again, nearly brushing Margaret.

They were close enough for Margaret to hear the labored breathing of whoever was wrapped inside the bundle.

They walked away from the fire and into the darkness. Needing to know more about what was happening, Margaret followed. The group stopped not far from the fire. Margaret moved behind a bush large enough to keep herself hidden.

The chanting resumed. The group placed the wrapped body on the ground at the base of a tree. They stood around the writhing body on the ground and chanted, looking back in the direction of the fire. If they saw Margaret, they gave no indication.

One of the naked men left and walked around to the other side of the tree they stood in front of. It was then Margaret recognized the tree and the purpose for being there became clearer.

The tree had a short, thick trunk that branched off into two separate directions about two feet off the ground. It wasn't *similar* to the tree in the conservatory, it *was* the tree.

The exact same tree whose leaves were holding her in place back in the real world.

The man came back around from behind the tree. He had rope wrapped across one shoulder and his chest and there was a flash of something in his hand. Margaret didn't need to catch a great glimpse of it to know it was a knife.

The chants got louder; the voices of the six people grew more intense.

The man with the knife bent and cut the fabric holding the body. A seventh naked person was birthed from the dirty canvas. When the person—it looked to be a man—was free and no longer wrapped up, one of the women stooped down and ripped a cloth from his mouth.

"Why are you doing this to me?" the man gasped as soon as the gag was out of his mouth.

The only answer was the continued chants.

"Please let me go." the desperation in the man's voice was palpable.

Margaret wanted to run for him. To help him in some way, but she didn't dare move. The last thing she wanted was to be in the man's place.

The three men hauled the captive to his feet. Then the six chanted louder as they forced him backward until his back hit the split tree. He fought against them, arms and legs kicking out, but the captive man was weak and six people were too many for him to fight off.

They held his arms and legs against the tree.

The knife flashed in the dim firelight.

Margaret's hand shot to her mouth, but she couldn't look away.

The man dragged the blade across the throat of his captive.

"Tie him up, quick," a female voice said.

The women held the dying man up against the tree as he coughed. Dark blood spurted from his slashed throat and dripped from his mouth, covering his chest.

The man pulled rope from across his chest. The other two men pressed their full weight against the dying man, so he didn't slump down to the ground.

The women worked fast, wrapping the rope around his ankles.

The blood seeping from his throat had slowed. If he wasn't gone yet, he was close.

"Quick," one of the men said. He tossed the end of the rope high into the air and it came down and slapped against the hard ground.

"Try again," a woman said.

The man tossed the rope up again and it wrapped around a branch above.

When the end of the rope came fluttering down, all six of them reached for it. They pulled hard and the man's body begin to rise feet-first.

As he rose, Margaret could see his feet were tied and splayed apart, the rope tied tight around each ankle.

The way he was tied allowed them to raise him up and kept his ankles apart, leaving him naked and spread-eagle, suspended above the ground.

When his head was about two feet off the ground, they stopped.

"Tie it off," a woman said. Movement. Someone tied the remaining rope to the lower branch, holding the victim in place.

There was silence as the naked murderers formed a semi-circle around the dead man hanging upside down, and also around the tree that Margaret knew all too well.

They looked from side to side as if making certain the others were ready, like some sort of ritual.

The chanting began again, quiet and low but growing louder with each second that passed until the six naked people were shouting at the tree and the dead body in front of them.

Margaret crouched down, her hands against her ears, and watched. Then, without warning, the chanting stopped.

"To the spirit that inhabits this tree," one of the women said. "We offer you this life—*this spirit*—in the hopes that you will leave us be. We ask that you refrain from calling us to you at night. We no longer wish to see the violent visions you have shown us. We no longer wish to see your glowing leaves or chant your unending chants. We wish to be free of you and, in accordance with everything we have learned about you, we offer a life as a way to show our gratitude."

The woman looked to the others and nodded.

"We thank you for your mercy," they all stated in unison. The chanting resumed. The six knelt in a semi-circle around the base of the tree, the dead man's slit throat dripping blood upon the grass below.

As they chanted, Margaret felt a stiff breeze at her back. The tree looked as though it grew taller and the branches longer, as if the tree itself was inhaling.

The chanting got louder. The leaves of the tree began to glow. First it was a soft dull green, but it became brighter until the entire wooded area was bathed in a bright green light more akin to daylight than night.

The body hanging from the tree swayed back and forth as the chanting continued. Then the body itself began to glow. Like the leaves, the light coming from the body gradually brightened.

Margaret crouched down lower behind the shrub, worried she'd be seen in the light.

The body began to convulse as if locked in some type of seizure.

Margaret backed away. This was getting too intense. She wanted to be back in the conservatory not seeing an event that had clearly happened sometime in the past.

The bodies of the six surrounding the tree also began to glow. Margaret took a second tentative step back, but she couldn't pull her eyes from the events in front of her.

"We're glowing," one of the six said.

"Oh no," someone else said. Their voices began to sound the same to her.

Joe Scipione

"We gave you what you wanted," someone shouted. "We were told you would let us go."

The six glowed brighter and there was an ear-splitting scream. Not from one or two of the six, but from all of them. They screamed in unison and Margaret watched as some unseen force squeezed them. The sounds emanating from their bodies were terrible.

Margaret put her hands on her ears again, wishing herself to be any place but there. The six bodies crumpled in on themselves, blood poured from their eyes, noses and ears, then began seeping out through their pores.

At least the screams didn't last long. In a matter of seconds, all six were dead in a massive pool of blood slowly soaking into the dirt.

Margaret was out of breath. Her chest heaved. She wanted to leave, needed to leave but didn't know how to do it. She sat on the ground, rocked back and forth, and cried, praying for her life to be extended long enough to get herself and Emily away from this evil tree.

"Please let me go," Margaret whimpered from dripping eyes and drooling lips. She squeezed her eyes shut tight but could still see the bright green light through her eyelids.

She continued begging, certain death was imminent.

∞

Margaret noticed the change in the air before she realized the green light was gone.

Still afraid to open her eyes, she sucked in a long, slow breath and let it out. She couldn't wait forever; she had to open her eyes at some point.

There was either death waiting for her or maybe a chance for escape. Escape from the conservatory and, when Emily got home, escape from the Hale House itself.

She just needed to open her eyes.

She did. And when they opened, she saw no bright green glow. There was only the warm golden sunshine through the window of the conservatory.

In front of her was the tree. The evil tree.

She'd seen what it could do, seen its past and wanted nothing to do with it. It was alive in a way plants should not be alive, and it was after her and Emily. Margaret understood that now. She backed away from the monstrous plant.

"I won't let you have my daughter," she said to it.

322

She didn't run from the conservatory, although she wanted to. Instead, she continued her slow retreat, never taking her eyes off the tree until she was out of the building.

Margaret slammed the door behind her and ran. She made it back to the house and packed up as much as she could, knowing she wouldn't get everything and not caring. There was still an hour before Emily would arrive home from school. Margaret wanted to be ready when she got there.

When the bus dropped Emily off, Margaret was in the driver's seat of the car with most of their things stuffed in the trunk.

"Mom," Emily said when she saw Margaret waiting. "What's wrong?"

"Get in," Margaret said. "I'll tell you."

She tried to sound casual. She didn't want to scare Emily. But the girl was intuitive and knew something was wrong.

"Oh no," Emily's face contorted right before she burst into tears. "Is it Dad?"

"Oh, no. No, honey." Margaret reached for her arm. "Nothing like that. Please get in. I'll explain. Your father is fine."

Emily got in and Margaret had shifted to car into first gear before the door was shut. She eased the car down the driveway and breathed a sigh of relief, feeling herself relax even with the conservatory visible in the rearview mirror.

Every moment the car moved forward, the further away they were getting from that tree.

"We just can't stay here anymore, Emily," Margaret said. "We will stay somewhere else."

Margaret guided the car around the corner, so the house was on their right.

Next to her, Emily was silent.

Margaret looked over in an attempt to see the conservatory one last time before leaving for good. Her gaze didn't land on the building housing the evil tree, because Emily took her attention first.

The girl was staring straight ahead, gazing out the front of the car. Her eyes were wide and unblinking.

More concerning though, was the fact that Emily's mouth was moving.

She wasn't making noise, but she was mouthing something.

In her head, Margaret heard the chants of the naked men and women and remembered one of them saying the tree called to them.

Margaret shifted twice and pressed down on the gas, shooting the car forward. They needed to get away faster.

Next to her, Emily began to chant, the same words the six were chanting moments before the tree killed them.

"No," Margaret said, pressing down harder on the gas as the car sped along the dirt road. "Emily."

Her attempt to gain the girl's attention did no good, and Emily's hand shot to the car door. The door flung open, and Emily dove out of the car as it sped away from the house.

"Emily, no!" Margaret shouted.

She reached across the seat to grab her daughter but wasn't fast enough. Emily was gone.

Margaret turned her attention back to the road just in time to see a tree right in front of the car. She slammed on the brake, but was too late.

The car smashed into the trunk of a massive tree.

The last thing Margaret saw was a bright green light and the trunk of the tree she'd hit, which was split in two about two feet from the ground.

Secret Garden
1959

The Bleeding Garden
William J. Donahue

The Rolls-Royce Silver Cloud made a hard left into the driveway and passed between two stone pillars, each bearing a pedestal with the likeness of a polished marble lion.

Daphne Hale, née Goulbourne, studied the statues from the backseat, only to realize they were not lions at all. The bat-like wings gave them away – dragons perhaps, or some other order of mythic beast, equal parts avian, mammalian, piscine, and reptilian, though eerily humanoid. The word *chimera* came to Daphne's mind.

Daphne thought of lions as the Rolls-Royce carved a path between two seas of parchment-dry vegetation. Waist-high grasses and wildflowers undulated like waves in the gentle wind. She imagined a three-hundred-pound jungle cat prowling the meadow floor for unsuspecting prey, teeth and claws at the ready.

As the limousine broached a modest rise, Daphne saw Hale House for the first time.

How she ended up in such an extravagant place, she could neither explain nor remember, only that she had earned it.

The Rolls-Royce squealed to a stop at the entrance of the sprawling home. The voiceless driver exited the vehicle and opened the rear passenger door, extending a gloved hand to help Daphne out. The edifice's size and severity left her in awe.

Yet, the closer she looked, she saw a dwelling in disrepair: more than a few slate shingles either missing or broken, sumac husks snaking up the façade, starlings roosting in the gabled dormers.

The home's front door creaked open, and out stepped a stout woman in an all-black jumper.

"Miss Goulbourne, I presume," the woman said. "My name is Nora Gladish, the caretaker of Hale House."

"Call me Daphne. Jeremy and I tied the knot months ago, I'm sure he told you. Finally yanked me from my perfect little existence in the city, though only God knows why."

"Some things you should know about Hale House. We keep it quiet, so you'll find no radio, phonograph, or television. Dinner's served promptly at five-thirty. Breakfast at seven-thirty. You'll figure out a way to feed yourself in the hours between."

Daphne struggled to parse Nora's coldness. Perhaps, once Nora realized that Daphne was of the same working-class stock – not an ounce of privilege until she crossed paths with Jeremy Hale – she would warm up a bit.

The driver fetched two suitcases and a pair of hat boxes from the trunk and ferried them through the home's heavy oak door. He tipped his hat to Daphne as he returned to his seat and left her on the stone porch in a cloud of exhaust.

Nora extended an arm, beckoning Daphne inside.

As Daphne crossed the threshold, the temperature seemed to drop twenty degrees. She shook the chill out of her body. The sound of the lock finding its seat echoed throughout the foyer.

"You'll find the master bedroom and bath on the second floor," Nora said.

"I'll make sure your bags find their way to you."

Nora disappeared down the hall.

Daphne's eyes scanned the ancient artwork adorning the rich mahogany walls. She took the staircase. Old wood creaked beneath her feet.

"Yoo-hoo," she called in a sing-song voice, just to see how far her voice would carry.

Something scurried in the wall behind the landing to the second floor. A rat, she presumed, probably one of many. The tear-shaped prisms of a crystal chandelier tinkled overhead.

She entered the master bedroom and went to the front-facing window to survey the empire of grass.

Her view at the day's outset had been much different: twelve floors up, surrounded by skyscraping towers of metal and glass, while humans tramped the concrete far below, ant-like.

As she inched open the window, a fragrant breeze lifted the lacy curtains. She fetched a cigarette from her purse and lit the tip. Her eyes closed with the first inhalation, the magic filling her lungs.

"Smoking is prohibited in Hale House."

Daphne nearly dropped the cigarette as she turned to see a figure striding toward her. Nora swiped the cigarette from between Daphne's fingers and extinguished the embers on the windowsill, wincing as she did so.

"Do you know when Jeremy is due back from London?" Daphne asked.

"Later this week, I'm told. Perhaps Friday."

"Until then it's just you and me?"

Nora held up the extinguished cigarette. "No smoking in Hale House."

As Nora retreated from the room, Daphne leaned out the window to light another cigarette. Each time, the wind snuffed out the flame. Finally, having succeeded, she took three long drags, and then hurled the cigarette's remainder to the gravel driveway below.

A creak echoed in the space behind her, and she expected to see Nora wagging a finger for defying orders.

But she was alone in the bedroom. Nothing but a faint whiff of turpentine.

∞

The next morning Daphne woke with the sun. She sat up in bed and contemplated her surroundings. She thought of her mother and the words she had shared years ago, when Daphne was no older than fifteen: "The world doesn't favor people like you and me: the wrong sex, the wrong color. Find a man to take you in – a kind one, if you can – and you'll suffer less. You'll grit your teeth through some of what's required, but it's a price worth paying."

Daphne had met Jeremy Hale at a speakeasy in the city in May 1958. They shared drinks, danced, and absconded to dark corners to exchange intimacies. Their meetings quickly became habit. He asked for her hand within three months.

Confident and classically handsome, Jeremy exuded wealth and influence, and she swooned over the imagined victories his assets might help her accrue. Her goal: to gain favor with powerful people as a way to hasten the slow pace of change.

She quit her job as a housekeeper and moved into Jeremy's high-rise apartment in midtown, overlooking the river, where she could pursue a purpose she had only scratched at before: fighting for equality.

Every morning, when she woke in her own bed, in a room with a view that made her look twice, she thanked the universe for her fortuity.

Good fortune aside, she had reason to question Jeremy's intentions. He had been married once before, though he preferred not to discuss Daphne's predecessor – how they met, why the marriage soured, the ex's fate after the divorce went through.

Her suspicions only deepened after she moved into his apartment. He spent the balance of their first six months as spouses in the air or on the road, traveling for business, and even when he was home, they rarely slept together.

She had been blessed with certain bodily assets, so why would he not make use of them? Such niggling thoughts had been pushed aside until the day he insisted they escape to the "family fortress" nearly two hours distant from the city she had grown to love.

Jeremy often spoke about how much he cherished Hale House, in part because the estate had temporarily fallen out of his family's hands nearly sixty years earlier.

By staying at Hale House even part of the year, he kept insisting, they would help prevent such a travesty from happening again.

As Daphne eyed the intricate woodwork of the bed posts and the wainscoting overhead, sinking into the firmness of the pillow and the softness of the bedsheets, she regarded her mother's wisdom as truth. Her mother had worked two jobs just to put food on the table every weeknight, and she died knowing none of the luxuries Daphne had come to enjoy.

"It's fine to help others and to do work that means something," her mother once told her, "but don't forget about yourself. When I'm gone, only one's gonna look out for you is you."

After completing her morning ablutions, Daphne dressed for breakfast. She found Nora setting the dining room table.

"I think I'll start the morning with a walk," Daphne announced.

Silver clanged against porcelain, and the clamor brought Daphne around.

"Take more than a few minutes and your breakfast will be cold as a witch's tit."

"As long as the coffee's hot."

"Don't wander far."

"We're surrounded by rolling hills, forests, the gifts of nature. I should get out in it, see if it suits me."

"Mountain lions, bears, snakes that bite. Maybe still a mohawked savage or two lurking in the foothills. People like you belong behind closed doors."

After exerting a surprising amount of strength to open the front door, Daphne stepped onto the front porch. She nearly tripped on the last of the stone steps and followed the driveway toward the road.

An unsettling feeling quickly came over her, as if the eyes of vicious beasts watched from the tall grasses on either side. Nora's ominous warning fresh in her mind, she turned and hurried back to the relative safety of Hale House.

She followed the path between the main house and the garage.

The path led to the formal gardens, which Daphne entered through an opening bordered by Italian cypress. Crabgrass and chickweed sprouted from the spaces between stepstones.

Ivy consumed an armless bust. Dragonflies hovered above the tea-colored water in a rectangular concrete pool, the waterline having dropped below the lips of potted water lilies, their desiccated stalks long dead.

It was as if no one had tended to the place in months, if not years.

She found the conservatory no better: countless glass panels broken, the branches of a dying banana tree poking through the ceiling, and an impossibly tall and thick tree that seemed far too large for the space, almost otherworldly in nature.

The oversized footprints of a canine marred the dried mud caking the floor, each toepad ending in an indentation made by an imposing claw. *A wolf,* she thought, though she did not know if wolves were native to the area.

A coyote then, or a rabid dog – something that would hunt her down and rend her flesh.

Her anxious steps led her toward the exit. As she looked about, wary of feral canines, a flash of color stopped her cold. The whisper of a cough sounded behind her left ear.

She stepped toward the bank of boxwoods to her left, and saw it again: a brilliant flash of red, bleeding through the hedges. She moved closer and, after the slightest hesitation, slipped through a seam between two boxwoods.

A hidden cosmos unfurled before her: a small but perfectly tended garden, blooming with starbursts of red, orange, blue, and green. Purple hosta and balloon flowers. Anthurium and blue wisteria. Caladium and hibiscus.

Bird of paradise and a dozen species of orchid. Some species defied the imagination, as if they belonged on a different planet.

William J. Donahue

Water cascaded over the lip of a two-tiered fountain. Clusters of bougainvillea climbed up the post of a trellis. Ruby-throated hummingbirds flitted from blossom to blossom.

The smells overwhelmed her as much as the vibrant colors.

Daphne had stumbled upon a corner of Hale House she could call her own.

∽

When she returned from the garden, Daphne was annoyed to find the dining room cleared. Somehow morning had come and gone, the hands of the clock having moved well past noon.

She found Nora in the kitchen.

"Who else might I find on the estate?" Daphne asked.

"A groundskeeper, perhaps?"

"No one here but me, with occasional visits from the master of the house. And you, for the time being. No one's done so much as trim a tree in four years, maybe five. The grounds tend to themselves."

Daphne wanted to ask about her discovery, because surely such brilliance required nurturing. She decided to keep the secret garden just that.

The final days of June passed with Daphne spending mornings at her writing desk. She penned letters to friends, peers, and community organizers back home in the city, partly to let them know she was still alive, but more so to inform them of her efforts to further their cause.

She filled pages with sharply worded pleas to congressmen and state politicians, to remind them of the injustices visited upon so many of Daphne's friends, neighbors, and family, and to underscore the need for equal protections under the law.

After all, she suspected her mother would still be alive – the cancer caught in time, if not prevented outright – had the world been different.

By noon each day, after she had stacked the envelopes on the foyer table for Nora to take to the nearest post office, Daphne would flee to the secret garden with a book plucked from the shelves of the library, turning pages beneath the trellis or beside the fountain.

She would leave only after the sun dipped below the horizon, her senses alight with the garden's intoxicating sights, sounds, and aromas. Her desire to linger chased away her ambitions.

The garden seemed to communicate with her through some unspoken language.

Stay, it said. *Stay with us.*

∞

The rumbling of a motor woke Daphne from a light slumber. She went to the window to see Jeremy climbing out of the Rolls-Royce's back seat. He breathed deeply; lungs swollen with crisp country air.

She slipped into her shoes and ran down the stairs, greeting her husband as he stepped across the threshold of Hale House. As she went to drape her arms around his neck, he protested her embrace.

"Please, dear," he said. He stepped past her and added, "After I've eaten."

Daphne followed him into the dining room and took a seat beside him.

"How was London?" she asked.

"Dreadful."

Her ebullient mood softened to meet his sullenness.

"It hasn't been much better here, to tell the truth."

"Forgive my absence," he said. He patted her hand. "Sometimes I forget that both of us have lives to live, one much different than the other."

Once they finished lunch, he led her upstairs to the bedroom and closed the door behind them.

∞

Six days had passed since Jeremy's return. Daphne sat on the edge of the bed, hands in her lap. Jeremy had just informed her of his travel plans. To California this time, though not for long. Her shoulders drooped as she remembered how quiet the house was without him.

He pinched her chin between his thumb and index, and whispered his pet name for her: "my caramel bride."

While she would never complain, she detested the sobriquet because it made her sound like a treat to be gobbled up.

"How much longer do we have to stay here?"

"Give it the summer," he said. "We'll return to old haunts once the weather turns its cheek. The winters here seem interminable anyway."

"But you're never here. I might as well live someplace that feels like I belong there, and not have to contend with that awful woman. I know you have business to conduct, but I shouldn't have to be cooped up with that witch. No offense to witches, mind you."

He laughed. "Nora can be a bitter pill. I'll have a word with her."

"It's not *just* her."

"I am sympathetic, my dear, but this place is sacred to me. I want you to be part of it."

Her feet carried her down the stairs and out the front door, toward refuge in the garden.

∞

After the last dinner before his departure, Jeremy retired to the library. She had offered to join him, but he made it clear he would rather be alone. She wandered the hall of the second floor, peering through the windows to the vast darkness beyond.

While she had never felt particularly welcome at Hale House, the feeling worsened after sundown.

Having had enough of the darkness and silence, she dashed down the stairs. She found Jeremy sitting at a desk in a shadowy corner of the library, scribbling in the pages of a leatherbound journal.

As she cleared her throat to announce her presence, he lifted his head and swiftly closed the book. She came behind him and palmed the ball of his shoulder.

"Is there something you need?" he asked sternly.

She removed her hand and said, "You're leaving tomorrow."

"And I can hasten my return if you let me do what I've come here to do. Now if you don't mind …"

"We've barely had time to talk. I've wanted to ask you about your friends."

"My *friends*," he repeated.

"State senators, fellow businessmen, people who can make things happen," she said. "I'd like to host them for dinner."

"To what possible end?"

"The world needs to move forward, to protect people with the same skin color as the woman you married," she said. "The people you rub elbows with can put the wheels in motion."

"I'm afraid other matters require my attention," he said. "Perhaps later."

"When?"

"Fine," he relented. "The dust will settle in August. We'll set a date when I return."

She retreated to the doorway, unsure of what else to say. He sat silently, eyes ahead, and waited for her to leave. As she padded into the hall, she heard the faint but frenzied scratching of her husband's pen carving up another page.

∞

Without Jeremy, one week bled into the next. Days began and ended in the dining room, the meals made bland by the sight of Nora's pinched face. The walls creaked and cracked from sunup to sundown. Shadows shifted on the dust-strewn floor as the hours passed.

She welcomed the dreary days, because the wind and rain disrupted the sameness and tamed the heat, but also because the dreariness better matched her mood.

If not for the garden, she would have succumbed to ennui. So many people around the world suffered and died each day, yet there she was, holed up in a modern-day castle, frozen in time and place.

She began to think that she would lose herself entirely if she did not leave Hale House, if only for a brief interlude.

At breakfast one morning in mid-July, she told Nora of her intention to visit the nearest town.

"What on earth could you possibly need?" Nora replied.

Time away from here, Daphne wanted to say. *And cigarettes*, though she knew to keep that to herself, too.

"Unacceptable," Nora added.

"When Jeremy is not here, consider me mistress of the house. You serve *me*, understood?"

Her expression unchanged, Nora replied with venom: "I serve Hale House."

"Mind me, Nora, or your days as an employee of this family will be few and difficult."

Nora waited a beat and said, "Teabridge is closest. Mister Hale's driver will take you. It's a fine little town, Teabridge. But do not linger too long, for your own good."

∞

Nora had been right about Teabridge. Quaint and quiet, the town's main street and surrounding homes had a distinct Bavarian character. As she walked the central thoroughfare, Daphne peered into shop windows and nodded to strangers as they passed, though each salutation went unreturned.

Her grumbling stomach begged for sustenance. She entered a luncheonette and took a seat at the counter. A loose menu sat on the countertop.

A waitress with a pronounced belly eyeballed Daphne and said, "We're closing soon."

Daphne checked her wristwatch. "It's one o'clock in the afternoon."

A cook in a white paper hat placed a plated sandwich on the cut-through sill. A bell dinged.

"Please," Daphne added. "I'm famished."

The waitress topped off a coffee cup for the man two stools down.

"Do you know Hale House in the next town over?" Daphne offered. "My husband is master of the house, and I am his wife."

"*Another* one?" the waitress asked.

"Surely our money is acceptable here. The chicken and dumplings will suffice. Please and thank you."

The waitress ambled toward the kitchen and leaned through the cutout to share whispers with the cook.

"You livin' in the spook house?" said the man sitting two stools down. Flakes from a biscuit clung to his lower lip.

Daphne eyed him contemptuously.

"My daddy worked the grounds of Hale House when I was a boy," he added. "Saw things there that scared the hell out of him. 'Unnatural things,' he always said. That word always struck me: *unnatural*. You see anything like that?"

Daphne shook her head and waited for her food to arrive.

"Haven't thought about it in years, the cursed place up on the hill," the man said. "'A ghost in every room,' my daddy always said, 'and twice as many roaming the grounds.'"

The waitress returned with Daphne's plate, suspiciously quickly, and nudged it across the counter. Daphne placed a napkin in her lap and lifted a mangled fork – two tines bent – nothing like the elaborate place settings she had gotten used to at Hale House.

She took two bites of a gravy-sopped dumpling, decided she did not like the taste, and delicately patted her lips with a napkin.

She undid the clasp of her purse and fished out a ten-dollar bill, which she placed behind the plate of mostly uneaten victuals.

As she stood and turned toward the door, a blur of movement caught her attention.

A woman in a purple hat passed swiftly by the window. A black woman. Two white men followed close behind. Daphne knew a chase when she saw one. The bell clanged behind her as she ran to even the odds.

∞

Daphne extended a hand for the young woman to shake. The woman looked no older than twenty, just a few years younger than Daphne herself.

"Cassandra Mott," the woman said, still visibly distressed from the encounter with her pursuers.

"How on earth did you turn up here, Cassandra Mott?"

"Bussed up from a small town in South Carolina. Spartanburg."

Daphne put a hand to her chest and said, "Montgomery, Alabama."

"Came here for a job as caregiver to some sorry sack of bones," Cassandra said. "Didn't work out – surprise, surprise. Let's just say the family didn't expect to find someone with such a *colorful* personality."

"You should head east, to the city. That's where I'd be right now if …"

Daphne chose not to finish the sentence, not wanting to admit the whims of a man governed her fate. Rather, that she *let* the whims of a man govern her fate.

"No one tells you, but it's the same story everywhere," Cassandra said. "Some places just take longer for the ugliness to wake up and show itself."

"Those boys," Daphne said. She nodded toward the two men across the street, the ones she had chased away.

They leaned against the wall of a haberdasher's, their stares sharp enough to cut glass.

"I know the type. You stand up to them once and they crumble like columns of sand. We better move along, just to be safe."

"Wherever I'm going, I'll get there on foot."

"You're welcome to stay with me until you figure things out." Daphne paused. "It's a big ol' house, emphasis on *old*. Probably haunted, too."

One of the men across the street spat onto the asphalt.

"Fine by me," Cassandra said. "Sure beats the alternative."

∽

Nora stood on the second step of Hale House's central staircase.

"No one said anything to me about visitors," she said.

"You have no say in the matter," Daphne said, Cassandra standing behind her. "She'll take a bed in the nursery. Or she can have a bunk in the servant's quarters. You have the whole third floor to yourself anyway."

"She's not welcome, upstairs or down," Nora said.

A mix of rage and embarrassment surged through Daphne.

"You are to treat her as a guest," Daphne demanded. "Treat her with the same kindness and respect you should be paying me."

Nora harumphed.

"You have been a shrew from the moment I crossed the threshold of this drafty old house," Daphne added. "Not another word. We'll be taking our dinner early this evening."

The caretaker waddled off, presumably to make a bed for the guest she did not want.

"You sure let her have it," Cassandra said with a smile. "She gon' return the favor later."

"A toad of a woman, that one, all bark and snarl."

∽

In the dining room the next morning, Daphne took a seat beside Cassandra, who sipped coffee from a dainty porcelain cup.

"You sleep just fine?" Daphne asked. Nora appeared with the coffeepot.

"Fits and starts," Cassandra replied.

"House creaks so loud and often, makes me think I've been transported to the belly of a sailing ship."

"Hale House is speaking to you," Nora interjected.

"Am I supposed to understand what it's saying?" Cassandra asked.

Nora departed for the kitchen without answer.

"Some place you've got here," Cassandra said. "So dang quiet, though. No music. No peals from a telephone. No knocks at the door. No children to make noise. Whole house, it's like one big *prop*. Know what it reminds me of?"

Daphne nodded, urging Cassandra to continue.

"It reminds me of the breath you take, the beat that passes, right before the bad thing happens."

Daphne dismissed the idea. She knew Hale House's flaws better than anyone, but she had grown to appreciate its charms.

Cassandra added, "Whole dang place is cold and dark and … colorless."

Daphne smiled and said, "Not *all* of it."

∞

Daphne led Cassandra through the fissure between the boxwoods. Cassandra brushed bits of detritus from her braids.

"No words do it justice," Daphne said. "In all my years, I never seen anything so beautiful. I call it 'my miracle garden.'"

Cassandra's line of sight drifted across the landscape. Daphne had trouble discerning the look on her guest's face, though the woman seemed unimpressed.

"A prank?" Cassandra said. "You're teasing?"

"I'm not sure I get your meaning."

"It's all dead, this place, just like the rest. Dry and withered, like a dead fish left out in the sun."

Perhaps Cassandra had seen better, or maybe she was immune to nature's brilliance. Daphne knelt by the fountain and let the crystalline water flow through her fingers.

The head of a flaming-orange koi broke the surface, its puckered mouth begging for food.

"Sometimes I can almost hear the earth speaking to me."

Cassandra's expression changed abruptly. Her body stiffened. She backed up a pace, then another, then she turned into a gallop and tore through the boxwoods, into the main garden.

Daphne followed a moment later, but Cassandra had gone – just the sound of heavy footsteps growing increasingly faint.

As Daphne approached the front porch, the front door squealed open and closed with force. Cassandra was halfway down the serpentine driveway by the time Daphne caught up with her.

The woman's dark complexion had turned ashen. Blood trickled from a scratch on the side of her nose.

"What happened?" Daphne asked.

Cassandra wagged her head fiercely.

"I saw a lot of strangeness back home in Spartanburg. What's in that back garden ain't no harmless thing."

"A ghost, you think?"

"Ghost, demon, something inhuman. Whatever it is, it's taken a shine to you."

Daphne touched Cassandra's bare forearm, and the woman nearly jumped at the contact.

"Your imagination's gotten the best of you."

Cassandra took Daphne by both arms.

"You in water so deep, you either too dumb or too proud to admit it," she said. "This place ain't no sanctuary; it's a slaughterhouse, and you on the killin' floor just waitin' for the devil in the white coat."

Daphne smiled in nervous response. She tried to wriggle free, but the woman's grip tightened.

"It *spoke* to me, Daphne, just like you said. It doesn't want me here."

Cassandra broke away, doubling her pace. Daphne decided not to give chase.

"Let me at least have someone drive you back to town," she hollered.

But the woman kept moving.

Daphne took a breath and shouted. "The voice. What did it say?"

Cassandra turned and opened her mouth. Daphne heard the words clearly: "It said, 'You'll burn, too.'"

∞

What horrors had driven Cassandra off, either real or imagined? Daphne had not spoken to Jeremy in nearly a week, and she would not bother to ask Nora.

If she wanted to know more about Hale House, she would have to find the answer herself.

Jeremy's journal, she thought.

Daphne crept into the library and sat in the chair at her husband's desk. She slid the blade of a letter opener into the seam between the desk frame and the top drawer.

The blade bent as she pried, and finally the drawer sprung open. Jeremy's journal lay on top of loose envelopes and paper clips, a second one just beneath.

She gently lifted both books from the drawer, opening the more tattered of the two to the first page.

The initial entry from 1956, three years earlier, began with Jeremy's benign musings about business and a maintenance project in the basement to address persistent flooding.

She thumbed forward to discover several pages filled with strange signs – "sigils," he called them, dozens of them – each one a mess of arcs, Latin characters, and jagged lines.

Jeremy's penmanship became illegible in the ensuing journal entries, the strokes somehow harried. Sentence fragments jumped out at her.

Opened the door and let them in ... no choice but to comply ... she must pay the price for my folly ...

Daphne struggled to make out a word that obscured the meaning of a sentence Jeremy had underscored, however sloppily. A moment passed before it came to her: *I have banished them from the house, but they have not gone far. Hidden, dormant, underground—waiting.*

She advanced to the second journal, less than half of which Jeremy had filled with his scrawling. Her name led off the most recent entry.

Daphne has proven worthy of my investment in her. Kind, elegant, stronger than I could have suspected, even courageous. A shame to see her go. Alas, they do not take no for an answer, otherwise they will come for me. I wish I had never–

"What are you doing?"

Nora stood in the doorway.

"The master of the house will return tomorrow."

"What is this place?" Daphne responded. "Who are you people?"

She imagined throngs of shadowy figures in robes and hoods emerging from the tall grasses out front, surrounding the house, intent on claiming her.

Cassandra's doomsaying conjured a clear picture in Daphne's mind: a beastly Jeremy looming over the blood-sopped floor of a slaughterhouse, a bolt gun clutched to his chest.

She stormed past Nora, up the staircase, into her room.

Jeremy had brought her to Hale House for some nefarious purpose, and she would not wait around to find out. She hurriedly packed a suitcase and dragged it down the stairs.

She found Nora Gladish blocking the front door.

"Whatever you're thinking, you can discuss it with the master of the house upon his return."

"Out of my way," Daphne said.

William J. Donahue

"I won't repeat myself." Nora crossed her arms.

"Woman, if you don't step aside, I will knock you down."

A moment passed between them. When Nora chose to stay put, Daphne cuffed her on the ear. Nora's head whipped to the side, but she did not relent.

Daphne cuffed her again, this time using her nails, but the blow had little effect.

As Daphne backed away, she tripped over her suitcase and landed on her elbow.

Bolts of pain shot up her arm.

"I told that silly man not to procrastinate," Nora said. "Now look at us, on the cusp of a storm he's brought upon himself."

Daphne got to her feet and ran room to room, ending up in the kitchen.

She went to the stove and turned on every burner. Gas hissed from the stovetop. She fished through the drawers for a box of matches, and she found it – atop a stack of letters Daphne had written.

Dozens of letters, unsent.

"Scheming *bitch*," she muttered.

As her quaking hand slid back the top of the matchbox, scores of red-headed matches tumbled to the tile floor.

The swinging doors opened and in walked Nora. She went to a table by the far wall and calmly dialed the rotary phone.

"It's time," Nora said into the receiver. "Would you like me to take care of it? … Yes, sir. … I'm happy to oblige."

The smell of rotten eggs found Daphne's nostrils – gas from the stovetop.

"I'll burn this whole place to the ground," she yelled.

"He was wrong about you, not as simple as he suspected," Nora said.

"No matter, I'm going to handle what he didn't have the spine to do himself."

Nora withdrew a ten-inch butcher knife from the knife block.

Daphne moved away from the stove and scoured the kitchen for a weapon. Nora stood between her and the knife block, so she settled for a maple rolling pin – a suitable cudgel.

Although she had never struck another person in her twenty-five years, she would enjoy beating this woman to death.

Nora backed Daphne into a corner.

"I'll break your skull open," Daphne said.

She held the pin like a baseball bat, ready to swing.

340

Nora slashed at Daphne. The blade sliced the side of her arm, just below the shoulder. The shock of it compelled Daphne to run. Nora took another swipe as Daphne bolted past.

A keen burning radiated from Daphne's left hand. A few seconds passed before she realized the knife had removed the tip of her pinkie finger.

She ran for the front door and struggled to yank it open, the handle warm and wet with her blood. Finally, the door parted, sunlight poured in, and she spilled onto the stone porch.

She briefly considered taking the driveway for the road, but then came the voice – the garden, *her* garden, calling to her.

She skirted the house, nearly tripped over a stepstone at the entrance of the formal gardens, and ran for the seam between boxwoods. The secret garden embraced her, bathed her in rapturous color.

Perhaps it was the adrenaline, but the colors seemed more luminous than ever, bleeding off the petals and dripping onto the ground.

Gravel crunched underfoot as Daphne saw Nora through the boxwoods. Evergreen fronds obscured her face, but the woman's intentions were clear: to enter the secret garden and face Daphne so one of them could murder the other. But she stayed put.

Daphne's bloody hand dripped onto the gravelly soil. Her ears picked up the faint trace of movement. Something stirred the soil at her feet. The earth seemed to *absorb* her blood droplets.

Her eyes returned to the space between the hedges, where Nora remained.

"You should know I have nothing against you," Nora said.

"Blame Jeremy's forebears for bringing that damned thing into the world, and blame Jeremy for waking it from its sleep. I give him credit for figuring out how to drive it from the house, and he may yet succeed in sending it back to where it belongs. Too late for you, though."

The first barb sank into Daphne's right calf, followed by another in her left ankle, straight through the bone.

To her horror, the soil crawled with black vines, each terminating in a star-shaped head with a fanged mouth at its center.

Tendrils slithered up her legs, around her waist, and tunneled through her flesh, entering just beneath the ribcage. Thorny branches shot through her forearms, wrists, the tips of her fingers, hungry mouths taking bites as the thing crawled up her throat, into her skull, toward the meat of her brain.

Just before blindness turned the world dark, the veil dissolved.

Every stitch of color sapped from her surroundings, the garden revealed its ghastly form, as it no longer had any need to deceive her.

Only then, when the ground gave way beneath her, did she realize her mistake.

∞

Nora waited an hour to enter the secret garden through the break in the boxwoods.

She found it exactly as it had been before that poor woman got dragged to her doom: tangles of dead vines, falling-down trees, and desiccated shrubs, all drab and brown, except–

A small green shoot poked through the soil, from the precise spot where Daphne had drawn her last breath.

The shoot had sprouted a flower, each multicolored petal – turquoise, ruby, magenta – rimmed with black.

Nora smiled and went to fetch the watering can.

Chapel
1932

Apparitions and Starshine Gods
Mercedes M. Yardley

Nobody ever said, "You can stay in the haunted chapel, if you like. It's full of ghosts and sorrows. It's full of faith and loss." Perhaps if those had been the words used, Bevin would have made a different decision.

But the serious young man, who introduced himself as Rowan, said something else entirely.

"I have a place to stay," he said. His eyes were piercing.

"There will be a bit of money and a roof over your head if you would like it. It's the chapel amid the grounds."

Oh, what joy! Oh, what a blessing! The heels of Bevin's shoes were worn down from walking and her ribs stuck out in what wouldn't be a desirable way until fifty years later. She was followed by ghosts, haunted, yes, but they were of her own making.

"Really?" she asked Rowan.

"Really," the woman answered. "Just take care of the chapel and you can stay in the small room there."

The room was, indeed, tiny. There was nothing but a sink to wash in, but a sink would certainly do. The bed was narrow and hard and neat as a pin. The blanket was rough but warm, and more importantly, hers. Bevin hadn't seen anything more beautiful in a long, long time.

She rose with the sun and dusted the pews. She scrubbed the altar and made awkward conversation with the life-sized Jesus statue nailed to a wooden cross.

"Hello, your grace. Or God. Mr. God? I'm not quite sure what to call you. I mean no disrespect, sir," she said, and put her head down as she worked. As expected, the statue said nothing.

She sewed and read, took walks about the cemetery outside, and often stared at the tall, splendid house on the property. Hale House, it was called. She believed it was where mysterious young man lived, but she couldn't be sure. There was something sophisticated about it. Tasteful yet sinister. She felt that if she climbed the front porch and stepped inside, she would most certainly lose her way.

"I believe there's something wrong there," she told Jesus, but His gaze didn't slide toward her. He continued to look morosely at the heavens, the crown of thorns heavy on His head, and Bevin wondered if all His suffering was worth it.

One day Bevin came back from the shops. Her bags were light, as were everyone's at the time. She had a little bread and potato, and that was pretty much it. But it was bread! It was potato!

Her stomach wouldn't turn on itself and she would feast and feast and feast for days on this bit of food. And when she ran out again? Why, back to the shops.

What joy there was in familiarity. It wasn't mundane at all.

She combed her hair neatly with her wooden comb and brushed her dress until it was free from lint and wrinkles.

She sat down across from Christ to have tea.

"Mr. President Christ," she began, and was quite careful to keep the crumbs from falling onto the altar. She was a lady, after all.

"You're the only one I really talk to. And I've grown rather fond of you as of late."

She drank her water and patted her lips gently.

"The last year hasn't been so good, you see," she admitted. "Quite a lot has gone on."

She paused and peered through the stained-glass window at the stately house outside. The window was a thing of beauty, depicting a picture she didn't understand. Most likely saints, she thought. Or God Himself, maybe, if He looked anything like a man. Although if you were God, why look like a man at all? Why not look like starshine?

"The economy hit us hard, you see. My family. My mother and father. I have sisters and brothers, too. Several, even. We sisters all look alike. My brothers, not so much."

The Christ statue was silent, his mournful eyes looking far, far behind anything Bevin could see.

"I had to leave them, to find my own way. To fill my own belly. I didn't want to admit that I was a burden to my family, but alas, it was true. Maybe that's what hurt most of all."

She looked at the wooden cloth wrapped around His loins. The shiny folds were full of dirt. She took her apron and wiped it carefully away.

"But I guess You understand what it means to sacrifice for others," Bevin said. "From the stories I've heard, anyway. I don't know much of them."

"It's not so bad," a soft voice said. Jesus shrugged on the cross. "Everyone is going to die anyway. It might as well be for a good cause."

Bevin, when retelling the story later, would want to say that she jumped. She would want to say that she was taken aback, gasping at this thing that simply *could not be*. But, she would eventually admit, it didn't startle her at all. It felt just right.

"That's a sensible way to look at it, I suppose," Bevin said politely to the talking statue that couldn't possibly exist.

"And you do seem like a practical man. Er, god. Being. Ghost?"

Jesus nodded and then winced, for the crown of thorns was plaited quite tightly.

"Tell me why you're here," he said. "Why you're really here."

He wiggled His nailed hands.

"There's nowhere for me to go. I have all the time in the world."

"I couldn't possibly," Bevin demurred.

"My life is the most boring little tale."

"Oh, no, I find you quite fascinating," Jesus assured her.

"Look at how you bustle around the place. You keep it beautiful and clean. You bring in fresh flowers and sing as you sew. You smile at everyone you see, and it doesn't matter to you if they don't smile back or if they scream in horror at the missing pieces of your head and arms."

"Oh," Bevin said, and went rather pale.

"Ah, you didn't realize you were dead," Jesus said.

"I understand. It's rather shocking for all of us."

"Mr. Emperor Christ, sir, I rather thought that part was a dream," Bevin said softly.

"A rather terrible dream. It had to do with hunger and fury and train tracks, and the rest is rather…well, it's quite vague."

Christ was silent and she was silent, and Bevin looked closely at the pieces of herself that weren't quite there anymore.

Such an unusual thing to be aware of, surely.

"Am I going mad?" she asked, and was rather relieved when the giant statue of Jesus Christ didn't answer her.

It seemed like the sanest response.

"But I like it here," she decided. "Rowan said I can stay if I care for the chapel, and I shall do so just as I promised. I enjoy the darling little mice and the breeze and this lovely Ghost Christ, who seems to be very kind. Unless I'm forced out, I never want to leave."

And being the kind sort, Bevin took a small flame and lit a candle every night.

She placed it in the chapel window to guide other lost souls who were looking for a place to rest. The more the merrier, she thought.

And that was that.

For whom would be monster enough to force a caring young woman out of her sacred home, I ask you?

Who would ever do that? Bevin was safe. For the time being, at least.

And while one might say that nothing lasts forever, well. Lasting for a while is sometimes good enough.

Mausoleum
1823

The Life and Death of Josiah Hale
Heather Daughrity

Josiah Hale stood, lightheaded and swaying, over the body of his wife, watching as the blood drained slowly from her wounds.

Wounds that he had inflicted.

Josiah's hand shook. The knife he held loosely in his fingers tapped against his leg. Crimson droplets fell to the ground with each palsied tremble.

The sounds of the night rose up around him, loud in his ears. Cicadas sang their last whining cries; crickets filled in the empty beats with their own shrill chorus. Tree frogs added their staccato trills while their cousins the bullfrogs rounded out the song with low, throaty croaks.

But above these sounds, loudest of all in his ears, Josiah's blood pulsed, rushing loud as a river through his veins. His heart pounded in his chest, a terrible drumbeat of panic.

Josiah stared into the darkness, biting back the fear that rose in him like bile at the thought of being found out. He strained his hearing, trying desperately to pick out any sounds of approach, any indication that his horrible crime was about to be discovered.

There was nothing. No footsteps, no human voices. Only his own heartbeat, and the insects, and the frogs. And Amelia.

Josiah shrieked, a high, frightened noise that would have embarrassed him if his senses hadn't already been overwhelmed by terror. Something had touched his foot, his leg. He looked down, gasped, and tried to back away from the dead body on the ground.

Because she wasn't dead.

Not yet.

Amelia's pale hand gripped Josiah's ankle, smearing bloody fingerprints across the fine fabric of his pant leg.

Josiah lifted his eyes slowly, filled with dread at what he would see but compelled to look just the same, to his wife's face.

Amelia was pale, even paler than usual, a ghostly visage in the flickering light of the single lantern Josiah had brought on this godforsaken mission. Thin streams of blood trickled from both corners of her mouth, and a shallow breath hitched raggedly in her throat.

Her eyes fixed upon Josiah, boring into him with an intensity that frightened him more than anything else he had experienced this night.

There was something in those eyes, a feeling, an emotion, some unspoken message he felt sure Amelia was trying to convey. Was it fear? Confusion?

Perhaps, he thought desperately, *it was forgiveness.*

Then Amelia managed to rasp out five final words which left no doubt whatsoever in Josiah's mind concerning her feelings toward him.

"Burn in hell, Josiah Hale."

Not forgiveness, then.

∽

Earlier

He should never have ignored the whispers.

The rumors.

The warnings.

He should have listened when the old women, wrinkled skin the color of coffee mixed with cream, had peered up at him from beneath their wiry white eyebrows and told him the flaws in his plans. Told him that he was destined to fail. That he was inviting ruin and despair upon himself and his household.

But he hadn't.

He hadn't listened, and he hadn't stopped.

He had continued with the clearing of the land in the midst of his newly-acquired property. Continued with the building of the grand house.

His house.

Hale House.

He had continued despite the grim predictions.

Despite the troubles and the setbacks.

Despite the accidents, the injuries.

The deaths.

It had taken the builders just over a year to finish the great edifice known as Hale House. In that year, nine men had met their demise, some through almost-explainable occurrences, falling from high walls or being crushed beneath heavy blocks of stone. Some from instances less easy to rationalize, like the stonemason who went running and screaming from the house, pounding his own chisel over and over into his gushing eye socket. Or the two brothers who, without warning, began to attack each other with hammers, leaving a bloody, pulpy mess on the floor of the entry hall.

Josiah had managed to explain it all away, at least in his own mind.

It couldn't be true, what the old women had said.

The land couldn't be cursed, couldn't be evil, couldn't be home to an ancient malevolence that the native peoples of the land had possessed the intelligence to stay well away from.

It just couldn't.

He had worked too hard to get to this place, too hard to rise to this level of wealth and respect. He had spent too much money on this damned house.

Besides, evil and ancient spirits didn't exist.

Except that they did.

∽

How proud he had been when the house was finished, when he had finally brought Amelia, with little Jeremiah squealing and squirming in her arms, to see their new home.

Amelia had remained tight-lipped and stoic in the face of the beautiful house with its polished floors and shining woodwork and expensive furniture. She'd had no desire to move beyond the edges of the city, no desire to leave her family and friends behind. She knew her place as his wife and would not dare speak her displeasure aloud, but the look on her face said enough

Still, he had persisted, determined to enjoy their new home. At least Jeremiah had seemed to like the place, delighted at the echoes of his own voice as he shouted nonsense words and ran about on his small, chubby legs.

Amelia had followed her husband as he gave her a tour of the home's many rooms, Jeremiah trailing along behind them, but she had never cracked a smile, never uttered a word, not until she paused on the second-floor landing, announced that she had a headache, and disappeared into the bedroom to lie down.

Josiah had sighed, half-angry, half-resigned, and continued down the stairs to the first floor, with visions of a quiet afternoon spent in the library with a good book and a glass of whiskey.

Young Jeremiah Hale was left, as usual, to his own devices.

∽

The occurrences had started that very night, and had continued every night thereafter.

Every single night.

∞

Sounds.

Lights.

Strange vibrations in the walls.

Heavy paintings fell, loudly, from their mounts.

Glass ornaments crashed to the floor, scattering shards into dark corners.

Things – important things, like Josiah's pocket watch, Amelia's embroidery hoop, Jeremiah's favorite ball – went missing only to reappear days later in the most unlikely places.

But it was the dreams that disturbed Josiah the most.

The dreams, and the laughter.

∞

He first heard it a week after moving in. Josiah was standing in the game room, lost in thought as he gazed out over the grounds. In his hand, he held one of his finest cigars, the smoke swirling lazily out the open window. He had just stepped to that same window when the sound came to him, low and dangerous, moving slowly on the heavy air.

It was unmistakably laughter, though the kind of laughter that made Josiah picture dark men hidden in darker alleyways, flashes of rotting teeth in sinister smiles.

His eyes scanned the night beyond, pinpricks of stars and a cloud-covered moon doing little to break up the darkness.

The sound came again, a rumbling chuckle, a dismissal and a threat rolled in tar and delivered, thick and dripping, into Josiah's ear.

Movement in the woods beyond the house caught his eye. As he peered out, his heart pumping fear like poison through his veins, the trees seemed to shift and sway as something much larger than a man pushed its way from one end of Josiah's vision to the other.

The movement stilled. Josiah's heart froze in his chest as two glowing yellow eyes blinked into existence six feet from the ground, just at the edge of the forest.

Josiah knew, somehow, that whatever lurked in the woods was watching him, a figure, a being, a presence beyond classification staring up at him from the trees. The particular yellow of those eyes whispered images into Josiah's mind, images of sick rooms and death beds, of filthy children in tattered clothes, of once-beautiful women now covered in open sores smiling up at him with toothless gums.

He backed away from the window then, closing the shutters and pulling the drapes tight, blocking out the eyes and the laughter and the oppressive heat of the night.

But he had heard the sound again. Had seen the eyes. Had watched as the trees parted before some invisible presence that stalked in circles around his beautiful, perfect, cursed house.

Many, many times.

No one else ever seemed to hear or see them, no one else seemed to notice. Josiah pondered and then rejected the thought that perhaps it was all in his head, and he was, quite simply, losing his mind.

He could have lived with the laughter and the constant feeling of being watched.

But he could not live with the dreams.

They plagued him nightly, strange visions that filtered into his sleep with startling clarity.

The dreams took place within his own home, although often in surreal, alternate versions of the rooms he had taken to pacing in the daylight hours. They featured people had never met, strange faces he had never seen in his waking life.

They were all horrible.

Sorrow and anguish, grief and longing, torturous pain and violent death. Screams and sobbing and odd snatches of music, and always, always, beneath it all, that low growling laugh.

A crooked old man chased a young boy through the halls, each footstep a pounding piano note in a music that Josiah could not quite recognize.

Atop the widow's walk, a woman with wild eyes and an uncanny smile bent over the chimney, whispering strange words into the dark hole before her as a baby's cry echoed up from that same dark chasm.

Animals from the wilds of Africa roamed the house, bowing in reverence before a woman painted in blood.

A young boy fell, again and again in an unending loop, from the branches of a tree at the edge of the clearing. A woman Josiah understood to be the boy's mother stood on the ground beneath him, reaching her arms out as if to catch the child, but pulling back at the last moment so that the boy's body broke against the tree's massive roots.

Strange dark shapes moved in the shadowy depths of the dining room mirror; sharp knives fell in showers onto the blue-flowered rug of Jeremiah's nursery; blood erupted like a geyser from the sink in the kitchen; a strange, lifeless woman stared at him from the darkness of the attic.

∞

Josiah didn't know how long it had been since he had managed to sleep more than an hour at a time. Most nights he sat awake till dawn, wrapped in blankets yet still shivering, as dark laughter echoed around the walls of the house, as the presence – the spirt, the evil, the source of his torment – crept through the dark branches of the tangled forest beyond.

He didn't know how much longer he could take it. He barely saw his son, saw his wife even less.

Jeremiah, though surely well cared for by his new nurse, had become wild, uncontrollable; a darkness seemed to look back at Josiah out of his little boy's face.

Amelia barely left her bedroom, taking all her meals in bed. She had grown alarmingly thin and pale. Josiah couldn't remember the last time they had spoken a word to each other.

Josiah sat at the dining table, a plate of untouched food congealing in front of him. His arms rested, crossed, on top of the table; his head lay atop his arms.

He raised his head only slightly when Cook walked into the room to fetch his plate. His eyes were red-rimmed and set deep within the bruised shadows of his gaunt cheeks. Even to raise his head those few inches off the table seemed to take every bit of strength within him; after a moment, he dropped his face back onto his arms.

It took him a moment to realize that Cook had not come to take the plate. Shifting his eyes, he looked toward the door. She stood there still, gazing at him intently, her arms crossed, face troubled.

Josiah stared at the woman, too tired to yell at her, too tired to tell her to do her job and leave him alone.

She approached him slowly, hands wringing together in front of her, and lowered herself until she crouched on the floor next to him, looking up cautiously into her master's eyes.

She began to whisper then, to ask questions. Josiah, against his better judgment, against his upbringing and societal position, answered her honestly. He began to weep as he spoke, finally unburdening himself of the torture and turmoil he had held inside for weeks.

And then Cook offered her words of wisdom.

Two months earlier, Josiah would have beat the woman for her audacity.

Now he was only grateful.

Grateful, and presented with a horrible dilemma.

∞

The spirit which inhabited this land had been here long before man of any color came roaming through the swamps and cypresses, she told him. She could feel its power, its malevolence, its desire for death and destruction. He should never have built his home here, should never have disturbed this sacred space.

There was only one way to rid himself of the curse he had called down on his own house, only one possible way to appease the spirit which stalked the woods.

Sacrifice.

Josiah had taken something from the spirit. Now he would have to give something back.

Something he loved.

∞

The next morning, Josiah, having slept fitfully as usual, sat once again at the dining table. Cook entered the room, followed by the maid, each carrying trays of food that would almost certainly not be eaten.

Jeremiah came tearing into the room just then, slamming into the wall and careening off again, shrieking a high-pitched squeal as he ran. His nurse came rushing in behind him, trying to catch the child as she apologized over and over to Josiah for the disturbance.

Cook stood motionless, tray still in hand, while the nurse regained control of her charge. Her gaze caught Josiah's, then swept purposely and intently to the place where Nurse had cornered the boy.

Josiah followed the woman's eyes. He knew what the look implied.

To end his torment, he would have to sacrifice his own son.

∞

He couldn't do it. No matter how exhausted, how distraught, how close to the end of his rope he knew he was, Josiah Hale could not murder his own son.

But he had an idea.

He needed to sacrifice something he loved. It did not have to be Jeremiah.

It could just as easily be Amelia.

More easily, even.

∞

Josiah thought about it all day. His head nodded off repeatedly as he sat before the windows in the library, but always he brought himself back to consciousness with one thought in his mind: that night, when darkness fell, he would lure his beloved wife out of the house, to a private spot, and there he would kill her.

He would have preferred one of the less messy forms of murder, poison or strangulation or something of the sort, but Cook had insisted that he must spill the blood of his sacrifice onto the ground outside the house. The blood was essential; it would soak into the earth and thus appease the spirit that haunted him.

A gun would bring the help running.

It would have to be a knife.

He also needed the perfect place to do it.

Outside, away from the house a bit – but not too close to the tree line.

It came to him like a lightning strike.

Of course. He knew the perfect place.

She would die quickly, quietly. He would explain to her why it had to be done. He would make sure she knew that her death would provide a better life for her husband and son. She would lie down on the bare earth then and simply allow him to puncture some important part of her, would lay quietly while her blood drained into the soil in order to save her child.

And if she didn't, well, she had barely been out of bed for the last month anyway, and had wasted away to a mere wisp of a woman.

Even if she fought, she would be no match for him.

He would fix this, would end it tonight.

And then, finally, he could sleep.

∾

Josiah ate dinner that night like a man already renewed. He devoured the dishes almost as quickly as they were set before him, juices running down his chin and fingers and soaking into his fine silk shirt.

Cook kept her eyes averted.

Night fell. Jeremiah and his nurse were tucked away safely in the nursery.

Cook and the maid retired to their quarters on the third floor.

Cook raised her eyes to Josiah's as she passed him, a bold risk; he simply stared back at her and nodded.

An hour passed, an hour of unbearable, silent anticipation.

The presence in the woods remained quiet. Josiah felt as if the spirit, the woods, the whole world beyond Hale House's darkened windows, all were caught within a held breath, in the moment just before something happened which would change everything, something which could not be taken back or undone.

But he was tired. He was so, so tired.

Certain that the rest of the household slept, Josiah entered his own bedroom and walked to the bed he had not shared with his wife in weeks.

Amelia lay with her face toward the windows, her dark hair spread out across the pillow behind her. Her eyes were large and vacant, her mind drifting somewhere beyond the walls of Hale House.

"Amelia. Amelia, you must get up. You must come with me," Josiah whispered, pulling the thick blankets away from his wife's frail frame.

Amelia stirred, eyes slowly focusing on her husband. She said nothing, only frowned at him, her eyebrows coming together sharply.

"It's Jeremiah," Josiah said, a half-truth. "You have to come and help him. We need you."

Amelia's expression grew more confused. Her mouth opened and closed once, twice. No sound came out.

Josiah noticed for the first time the utterly haunted look of his wife's face. Perhaps he had not been the only victim of the spirit's torments.

Perhaps Amelia had been suffering through torment of her own.

Too late to consider such things now.

Josiah pulled Amelia from the bed. She weighed next to nothing, and it was no work at all to support her out of the bedroom, down the main stairs, and out onto the grounds.

Josiah half carried his wife as he led her around the side of the house, through an opening in a low iron fence, and right up to the entrance of a structure which spoke to Josiah's own sense of self-importance.

Made of stone to match the house which loomed beyond it, the mausoleum stood alone within the ground Josiah had dedicated as the family cemetery. Carved into the stone above a heavy, barred door, the name HALE stood out in stark relief as Josiah struck a match and lit the lantern he had left on the mausoleum steps earlier in the day.

Amelia slumped to the ground before those steps, leaves catching in her long hair, chest heaving with the exertion of walking so far.

Josiah pulled the knife from its hiding place within his jacket. Amelia's eyes widened as the lantern light glinted golden off the weapon's blade.

Words poured out of Josiah then. He tried to explain what he was doing, why he had to do it. He begged her to agree to it, to die of her own free will. He told her what a wonderful gift she was giving her son, what a wonderful gift she was giving him.

Amelia, unable to stand on her own, tried to crawl across the damp, mossy ground. She moved mere inches.

Josiah sighed.

He grabbed her ankles, yanked her back toward himself, hard. She cried out, a sad, mewling complaint.

Josiah turned her over, straddling her waist, gathering her wrists together and pinning them above her head with his left hand.

It was as he had predicted. Amelia had no strength, no fight left within her body. Josiah plunged the knife into her again and again, slowly at first but then much faster. She whimpered with the first few hits, then went silent.

Amelia's white nightgown soaked through with blood, blooming patterns of ruby flowers that spread outward from her middle.

Finally, Josiah stopped. He stood and stumbled back a few steps, head swimming, vision drifting in and out of focus.

After the scare in which Amelia grabbed his leg and use her last breath to damn him to hell, Josiah took a few minutes to sit on the ground next to her cooling body.

Then he pulled a great iron ring from his pocket and unlocked the barred door of the mausoleum. He dragged Amelia's body, hesitant to get her blood on him any more than he already had, trying to move her while touching her as little as possible.

Through the small front vestibule and into the deeper space beyond, Josiah Hale hoisted his wife's corpse, depositing it finally on one of the biers cut into the deep stone of the outer walls.

Josiah hurried from the mausoleum, wiping his hands on his pants, frantic to get away from the reminder of the crime he had just committed.

No one needed to know. He could say she had died in her sleep. She had no family or friends nearby to argue the fact. He could say he had interred her in the mausoleum himself in a private ceremony of grief. He held the only key. He would keep it with him always, every day for the rest of his life.

Josiah closed the iron gate behind him and locked it. He gulped in great lungful's of air, his abundant dinner threatening to rise back up the way it had come.

He looked out toward the woods, searching for the yellow eyes, listening for the inhuman laughter.

Nothing.

He'd done it.

Oh, God. He had done it.

∞

He hadn't done it.

At first he couldn't understand why it hadn't worked.

Why the dreams and the laughter and the torment and the pain had come back again the very next night.

But Cook knew.

The sacrifice had to be something he *loved*, she told him, a look of disgust in her knowing eyes.

He hadn't loved Amelia, not truly.

If he was honest with himself, he wasn't even sure he loved Jeremiah.

He could not bring himself to sacrifice the one thing he did, without doubt, love.

Himself.

∞

Josiah Hale lived on, growing more reclusive by the year, until finally he ceased leaving Hale House altogether, retiring to his own bedroom to lie awake, staring at the ceiling, at all hours of the day and night, in the same bed where his wife had wasted away.

He continued to hear the laughter. He continued to live through nightmare after nightmare, the old ones which he had grown almost numb to as well as new ones which appeared every few years to jolt him into new states of despair.

A man tied to a tree, drained of blood before a crowd of chanting figures.

A woman who seduced him in his own bed, only to rot away into putrescence beneath his hands.

A creaking rope slung over an attic beam, a shadowy silhouette swinging back and forth in the silvery light of a candle set on a windowsill.

A great mass of loud and panicked confusion in the ballroom, screams and cries as a crowd of people pressed uselessly against each other, trying to escape a tragic destiny.

Chess pieces that moved themselves; books that opened and closed like mouths, laughing at him as bloody ink ran down their pages; strange plants, toxic poisons, scratch marks on the walls.

Worst of all were the dreams of his family.

Amelia roamed the rooms and grounds of Hale House, a tragic apparition in a blood-stained nightgown, her mouth opening and closing in mute speech. Though Josiah could never hear her words, he recognized the look on her face all too well.

She would never forgive him.

Never.

More disturbing still were the visions of his son, Jeremiah. Over the years, the rambunctious toddler had grown into a quiet, withdrawn boy who spent all his hours alone in the dark rooms of Hale House or wandering among the trees which surrounded the property. Once grown, he had surprised his father by announcing his dreams of becoming a doctor.

Josiah had supported his son in this, though the idea had sent a frisson of cold fear deep into his belly, for in his dreams his son stood over faceless patients, inflicting unspeakable pain on their writhing bodies while from his mouth issued a deep, malevolent laugh that Josiah knew all too well.

Jeremiah spent five years attending medical college and returned home just in time to bury his father.

Just in time to lay his father's stiff body on the bier above his mother's desiccated remains and lock the door behind him.

Just in time to take ownership of the family estate, and to begin to make changes of his own.

∾

The ghost of Josiah Hale watched helplessly as his son walled off one end of the third-floor attic, creating a secret room, a private place where he would one day perform unthinkable experiments on those unable to stop him. Across the attic, the bloody spirit of Amelia Hale stared daggers of hate into her husband's immortal soul.

Then Josiah hid himself away within the thick stone walls of his mausoleum. Here he would live out the ceaseless days of his tormented existence, while the tragic dreams that had haunted his life turned into tragic realities in the world beyond the crypt.

∾

Jeremiah Hale stood in the secret room on the third floor of Hale House. He cut into the beautifully dark skin of his first unwilling patient – bound, gagged, and strapped to the operating table. As the patient screamed in pain and terror, Jeremiah laughed, and his laugh echoed through the rooms of Hale House and beyond, through the dark and tangled woods, the sound heavy on the air, sticking like tar in the ears of all who heard it.

Farewell

Ah! You're back.

Did you give Josiah my message? Thanks so much. It's always a bit of a hassle, having to send the messages through someone else, but he's refused to listen to *my* voice since the day he murdered me.

Til death do us part, indeed.

But that's all water under the bridge now.

∞

Did you enjoy your tour of our beautiful home?

Oh, good. I'm so glad.

What's that? You need to be going now?

What's the hurry?

Ah, you have a life to live.

How lovely that must be.

Well, go on then.

The gates might let you out.

Or then again…

They might not.

That's alright.

I quite like you.

I'd be happy to have your company.

Here in the dark of Hale House.

Forever.

About the Authors

Christy Aldridge

Christy Aldridge is the crowned Southern Belle of horror, conjuring spine-tingling tales from moonlit porches and Spanish moss-draped oaks. With four feline phantoms, a faithful hound, a quacking duo, and Lily, her emotional support chicken, she orchestrates her own eerie menagerie. Anthologized in chilling collections such as *25 Gates of Hell* and *These Lingering Shadows*, Christy's craft lies in creepy twists and dark tales. Her latest novel, *The Breaking of Mona Hill*, invites you to a world where the line between Southern charm and unsettling fear blurs with every turn of the page.

∞

Brooklyn Ann

Formerly an auto-mechanic, Brooklyn Ann thrives on writing romance, urban fantasy, and horror novels featuring unconventional heroines. Author of historical paranormal romance in her critically acclaimed Scandals with Bite series; urban fantasy in the cult favorite Brides of Prophecy novels; rockstar romance in the award-winning Hearts of Metal series; and horror in the B Mine series, horror romances riffing on the 1970s and 1980s B horror movies that feature a Final Couple instead of a Final Girl.

She lives in Coeur d'Alene, Idaho with her gamer son, rockstar/IT Guy boyfriend, three cats, a few project cars, an extensive book collection, and miscellaneous horror memorabilia.

She can be found online at https://brooklynannauthor.com as well as on Twitter, Facebook, Mastodon, and Instagram.

∞

Simon Bleaken

Simon Bleaken lives in Wiltshire, England. His work has appeared in magazines, ezines and podcasts including *Lovecraft's Disciples*; *Tales of the Talisman*; *Dark*

Dossier; *Strange Sorcery*; *Lovecraftiana*; *The Horror Zine*; *Schlock Webzine*; *Night Land*; *Weird Fiction Quarterly* and on *The NoSleep Podcast*.
He has also appeared in the anthologies: *Eldritch Horrors: Dark Tales* (2008); *Space Horrors: Full-throttle Space Tales #4* (2010); *Eldritch Embraces: Putting the Love Back in Lovecraft* (2016); *Kepler's Cowboys* (2017); *Twilight Madhouse Vol. 2* (2017); *The Shadow Over Doggerland* (2022); *HellBound Books' Anthology of Science Fiction Vol.1* (2023); *From Beyond The Threshold* (2023) *Eldritch Investigations* (2023) and in the forthcoming *Horror Zine's Book of Monster Stories* (2024).
His first collection of short stories: *A Touch of Silence & Other Tales* was released in 2017, followed by *The Basement of Dreams & Other Tales* in 2019 and *Within the Flames & Other Stories* in 2019.

∽

Jay Bower

Jay Bower is a horror author living outside St. Louis, Missouri in the forest of Southern Illinois. He spends his time reading, writing, and convincing his wife the dark stories he writes do not involve her.
One time punk-rock skateboarder and heavy metal kid of the '80s, Jay approaches his work with the same indie attitude as those early punk bands.
He's the author of several dark novels and short stories. He can be found at jaybowerauthor.com.

∽

Clay McLeod Chapman

Clay McLeod Chapman writes books, comics books, children's books, and for film/TV. You can find him at www.claymcleodchapman.com.

Heather Daughrity

Heather Daughrity loves all things macabre, dark, autumnal, and horrific. She lives with her husband, author and publisher Joshua Loyd Fox, their extended circus of children and pets, and more books than any one house can hold.

She is the author of *Knock Knock*, *Tales My Grandmother Told Me*, and the upcoming *Echoes of the Dead: Collected Hauntings*, as well several short stories published in various anthologies.

She splits her time between Southern Maryland and her native state of Oklahoma, where she spends her days writing, editing, gardening, and keeping her family's head in the clouds, but feet on the ground.

Visit Heather Daughrity for book and tour news, to purchase her varied writings, see her appearances, peruse her professional book reviews, and contact her for editing services at www.parlorghostpress.com.

∞

Joe DeRouen

Joe DeRouen (joederouen.com) is a best-selling author of contemporary fantasy and horror novels. His most recent release, *The Small Things Trilogy Omnibus*, has enjoyed strong reviews and currently has a 5-star rating on Amazon. His other works include stand-alone novels *Leap Year* and *Memories of a Ghost*, as well as *Odds and Endings*, his collection of short stories and novellas.

Joe was born in Carthage, Illinois, and currently lives in Rogers, Arkansas with his wife Andee, their son Fletcher, and their cats Archer and Biscuit. Joe is a freelance writer, editor, and web designer. In addition to writing, he enjoys listening to music, collecting Mego action figures, and playing video games. When he's not crafting words, you can usually find Joe playing City of Heroes Homecoming on his PC or Pokémon Go on his phone.

William J. Donahue

William J. Donahue is an editor, feature writer, and kitten foster who has not been the same since watching John Carpenter's *The Thing* as a ten-year-old. His published works include the recently released novel *Only Monsters Remain*, as well as two previous novels: *Burn, Beautiful Soul* and *Crawl on Your Belly All the Days of Your Life*. He lives in a small but well-guarded fortress in Pennsylvania, somewhere on the map between Philadelphia and Bethlehem. Although his home lacks a proper moat, it does have plenty of snakes.

∽

J-F Dubeau

Designer by training, marketing director by trade, J-F is addicted to writing and there is no cure. The author of A God in the Shed and Song of the Sandman, he's also the 'writer of wrongs' behind the Achewillow cozy horror podcast. Short stories are a new thing to J-F., a quick fix between longer projects to help keep withdrawal symptoms at bay.

Fascinated with characters and their stories, horror is a natural fit. It's a dark blanket be draped over other genres, drawing out the themes and topics that would otherwise remain hidden. Ultimately, J-F. strives to tell tales of terrible beauty, and beautiful terror.

∽

Joshua Loyd Fox

Joshua Loyd Fox is the author of several novels including *I Won't Be Shaken*, *Had I Not Chosen, Amongst You, To Build a Tower*, and *One Becomes a Thousand.*

He is also the author of the upcoming *I Don't Write Poetry: A Collection*, his first book of poems, and Book V of the ArchAngel Missions, *Unto This Mountain*. His short stories, *The Book of the Tower and the Traitor,* a companion series to The ArchAngel Missions, can be found on Amazon Vella.

Joshua Loyd Fox has been a soldier, a Master Aircraft Mechanic, a cook, an amateur MMA fighter, and most recently, has worked as an Engineer, a Technical Writer and a SME for the US and foreign militaries on missile defense systems.

He and his wife, author and world renown editor, Heather Daughrity, split time between NE Oklahoma and Southern Maryland where he can be found with a fine cigar, an even better whiskey, and feet up next to a wood fire on most evenings. Find all of his work, as well as public appearances and his master class series at www.joshualoydfox.com

∞

Jennifer Anne Gordon

Jennifer Anne Gordon is an award-winning author and popular host of the Vox Vomitus podcast. Her debut novel *Beautiful, Frightening and Silent* won the Kindle Award for Best Horror/Suspense for 2020, Best Horror 2020 from Authors on the Air, and was a finalist for American Book Fest's Best Book Award- Horror, 2020. Her novel *Pretty/Ugly* won the Helicon Award for Best Horror for 2022, the Kindle Award for Best Novel of the Year (Reader's Choice). Her collection The Japanese Box: And Other Stories was an Amazon Bestseller. She is also a featured essayist in Diane Zinna's upcoming book Letting Grief Speak.

Jennifer is a member of Mystery Writers of America, and the Horror Writers Association (where she serves on a jury for the Stoker Awards) and is the Agents and Editors chair of the New England Crime Bake Committee.

Her personal essays on grief, trauma, and horror have been published in The Horror Tree, Ladies of Horror Fiction, Nerd Daily, and Reader's Entertainment Magazine.

When she is not writing, she spends time in her haunted house in New Hampshire with her husband Roman, and their silly dog Lord Tubby.

For more information you can visit her website at www.JenniferAnneGordon.com.

She is represented by literary agent Paula Munier at Talcott Notch Literary, and Mickey Mikkelson with Creative Edge Publicity.

∞

Gage Greenwood

Gage Greenwood is the best-selling author of the Winter's Myths Saga, and *Bunker Dogs*. He's a proud member of the Horror Writers Association and Science Fiction and Fantasy Writers association.

He's been an actor, comedian, podcaster, and even the Vice President of an escape room company.

He lives in New England with his girlfriend and son, and he spends his time writing, hiking, and decorating for various holidays.

Find out more, or contact me: www.gagegreenwood.com

∞

Justin Holley

Justin Holley lives somewhere on the Cass Lake chain of lakes with his wife, and also a rather large Daneiff named Nu and a clever but tiny Devon Rex named Jinx. Justin is the author of the novels *To Cut A Man*, *Hellweg's Keep*, *Blood from the Stars*, *Tethered to Darkness*, *Seven Cleopatra Hill*, the three-book Bruised series, and several short stories.

∞

Jo Kaplan

Jo Kaplan is the award-winning author of *It Will Just Be Us* and *When the Night Bells Ring*. Her short stories have appeared in *Fireside Quarterly, Black Static, Nightmare Magazine, Vastarien, Horror Library, Nightscript*, and Bram Stoker award winning anthologies. She has also published work as Joanna Parypinski. In addition to writing, she teaches English and creative writing at Glendale Community College and plays the cello in the Symphony of the Verdugos. Currently, she is the co-chair of the Horror Writers Association's Los Angeles chapter. Find her online at Jo-kaplan.com.

∞

Ronald Kelly

Born and bred in Tennessee, Ronald Kelly has been an author of Southern-fried horror fiction for 37 years, with fifteen novels, twelve short story collections, and a Grammy-nominated audio collection to his credit. Influenced by such writers as Stephen King, Robert McCammon, Joe R. Lansdale, and Manly Wade Wellman,

Kelly sets his tales of rural darkness in the hills and hollows of his native state and other locales of the American South. His published works include *Fear, Undertaker's Moon, Blood Kin, Hell Hollow, Hindsight, The Halloween Store & Other Tales of All Hallows' Eve, After the Burn,* and *The Saga of Dead-Eye* series. Kelly's collection of extreme horror tales, *The Essential Sick Stuff,* won the 2021 Splatterpunk Award for Best Collection. He lives in a backwoods hollow in Brush Creek, Tennessee with his wife and young'uns.

∾

Marie Lanza

Marie Lanza writes fast-paced horror and thrillers. She is the author of post-apocalyptic series Fractured, the short story series The Colony, along with other short stories part of larger anthologies. She also writes in various genres as a ghostwriter bringing others' visions to life. Marie is always creating, whether it's for a new book series, feature film, or television. She currently resides in Los Angeles, California with her husband and two daughters.

To learn about upcoming book releases and projects for Marie Lanza, visit her website. www.MarieLanza.com or Marie's Amazon Page.

∾

Caitlin Marceau

Caitlin Marceau is a queer award-winning author and illustrator based in Montreal. She holds a Bachelor of Arts in Creative Writing, is an Active Member of the Horror Writers Association, and has spoken about genre literature at several Canadian conventions. Her work includes *Femina, A Blackness Absolute*, and *This Is Where We Talk Things Out*. Her novella, *I'm Having Regrets*, will be coming out later this year and her debut novel, *It Wasn't Supposed To Go Like This*, is set for publication in 2023. For more, visit CaitlinMarceau.ca or find her on social media.

D.E. McCluskey

Born in Liverpool in the UK, Dave McCluskey left school and began working in a music shop selling guitars and drums and playing in local bands around the Liverpool music scene. When he realized that fame and fortune, and rock god status was proving rather elusive, he went to university leading to him wasting almost 30 years of his life messing around with computers.

He became a novelist later on in life having been an avid reader since he was a child. He writes as DE McCluskey, mostly in the genre of horror (mainstream, extreme, and comedy), although he has been known to dabble in thrillers, romance, science fiction, fantasy, and also children's books (written as Dave McCluskey).

He began his writing career creating comics and graphic novels, thinking they would be easier to write and sell than traditional novels (how wrong he was). He then made the switch into the media of novels and audiobooks and has not looked back since.

His books include the highly regarded *The Boyfriend, The Twelve, Cravings, Zola*, and the historical thriller *In The Mood for Murder*.

Dave remains an avid football fan although sometimes he wonders why, and he has been known to lurk around the stand-up comedy circuit in the North-West of England.

He lives at home with his partner, their two children, and a sausage dog with his own future children's book series, called Ted (Lord Teddington of Netherton).

∞

Jeremy Megargee

Jeremy Megargee has always loved dark fiction. He cut his teeth on R.L Stine's Goosebumps series as a child and a fascination with Stephen King, Jack London, Algernon Blackwood, and many others followed later in life. Jeremy weaves his tales of personal horror from Martinsburg, West Virginia with his cat Lazarus acting as his muse/familiar. He is a member of the West Virginia chapter of the Horror Writer's Association, and you can often find him peddling his dark words in various mountain hollers deep within the Appalachians.

Joe Scipione

Joe Scipione lives in the suburbs of Chicago with his wife and two kids. He is the author of the Mr. Nightmare series, *The Life and Times of Edward Morgan, Zoo: Eight Tales of Animal Horror, Decay,* and *Never Dead.* He has had short stories featured in numerous anthologies and is a member of the Horror Writers Association. When he's not reading or writing you can usually find him cheering on one of the Boston sports teams or walking around the lakes near his home with his dog. Find him on Twitter or Instagram: @joescipione0 or at www.joescipione.com.

∞

Samantha Underhill

Samantha Underhill is a multifaceted artist, researcher, and educator whose heart beats to the rhythm of the dark and beautiful. Hailing from the enchanting foothills of Appalachia, her soul resonates with haunting melodies and stirring folklore. In the tapestry of her identity, duality weaves its intricate threads. Her bright and vivacious personality externally often hides the dark storms within. A balance between light and shadow, her complexities endear her to those who know her.

Sadness of the Siren was the first of Samantha's non-scientific works in publication. It is testament to her emotionally evocative writing. Jonathan Maberry has said of her work, "...with any given piece there are visible layers. You can read [her work] one day and then on another day, or in another mood, read it again and there has been a magical transformation. The meaning of [the writing] has changed."

In Samantha's work, feelings bleed onto the pages – every word, a brushstroke from the inkwell of the heart. Since her initial publication, she has achieved unexpected feats. Her short stories and poetry have found homes in illustrious literary journals including the renowned *Weird Tales Magazine, Weird House Magazine, Borderless Journal*, and a myriad of poetry anthologies.

Yet, Samantha's artistry extends beyond the written word. Her voice, haunting and soft, has found its way into diverse realms. Much of her professional narrations can be found produced by BBV Productions, connected to artists like Chris McAuley and Claudia Christian. Her voice work from characters, to narrations, to advertisements and beyond are a testament to her creative versatility.

For more information on her artistic universe, encompassing both her written and spoken works, we invite you to visit her digital space, https://samreadsandwrites.weebly.com/ where darkness and beauty entwine in an eternal dance.

∞

Mer Whinery

Mer Whinery is a storyteller of the rural macabre from southeastern Oklahoma. He enjoys sunny autumn afternoons and wandering about in forlorn burial grounds, dressed all in black with a thoughtful look upon his face. He loves horror video games but covers his ears if they get too loud and relies on his oldest child to get him past the jump-out parts.

He is the author of *The Country Girl's Guide to Hexes and Haints, The Little Dixie Horror Show* and *Trade Yer Coffin for a Gun.*

He resides somewhere in Oklahoma with his wife Annie and his two sons Kameron and Harper.

∞

Mercedes M. Yardley

Mercedes M. Yardley is a whimsical dark fantasist who wears red lipstick and poisonous flowers in her hair. She is the author of numerous works including *Darling,* the Stabby Award-winning *Apocalyptic Montessa and Nuclear Lulu: A Tale of Atomic Love*, *Pretty Little Dead Girls*, *Love is a Crematorium,* and *Nameless*. She won the Bram Stoker Award for her stories "*Little Dead Red*" and "Fracture." Mercedes lives and works in Las Vegas. You can find her at mercedesmyardley.com.

Printed in Great Britain
by Amazon